DESPAIR

Pathfinder Media Group
Harrisburg, Pennsylvania, USA
media@pathfinderops.org
legacyofsorrow.com

Despair – Volume IV of The Legacy of Sorrow

Disclaimer:

All characters and events portrayed in this book are fictitious. Any similarity to real persons, living or dead, is purely coincidental, and not intended by the author.

The content of this book or series may cover controversial or sensitive topics to include assault, violence, addiction, loss, trauma, SA, suicide, or other potential triggers. Readers' discretion is advised.

ISBN (KDP Paperback): 978-1-970018-15-8
ISBN (Kindle eBook): 978-1-970018-19-6

Though these books detail a long and bloody war, I've been through battles of my own as this series was written across more than a decade and a half of my life. For those who stood by my side, those who believed I could finish the fight, and for my readers who face their own battles, this story is for you.

While the evils that raged in my mind and battled for control
had yet to win their war, I was out of time to wage it.
Against the overwhelming enemy of a thousand thoughts
and countless emotions, I was outmatched.
Wars against ourselves are never won through the brutalities
of force, but end in the same punishments for their prisoners
as in our external conflicts.
Death, it seems, spares no one.
In each imagined battle, I took solace in the strength of the
fight in spite of dying prayers that a victory would be sung.
But in this war…
No victor would be declared.
No conqueror would reign over the new lands of a forsaken
mind.

In agony, I draw my breath and draw my sword.
In torment, I charge into battle to face myself one final time.

In this, I find my despair.

TABLE OF CONTENTS

UNIFICATION

VIOLET

I didn't care as much as I should have about being late to the meeting, but I didn't feel obligated to attend, as the entire city knew to leave me alone in my unsettling isolation. Since I had largely – at threat of bodily harm to others – been left alone over previous days, I was able to take my time and gather my thoughts before ambling back down the hall and crossing the short distance to the nearby conference room. Vanaheim's arboretum felt more alive than Aerael's ever had been, but the scene of its existence just reminded me of what was lost to us.

New city. Old lies.

It wasn't a pleasant experience to watch everyone's eyes turn to me as I pushed the doors open and squeezed through before darting to the back of the room. I had decided to show up only to gain the information necessary for me to follow what was going on before heading straight back to my room, and was in no mood to socialize with anyone present.

At least Kara's not here. My…mother. Even the thought of it…

I struggled to ignore the cynical, bitter thoughts in my head and focused the best I was able on the conversation at hand.

Eric's laptop was set up on the conference table, and an informal huddle took place around it rather than the traditional placement of everyone at seated positions around a large area. Yuri's face was shown on the screen and was deeply involved in a conversation with Tony, who stood at the front of our group.

"Are you sure you can handle this? We're asking a lot of you." Yuri asked, turning to a young, blonde female sitting next to him on the screen. "Miss Goss is prepared to help you, but-"

"This needs done. Period." Tony interjected, adjusting the laptop's screen. "The maneuverability of those F-35s can't match an F-22 or an F-18, not by a long shot. That means if Legacy has either, our pilots are dead. We can't afford for that to happen." Jalix decided to speak up, asking a question to Tony.

"You're *sure* you can do this? You're modifying an aircraft meant to travel at Mach speeds."

"I can do it." Tony replied, nodding. "I already have a few ideas. I want to start by modifying the thrust vectoring for better control on tight turns. That, along with some tweaks to the engine and powerplant, will get us a start. It'll help even the odds, and Vampyres should be able to handle the increased G-forces more than humans could. If I can get my hands on the technical manuals, I can also find some ways to lose extra weight from equipment or systems onboard that we won't need."

Do I really need to be here for this? I'm barely following what they're talking about.

"And I have another project in mind to avoid the surface-to-air systems, as well as Legacy's aircraft weapons' locks. Think of headphone noise-cancelling, but with radar. If I can design the system I want to, with Eric's help, we can make it nearly impossible for weapons to lock onto those aircraft. So we'll have stealth aircraft capable of near-peer dogfights that can't be targeted by radar-guided weapons. We'd be nearly invincible. At least long enough for the first strike against Legacy's forces. I can't guarantee that we can outmatch Legacy's aircraft in a straight-up fight, but I can give our pilots as much of an edge as possible." Tony sounded extraordinarily confident, and his voice reassured the group as a whole. Val was thinking about the concept, but his eyes were as tired as anyone else's and still weren't totally focused on what was going on. Sonya seemed to be the only one other than Jalix to follow completely.

"Alright. Tony's yours. Get it done." Jalix spoke up again.

"I'll head out in the morning." Tony said quietly, shaking Jalix's hand and clapping his shoulder lightly. He went to leave, stopped by Sonya as she chuckled and gave him a brief hug. A small line formed behind him, with Val next and Krystal standing with Amy at the back. They both looked at me instead of Tony, giving me a small wave and a look of pity I didn't appreciate. My scowl discouraged them, both of them looking away and mumbling to each other.

Even my two best friends want to talk to each other more than to me.

I rolled my eyes, backing up even further and leaning against the farthest wall of the room. Yuri spoke up and I listened without watching the interaction.

"Miss Goss had an idea for keeping our rotary craft hidden."

"I'm listening." Jalix replied. "Sonya, come listen to this one. I want a second set of ears in case I miss anything." Out of the corner of my eye, I saw Sonya step back toward the computer and allow Val and Tony to exchange quiet words. The blonde girl on the screen started explaining parts of a plan that I didn't have the context to follow.

"So what if we took tarps and painted them to match the main Quantico runway? We'll stretch them and mount the tarps on tall poles so they're flat and smooth while being off the ground by fifteen feet or so. We store the aircraft on the runway itself, under the tarps, but the satellite images won't be able to tell a difference. At least, unless someone knew exactly what to look for. There will be space underneath for maintenance and exercises, and it'll all be hidden to the skies."

"That's genius." Sonya acknowledged. "Couple of kinks to watch out for, but great overall."

"Agreed." Jalix concurred. "You can do a few test runs before the Blackhawks get there from Pennsylvania and use drones to mimic what the satellites would see.

"That's exactly what we were thinking." The blonde woman replied. "Okay, awesome. We'll get everything started, then. Everyone is excited to have work to do."

"Work quickly." Jalix warned, looking at Val as he approached. "We have time, but that could change at any moment. I don't want to get caught halfway through a plan. Treat every day like we go to war tomorrow."

We're at war already. You weren't the one to see New York go up in nuclear fire.

"Stay safe, Jalix. Stay safe, all of you." Yuri acknowledged the group before the screen went blank, returning to the laptop's default program for video calling. Krystal and Amy had stepped back from Tony, allowing him free passage to the door of the conference room. Instead of leaving, he looked around for a moment before seeing me and approaching slowly. No one else bothered to watch, unwilling to feel more awkward than they already did.

"Hey." He said quietly, his brow furrowed deeply.

"Hey." I mumbled, trying not to be rude. "When will you be coming back from Quantico?"

"Not sure." He muttered. "Whenever the work's done. And in this case, the sooner the better. But I have people to train, too." He sighed, running a hand over his face as stress started to catch up to him. "You know…" He started, leaning in to speak quietly. "I don't have a stake in your personal life. We're not buddies. And even Ka-…your *mother* and I…never got close." He took in a short breath. "I spent too many years telling myself that as quickly as I could have been dead as a human, I would be dead again as a Vampyre. I was saved from a burning car and dragged into a war. One hell to another. And I'll give you one piece of advice I should have told myself a long time ago. Before my brother became as bitter as I was." He turned his head, speaking in short sentences. "It's not worth the anger. None of it is. Anger is bullshit. Love who you can, while you can. You have parents now. Appreciate that. Before this new war kills one, or both of them. Life's too damn short." I stared at him blankly, the blunt and honest truth too much of a candor to fully comprehend in the moment.

"Yeah, I-…I know. I just-"

"I know what you *just*. Get over it. Alright? These people deserve your love just as much as you deserve theirs." He beckoned to Jalix, laughing as he made a joke with Val about something. "Go enjoy it." He finished, nodding once and making his way through the room and into the main hall.

He's right. And it's nothing you don't already know. But I don't think Tony has ever dealt with the kind of…betrayal I'm going through. Still, he has a point. I do love them all so much.

I breathed heavily for a moment, fighting the aching lump that continued to return to my throat and was made worse by Val replacing Tony at my side. I still felt awful for yelling at him and saying the things I did about Alice, but I also knew he would have forgiven me since last we had spoken. He stood awkwardly, heavily desiring to speak with me and undecided on how to broach the silence.

"You should eat." He decided.

"I'm good." I returned curtly, trying to find a good opportunity to escape the fading and unnecessary social gathering in order to retreat to my room. He winced, making another attempt.

"I-…you really should get some food."

"No, Val." I insisted, crossing my arms. He nodded slowly, turning to walk away when my thoughts started to make sense of the exchange.

You selfish bitch, he's not doing it for you. He wants someone to talk to. We're all suffering at what's going on in the world. He was lied to just as much as you were. Don't be such a self-centered asshole.

"Val…" I started apologetically as I mentally chastised myself for not recognizing his intent. He turned around, his eyes more hopeful than I thought they would be. "I could go for a quick bite. Sorry. I'm…I don't mean to take my mood out on anyone else."

"Why do you think I came to you?" He chuckled softly, his tone low and quiet. Jalix's eyes darted over to look at us briefly before Val tapped my shoulder and gestured to Sonya with his head. She was watching both of us, and started to walk toward us as Val spoke again. "You mind if she joins? She missed you like hell."

"Yeah. By all means." I did my best to smile at Sonya's approach, her typical sense of affection having faded to a wary wave of her hand.

"Hey." She said quietly. "How have you been? I haven't seen you since…well, for a few minutes in Krystal's room. We haven't really had the chance to catch up."

"I'm good. All things considered." I wrapped an arm around her shoulders, touching my temple to hers. "How about you? Heard you threw a tank at some Tortured."

"Yep." She nodded, failing to elaborate. "Yes, I did."

"Burgers." Val hinted, beckoning to the door. "We need them, someone has to have them."

"Raven said the bistro near our quarters has some good food." Sonya suggested, pointing to the patio-style seating outside of the doorway as we left the conference room and walked across the concrete floor. "God knows I could use it.

I've been living on MREs and Vampyre medicine for way too long."

"That's your own fault." Val scolded. "When we packed for D.C., I told you to pack snacks."

"Yeah, and I didn't feel like taking an extra sixteen packs of instant ramen. Did you *see* how bare Krystal's kitchen was? No wonder Jalix's cooking was always shitty. He had nothing to work with." I smirked at the banter, feeling the friendship between them fuel a more positive note as we approached the restaurant. A waiter was already prepared for us, meeting us outside the front doors and speaking with an overabundance of cautious respect.

"Good afternoon, Mr. Valencia. It's an honor-"

"Burgers." Val interrupted, sensing that the employee was going to vastly overestimate what we expected of him. "We need them, you've got them. All we need is a table and some food, no need to make a big deal out of it."

"Of course. We have VIP seating inside for Raven and her-"

"Right here works." Sonya raised her eyebrows as she slowly and obnoxiously pulled a metal chair across the concrete floor with a drawn-out screech and sat down at the nearest table. It looked out into the rest of the main hall, letting us take in the view of passers-by. The employee grimaced, his eyebrows messily scrunching together in an awkward state of confusion before handing us the menus he held. I took one of them gratefully and sat down across from Sonya, letting Val take the seat facing the restaurant doors.

"My name is Vishnu, and I'll be your server this afternoon. Our specials today..." The waiter started hesitantly, waiting for another interruption. We let him continue, relaxing in our seats and taking a moment to appreciate the normality of getting food together once again. "Are a truffle and basil Fra' Diavlo with foie gras and a duck breast with beetroot-raspberry sauce, served with watercress and roasted parmesan asparagus."

"Bur." Val enunciated, raising his eyebrows. "Ger."

"Right, sorry." The waiter apologized. "We have black bean, plant-based, or turkey-"

"No, dude…just-…a regular cheeseburger. None of this fancy stuff." Val clarified.

"I'm sorry, sir, but our offerings don't include-"

"Listen to me very closely." Sonya slapped her menu onto the table and lifted both hands. "In the kitchen, within those refrigerators, is there ground *beef*?"

"Yes, but-"

"Okay, perfect. You're going to tell whoever is back there to shape half a pound of it into a patty, then char it on the grill until it's medium-well. You're going to put it between two halves of empty-carb bun with a slice of American cheese, and you're going to add lettuce, tomato, and mayonnaise. Is that…*perfectly* clear?" Sonya's eyes slowly grew wider, her sense of wild-eyed impatience burning a hole in Vishnu's face as she stared at it. "And add French fries-…you know what? I'm going to explain this. Have them take a few potatoes, slice them into strips, and deep-fry them to hell and back before covering them in salt. A lot of salt, okay? Like-…no, just bring out whatever container of salt you use in the kitchen. The whole thing." The waiter looked more and more afraid as Val and I sat in sheer enjoyment and watched the interaction. He realized Sonya was done speaking for the time being, and unwillingly prodded the beast in her eyes further.

"Ma'am…we don't have American cheese here. But…I could give you Swiss?" He winced, waiting for her rebuttal. She contemplated the exchange for a moment, squinting slowly before approvingly nodding.

"Fine. Add eight strips of bacon." She decided. "At least." He opened his mouth to reply, but instantly regretted his decision as she throatily barked at him. "You *do* have bacon, right?" One of her legs crept out from under the table as if she was going to lunge at him.

"Yes- I…we have bacon. But we don't have any hamburger buns. Is a brioche roll okay with you?"

"Oh, hell yeah. Brioche rocks my goddamn world." Sonya relaxed in a heartbeat and picked up her menu again, shaking her head as she read over the extravagant dishes. "Three of those." She finished, peering over the top of the menu. "And three full-sugar root beers." Vishnu nodded once, scurrying to the inside of the restaurant before she could torture him any further. Val chuckled, tapping her on the arm.

"You went too easy on him. Could have thrown a tank at the guy with just your brain again. We could have made a Vishnu-burger with what was left."

"I am officially calling whatever comes out of that kitchen a Vishnu burger." Sonya cheerily replied, dropping her menu again to look at me. "Sorry. I'm…hungry."

"Me, too." I laughed, propping my head on my hands and leaning into the table. "Tired. Hungry. Bitchy."

"Same." Sonya agreed, sighing in a deep breath of attempted calm. "But I was going to make sure you and Val could try and establish your old routine."

"I almost forgot about that." I laughed, looking over at Val. "Monday night burgers and Wednesday night wings. The best way to ignore the world going to hell."

"The good ol' days." Val reminisced, leaning back in the wrought-metal chair. "The days before the outbreak, before the breakdown-"

"Before I knew Kara was my *mother*." I sneered, staring at the menu as if I had any interest in reading it. They both grew silent, and while I felt awkward for souring the mood, I knew that it was the topic that bothered all of us.

"I should have known." Sonya said quietly, sighing and spreading her legs out under the table to stretch.

"There's no way you could have-"

"No, not-…Kara said something recently, and I didn't really take it to heart. Not really." She interrupted my protest, looking over briefly at Val. "It slipped my mind until that…staged act with Legacy. She…god damn it." She shook her head, looking at the ceiling and trying to remain emotionally neutral. "It was when we rescued…our group of women. From the Tortured."

"Thank you again. A thousand times over, we owe you guys more than we can ever repay." I emphasized, reaching out to touch her hand. The scenario still seemed too impossible to be true, only ever meeting reality in my brain on the few occasions I had seen Alice's distant and troubled eyes since the event.

"Don't thank me. You're family. As damn close to a blood relation as I'll ever have." She replied. "But Kara is the one to thank. I…I didn't actually know what was happening. We were catching up to you guys, following the GPS tracker on Tony's van to meet up with you all, and we ended up driving *past* Kane-Hudson, past Vanaheim, just to meet with you as soon as possible. Kara-…your mother-" She corrected herself mid-sentence.

"It's…Kara is fine. Still a bit too soon." I confessed, my eyes darting forward to avoid whatever look Val wore.

"Kara was still sedated from whatever drugs Legacy used to sedate her, but we found the van by the side of the road. Bloodstained from where Krystal was stabbed, a pool of blood from where you bit Rachel…and you were all gone. I panicked." Her eyes lost their focus as she retold the story. "Tony had just woken up, but once he saw what was going on, it was like he was never injured. Just…this energy I had never seen when he went to the other vehicle and *commanded* that they gear up for a fight. I knew we needed her, so I grabbed Kara and I yelled at her, shook her. I kept saying *Amy needs you.* I just yelled at her over and over again, *your daughter's in danger.* And when she finally woke up, her eyes fluttered…and then they snapped open. She just looked at me…" She shook her head as I looked up, watching her brow furrow in confusion and remembrance. "And said your name. She just whispered…*Violet.* And then she took off in a sprint. I remember…she looked at the blood on the van, then at the puddle of it on the road. She tilted her head and smelled the air like a damn wolf. We sprinted up toward the buildings and finally we heard Alice scream." Val visibly grew uncomfortable, shifting in his seat and breathing heavily. It was unlike him to appear so anxious, so unnerved by a retelling of events despite knowing his wife was safe and within the city. Sonya attempted to shift the tone of the story. "Tony and the others cleared you all out of the building. And I thought Kara was going to lose control, the way she only had done a few times before."

"Like when she rescued me and Jared from Schillinger in his warehouse. God, that feels like a lifetime ago." I realized, details from my past starting to make sense.

"Yeah…but she didn't. She focused on Alice. I think…because Kara had been through it. She knew what Alice was going through. And she wanted Alice to have closure the way Kara never could."

"Hey, can we-…" Val made a circular motion with his hand, visibly nauseous and at risk of walking away from the table.

"Val, I'm so sorry." She apologized. "I know this isn't any easier on you to hear, but…you deserve to know the full story. And that we did – truly – move as fast as we could."

"I know." He mumbled. "I blame none of you. Not even Raven. I blame Legacy, I blame the Tortured. Not any of you. I'll always be thankful that my wife is here, and alive. We'll work through the rest." He lifted his head in defiance, courage taking hold of his eyes and chest.

Alice…why do I keep thinking about her more than the others?

My brain struggled with a series of brief memories, trying to make sense of them before my eyes widened and I caught up with the reality of a majority of my life.

"They were trying to tell me all along." I whispered, my throat growing tight. I snarled at Val, angry at the realizations and wishing I had let my memories rest in the recesses of my mind. "When we were at Krystal's mansion, down in her gun vault, do you remember what Alice said to us? That we'd make a lot of mistakes judging people by who their fathers are?" The sadness in his face was accentuated when he realized she had been trying to tell him, as well, in a language that no one would ever decipher. "And I remember…so many years ago, right before Kara died. Krystal and I were at her mansion because she was…she was grieving that Kara would never be with her, that Kara had married Jalix the night before. But the next morning, Krystal got a phone call from Kara before everyone went after Kilkovf. She told Krystal to get to the cabin where Kilkovf was, and to stay out of sight. But she said that, whatever else happened, *not* to bring me under any circumstances. I had always wondered why." I gritted my teeth, my fangs starting to push against my gums. "I remember as she was laying there…dying…she said she loved us all so much. But she looked right at me, and she wouldn't look away…" I sniffed hard, trying to quickly change my mental state and avoid any sign of emotion. "Things are just making more sense now." I sighed, shaking my head.

"To all of us, Vi. You're not alone. You do know that, right?" Val asked, leaning forward and tilting his head toward me. "My sister was forced to have a child, fathered by our avowed enemy. A monster, even before that. The literal thing that started the Vampyre race."

"Yeah, and I'm a part of that." I whispered shamefully.

"Don't you dare." Val growled, tears welling in his eyes. "Don't you *dare* take that onto your shoulders. There's nothing of him left in you."

His cold, evil eyes…

"His eyes…" I realized in a horrified whimper. "I have his eyes. I…I've always *hated* my eyes."

He is as much a part of you as Kara. You're part monster…part machine.

"No, Vi. You have *my* father's eyes." Val corrected, staring at my irises in wonder. "I don't remember much of him, but one of the things I sold to help Kara and Sonya run and start a new life was a painting of my father. And I'll always remember the darkness, the intensity of the paint used for his eyes. Almost black, but not quite. The color of…strong coffee. Of bittersweet chocolate."

"All I know is that I don't have Kara's. Or her strength, her bravery, her leadership-"

"Violet, you don't have much of anyone else in you at all. You're as unique a diamond as any one of us." Sonya's brightness shone through my despair for a moment long enough that I absorbed her words. "You're a lot like me. This city-" She rolled her eyes. "The other city. Our people, our family, whatever. Life. Life gave you your soul. You just needed the genetics to shape it all. A body to hold your life, your experiences and memories, your emotions and feelings. No one, and I mean *no one* cares where you got your body. Whether you were a foster kid from scumbag, deadbeat parents or a reclusive billionaire's heiress, you're loved because of *who* you are. Not *what* you are. And if you believe for a second that there's anything of Schillinger in you, then you're just an idiot. And that would *have* to come from the genetics you share with your uncle."

"Yeah, you'd have to be an idiot." Val enthusiastically agreed. "Wait, what?"

"Nothing."

"Did you call me stupid?"

"I didn't call you smart, big guy."

"Says the blonde with no memory."

"Says the chick who can throw *tanks* at people."

"Technically, I could-"

"With her *brain.*" She beamed, defeating Val in a quick battle of words before our food exited the front doors of the restaurant on Vishnu's arms.

"Here we are…" He groaned, the faint edge of disgust on his voice as he placed the plates in front of us and quickly walked away. Sonya immediately ripped the top bun from her sandwich, delicately peeling back layers of bacon, cheese, and toppings as Val and I watched with keen interest. Sonya's face relaxed inch by inch until she replaced the top bun and took a gargantuan bite, a drop of grease rolling down her chin before being wiped away briskly with a napkin. She chewed viscerally for several seconds, swallowing and placing the burger on the plate once more.

"Where's my drink?" She whispered, the wicked venom of violence on the tip of her tongue. No sooner did the words leave her mouth than did Vishnu appear again, balancing three tall glasses on a tray. She nodded satisfactorily and took a long draught before he could fully disappear again, leaving him with the resonating echo of a loud belch as he disappeared into the restaurant once more. "I am happy." She murmured pleasantly.

"Vishnu burger good?" Val asked, reminiscent of a caveman.

"Tasty Vishnu." Sonya confirmed, devouring another massive quadrant of the sandwich. I picked up a fry instead, tapping it against my plate and visibly watching salt grains fall off before munching on it and contemplating Sonya's words.

Grand scheme of things…I'm still me. I don't like being lied to…but maybe it was better I found this out once I was emotionally responsible enough to handle it. Maybe I would have reacted differently twenty years ago when Krystal was a…more anarchic influence. When I was still ignorant to a lot of things in life. When I was just barely grasping the scale of things.

"Thank you." I said appreciatively, looking at both of them.

"Not a problem. Sometimes you have to make a few threats to get a good burger." Sonya said, chewing with one side of her mouth.

"No, I mean-…you know *exactly* what I mean." I chuckled, realizing that she didn't want to revisit the more emotional side of the conversation.

"You know, I grabbed Sonya for lunch because I didn't want to get all mushy." Val said pointedly, picking up a fry as I nodded to his plate approvingly. "Do we have any-" He stopped as Sonya tapped his shoulder, pointing at the near side of the hall and bringing attention to Jalix, who had left the conference room and was approaching the area outside the restaurant.

"Hey, brother." Val reached a hand around to the other side of the railing, calling out to him and encouraging Jalix to come over and shake his hand.

"Looks like you guys are enjoying yourselves. Glad someone is getting time off." Jalix's complaint was made with the intent to express satisfaction that we were using our time well rather than to complain about a lack of recreation on his part. I took notice of his unwillingness to look at me, the brief comments turning into awkward silence quickly.

"Try a bite." Sonya suggested, holding out the remnants of her sandwich. Jalix didn't hesitate, contemplating the flavors before nodding.

"Damn. That's *good*." He declared, chewing with one side of his mouth.

"Vishnu burger."

"Bless you."

"Made from waiter meat."

"Oh." He frowned briefly after swallowing, reaching over to steal one of Val's fries as a palate cleanser.

"Grab a seat, man." Val gestured at the chair to my left.

"I should be going-"

"Come on. Sit." I patted the chair, trying to allay any concerns of my anger. He seemed surprised to hear me speak, looking over at me with hesitance.

"You know me, I can't sit still longer than five minutes. And besides, I have a lot to work on right now."

"You have time." Sonya said pleasantly, but firmly. He sighed, making his way around the short, dividing fence between the restaurant patio and main hall and approaching our table. Vishnu barreled out from the front doors, approaching Jalix at a significant fraction of the speed of light.

"Mister Kane, it's a pleasure to-"

"Vishnu." Sonya warned teasingly. "Relax."

"Right. What can I get you, sir?"

"Iced coffee would be great." He pulled out the chair and took a seat, leaning away from me with an uneasy look on his face.

"Oh, we don't have-...*right* away." Whatever the restaurant didn't have, the fact changed after a brief glare of death from Sonya. Each time he entered or exited the restaurant, it was as if his speed increased, the doors swinging shut before any of us could react.

"So did you get that from Kara, or did she get that from you?" Jalix asked, chuckling. "The whole, I-get-what-I-want-or-you-die attitude."

"Bit of both. I brought the innocence, Kara brought the crazy eyes. The sarcasm came from Val."

"*No* way, I'm not a sarcastic person."

"I've gotten those crazy eyes before. Not fun, even as her husband."

"How bad?"

"Drank the last of her coffee while she was in a meeting. Thought she was done with it, and I was *very* wrong."

"You should have known better than to get between Kara and her coffee."

"It was her sixth cup that *morning*."

"Not after that, it wasn't." I couldn't help but to laugh with them, remembering more than once the late nights and early mornings during the initial stages of the outbreak. Jalix's face softened, asking me a question without looking over.

"Holding up okay? You've...been through a lot."

"We all have." I replied quickly, needing no more pity from anyone else. "We're at war again."

"War is easy. Family is hard." He returned, finally making eye contact. "I would know. I started with all of you by going to war...then losing my family. I'll take a fight any day of the week."

"I know. It shows." I pointed to a spot on my neck, the barely exposed mark of a wound exposed on his own. "You shouldn't be the one asking. You should be the one taking a break."

"I'd love to. And I will. But we have some things to iron out first. Tony needs to work on getting our aircraft combat-ready, Raven and Kara are coordinating refugee efforts from NYC, and I need to apologize for keeping the truth from you." I had assumed that only an act from a higher power could have kept Sonya from finishing the last bite of her food, but she stopped with the morsel only inches from her mouth and frowned, placing it back on her plate. "From...all of you." He corrected.

"Tell *her*, not us." Val said quietly, looking away.

Man...he really is just as hurt as I am. So is Sonya.

"I'm telling all of you." He reaffirmed, patting his palm against the table. "It hasn't been easy, but we had our reasons. Raven was dead, so we thought. Amy was *our* first child. And Violet was always a member of the family. Not much else needed said."

"It's not about that. But we expected you, of all people, to be honest with us. After keeping a secret like that, it gives a person doubts." Val responded.

"Of all people?"

"Kara was always known to be a bit of a…mystery. We expected it. And Alice kept a lot of things – I'll say *private*, especially when it came to her patients – but we just didn't see it coming from you. *I* didn't see that from you." Val was even-tempered, but wanted to resolve things honestly.

"It wasn't personal, Val. I made your sister a promise, and I made that promise to keep Violet safe. Even if the outbreak hadn't spiraled out of control, we couldn't have been a hundred percent sure that our enemies were dealt with. We wanted to give it some time."

"How much time did Kara need, Jalix?" I asked finally, unable to remain neutral. "I lived with you all for years. I was around for even longer. When would it have been okay?"

"Vi-"

"And to be honest, I'm bothered less by who I'm related to than I am the reasons we were in that war to begin with. How much of Kara's pursuit was really for her people, and how much of it was for revenge? From what I hear, she really amped up the assassin aspect of things after, uh…wow, right around when I was born. *What* a coincidence."

Be nice.

"I'm not trying to argue. I'm trying to help everyone see how many things this secret has affected." I finished.

"Believe me, I know." Jalix wasn't excited to discuss the topic, but understood well what I meant. "Even more so with whatever Legacy has going on. I'm still wrapping my head around the fact that Amy's version of the virus came from me, and that they experimented on me when I was in Schillinger's lab. That my daughter inherited some mutation from me. I'm at least thankful it led to something positive." He shrugged with one shoulder before placing a hand on top of mine. "We all have way too much to mentally handle at the moment. But I at least need you to know that Kara and I are here for you. Not as your mother and her husband, but as friends."

"That sounds *so* weird. No offense." I winced at his phrasing, trying to wrap my head around it.

"I know, especially since I'm only…what, four years older than you?" He asked. I nodded, the math checking out while Val and Sonya suddenly looked back and forth between the two of us in realization. I grimaced, nodding.

"Yep. Vampyre ages are…weird. Numbers mean a hell of a lot less. I'm starting to see what you mean, Val." I referenced an earlier comment he had made.

"I said what?"

"When we left Aerael with Krystal, you said there's a point of age at which a person's experience is measured differently. Where they see things in a completely different light. That's starting to make sense."

"Oh, yeah." He recalled. "I do drop the odd pearl on occasion."

"Sounds way too smart for something that you'd say." Sonya jested, flicking a French fry at him.

"Well, it made sense. And I hope you didn't take it personally, Vi. But Jalix was in combat and held a college education while you were overcoming a stutter and painting with Krystal. We didn't facilitate your growth well as a person. We kind of…assumed you had all the time in the world. That you'd never *need* to grow up. Like Krystal, in a way."

"Krystal was a lot more mature than you guys ever recognized." I argued, disagreeing with Val's last point.

"Removing the drugs just exposed it more and more. As she finally got over Kara, that veil lifted. Her problem was that she didn't have purpose. She had no way to hide from the world, no way to mask her pain, and then had nothing to drive and motivate what was left. She was…a hollow shell of her potential." It was hard discussing Krystal's mindset and attitude in the days after Jalix came to the city, and harder still to think about her slow descent into suicidal madness.

"And I owe *her* an apology, as well. Because I should have known she'd become exactly the person we all knew she could be." Jalix responded, staring a few inches above Val's head as he spoke. I looked over to see Krystal and Amy leaning over the railing, huddled together and amusedly listening to us speak.

"Oh, shit. Sorry." I apologized. "I didn't see-"

"Thanks for being honest, Vi." Krystal said, giving me a thumbs-up. "I don't mind people talking behind my back when they're being honest. It's all those lies Val makes up that drive me *nuts*."

"Did you know Krystal is an amazing person?" Val quipped.

"See? Lies." Krystal finished the joke, patting him on the shoulder. Our focus shifted to Amy, who took a second in deciding who to address.

"Hey, dad." She waved softly, gesturing to Krystal. "Brought a friend home. We actually came to the meeting to steal Violet, but you guys got to her first, I guess."

"You can have her." Jalix said dismissively. "All she wants to do is talk about her feelings."

"That's what *I* said." Val added. I took the opportunity to slide Jalix my burger, standing up and brushing the crumbs from my pants.

"I'm going to go hang out with them for a bit. I need sleep…really badly. So I'll talk to you guys in a bit, I guess?" It was weird leaving them in place, having been used to goodbyes that would last weeks or months. The feeling was apparently mutual, as no one knew quite how to address the departure.

"I love you, Violet." Jalix decided quietly. "*We* love you. And we always will. You may be Kara's daughter, but that makes you *my* family. I love you as much as I do Amy and Kara."

"I know." I smiled, briefly putting my hands on his shoulders as I walked behind him and faced the group. "I love you all, too. Tell Alice hi when you see her." I said to Val, stepping into the main hall with Krystal and Amy.

"Still want me to punch her in the face for you?" Val called, referring a previous threat during a fit of anger. The table glared at him, and I heard him try to clarify the situation as we walked away and left him with the uncomfortable explanation.

"They seem like they're doing well." Amy commented, wrapping an arm around my waist and pulling me in for a small hug as we walked. "Everyone seems…happy. Under the circumstances."

"With those criteria, it doesn't take much to be happy. Hot showers, cool beds, and good food are gonna go a long way. Tensions will ease. It'll just take time." I affirmed.

"Anyone see Kara yet? Or Alice?" Krystal asked as we turned into the hall of our living quarters.

"No." I replied, realizing that neither were at the meeting. "I think they said Kara's in her room…" We all looked over at the door as we passed, not daring to approach it yet and keeping our voices low. "But I haven't heard about Alice. Probably with the other doctors, still."

"Val will take good care of her. She may have asked for space. Otherwise he'd be there with her." Amy justified.

"Very true." I nodded, looking at the small placard next to the door that denoted my room. "Hang out in here for a few? Then, seriously, I need to get some sleep."

"As long as I can use your shower." Amy replied. "I want to hang out with you all, but I can't stand to be in my own skin at the moment. I am *gross*. Krystal's a good workout partner, but she knows how to wear someone out."

"Need to test my shoulder." Krystal shrugged passively. "Can't go easy on you if I'm going to get a good workout in." She stuck out her tongue at Amy, who returned the gesture as they both chuckled.

"Oh, right." I replied, opening the door and allowing them to walk inside first. "How's all that been? How's the shoulder and the...weird, touchy-memory-stuff with you two?" As we entered, I was finally able to appreciate that my apartment had been furnished by someone who knew my tastes intimately. While it had been ignored over previous days due to my emotional distress, walking through the door finally felt like home.

Dark, muted colors made up a majority of the furniture while the vivid and bright colors I needed in my life were sprayed onto the walls through countless pieces of my old art. Above the gas fireplace, directly in the center of the living room, was my most esteemed piece of art and had been framed especially for this location. Krystal smiled as her eyes met it, letting the waves of pastel purples and deep indigos create the backdrop for a thin, ghostly white image of the woman holding the rose. Attention was drawn toward the center by the clarity and vibrancy of bright red paint that created the trail of blood flowing from the woman's fingers down to her wrist by way of sharp thorns.

"Damn. This is a lot nicer than I expected." Krystal commented. "Shoulder is great, to answer your question. I have my mobility back, but I'll probably have to keep an eye on it. And the touch thing is..."

"Diminished." Amy finished. "Greatly. Shouldn't be a problem anymore. Is that a piano?" I looked in the corner of the room and saw an ebony-finished baby grand piano in the corner, polished and adorned with a bouquet of artificial flowers. "Since when do you play?

"I don't. But *you* do. Eric – who I am assuming set up all of our rooms – must have suspected you and Kara would be visiting my room rather frequently. He really must have been watching from a distance."

"That is…both sweet *and* creepy." Krystal remarked, taking a closer look at the instrument. "Holy shit." She pulled back, tilting her head before pointing. "That's Kara's. I'd know it anywhere. I mean, it's cleaned up and refinished a bit, but that is definitely the one she had. She moved it to Jalix's apartment when they first got together."

"I knew it seemed familiar. If it's hers, it was in Aerael for a while after I was born. It's how I learned to play." Amy explained. "It looks so much nicer now. She had it shipped to Krystal's manor when I got busy with medical work and couldn't play as often, but the truck never arrived. We figured it was stolen or something."

"It was." I chuckled. "Just stolen by our friends. Man, we have weird lives." We laughed, taking seats around the living room at random and creating a small triangle across the couch and armchair. I took a deep breath, enjoying the sweet smell of a new home, which this time was reminiscent of warm cotton and brilliantly clean linen. It was a moment of comfort similar to the first steep of a good tea, and let me soak into the room a bit further as we sat in perfect silence to absorb the peace.

"Mm." Krystal's head was tilted backward on the couch, using the cushion as a pillow to rest her eyes for a moment.

"Yeah. Same." Amy said quietly, her position on the armchair equally as comfortable-looking. "I am *so* tired."

"Not as tired as *they* are." Krystal sat up and nodded to the door. "I want to avoid them all for a little while and let them get some sleep. The Counsel has only been here a few days, and only half of us have even paused to catch our breath from…recent events." Krystal took a deep, shuddering breath, beckoning to the three of us. "We were unconscious when the Tortured…kidnapped us. All three of us. Jalix and Val were on the front lines of a battle. Sonya and Tony right before it. Alice went through literal hell. Kara's the only one to be on the okay side of things, and even that has been diminished a bit since our most recent meeting with Legacy."

"You forgot Raven." Amy said quietly. "She was there with Alice, too."

"Still don't know how I feel about her." I added. "Not saying she deserved any of that, not at all. Just in a general sense, I guess I'm wary."

"She was always an unknown." Krystal agreed. "We didn't really know much about her until Schillinger went public. He did a good job of keeping her hidden. But I suppose it's not out of the question that she only did what she did for the glory, the money, the luxury. Especially if she was raised in that environment. I don't know. I could see either side of it, and that's a problem."

"We're together on that one. I think with this…" Amy waved a hand around her. "It sort of scrapped a lot paranoias I had. Inviting the entire enemy team onto your home turf and letting them take over doesn't sound like anywhere close to a good idea for the bad guy."

"Neither does letting us know she even *had* a home turf or…that she was alive, at all. If she was working with Legacy, it would have been way too easy to turn us in or kill us. At this point, it wouldn't make sense." I rubbed my brow. "I'm conflicted. I think there's always going to be a…caution used with her."

"As there should be." Krystal assured. "I don't think Eric ever wanted to follow her, either. He's intelligent and would have had his own safeguards. If he saw her without supervision for that many years and didn't feel the need to keep us away…there are too many things saying that she's okay."

"I can settle with that." Amy agreed. "Not much we can do, anyway. All the things that would have gotten us killed have already happened. I still can't believe New York is gone."

"Not all of it." Krystal tried to recover the positivity of the conversation. "A part. But parts can be fixed. Buildings rebuilt. People healed. Dead mourned. We'll get past this. The city is still standing, just…scarred."

"Sounds like most of us." I commented. "Scarred but still standing."

"Shaken but unbroken." Amy concurred.

"Your father said you told him those exact words." Our heads snapped over to realize that Kara had somehow entered the room, as silent as something could be and without a sign or trace that she had entered.

"You are really goddamn scary, mom." Amy chuckled, standing up and making her way over. "Even when you don't mean to be."

Mom. The same word I should be thinking, that I should be feeling. But I don't. Maybe I did when I lived with her and Jalix at Krystal's mansion, but something's changed. Something's different. I can't get over that my father…half of me is a monster. Half of me is pure evil.

"Hey, Kara." Krystal waved, her head falling back onto the couch again. "Mm."

He was so malevolent that he ruined who Kara was. He transformed her very essence. And that horrifying person gave rise to me. Is part of me. How could I ever be a whole person when I'm half cruelty and half Sorrow?

"Hey." I tried to say pleasantly, ignoring the thoughts that rolled around in my head after looking at her. I couldn't stop noticing similarities between us, from the color of our hair to the shape of our noses and the athletic physique we both had. Although she stood a few inches taller than me, I couldn't unsee my own reflection as an older, wiser, and deadlier version of myself.

"Hey." She replied quietly, taking notice to the fact that I said neither *Kara* nor *mother* and had instead chosen to be impersonal. She turned to Amy in an attempt to escape the clear desire to pour out her emotions.

"So how are you?"

"Filthy. I'm gonna go shower." Amy either decided to give us time alone or had gotten fed up with her appearance, standing up from the armchair.

"Oh, I just wanted to talk for-"

"Mom. Listen to me very carefully." Amy said firmly, clasping her hands together. "I swear the two of us are fine. We're good. No hard feelings, no resentment. But please, I just spent the last few hours sweating my *ass* off, and I cannot-"

"Go." Kara chuckled. "Sorry. Go take care of yourself. You've earned it."

"Imma use your bathroom." Amy whispered to me as she walked past, closing the door behind her as the spray of water echoed around the room. "Marble? God actual *damn*." She called, inciting another chuckle from our new trio.

"I think Eric wanted to spoil me with my own space." I remarked to Krystal. "Since I lived down in the residential area for so long. And without Jalix needing his own place or…or Jared needing one…" I let the sentence hang, grimacing at the pain of his death's familiar sting.

"I miss him, too." Kara said, a gentle smile on her lips. "He was…he was funny. I remember that first. But he was also kind, kinder than so many others. He and Val made a good team. And you made him happy, too." She looked at me. "He talked about your mission in Los Angeles for so long. He was terrified, and it was a horrible thing to go through. But the time he spent with you was something he never forgot." I smirked, thankful for the remembrance. "I'm…sorry. Vi." She finished, finally speaking her mind.

"Don't be." I argued. "You had your reasons."

"They weren't good ones."

"And that's partially because of *me*." Krystal stopped Kara from continuing her defense. In surprise, we both looked at her. "My influence over both of you was…terrible. Awful. I was holding Kara back from being able to move on with her life, and I was tethering Violet to a childhood she never had. I was doing *exactly* what I shouldn't have done."

"You were *there* for both of us." I returned. "You were the only one that wasn't scared to speak your mind, the only one to confront either of us when you sensed something was wrong."

"She's right." Kara added. "You tethered me to reality. Instead of letting me – quite literally – get away with murder. You reminded me of the humanity in all of us."

That's exactly what Raven told Krystal.

Krystal nodded, but didn't accept any positivity from the response.

"None of this is your fault, Krystal. You saved both of us from being people we didn't want to be. I need you to understand that. The only reason I'm still struggling…" I started, trying to find a way to approach the topic and turning to Kara. "…is that you…abandoned me. But you saved me. I saw you as my guardian, but you were the one who left me in the first place."

"It wasn't like that at all." Her face grew red, and she sighed, understanding that she wouldn't be able to get through this on logic and reasoning alone. "Alice said she was going to tell the story, but I guess you weren't there. The long and short of it is that I was…traumatized. According to Alice, I had some intense PTSD and shock, and I wasn't fully lucid for a while. The decision to hide you wasn't mine.

It was Sonya and Alice's. And because of everything that was happening…they kept you hidden. Even from me."

"Why?" I asked quickly. I already knew the answer from the brief conversation with Sonya earlier, but I wanted to hear things in her own words. "Why couldn't they tell you?"

"I was already suffering from the…event. I hadn't recovered, I was in the darkest place of my life. Adding a child to that, any child that would be close to me…would only bring out the darkness in you. It would have brought out Schillinger's side in you." She sat down next to me, clearing her throat. "And they were right. Because I was getting closer to his way of thinking than I should have. Victory at any cost. And just like *you* having Krystal and Amy to keep you sane, I had Alice and Sonya. They did the right thing. Because you're here, now. And I could never have asked for a daughter as strong, as beautiful, as witty and talented and passionate as you are. You've become the woman I always wanted to be. And I'm so, so proud of that, Violet." I leaned into her, for the first time feeling and understanding the instincts she had to keep at bay for so long.

"I love you, Kara. I always have, and I always will." I paused. "It might take me some time to get over my own negative thoughts, but nothing will keep me from valuing you all the way I always have. You, and Jalix, and Val…"

I exhaled softly, the warm breath escaping from my lips in a soft attempt to avoid crying. I felt like every ounce of emotion I had was expended, and that no amount of talking about things could make me feel any more than I had felt in the last few days.

"Krystal!" Amy called from the bathroom. Krystal sat up, confused, and looked at the door.

"Uh…yeah?"

"C'mere. I'll show you what I was talking about for your hair."

"Oh!" Krystal jumped up, trotting over to the bathroom and escaping into the steam, leaving Kara and I alone.

"I guess I get why you asked me those questions back in the conference room. After I attacked Rachel. You wanted to see if I had lost control the way you used to." She nodded slowly.

"Yeah. I wanted to make sure I hadn't left a bad impression. I *am* proud of you for holding your ground against Rachel, though. From what I hear, it was impressive."

"I didn't have another option. These guys, the…Tortured. They're so much faster and stronger than we are. And then what they tried to do to us…I'm worried about this fight."

"We'll be okay. We just need to do the jobs Eric asked us to do. We need to learn and train, then fight and win. We'll do this." She sounded confident, smirking as she stood up. "What's the worst that happens? I die again?"

"Didn't stop you the first time."

"Exactly." She looked around the room, taking quiet note of the piano with curious eyes. "But for now, you all should get some rest. We can get started on things tomorrow. Jalix and I are going to go see Alice. She's doing fine, but she needs help with some unrelated stuff."

"Is she actually-"

"She's *actually* fine." She interjected. "Sonya had a long talk with her. She's got all of us and Val to lean on. It won't be perfect, and there will be nightmares and hard days. It'll be difficult. But she'll get through it and be the person she's always been. She has a purpose and a motivation to get the cure finished, and she's going to use that to distract herself and cope with things."

"As good a thing to work on as any."

"Yeah, it really is. Anyway…I'll be around. Even if I'm busy, you can feel free to come visit."

"Sounds good." I gave her a small wave as she left, closing the door behind her and leaving the faint aroma of vanilla and rose petals. I picked up on the quiet chatter between Amy and Krystal, muttering to themselves in the bathroom.

"-just seems like a lot of conditioner."

"It'll help the ends from splitting, trust me." I leaned my head back on the couch, blissfully following a gentle conversation between my two best friends and finding peace that I had them in my life.

INDUSTRY

TONY

I trotted away from the mess of running water that fell from several feet above me, moving to stand closer to the center of the tarp and shaking the front of my shirt rapidly so it would dry.

"We need to get those tarps at steeper angle." I pointed up, nudging Yuri and breaking him away from his conversation. He looked up, noticing the same bulging collection of water that I did, sighing at the pouring rain around us. "The rain keeps pooling in low spots."

"We will need to wait until the weather stops." Yuri decided, texting someone briefly.

"Rain. In November." I shook my head. "As if it wasn't miserable enough." Yuri chuckled, shaking his head at me.

"You complain too much."

"Thanks, it's what I'm known for. Now where are we on those materials? I needed them days ago and it's putting us behind-" I started discussing the issues that were most pressing, and started to get tired of the interruptions as he cut me off.

"They are on the way. Your schedule is not realistic, my friend. You want everything done *now*." He tried correcting me as we made our way to the inside of the hangar and took a break from the rain. One of my engineers looked at me from across the width of the building, signaling that he needed to speak with me. "We have time."

"No. We don't." I said curtly, removing my sunglasses and squinting briefly at the fluorescent lights of the hangar. "We're *borrowing* time. There's a difference. Could be taken away at any moment."

"Then live in those moments that our time is not taken." He smiled, trying to lighten my mood. "You will be a happier man for it."

"I don't need to be happier, I need to be faster. I need everyone *else* to be faster." I sighed, waving a hand dismissively before jogging over to the pile of technicians and engineers working on the back end of one of the two F-35 aircraft inside the building.

"Afternoon, sir." The tech started, pinching his fingers to zoom in on a piece of a digital schematic. "We need to replace a fuel-regulating valve *here*, but we can't find one that meets the specs we need."

"Then make one." I advised. "We just got all the fabricating equipment we should need."

"We do, but we don't have the material yet. We're short on titanium, carbon fiber-"

"It's on its way. Yuri just told me. If it needs to wait until tomorrow, help my brother with-"

"No! Stop telling them to help me!" A familiar and demanding voice called out from a tight space in the aircraft, accessed by a ladder leading to a gap in the turbines. Eric slid out, somehow clean in spite of the work he was doing. "One person can be up here at a time. *One*. And I don't need people pestering me for stupid shit."

"Then don't complain when things aren't done on time." I fired back, annoyed with his apparent feelings of success in spite of our obstacles.

"Tony. We're ahead of schedule. Jesus, lose the attitude." He groaned, making his way down the ladder. "The anti-radar systems are literally built and ready. I'm just trying to find space and placement. Takes time. Deal with it. The alternative is that our pilots last about eight seconds in the air when we have to go up against F22s."

"So glad you came." I grumbled.

"So glad I'm here for the week." He returned, a different technician making their way up the ladder with an elaborate-looking device. "Do you have the thrust vectoring issue figured out yet?"

"We need parts. But yes, once they're installed, we should be good. Everything else is as done as can be. At least we're not dealing with the older generation of these things. We'd be screwed." I pointed out. A blonde head of hair and bubbly voice made her way through the air as the cockpit roof opened and Layla began gushing about something unrelated to her assistant standing below the jet.

"We only need them for an initial airstrike and chasing away anything else in the sky. Hopefully, we won't need them in a long engagement." Like everyone around me, Eric sounded unreasonably optimistic, and I doubted his seriousness in the perception of our circumstances.

It's like no one here knows the battleground we fought through to get here. The effort to take Quantico, the massacre at D.C. The nuclear strike at New York.

My phone rang, with Jalix being the caller and no previous explanation as to what reason he had to get in touch again. Since our next check-in wasn't for another six days, I tapped Eric and ran to Yuri as I answered the call. Layla clambered out of the aircraft, rapidly descending the ladder on her side and making her way over as Jalix started speaking.

"Tony! What's up, man? How are you guys holding up?" I was pleasantly surprised at his tone.

"Uh…decently, I guess. Making good progress. Some delays, but we're hard at work." I heard him chuckle on the other end along with several others at my answer.

"Relax, Tony. We're calling with good news. I'm here with Val, Sonya, Kara, and Alice. Say hi."

"Hi!"

"Hey, Tony!"

"What's up, dude?"

"Hey, guys." I smiled at their voices, missing the camaraderie of our team as one cohesive unit. "What's the good news?" Eric asked eagerly.

"We're all here, by the way. It's Yuri, myself, Eric, and Layla." I added.

"Perfect." Jalix paused, listening to one of the others speak for a moment. "Yeah, so that supply delivery…was something I wanted to apologize for. I know you're waiting on materials, but I had them take a detour. We picked up something a little bit extra, but they're almost back to you."

"Extra…?" I asked, wondering what would have been more important than the aircraft parts.

"Yeah. Cool shit." Val butted in, taking over their end of the conversation. "You remember when Schillinger had that big-ass missile thing back when he first tried to go after D.C.?"

"The baseball stadium. I'll never forget that misadventure. Or building your bobsled." I taunted.

"Well, Alice and Amy started talking about dispersion for the cure, and we're stealing Schillinger's old plan. Once we take D.C., we're going to use one of those launcher platforms to scatter an aerosolized version of the cure across the city so it hits all of us at once. The Tortured, the civilians, and us. Alice said it'll create a faster spread than any other options. We stole one of the launchers from the same place we got the Blackhawks from, the military base in Pennsylvania. Now, it was decommissioned and stripped of a lot of parts when we found it, but they grabbed the repair manuals, technical specs, user handbooks, everything. Think you can get it operational?"

"It's going to need to be modified, too." I added. "We're not launching missiles, we're launching gas canisters. Different propulsion, different type of load, probably a new firing mechanism. We can do it, but it'll take another month. And I'll need to call the shots on exactly how we load the virus because I'll need to make custom canisters to fit the device." Alice decided to chip in at my statement.

"Make the canisters empty, just provide a way to fill them. We'll fill and load them onsite when the weapon's in place. That way, we can keep the cure safe and out of the way during the fight. We'll bring it in and fire everything off once the battle's over, or at least when there's a *very* clear opening."

I nodded for a moment at her explanation, thinking about ways I could make it work. One of Yuri's captains came into our huddle from outside, shaking off the saturating rain and listening to the call by our side. Yuri nodded to him briefly, watching him throw an armored vest into one of the lockers from the row we shared.

"We can do it." I decided. "Give me another month, and Alice, I'll need some more details on the chemicals you'll be using. However you're keeping the cure virus suspended and alive. Need to make sure we do this right or we'll end up frying whatever's inside."

"Sounds good. We're wrapping up the last details today. We should be ready for manufacturing by tomorrow night. I'll have one of my assistants send it over to your email by the end of the day." She affirmed.

"We get assistants, now?" I meant to make a light joke on the topic, but was immediately berated by my colleagues in unison.

"You fired yours."

"You fired yours."

"You fired yours." I grimaced at their voices, and should have expected the response.

"Doctor *Weiss* has other talents. Best used in Vanaheim." I said slowly, trying not to re-hash the argument. "Speaking of, where's everyone else? Violet's not at your meeting?" There was a long, uncomfortable pause before Jalix spoke up.

"We have things handled. Been a…bit of two sides to things. Kara and I, along with Val, Sonya, and Alice have been working one end while Krystal, Amy, Violet, and Raven work the other half. We're trying to give them some more free time."

"Meaning that you're trying not to bother them with your issues." I articulated. "Sheltering people didn't work out well in Aerael. Now you've got the kids split up from the adults?"

"We're not sheltering them." Kara defended. "But we've done this before. All of us. We know the stresses, we work well together. If we let them do the small things, it gives us time to make the higher-level plans and iron out the larger details."

"Letting you take responsibility when things go wrong." Eric added, taking my side for the first time in a long occasion. The silence from the other end of the phone was resounding. "How predictable."

"They need to have lived a life, Eric. As short or long as that may be. Let them live it." Kara's argument was poignant and short, allowing us a change of subject.

"We will do what we must, Jalix. We are rich in the commerce of war. We will be prepared for it shortly enough." Yuri brought the conversation to a close, deciding that results would likely go nowhere from arguing and debating.

"Sounds good. Stay in touch if you guys need anything else." Jalix hung up, leaving the five of us huddled around a workbench in the corner of the hangar.

"Sounds like we're going to need to shift some plans." The soldier shifted the sling of his rifle to a higher spot on his shoulder, speaking to Yuri. "I have everyone either running close-quarter drills or going through the gear to start issuing everything out. We have a bit, if you wanted to talk."

"That's why I called you, Marcus." Yuri motioned for all of us to follow him, heading through a door in the back of the hangar that led to the administrative building attached to it. It was nice to finally hear the rain grow distant, although the silence was disconcerting while the few soldiers and techs worked inside the office space. "We need to go over a few things. More than a few, now that the plans have changed." The front of my shirt was cold in the dim office, still wet from the river that spilled on me and chilled by the building's fans. Layla seemed to be taking in the warmth, rolling her shoulders and enjoying a moment free from her cockpit.

"Hopefully for the last time." Eric added firmly. "A bigger force is a good thing, but it means we have a harder time changing that up. Six hundred people can't swivel on a dime and change up their mission."

"And that's just what's here at Quantico." Layla agreed. "The soldiers here get one side of their training, but the technical aspect of gearing up for the fight is happening at Vanaheim. I'm sure it's no easier for them." We walked up a flight of stairs, moving into Yuri's office and standing around the massive table that held our map of Washington, D.C. Several plastic sheets were placed atop its surface and a pile of wet-erase markers were banded together on the edge of the table for highlighting and marking its surface without making permanent changes.

"Well, as much as I don't like Jalix randomly making that call without checking first, it's a good idea overall." Eric started, handing out markers in unique colors to each of us. "I've been staying in touch with Raven. Not much else has changed. Whether that's good or bad, we'll find out. But let's…let's run it from the beginning, assuming nothing, and go at it with a cure-based approach instead of one based on the attack alone." He took a short breath, twirling the marker between his fingers as he often did with his pens. "We've got one main target, and that's Legacy in the White house. He wants Kara and Amy to dictate the world and be used as a cure, respectively. As soon as he has them in his hands, game's over. He drops nuclear bombs on the remaining U.S. cities so there's no way for the world to retaliate, then blows them away, too. Whoever is left will be converted to a Vampyre and all under his – or Kara's – control, using the cure as a vector to occasionally purge the population. Which…is not what we want."

"Oh, it's not?" I asked sarcastically. Eric glared at me while he continued.

"While he thinks Kara and Amy are on the west coast and chases the ghosts we've left him, we have enough time to get our pieces set on the board, as well as examine the ones Legacy has. Yuri, that's you."

"Well…" Yuri started, pointing to a spot above the White House on the large map. "Legacy has a bulwark of civilians to his north that prevents us from attacking that way. The Potomac river is to the west, which leaves us a south and east-oriented attack. His personnel are garrisoned in the historical and museum buildings to the east, and his ground security is entrenched to protect the open zones on the south side. That security consists of armored vehicles, machine gun nests, and two anti-air missile platforms."

"Along with like…twelve hundred drug-fueled super-Vampyres." Layla added, scratching her scalp to undo the messiness caused by wearing her helmet a few minutes prior.

"Agreed. Factor Five, although a useful asset on our side for healing any physical damage, is being misused by the enemy side to increase their strength and speed. Thankfully with how it affects them, along with the torture they went through to brainwash them, they're a lot more careless."

"Careless, but durable. I watched more than one get shot in the chest and barely flinch." I added. Yuri paused, pointing at me briefly.

"That's right, you were there when I helped your friends escape with the data we needed. You've seen just how difficult it can be."

"They're animals. There's little else to be said. The Tortured are not something we want to take on without an advantage. And considering we have none-"

"Have none?" Marcus asked with incredulity. "You have a friend that can throw tanks with her mind-"

"Two of them."

"A friend that can set things on fire-"

"Technically, she's a doctor."

"And one *very* attractive blue-haired comrade that can freeze things solid." He smirked, and realized that I wasn't about to add anything to that description of Krystal. "You guys have a huge upper hand. We're just foot soldiers."

"Which is what's going to win this war." Eric warned. "Those people you mentioned may be the best of the best, but they're leading. Advising. They're still only a handful of people, and won't turn the tide against Legacy's army on its own. Our ground troops will, along with the air power we've managed to wrangle."

"Agreed." Yuri took over again. "Those troops will be split into two parts. The bulk will be with Valterius, who is training his team leaders and vehicle drivers in Vanaheim.

They will have the heavy vehicles and firepower moving upward from the south. I will have a portion of what remains, using our Blackhawk helicopters to bring them in from the east side and take the garrison buildings from the top down. Whoever is flushed into the streets should be annihilated by Val's forces. Now, before we can get there, I think we have some kinks with the air superiority to work out. Layla, how is your work with Jalix going?"

"As well as can be." She sighed. "Andrea and I are going to be flying the F-35s here to drop a strike on both of Legacy's anti-air missile platforms. That should let the Blackhawks fly in. From there, we're going to start an air patrol to ensure Legacy doesn't have any support from fighter jets. If he does, we'll handle them. Since F-35's aren't made for air-to-air combat, the new modifications will let us compete if we need to." She tilted her head. "I don't foresee it happening, though. If anything, Legacy will need air-to-ground support, which flies much slower. Now *that*, we can handle easily."

"That airstrike will open the fight." Yuri continued. "At either Layla or Andrea's confirmation that the strikes against Legacy's missiles are successful, the Blackhawks that are hovering just out of reach will move in, and Val will push from the south to take advantage of the initial damage. As my unit clears the garrison buildings, we'll be securing holding areas for Val's casualties. From there, we continue to push slowly from the south until we reach the White House. At that point, Marcus comes into play." Marcus cleared his throat, nodding.

"Yeah, I should have a team of twelve ready to go at the front of Val's firing line. Our best soldiers. We'll breach through the grounds and start sweeping the building to find Legacy. We'll be joined by people like Kara, Sonya, Val, and the rest of the leadership. Once we take the White House, we'll transition to holding our ground and moving slowly to clean up what's left around the city."

"Which wraps everything up in a bow *except* this new variable." I pressed. "Our missile launcher is different than what Legacy has. His anti-air platforms are trucks with mounted, pre-established explosives. What Jalix is talking about is a towed system that we're apparently going to have to load and fire off once it's in place. It's an entirely independent system. That means it's slow, and it's vulnerable."

"So we put it at the back of Val's unit." Marcus shrugged.

"Too easy for a couple people to flank and wreak havoc. It'll have to be about three-quarters of the way back. We need protection from behind, as well. And as far as positioning…honestly, the White House grounds themselves would be a fine staging area." Eric uncapped a blue marker and drew a dotted line along Val's path. "If Val goes through here, Marcus' team can breach the perimeter fencing and get in while we tow the platform through and start setting up. Everyone outside of the fence goes on defense to protect the cure's escort and the firing platform."

"That's perfect." I nodded. "We just set up a perimeter and hold on long enough to set up. Maybe…if I run assembly and disassembly drills with a team of my techs, we can get the setup time down to five minutes."

"Five minutes? That's impressive." Layla complimented.

"Five minutes is eight years in a firefight." I returned.

"It's fast enough." Yuri decided. "Once we load the cure and get-"

"It's more than that." I interjected. "Schillinger's old plan was pretty dumb to begin with, but he had more steps involved than it seems. The targeting system has to be recalibrated completely. We're not firing short-range missiles at jets, we're just launching metal cans. Hell, a regular mortar tube would work if it had to. But this way, we can get dozens of them fired in a short time. Now, we only need a mile or so in trajectory, and it's going to be pointless if we start landing the gas on rooftops or empty alleyways. We need to hit intersections, major roads, points of travel. Places people will walk through. We need to infect as many people as possible, as fast as possible. When those civilians start fleeing to the north, they'll spread it across the country as they escape to other cities."

"This sounds familiar." Eric grimaced. "Project Cerberus. Same words, same plan, different intent."

"Why aren't we hand-delivering the cure?" Marcus asked, shrugging. "Or planting the canisters as we go?"

"Risk of being a target, of them getting destroyed, misfiring. And from what I know of last time, they have to be kept refrigerated. Like...*cold.* So leaving them to sit for later is going to quickly kill the cure virus inside."

"And converting us to humans too quickly will only make Val's forces get demolished. So we can't start gassing the bulk of the fight. This is the only shot we have, but it's a good one." Eric and I explained the situation, remembering more and more pieces from Schillinger's first major attempt on the world. "Last time, Schillinger's people manually aimed using fixed-point pneumatic struts. We'll have to go digital and install a computer system with pre-planned coordinates."

"Alright, so we have the airstrike on the missile platforms, then the rush of troops from the east in helos and the south in heavy vehicles. South team pushes to the White House where we clear and set up for the cure. It sounds...too easy, in theory." Marcus summarized. "What if Legacy's launchers aren't disabled by the air strike? Or we miss?"

"I'll hit them." Layla said firmly.

"Just in case." He allayed, showing his hands in friendliness. "Not doubting you, or Andrea for that matter. We just need another jet pilot as backup."

"We do have a…lead." Yuri winced, hesitating in deciding on whether to say anything at all. "I- well, Jalix actually, has an old friend in Colorado. Retired Major Hamilton, F-22 pilot. Lives off the grid. Jalix sent a message to Nellis Air Force Base in the hopes they can reach him sometime soon." We all waited, trying to see what his hesitance was stemming from.

"And…?" Eric probed.

"*And* nothing. At least, not yet. That's the problem. Nellis still has an F-22 that's flyable, but…we can't count on whether the guy is even going to respond or not."

"Okay, but why? Every Vampyre in existence needs to fight. Why wouldn't this guy want to answer the call to duty?" Eric questioned. Yuri sucked air through his teeth.

"It's not exactly *his* fight. He's…a bit of an oddball. When I say retired, I mean *retired.* Moved into the Rockies to hide from the world. Guy living on his own for that long with no visitors, and certainly no flight practice in the last thirty years, he's going to be rusty at best. Unreliable at worst."

"Nonexistent at worst." I corrected Yuri. "We can handle rusty. If he can stay in the air, it gives another show of force and keeps other aircraft away from our airspace. We don't need much else."

"You're saying he'd be bait." Layla realized, turning on me with hostility. "He'd be a distraction for them so Andrea and I can-"

"Yeah. If it gets the job done. No one's going to force him." I stood behind the principle of my statement, knowing that everyone else was at no less risk. Yuri tried to change the subject quickly to avoid things growing hostile between us.

"Layla. How's the pilot training for the Blackhawks? How many can we get in the air? I think we're over halfway done on assembling the aircraft themselves."

"Two. Right now." The room grew silent again at her answer.

You've got to be kidding me.

"What?" She shrugged, looking at each of us. "I'm not a rotary-wing pilot. We have *one* guy that can actually fly them and he's training and teaching as fast as he can. Only one student managed to pass a test flight in the simulator-"

"So they haven't even conducted a *real*...test flight?" Eric groaned.

"Uh...no? Look outside, genius." She pointed to the windows, watching the rain roll off the tarps and onto the runway. "Not only is it a miracle that we shipped twelve aircraft in pieces from Pennsylvania with no one noticing, but we covered them in tarps to *hide them*. We can't just start flying them around. What, do you think Legacy's patrols are just going to ignore a drunk-looking Blackhawk doing practice runs? Those simulators are damn good, it's the only training they're going to get. And with Vampyre reflexes and enhanced fine-motor control, I can promise you it's easier than learning as a human." She sighed. "We have twelve craft, should have fourteen pilots in case anything happens to one of them. I do...I do genuinely expect them to be ready. Another month, maybe six weeks."

"If...that's time we have." I added quietly, staring at the map.

"Make sure your lead pilot is with Jalix on his personal ride." Eric added. "We can't take any risks. Guy in charge needs the best pilot." We sat in silence for a long moment, each of us second-guessing aspects of the plan and pieces that were still missing.

"What do we expect casualties to be like?" Marcus finally asked. The gloomy question hung heavily in the air, unanswered and disheartening.

"No one's going to know. That'll be up to Alice and Amy's teams. Hell, if Krystal and Amy can be separated for more than five seconds." Eric joked. I chuckled, knowing what he meant. "They're…they're going to do what they can to keep the fight going. But Amy can't be on the front lines, even with her healing powers. Can't take the risk of capture. Or worse." Eric pulled out his cell phone to open a document. "They have…thirty nurses, eight of those still being trained, and five doctors, not including Alice and Goodson. Raven managed to pull some from refugee volunteers after New York. It'll have to be enough."

"That's actually not bad." Marcus chimed. "My team has a medic, so we can handle the frontline of Val's…assault." He turned his head, walking toward the window and staring distantly at something past the airfield. He tilted his head as if he were listening to something, but all the rest of us could hear were drops of rain against the glass. We waited for a moment, hoping he would say something before he turned again to face outside and peered through the rain. "Something sounds off."

"I hear it, too." Layla agreed, turning to us. "Thunder? No…sounds like gunshots, distant. Getting closer, fast."

"Tortured patrol?" I didn't wait for an answer before turning around and running back down the stairs.

The rest of the team followed me, close behind as we made our way back through the hangar. I was the first to throw open my locker door, trying to stay out of everyone else's way as they did the same. We could hear noise outside as engineers dropped their tools and started shouting to each other between the aircraft. Each of us either grabbed a rifle or a pistol from our personal kits and sprinted out of the hangar to follow the crowd that accrued near the edge of the airfield. As I left the cover of the tarps, I put my sunglasses back on to protect my eyes from both the rain and clouded sunlight before strapping my pistol holster across my leg. Marcus managed to gain the lead, taking point as we moved toward the intensifying sounds of an impending fight.

"Shit!" I heard Yuri hiss from behind me. I turned around, watching him shake his phone with a sense of incensed violence. "If it's the returning team, they haven't contacted me. Why?"

"I don't know." I breathed, finally starting to make out the scenario while it barreled toward us.

On the main road leading to the airfield, four vehicles started making their way into view from behind the buildings of the base. The first was a heavy truck hauling Jalix's missile platform on a towed trailer. The next vehicle was an armored truck filled with the retrieval team, who was much more focused on shooting at the pursuing pickup trucks than driving in a straight line. The heavy vehicle veered to one side, breaking away from the chase and nearly tipping the trailer behind it. The patrol vehicle became the pack leader, its occupants doing their best to take suppressing shots against withering gunfire. The remaining three vehicles were maintaining their speed, bringing the fight toward the hangar faster than we initially expected.

They're headed straight toward the airfield.

"Open up!" Marcus yelled, lifting his rifle and trying to find a point of aim that would allow him to hit one of the pursuing vehicles without shooting at our own people. "We can't let them get to the runway!"

"That part's too late." I realized, grabbing Marcus's shoulder and pulling him away from the path the vehicles took: a straight line from the road into the side of the runway. The traditional protective barriers had been removed to tow the helicopters along that same route and were yet to be replaced, leaving it vulnerable to speeding vehicles.

While the driver of our team's vehicle was aware of the airfield's layout, the pursuing trucks were not, and couldn't recalculate in enough time to avoid skidding into the side of unfinished helicopters at the north end of our tarp-covered construction site. One truck impacted at a steep angle, smashing into several tent poles from the side of the airfield before stopping against an unfinished Blackhawk and causing tremendous damage. The other vehicle was luckier and skidded several yards first, only lightly grazing the second Blackhawk before braking and losing its passengers to a dismounted gunfight. Half of them took notice of us and started shooting while the others took aim at the patrol vehicle. The tarps around them fell, obscuring our view of the combatants and inciting our group to sprint toward them. I ducked to my right, entering the shaded maze of huddled mechanics, spare parts, and tools while I made my way toward the sound of firing rifles.

"Tony, on your left!" Yuri called out. I drew my pistol and whipped to my left, watching one of the Tortured sprint past me on the other side of the tarps and attempt to rush the hangar.

Lift. Line up. Trigger squeeze.

With the first of what sounded like many being dispatched, I pressed forward until reaching the first damaged helicopter. Marcus fired off another few shots, followed by Layla, who provided him with suppressing fire while he reloaded. I took a moment to examine the scene, one of our helicopters now defunct.

Shit. This thing's decimated. It's going to take weeks to fix, and we don't have the material to repair it anyway. They just took one out of commission entirely. Wait, no…they saw the opportunity…and did it on purpose.

I rounded the corner, aiming the handgun at the interior of the first vehicle before seeing their bodies strewn across the hood and smeared across the fuselage of the helicopter. The impact was hard enough to eject them, and none had made it through the ordeal alive. Even with their enhancements from Factor Five, the amount of blood that gushed from their devastating injuries wouldn't have let them live for longer than a few seconds.

Good. Bastards should have worn their seatbelts. Truck has five seats, I count five bodies. Other truck would have been at capacity, and I already took out one of them. Marcus, Yuri, and Layla were shooting at the rest.

I took a breath, making my way out from the collapsed tarps and seeing Eric approach me from the left side. He carried a rifle and walked with me toward the last truck, whose occupants were now deceased a few dozen feet ahead in their vain attempt to run north toward the vehicle containing our own people. I sighed quietly, holstering the handgun and calling out to the stopped transport.

"You guys okay?" I yelled, slowly watching a shaky thumbs-up make its way into view through one of the battered windows. Our group approached theirs as the driver climbed out and promptly vomited all over the rear tire.

"We're alright." The passenger called, jumping out and running his hands through his hair.

"What the hell happened?" Yuri demanded, trying to keep an even temper. "You guys were supposed to keep a low profile. How the hell-"

"They were watching the base, sir." A young woman climbed out from the backseat, struggling to remove her ballistic vest. "Legacy was waiting for us to make a move. Those Tortured were a few miles out from Quantico on the side of the road. Watching. Nothing we could have done to avoid it."

"How would he have known?" Marcus asked, sliding his hands into the top of his vest for comfort. "We were careful, we had recon and security far enough out that we would have seen Legacy's men watching us."

"I don't have an answer for you, sir." She swallowed, still struggling to breathe normally. She tossed her vest into the truck and leaned against the frame, closing her eyes and sighing heavily.

"Well…Legacy knows about it now. He knows…everything. The launcher, the-"

"I don't see how, sir." She interjected, taking a step toward Yuri. "Anytime they could have had the opportunity to contact Legacy, we opened fire. They seemed too focused on the fight. Too distracted to contemplate anything else or bother with anything other than killing us. We counted shots, and I don't think any of them stopped to bother with a phone call." She gagged, the adrenaline finally leaving her system and taking a toll on her body. The driver composed himself and looked at Yuri after wiping his mouth.

"If Legacy found out, sir…I don't see how it would have happened. We did everything we could, opened fire at every chance we had. And now they're dead."

"You did well. All of you." Yuri concluded, palming the driver's shoulder. "You've taken your first steps in defending our way of life."

"We should examine their phones." Eric suggested to me quietly. "We can check to see if anyone made a call in the last fifteen minutes. I'll get a couple techs together to get through any passwords." He pulled out his own phone and dialed a number, looking back at the hangar and stepping away from us.

If we get out of this, it'll be a miracle. Otherwise, we're going to see an army at our doorstep in a few hours.

"Have your trainees stop what they're doing and take up positions around the base. Rotate them out as they need rest, but I want eyes everywhere for the next while." Yuri looked at Marcus, issuing him an order.

"Yes, sir. And I'll have my scouts head up the road to keep any new surprises from hitting us. If he's coming, we'll have some warning." He nodded to Yuri and took off running toward the hangar. Layla looked back at the wreckage at the north end of the construction site and sighed.

"One of those Blackhawks is unsalvageable."

"Use it to repair the second one that got hit. Get the pilots and have them participate so they can learn more about the repair process. I'll have my engineers focus on getting the tarps repaired first, and we'll get rid of the bodies and trucks." I sighed, shaking the rain from my hair.

"Speaking of trucks..." Layla started, watching the previously-swerving transport vehicle roll toward us slowly, making its way to the head of the airfield and slowing to a stop in front of us. The flatbed trailer seemed largely undamaged, as did the weapon strapped down on its surface. The canvas cover for the truck's attached cargo bed was peppered with holes, but appeared to have tolerated the gunfight and erratic driving as well as could be expected. The driver climbed out, quickly making his way over to the occupants of the recon vehicle.

"You guys okay?" The driver asked. The young woman from before nodded, smirking.

"Yeah. We're good. Glad to see you guys are alright." She paused, glancing at me briefly. "Want to tell him?" She turned back to the driver of the transport, who smiled and turned his attention toward me.

"I don't like the guessing game shit. What do you have for me?" I asked curtly, not feeling the need to waste time. The cargo driver pointed to the back of the colossal truck, gesturing with his thumbs.

"Everything, sir. We got almost everything you needed and *then* some. One of my guys had the bright idea of trying to get some of the rockets for this missile system. Now I *told* him..." He guided me to the back of the truck, pulling out a ladder so we could climb into the back and view its contents. "That the ammo supply points would be locked down, the uh...ammo bunkers on the base where they store all the fun stuff we'll need for the fight. But it turns out, those doors were designed for the security to be electronic. So we took a detour with some bolt cutters and torches." He spoke to me as we climbed up before he pulled back the plastic sheet covering a set of cheap-looking wooden crates. Bits of plastic filler and natural fibers stuck out from the enclosure, indicating that they had been opened. "We have the original ordnance for the missile launcher. You can use those-"

"To reverse-engineer the viral canisters."

"And you can even use the original propellant." He spread his arms, happy with his loot. He held up a single finger, leading me into another discovery. "One more thing for you, sir." The cargo bed was stacked from floor to ceiling with boxes, crates, and totes, but one of the black boxes was near the edge and had bands of strapping to hold it in place. Nothing was piled on top of it, likely so it wouldn't break under undue weight. I waited with anticipation, hoping it would be as useful as the previous bounty. After unclipping the straps, he popped the latches of the box open and stepped to the side, letting me take in the contents without his disruption.

"Is-...is that what I think it is?" I asked, kneeling to look at the device.

"Yes, sir. I know we don't have any Apache pilots, but I thought we could retrofit it-"

"Onto Jalix's Blackhawk." I finished, nodding. I looked back at him, in disbelief that any of the crew we sent were intelligent enough to consider the option of salvaging the particular piece of equipment. "You do realize that *this*...could virtually guarantee a hit on our initial airstrike?"

"Yes, sir. Chris and Vivian were the ones to think of it, I just helped pull it out of secure storage."

"I don't care who the hell thought of it. This might just win us the damn war." I looked back at the intricate system of complex sensors and cameras, in awe and nearly afraid to move it.

It's going to take a colossal effort to integrate this with anything other than an Apache, but if we can pull it off, we'll have a tide-turning advantage.

"We figured the infrared and radar in that sensor system would help mark the targets for the pilots, plus the radar and thermal tracking could end up giving us an advantage to hit the heavy vehicles on a second pass." He added, kicking another box. "Especially because of these." I paused, closing the case and standing up to look at him directly.

"Stop doing that shit. Don't lead into it, just *tell* me what's in the goddamn box." I growled, hating anticipation.

"Sorry. The rest of the truck is either titanium for your engineers or rifles, pistols, and carbines for the fight. But this box...we managed to grab some Mavericks while we were stealing from the ordnance bunkers."

You did...what?

"Mavericks. As in-"

"AGM-sixty-five-delta Maverick air-to-ground missiles, yes, sir. For Andrea and Layla." He tapped the crate with his foot as if discussing a new part for his car instead of armament capable of targeting a vehicle with deadly precision from several miles away.

"Is there anything else that you'd like to tell me is in here? A golden goose? A unicorn? How did you idiots manage-"

"There is *one* thing we couldn't get." He grimaced, interrupting my brief moment of happiness. "What?"

"We couldn't fit the raw carbon fiber materials in here. But hey, we got everything else-"

"You're fired."

REVELATION

KRYSTAL

Even through the glass, I could almost feel the hot, panting breaths from her open mouth, a ravenous set of fangs clenched with both anger and pain as she writhed on the hospital bed.

"The sedatives I've been using won't keep her out for longer than a few minutes. At the levels we'd need to keep her unconscious, I'd be worried about toxicity. The…deadly kind." Alice added, shrugging and gesturing at the intensive care room behind the window. "I don't know what else to do. I'm just going to have to manage the pain-"

"No." I argued quietly, watching my ex-lover roll on the bed in agony and cry a short, howling burst of air before shaking violently and gripping the side of the mattress. "She was an addict. Worse than I was. Replacing one addiction with another will do more harm than good. And we both know that only the strong stuff is going to put a dent in *that* kind of pain."

"Then what do you want me to do?" She was asking me honestly, desperate to keep Rachel's hold on sanity alive. I sighed, combing over a brief set of options in my head and coming up empty-handed.

"Let me *out*!" Rachel screamed, barely audible from where we stood. Her voice was desperate, a type of anguish only heard in the moments when a person suspected their own death was imminent. "Please!" It asked for nothing specific, but howled for a chance to be free from the pain she suffered. I watched the thick mat of brown hair flail from side to side as she tried to break free of the pairs of handcuffs and leather bands before quitting and crying loudly.

"Let me in." I said to Alice, watching her eyebrows approach the ceiling.

"Nope."

"Please. I'm the only one that knows what she's going through. And seeing a familiar face might-"

"*Familiar* in this case…might not be best." Sonya mumbled, reminding us of her seated presence behind us.

"I know her. She's not going to hurt me. She wanted revenge because of these drugs, because of this Factor Five addiction, not because of how she actually feels." I was hoping to convince both Alice and myself, and succeeded at one of them.

"Fine. But Sonya goes with you. I just need to know *exactly* what's going on from her perspective. I have all the technical measurements, but I need to hear it from her. Pain, type of pain, discomfort, itching, fatigue, *anything* is going to help if we have a chance at doing this for more people." My sister's sense of goodwill became more noticeable, the lab coat she wore accenting even further the enthusiasm she bore for her profession.

"I'm going to be honest, those odds are low." Sonya stood up, preparing to enter the room with me. "We're prepping every person willing to go to war against them. I don't foresee a lot of survivors. And the ones that *do* make it…they're programmed to kill us. Raven has someone bringing what's left of the Catalyst data, an old colleague I guess, but I'm not sure how much it'll help."

"We're going to find out if Legacy's programming can be broken." I reminded. "I want to smash through this."

"We've had Rachel in Vanaheim for eight weeks. I can't taper off the Factor Five dose any slower. I'm dropping it by five milliliters a day and she's in constant agony. Any more than that and her organs start failing, cancers crop up, it's…this is a mess, Kryssi." She looked at me with a mixed sense of despair and failure. "I don't know what else to do."

She thinks this is her fault; that she invented Factor Five and the enemy is using it against us because of her.

"I need you to know that you didn't cause any of this." I started, gesturing to Rachel's room. "This is not how you designed the drugs to be used. It's no different than when I got hooked on-"

"And that was *also* my fault, Krystal…I mean, I claim to be the only doctor that can do these things-"

"And you are. Without a doubt. But you can only control what you *do* for the patient. Not what they do to themselves. You treated me for an injury the best you could. Saved my life for the *second* time, at that point. I chose the rest. I chose to keep using. Not you." She seemed relieved at the fact that I was taking responsibility for my own addiction, and even more so that she wasn't regarded as being at fault for starting the downward spiral in my life. "But this is a team effort. Medicine is a team effort. If we need to go in there and break the mental barrier, so be it. That's medicine, too."

"Yeah, well…" She crossed her arms and sighed, looking at a display briefly as it beeped. "I'm not giving you a license to practice anytime soon."

"Why not? Amy got one. If she can do it, I can." I teased, patting Sonya on the shoulder so she'd follow me to the door.

"Amy studied for a very long time, and she's *much* more cautious than you are."

"Tell her that on karaoke night at the nightclub. And don't let her near tequila." I warned, opening the door that separated us from Rachel's moaning figure. She was contorting repeatedly, a series of motions in patterns that would have ripped muscles and tendons on most humans, but on her had been repeated for days on end unless an hour of sleep forced her into a nightmarish pause. Sonya approached alongside me, staying close enough that I knew she was taking on the responsibility of being my bodyguard.

It's fine, Sonya. We'll be okay.

Without warning, Rachel's body swiveled all at once to look at the two of us, glaring with a seething hatred.

"You." She whispered, groaning quietly before hissing at me again. "Thought you were dead."

"Nah." I said casually, waving a dismissive hand. "You actually ended up fixing my bad shoulder. I came here to thank you." Her pupils flashed quickly from dilated to constricted and back, an unhealthy flickering of her irises as she looked between my eyes.

"Why are you here?" She grunted, beads of sweat pouring from her brow.

"We came to help." I said honestly. "I can't give you Factor Five and I can't give you any hard drugs. Is there anything else that would help?"

"A quicker death." She snapped, a whimper shortly after. "Kill me now."

"We're trying to *save* you." I reassured. "We know what Legacy did to you, and we want to find a way to reverse it." She seemed to fall still for the briefest moment, even her trembling coming to a momentary halt.

"You don't know what he does to us." She said in a breathy whisper. There was something horrifying in her tone of voice, a primal fear that made Sonya and I equally uncomfortable hearing. "There is no reversing it. There is no going back. We are immortal…and then we are dead." She swallowed. "There *is* no saving me."

I can't even see anything left of the person she used to be. It's just…a wounded animal.

"Rachel, I…I want to know how you're feeling. Besides like shit, I already know that."

"How I feel? I *can't* feel." She started to shudder again, her leg jerking at the knee before straightening out again. "I know where my body is, but it's…beyond me. I can…barely control myself. Speaking…breathing…it's all I have left. I can't fight back, I piss myself. I have nothing left." She paused, looking at Sonya. "And somehow, there's…still so much pain."

"What kind of pain? And where?" Sonya asked, pressing harder than I was.

"We can't help you unless we know." I explained, softening my tone. Rachel was quiet for a moment, dealing with a fit of movement before turning her attention back to us. She stared at me for a long moment, the only thing left in her eyes being a sense of hopelessness.

"It can't *be* described…" She licked her cracked lips, sniffling. "The pain is in the soul. In the spirit. It infects the body, but it's not *within* the body. It's like broken glass in every thought." I heard Alice faintly rap on the glass, drawing our attention away from Rachel for a split second. I sighed, looking back at the suffering woman.

"I'll be back. I don't know when. But we're going to try and help. Okay?" I raised my left hand and placed it on her brow, trying to let a cool flow of energy radiate from my hand without overwhelming her skin with new sensations. She inhaled sharply, then sighed deeply.

"Thank-…thank you. Krystal." Her breaths were labored, only partial lungfuls of air entering her mouth when her body allowed. Wanting to see what Alice needed and simultaneously escape watching the gruesome process of a slow death, I made my way across the dimly-lit hospital room and opened the metal door, closing it behind me and standing on the other side of the glass again. Alice stood with her cell phone in one hand and the other on her hip in an irritated fashion.

"Of course *this* is when Jalix needs all of us for some meeting." She clicked her tongue disapprovingly. "Sorry you couldn't get anywhere with Rachel. If it wasn't for Jalix, I'd have let you stay in there for longer. Her description was…interesting. I'll take it into account and do some reading."

"I needed an excuse to get out of there, anyway." I shook my head in disbelief, watching Rachel's fits of pain start again.

"Are you…okay?" She asked, gesturing. "I know she's an ex, but she *did* try to kill you."

"I know." I sighed, running both hands through my hair and lifting the mass to allow air to rush over my neck. "But there used to be a person under there. Someone I knew. And to see the body there without that person inside is…it's like staring at a corpse." Alice was in the middle of a reply to her text when she stopped, looking up at me slowly.

"I know that feeling well." She started. "Very well."

"We all do." Sonya finished, raising her eyebrows.

That's what it was like when I was in my coma.

"Jesus…" I said in both awe and sympathy, not realizing that they had been through a similar experience with me. "I can't imagine what it must have felt like…" I paused. "…to see someone *so* amazing-"

"Here we go." Alice rolled her eyes and started removing her lab coat, leaving the observatory and walking down the hallway at a brisk pace. I followed, pressing the joke to lighten her mood.

"-so courageous and brave-"

"I'm *so* glad your ego's back."

"-not to mention attractive-"

"Debatable."

"-to be lying there like a supermodel-"

"Averagemodel."

"-rude, waiting to be awoken."

"And you *were* awoken. To a broken-ass city and a bunch of seizures." Sonya teased as we entered an office, letting Alice change briefly into a tan jacket instead of her lab coat.

"I didn't see *you* there, missy." I antagonized the situation even more, pressing my luck with how much I could irritate the two of them. "Off gallivanting around for no reason."

"Gallivanting…?" Alice asked incredulously. "*Dicking around* is what you'd normally say. Or something far more vulgar."

"I doth protest to thine image of mineself." I pulled my phone from my pocket, reading Jalix's text before replying.

Krystal, we need you guys in a meeting. Main conf. room, make sure Alice comes with you and doesn't get distracted with her medical stuff. Thumbs-up emoji.

"I am but a fair and proper lady, and I act as such." I scolded Alice pompously, tilting my nose in the air.

We're already on our way, Major Dumbass. Give us a damn second.

I sent the message back to Jalix, basking in the beloved irony as a newly recruited nurse I had seen several times before walked into Alice's office.

"You paged me?" She asked inquisitively.

"Yeah, I need you to take over. Counsel's meeting. I don't want to try any opiates, but we can try to start her on twenty of diazepam instead. I'm out of other options. It might take the edge off and prevent her from hurting herself. Maybe let her sleep for a bit." Alice's voice was saturated with pity.

"Sure thing, ma'am." The nurse replied, looking over at me and smiling. She tucked a strand of hair behind her ear, an auburn with occasional strands of deep purple, and stared at me for a moment with intense blue eyes.

"Hey, Krystal." She said after a moment, apparently expecting me to speak first.

"Hey, Emily! How are things?" I tried to be friendly, but wasn't overly familiar with her and barely knew her name.

"Things are good. Busy, you know?" She giggled. "Trying to find things to do after hours. Might hit the nightclub later."

"Yeah, the club usually has some pretty fun events. Tonight's beer and wings night, I think? Sounds like a great way to blow off steam." I wasn't sure where the conversation was heading and made my best effort to be social, but had apparently said something wrong as she pursed her lips and nodded, walking away quietly. I shrugged in confusion, glancing at Alice for guidance. Her smile was abundant and smug.

"It's been *that* long, huh?" She finally said, prompting a loud and aggravated sigh from my mouth.

Oh, she was hitting on you.

"I…yeah, I should have picked up on that one. Sorry."

"Apologize to *her*, hon. That was rejection if I've ever heard it." Sonya taunted.

"Well you *haven't* heard it, so butt out." I hit back, poking fun at her lack of intimate relationships. "I do feel bad, though."

"You can always make it up to me?" Emily's voice was raised into a hopeful tenor as she rounded the corner again, this time holding a clipboard and rocking back and forth on her heels. "Sorry, I wasn't eavesdropping. Doctor Goodson is here." She made the last comment to Alice, but immediately returned her attention to me while waiting for a reply.

"Oh, I actually have plans for tonight." I grimaced, being truthful. "Maybe another time, though?"

"Sounds good, Ice Queen." She winked at me before walking away, her lab coat fluttering behind her as she disappeared.

"Not a chance." I whispered quietly, more to myself than to anyone else.

The quiet sound of tapping footsteps grew closer to the door, slightly uneven and as if they walked with a slight and nearly unnoticeable limp. Had I been occupied with anything else, I wouldn't have even noticed the irregularity. A woman rounded the corner quickly with a small box full of papers in her hand, dropping it on the carpet to the right of the door and throwing a fear-inducing glare at Alice.

"You're in my office." Her voice was more rough and shattered than Raven's, and had scars on her face to match.

From one side to the other, old and well-healed burns marred her face and were just enough to wrinkle the skin in a mottled pattern of damage. Her nose was crooked on one side, and one of her earlobes was missing entirely. While most of her hair was gone, I could see some faint strands of red that were intentionally shaved down since the rest had been burned away. I felt pity for whatever horrible event she had been through, but was on edge with her attitude toward my sister. "You can leave as soon as possible." She finished. Alice tilted her head, shocked at the level of disrespect she was being shown.

"Uh…I'm…sorry for the inconvenience. We had to borrow it for the time being, but I'll have some of the admin staff move my things to one of the empty offices at the end of the hall." Alice tried to foster patience, tested quickly as Dr. Goodson walked up to Alice's desk and stared into her eyes, slowly pushing every document on her workspace to the floor in a quiet flutter of paper. The box she had delivered was picked up and placed on the surface, her eye contact unbroken during the ordeal.

"Today." Dr. Goodson emphasized.

"Who the hell do you think you are?" Sonya chuckled, crossing her arms. "Do you have *any* idea who you're talking to?" Alice stared back and I watched her face grow from anger to curiosity as she examined the woman's facial features.

"I do." Dr. Goodson replied quietly. "But *she* has no idea who I am. Or why I bothered showing up to help." Alice continued staring, growing increasingly lost for words.

"I-…have we met? I don't recall your name-"

"Oh, I wouldn't expect you to recall. You weren't there at Schillinger's facility for *me*. For any of us. You were there for *Jalix*." Alice's eyes shot open, her mouth parting to say something before Dr. Goodson continued. "You had *better* things to do. Remember me now?"

"Tammy." Alice whispered, taking a step back and shaking her head. "You…you survived."

"No thanks to you. Or your…mafia family." She seethed. "Your husband told me to get back in my cell. That you'd come back for me. And you know what? I believed it right up to the point the thermite went off inside my airtight compartment. You might play with fire, but do you know how *hot* it was in that box?"

"Tammy, I-"

"It's *Doctor Goodson*. No amount of explaining helps." She returned coolly. "I don't care what your mission was, I don't care who you were rescuing. You ruined my life. Forced me to cut myself open and smear samples from a Project Catalyst strain against the wound to intentionally infect me. So *then* I was almost immortal, clawing my way out of a burning, airtight box." I interrupted the two of them, stepping in to quell the argument.

"Look, I have no idea what either of you are talking about, but we need to be on the same side. We already are, or you two wouldn't be in the same room. Mistakes were made by a lot of people. We need to put aside the grudges and get along for now."

"Says you. I can work, so long as you remember my name. Doctor Tamara Goodson. Hope it keeps you up at night." She growled at Alice, walking back to the doorway and making her exit angrily. Sonya and I watched for Alice to say something, but her expression of sadness and regret overcame anything else she could have put into words.

"Hey. Forget all of that. It's in the past." Sonya tried to reassure Alice, gently beckoning toward the door to remind her that we had an obligation to attend .

"*Forget* that…easy for the blonde chick with amnesia to say." Alice joked quietly, smiling gently as she brushed past us. I made a face at Sonya, wrinkling my nose at the level of intensity that Alice's humor could reach.

"Ooh, I feel *burned*." Sonya retorted as we walked through the passage of the hospital that led to the main hall. "How very like you."

Exiting the main doors, we could see the hall as a whole and paused momentarily. The smell of food filled the air while the bodies of citizens and recruited soldiers swarmed the floor from one wall to another. It was packed, with almost no room to move until several people took notice of us and rapidly shifted to allow us passage. My phone went off again, and I checked the message before stepping forward.

It's Colonel Dumbass, for the record. I got promoted because no one else was in the damn conference room as they were handing them out. If you don't get here on time, I'll be a General in no time. Hurry up.

I chuckled at Jalix's reply, glad that he was dropping the seriousness used in front of the recruits in favor of maintaining his personal image with the rest of us.

While his jokes about military rank were all in jest, he rightly acknowledged his position within the city as a leader parallel with Kara's stature. As we walked, I gave attention to the number of people and the logistics that Jalix had helped put into ensuring we could handle a higher capacity. The mix of Vampyres around us was obvious and split in three equal parts; some were refugees from the New York nuclear bombing, some were soldiers-in-training, and some were permanent residents.

"Damn. Busy today." Sonya commented, watching two teenagers lean against each other lovingly on a bench under a tree in the central arboretum. The holiday decorations lit the hall in an unusual array of colors, mainly red and green, and gave us the impression of a winter below ground.

"Recruits switched last week." Alice reminded. "These are all fresh from Quantico. They're still admiring the city." Their marvel was apparent, half of them staring at the arched ceiling in wonder as the lights bathed them in synthetic daylight. I was pulled from my musing observations with a tap on my shoulder, Amy evidently having been called to the same meeting.

"Hey!" I exclaimed happily, wrapping an arm around her shoulders while continuing to walk. "What's up?" I smiled at her, playfully flicking the snowman-shaped cluster of diamonds she wore to represent her passion for the holiday.

"What happened to breakfast?" She asked, grinning accusatorily. I grimaced, having forgotten entirely that Andrea and Violet had made plans for this morning. "Sleep in?"

"Didn't sleep at all." I corrected. "I was helping Violet with her dossiers last night before Raven texted me and needed some help with Rachel. Turned into an all-day thing with my sister." She chuckled, watching Jalix stand outside the door to the conference room and casually wave at us.

"Damn, sounds like you need a break. You're even busier than *I* am."

"Wine and Bitches meeting tonight. That'll be *plenty* as far as a break is concerned." I chuckled, pondering our past few outings.

"No karaoke tonight. No club, no going out. We're hanging out in *your* room. We all agreed this morning to take a break from partying." She lowered her voice as she walked by Jalix, not wanting her father to hear about his daughter clubbing with her friends.

"You know they don't care, right? You're a grown-ass adult-"

"It's just…they're my parents." She explained, looking around at the room and judging where she wanted to sit. "They don't need to hear about that stuff. They have this *image* of me, you know? The professional, the doctor, the innocent one-"

"You think *they're* innocent? Jalix almost destroyed Archangel the day after he came to the city in a drunken frenzy with Val. You don't even want to hear what he and Kara did to their room the night before their wedding."

"So I've heard…" She mumbled in disgust, shaking her head and pulling out a chair. I sat next to her, nodding to Val, Kara, and Raven across the table. Alice and Sonya took their seats before Jalix closed the door and approached the table.

"Eric and Vi not coming?" Sonya asked.

"Busy. Sorry." Jalix shrugged. "They know what's going on, but Violet is helping Eric coordinate the new dossiers and assign training down in the other conference room. They're going to be extremely busy for the next few days."

"Ah, gotcha." Sonya seemed satisfied at the answer. Kara stood up and joined Jalix at the head of the table, but stood behind him instead of taking a spot at his side. She crossed her arms while Jalix spoke, appearing uneasy about something.

Oh, this isn't going to be good.

"A few quick updates. First of all, Tony's doing great. Still nothing from Legacy after their last incident, which is good news. He's working with Yuri and Layla on the aircraft and training is going very well, minus some…hiccups. For only having eight weeks to renovate advanced combat aircraft…we're *way* ahead of where we expected. He should actually be returning shortly, and his techs are going to finish up the rest of the work."

"That sounds like really good news. Which means we're about to get…really bad news." Val suggested.

"Not bad news. Just…some changes." Jalix started, looking back at Kara. She approached the table, giving Amy a brief glance.

"I'm stepping down as the Commanding Officer for the upcoming fight. Jalix is going to be taking that role so I can be focused on the field." She didn't sound sad, but nearly had the impression of being apologetic. "Jalix and I had a long talk, worked with our plans quite a bit, and we realized I would be more of an asset as a fighter. So I'll be helping Jalix remove larger obstacles from the battlefield while he calls the shots from above."

"I have a personal Blackhawk being fitted with Tony's anti-radar tech, so I can fly above the battle and see things on a larger scale as we progress to take the White House. Raven and Eric will have drones, but it's not the same as having a person being there to observe." Jalix explained further. "Plus the Apache sensor that Tony was able to retrofit onto my aircraft will help the ground forces by giving them a view from the air."

"So who's going to be the Air Wing Commander? Haven't you been working with Andrea for weeks now?" I asked, having listened to Andrea's drunken rambling about their meetings on more than one occasion.

"Still me." Jalix confirmed. "I'll only need to coordinate the first few minutes, between the initial airstrikes and the arrival of the helicopters. After that, Yuri will have the helos and Andrea will call the shots on anything else in the air."

"And you're cool with this?" Val asked Kara.

"Very. I wanted to tell you all myself so there was no confusion as to whether I was being coerced or forced out. It's a decision Jalix and I made together, and it's for the best. Here in the city, we still have equal roles. But once the fight kicks off, I'll be on the ground with you guys." Kara justified.

"So you're just taking her job and she'll be with us during the fight." I confirmed, summarizing. They nodded, the explanation simple enough. "Easy enough."

"Couple other things on the agenda. Raven?" Jalix gave her the floor as she leaned forward, clasping her hands.

"Yeah. Um…Christmas is coming up. Fast. To keep spirits high, Quantico is doing a large-scale dinner and some fun events for morale. Games and movies and shit. I figured we could do something here, as well. It would give the trainees, refugees, and even the residents a nice break." She paused, swallowing. "Christmas Eve, tomorrow night. All of us plus Violet and Eric are going to get a large table at the close end of the residential portion of the city, and everyone else in the city is going to sit in the main hall. We'll have food and coffee provided by the restaurants and café, play some music on the speakers, but we want people to see you guys, talk to you…be reassured that things are going well and you're just enjoying the holidays."

"Things *are* going well and I *am* enjoying the holidays." Val remarked. "Plus it's beer and wings night at the club." He pointed to me subtly in question, and I shook my head in regret, inciting a brief look of poutiness.

"Then all the merrier." Raven sighed. "But there are a *lot* of people out there that see you guys as heroes. So it would be a cool experience to get to meet their leaders and idols before we head off to war." A loud beeping sound interrupted the peace at our table, Alice quickly whipping the pager from her pocket and standing up.

"One of my patients just went into labor, I have to go. Sorry. Fill me in later?" She pointed to Val, taking several steps away from him before his stare forced her to trot back to her starting spot and kiss him. "Please?"

"Of course." He chuckled softly, finally letting her go.

I'm so happy they're...back to the way they were meant to be. Blissful. Idyllic. Especially in light of her struggles, her trauma...

"The other docs can't handle Vampyre pregnancies yet?" Val asked Amy out of curiosity.

"She's trying to train the nurses on them, too. That way, they can do assists or handle things if a resident collapses when they're nearby." She explained.

"Oh, that's awesome. Didn't know she was training them on it." Val paused, looking back at Raven. "Sorry, I didn't mean to sidetrack."

"It's all good." Raven waved dismissively. "Christmas Eve dinner. Be there around four tomorrow. Food and music, autographs and photos, then we all go home for Christmas with our families. That's all I've got." Jalix looked at Amy, who unexpectedly stood up.

"My turn, I guess..." She started, her smile growing to a luminescent grin of absolute elation. "I've been working with Alice a lot these past few weeks...and I think we're done." She bounced once, looking around the room as we all shared the same look of confusion.

"You're done working with her? Why?" Sonya asked with concern.

"No, I-...I mean we're *done*. With the cure." She whispered gleefully.

"No shit!"

"Are you serious?"

"Oh, my God, congrats!"

The room erupted in cheers and praise, which forced a bright pink blush across Amy's cheekbones as she laughed. She waved her hands for everyone to stop, trying to speak again.

"Alice told me yesterday to announce it the next time we were all together. It's…a little bit different than what Alice had originally planned, but it works *way* better than we had hoped. So…" She tilted her head, and I could see that she was trying to dumb down the explanation for us. "Instead of inventing something to destroy the virus completely, we made a new one. This strain is as infectious as the one from the outbreak fifteen years ago, *but* it has a protein that blocks the genetics for all the normal Vampyre stuff. It's like Diet Vampyrism."

"Diet Vampyrism…" Jalix chuckled, shaking his head.

"Or Vampyre Light, if you prefer." Amy joked.

"Vampyre Zero?" Raven shrugged, playing with her hair and avoiding any seriousness.

"*Anyway*…You get infected with the virus without any effects. Doesn't sound like a big deal, but it means that it'll act as an immunity for humans against all the other strains, which is awesome. So no worries regarding a new outbreak caused by the isolated people that won't get hit with the cure right away. In *us*, however, it'll mutate our virus to make it like the new one. So we'll sort of de-convert over a period of a few hours when it hits us. It's a cure for the infected, and a vaccine for humans. Now…we still have a *little bit* of work to go on getting it up to the standards we need, but we're both confident with the way it's going. Long story short, we just need to find a way to store the concentrated cure to load into Tony's missiles. But we started mass-producing it here in Vanaheim and using some of the facilities upstairs in Kane-Hudson. It's ready, just not portable yet."

"Is that going to be difficult?" Val asked, still smiling.

"No, not at all." Amy explained. "We're just experimenting with a few methods before deciding. Everything else is wrapped up. We've logged the research and computer simulations in case it's needed again, but the rest of the project is officially shut. The previous samples have been destroyed and-"

"You *what*?" Raven growled. The table turned to face her in confusion. "Those samples are the key to our success and you *destroyed* them?"

"The formula for the cure is finished, Raven. Alice wanted to make sure there was nothing around for Legacy to use against us if the worst would happen." Amy spoke eloquently, but was extremely defensive.

"Why is that such a big deal?" Val asked, looking at them both. "We have our blood taken all the time."

"They're not blood samples." Raven explained, her voice stained with anger. "They were purified strains of Kara and Amy's virus. It takes months of dedication, trial, and error to distill something so pure into a usable form. If this doesn't work, it's going to set us back *months*. Maybe years."

"It works, Raven." Amy endorsed. "Beyond any doubt. Even Doctor Goodson was amazed with the results. We won't need to go back." Raven sighed, scratching the shaved side of her head before letting her fingers tumble through the long, black hair on the other side.

"If you say so." She concluded, her eyes distant in thought. "You'd better hope so."

"I'm positive. Alice and I have no doubts about this. We wouldn't let you guys down." Amy reaffirmed.

"Amy, that's amazing. You've worked really hard for it." Val said genuinely.

"You and Alice both have. Congrats, hon." Sonya stood up to wrap Amy in a hug while I sat in shock and gratitude.

They did it. After decades, almost a century of work. They finally did it. We have a chance at fixing things.

"Amelia Lynn Kane. You're going in the history books, you know that?" Jalix followed suit with Sonya, embracing her tightly in pride and affection. "I love you so much. I'm so proud of you."

"Thanks, dad." She whispered quietly, growing emotional and pulling away to take a deep breath. "We'll keep you guys updated on the status of things." Amy looked at me, her eyes sparkling with happiness as she leaned into my shoulder and took a deep breath.

"I'm so happy for you." I whispered, putting a hand on her head. "I'm going to *crush* my sister in a hug when I see her. Can't believe she managed to keep it quiet from us."

Joy. Hope. Faith. Appreciation.

I pulled my hand away and we both looked at each other, chuckling as the effects from her supernatural abilities gave me a glimpse into how she was feeling as I touched her skin. I couldn't complain, the raw happiness from the moment overwhelming all of us and deservedly lifting her mood.

"You still have a lot of emotions buried. Something that's bothering you. You okay?" She asked quietly.

"Yeah. Just…a lot going on." I decided, looking back at Jalix and Kara. Kara stared at Amy happily, understanding that it would be best to wait until the end of the meeting to give her a hug.

"That's all I've got, unless anyone else has world-shattering revelations." The group chuckled, Jalix indicating that we could depart. "Keep up the good work. Seriously." He looked around at all of us. "Yuri said the recruits we sent to Quantico are absolute, skilled professionals. That means we're doing something right. And it's going to save lives. So keep taking these jobs seriously, even when they seem to get boring. Keep following the training schedules and putting up your best effort. It's making changes. Show the recruits why we're legends and train them to do their jobs." He paused, bumping his fist on the table lightly. "We can do this. We have the cure. Now we just need to win the fight."

"I say we just send Jalix in." Val smirked, walking past Jalix to leave the room. "He can just solo the whole thing and escape on a mattress."

"Better than a bobsled." Jalix returned, referencing another critical mission from too long ago.

"I agree. Maybe you can give speeches until they die of old age." Sonya remarked, following Val out of the room. Raven hadn't moved, deciding to open a laptop and use the conference room as her temporary office. I stood up, moving to the side so Kara could give Amy a hug and talk quietly.

"I'm proud of you." Kara whispered. "You know that. Keep kicking ass, okay?"

"Well I came from *you*, so…" Amy joked.

"You'd *better* take some time off tonight." Kara warned, pointing to me, as well. "You two have been working overtime. I know *you* haven't taken a break in two or three days." I nodded sheepishly, knowing that she was right.

"Wine and Bitches meeting tonight. You're always invited." Amy suggested, trying to bring Kara into the mix. As usual, Kara shook her head gently and declined.

"That's something special for you guys. I'm not going to intrude. But thank you, as always. I host my own Wine and Bitch club. Singular." She chuckled. Jalix reached out and took Kara's hand, leading them out of the conference room.

"See you." Amy said quietly. She sighed, turning to me and gesturing toward the door. "After you."

"Tagging along today?" I asked, believing that she had work to do.

"I already texted everyone. We're starting our *meeting* earlier than usual tonight." She smirked. I looked back at Raven, who threw up her hands in disbelief.

"Yeah, texted *everyone*, okay." She complained, clearly left out.

"Sorry, I sent it in the *group* chat." Amy corrected. "Which you refuse to be a part of."

"The last thing I need is my phone blowing up with videos of you singing Missy Grey songs on karaoke night-"

"I didn't send-"

"Shaking your ass and downing tequila shots-"

"Okay, that's not-"

"Forty-five minutes before you have to train the nurses on open-thoracic surgical techniques." Amy cleared her throat, waiting for the chance to speak.

"I did not send those videos."

"I did." I chuckled, shaking my head. "Everyone did. I think Alice even got ahold of them."

"Explains why she was so upset when I showed up late that morning." Amy pondered.

"No, *that* was because you were covered in body glitter and smelled like a margarita." I clarified as we made our way out to the main hall. In the distance, I saw Dr. Weiss turn the corner and make her way down the hallway to my room.

"To be honest, I don't see how either of those things is a negative." She protested.

Girl's got a point. I've been there…more than once.

The silence was an awkward pause for both of us, Violet usually present with us to break any gaps with her witty comments. Her workload significantly higher than either Amy's or mine by being assigned to assist Sonya, we oftentimes couldn't see her until after hours, if at all during a given day.

"Sorry that Violet hasn't been available." I started. "I don't mean to hijack you from your sister."

"You're not. We all have crazy schedules. Sometimes I hang out with my parents, sometimes with my friends, sometimes with my *best* friend-" She gestured to me briefly.

"And sometimes with my lovely sister. It's a good way to share my time with everyone."

"Did you just call me your best friend?" I asked in shock, honored at the comment. She looked at me with contempt, her face scrunched up in derision.

"Yes?" She said the word like it was a question. "Why wouldn't I? You've been by my side ever since we showed up to Vanaheim. You're awesome. And you've given me more support than anyone, along with Violet."

"Yeah, but…" My heart still struggled to grasp how kind her words were, even though she meant to be casual in how she spoke. "Violet is the only person to have ever said that about me."

"Well, now you have two besties. Deal with it." She stuck out her tongue at me, rounding the corner and waving to Brynn. I smiled, losing myself to my own thoughts as I realized the ever-growing circle of people my life had encompassed.

You're becoming a better person.

***

With a great deal of defiance, I ignored the angry churning in my stomach and poured another round of shots, letting the last of the bottle drip a few extra drops into the one that I would hand to Raven. Although I was more than willing to be intoxicated, most of my body had decided otherwise and was choosing to attack my personal decisions instead of letting me enjoy the evening.

I have to eat something first. I haven't had any food all day.

"Alright ladies, fresh from the udder of the vod-cow." I turned back to my small bar and its guests, handing out the shots yet again. They were taken gratefully, downed while mine sat behind me on the kitchen counter. Not a single one of the women sat with the taste, chasing it with sips from their wine glasses and grimacing.

"What's with the bad jokes? Are you Violet, now?" Andrea commented, Violet shooting her an open-mouthed glare.

"I *just* got here and you're already gonna start with me?" Violet chuckled, raising her glass. "I respect your wits, but you don't have the guts to match."

"I fly combat aircraft for a living, hon." Andrea rebutted before groans from the group effectively shut her down.

"Jesus, *again* with this…" Raven groaned.

"Andrea, is there a single other thing about your personality worth bragging about, or is it checked with your luggage?" I taunted, the group laughing and taking my side of the situation. Andrea laughed with a sense of self-consciousness, nodding with fairness and discontinuing her argument. I picked up a few crackers from the shared plate of hors d'oeuvres and set them on my palm, munching quietly to absorb some of the alcohol. While I had consumed less than any of the others by far, my tolerance was much lower and I was perfectly fine with beginning to sober up as the rest of the party doubled down.

"'Nother shot, Krys?" Amy asked, looking at me enquiringly.

"Eh, I'll stick with wine. Stomach." I mumbled, no one pressuring me to change my mind.

"Well, does anyone have a topic for the evening, now that our esteemed guest is *finally* here?" Brynn beckoned to Violet, who stood from her stool and bowed sarcastically.

"Thank you for the introduction, Dr. Brynn Weiss, biologist to the stars."

"I've been curious actually, and afraid to ask. Relationships." Andrea started. "Let's talk body count."

"Virgin."

"Celibate."

"Virgin."

Amy, Brynn, and Violet all responded quickly, their answers evidently surprising Andrea.

"Really? Amy I kinda suspected since she's so uptight, and Brynn's I knew, but *Violet*...you surprise me. Really haven't found a worthy guy yet?"

"Nope!" Violet replied enthusiastically to Andrea's extremely personal question. "Dated a few, couple months at a time. They all suck. At least, so far."

"I'm not uptight." Amy defended after a slight delay, taking offense.

"Huh." Andrea contemplated Violet's explanation. "Mkay. Fair answer."

"I'm *not* uptight. I have fun." Amy tried standing up for herself, no one buying into it and ultimately agreeing that her sense of academic intellect and outstanding moral character unsurprisingly diffused into her personal decisions. The silence lingered for a moment and turned the attention to Raven and I. Raven raised her eyebrows and tilted her head at me, requesting that I go first. I declined silently, shaking my head rapidly while the others chuckled at our quiet battle. Raven smirked, sighing and taking a long drink from her glass, smacking her lips and preparing herself for the answer.

"No serious relationships." She kept smirking, although her demeanor for most of the night had been her typical, aloof self. "Had a few flings here and there. Guys I met were never...good enough. I was looking for someone that wasn't intimidated by me. Couldn't find it."

"Ever try not being a bitch?" I raised a brief toast to Violet's question before munching on another cracker.

"Nope. Worked out well enough for me. And to answer your question, if you must know, I've been with six guys. And...one girl. Once. Wasn't a huge fan of the experience, but she had an incoming investment, good taste in liquor, and an amazing ass. Still wouldn't do it again." She rushed the last part of the sentence, Andrea seeming to be satisfied with the answer.

"We all get curious. It's not for everyone." Andrea shrugged. "And a good booty is always nice. But speaking of chicks, how about you, Krystal?"

"Great segue." I groaned. "Three." I mumbled, taking another drink from my glass to avoid elaborating any further.

Andrea always, always wants to talk about this girly sleepover shit. Does no one else like guns? Or cars? Hell, she's a Marine, she has to like guns. Wait, does that only come with being a lesbian? No, plenty of straight chicks like guns. Raven likes guns and she's straight. Ish. Plus Violet used to love my car collection. Aw. I miss my car collection.

Lost in my tipsy thoughts, I failed to recognize that everyone was staring at me with a level of intensity that made me extraordinarily uncomfortable. My eyes grew wide while I waited for an explanation, trying to figure out why the hell I was being targeted from my response.

"Can I help *any* of you?" I asked in vain.

"How old are you?" Raven finally asked.

"Uh…two-sixty-eight." I was still confused as to their reaction.

"Damn, you're old." Brynn chuckled. "Hope I look like you at that age."

"So you're two hundred and sixty-eight years old and have been in *three* relationships?" Andrea clarified.

"I mean, I wouldn't call them relationships, per se." I clarified. "I haven't been in anything serious, no. Rachel is my most recent ex, about a decade ago-…well, a decade before the outbreak, sorry. I had…" I recalled some of my memories that were nearly lost to time, too many crazy missions and life-changing events since that point to remember clearly. "Another girlfriend I had was on and off for about a year. Maybe a year and a half. She made it pretty clear that she was around for the money and glamour. Wait, why is *my* answer so fascinating?"

"It just…seems low." Andrea whispered. The rest of the room cackled as I gawked at her for the audacity of the statement, backing up against the kitchen counter and crossing my arms.

Why does everyone assume?

"Wow." I chuckled, seeing no sign of the laughter slowing down.

"I'm only laughing because I knew the answer, and their reaction is hilarious." Violet struggled to keep her glass upright, doubling over against the bar as she wheezed. I shook my head in comedic dismay, waiting for the dust to settle and Andrea to finally pony up her own answer.

"Let's do another round." Brynn requested, sliding everyone's shot glasses back to me. "In honor of your social honesty and sexual temperance."

"Oh, hear, hear!" Amy toasted enthusiastically. I sighed and grabbed a new bottle of vodka from the refrigerator, the bright blue bottle staring at me in disappointment as I cracked the seal for my friends.

"And just out of curiosity…" Brynn added, burping quietly. "*Sheer* scientific curiosity…how do you not freeze your…partners? With your abilities, I mean."

"Hot tubs, hot springs, and hot showers." I answered, leaning into the brutal discussion and embracing the lack of escape from it. I disbursed the drinks, once again leaving myself out of the mix. "Ended up freezing the pipes in more than one hotel, but I kept the babes nice and toasty. Never actually done it in a bed for that very reason. And speaking of pipes, *your* turn." I pointed to Andrea.

"Nice segue." She mocked. "I feel bad for answering now. I didn't expect to get those answers." She sniffed the new shot, quickly realizing that the action was a mistake and visibly questioning why she had done it in the first place.

"What answers did you expect from them? Figured Raven had more fun?" Violet asked, a devious look in her eyes as she glanced at Raven. "You can't tell me those scars are the only throat damage-"

"Don't you *dare*, you little shit!" Raven yelped, punching Violet in the arm repeatedly as we all roared in laughter.

I needed a break like this. And watching Raven suffer at the hands of this discussion…all the better.

A quiet knock on my door was almost missed by all of us, but gathered my attention as the only one who wasn't drinking heavily. As I made my way to the door, Violet continued to badger our guests.

"Andrea, you never answered."

"Ugh. Twelve. And now I feel sleazy."

"Why would you? You're almost forty-eight years old…" The discussion behind me continued as I left the room and opened my door to reveal a tall, handsome-looking young man holding an exceptionally large black tray. It was covered by a plastic sheet, the faint white distortion of condensation obscuring what its contents were.

"Delivering a platter request from *Zan'nin*?" He asked, gesturing to the tray. "Catering for a…meeting…?" He smirked as the women behind me erupted in laughter again from around the corner.

"The…Japanese bar? We didn't order any food. Who put in the request?"

"Ah…really not supposed to say." He grimaced.

"O…kay. Are you sure it's the right meeting? I think Eric is doing telecom training down in conference room two-"

"The order was for your room, specifically." He clarified.

Who the hell-

"Amy and Violet have been eating all day, Brynn wouldn't order food without asking the group, and Andrea is drunker than shit. Since I didn't order it, I'll thank Raven." I deduced, taking the three-foot-long tray from his arms. "Jesus." I mumbled, noting the weight.

"There are smaller containers and lids in there so you can refrigerate anything left over, as well as utensils and napkins." He said, turning to leave.

"Thank you." I called, closing the door. "Raven." I summoned, walking back around the corner to the bar. She sat up, raising her eyebrows at me while the other girls picked up their drinks to make room for the tray. "*Thank you* so much for your kindness and good heart." I goaded.

"You got us sushi?" Amy asked, her eyes lighting up with happiness.

"No, I did not." Raven insisted. "Whoever ordered it-"

"Delivery kid had a bad poker face. Better luck next time, tiger." I popped the lid off the tray, letting everyone grab chopsticks and dig in.

"Damn. Thanks, Raven. This was nice of you." Violet acknowledged.

"I didn't-…ugh. I'm never being polite again. The stuff in this corner is for you, by the way. Kosher." She mumbled to Brynn, grabbing a piece of sashimi from the edge and dipping it in soy sauce. Brynn smiled gratefully, thankful that her dietary needs were considered. "Getting harder and harder to come by good ingredients." Raven continued, staring at the vibrant red color of the tuna. "Going anywhere south of here is tough without raising Legacy's alarms, and since New York…" She shook her head, popping the piece of fish in her mouth and savoring its flavor. I picked up some chopsticks, partaking in the food.

"Gotta love the bad guys making promises. Says he'll pull back his patrols, but we can't even make it to Charlotte without seeing six of them." Amy griped. "I know he sent quite a number out west, but there's no rest for the wicked on the east coast, either."

"Homicidal maniacs tend to do shit like that. Should have seen the last one. Here's to you, being dead as all hell, dad.

Rest in pieces." Raven raised another piece of sashimi, being unexpectedly joined by Violet.

"Rest. In. Pieces. You piece of paternal shit." Violet chomped down on her bite of food, two drops of soy sauce dribbling down her chin.

"I keep forgetting about that part of things." Brynn observed, holding a piece of salmon with her utensils. "That this is a…second war. That this time, the enemy is fueled by super-drugs and led by someone with two lifetimes of experience."

"Time doesn't mean experience. Our family has no equal when it comes to experience, where Legacy is still an infant. A terrifying one, but an infant nonetheless. His troops are what concern me." I added.

"Why's that?" Amy looked up at me, giving me her undivided attention. "We have abilities, powers…a reason to live past all of this. Conscious thought and choice and free will. They don't."

"They just seem…physically evolved. Everything we have, they have on a higher level. Reflexes, speed, strength, healing, everything. They're like another evolution of Vampyres, the same way Vampyres came from humans." My response was seen as intriguing by Amy.

"If Factor Five increases these Vampyre traits, if they seem more evolved…does that mean we'd become them someday? Is that our virus's next evolutionary step?" She asked, inciting a new, purely philosophical discussion.

"No way." Andrea defended, shoving a piece of sushi in her mouth. "We have soul. We have passion and a love for living. Those guys are animals. They run on instinct."

"True. But have you met my mother?" The table snickered, but Amy pressed on. "No, seriously. We-…well, those that were around at that time, regarded her as the best. The most evolved. And her emotions were largely suppressed. So it begs the question, does the next phase of our evolution look like what we're fighting against?"

"I think the difference is choice." I contemplated. "We can choose to press on and grow, and the Tortured can't. They've been broken of that ability and forced to undergo their changes. If we're allowed to continue naturally, I think we'd go another way. The same way your mother chose to become who she is today."

"Well…I guess we'll never know." The table paused, coming to a complete standstill at Brynn's words.

The cure…it'll make us all human again.

"Right." I shook my head. "Forgot about that. Then…I guess the discussion is moot." I chuckled, hiding the insecurity that came with the fear of becoming human and losing the precious qualities that made me one of the leading Vampyres of the city.

What will I lose? My decision-making? My analytical skills? My health and appearance? What's going to catch up to me first? How long until I realize that my life is on a timer?

My negative thoughts were cast aside by another knock on the door. I groaned, unwilling to walk the distance over to the door again.

"Come in!" I stood in my comfy spot against the kitchen counter and called out. After a moment, Val poked his head through the doorway and started to speak.

"Hey, I-"

"Are you wine?" Violet interjected.

"Uh…no?" His response was understandably confused.

"Are you a bitch?"

"No…"

"Then you do not belong here." Raven chuckled at the exchange, tugging at the sleeves of her designer sweatshirt.

"What the hell is *here*?" He asked, beckoning to the gathering.

"Wine and Bitches club." I explained. "Would have been wine and cheese or wine and charcuterie but Dr. Weiss is Jewish and Violet is lactose intolerant."

"Plus *charcuterie* is way too many syllables after drinking all night." Violet finished. Val sighed, running a hand across his face and wrinkling his nose at the smell of vodka, rosé, and sushi.

"I just need to borrow you." He said to Violet, defeated in tone. "Eric needs-"

"Don't, Val. Please don't." Violet begged, whining. "I helped deal with Sonya's nightmare dossiers all day. I've been here for like twenty minutes."

"I know. I have to be there, too. He's laying out the assignments for comms and their personnel for each of the vehicles and convoys. He wants you there to make sure everything adds up."

"Then…that actually requires me, as well." Brynn stood up unsteadily, grabbing another piece of sashimi. "I have to pass along any of that info to Tony when he gets back so we can make our own plans." She explained. Val nodded, giving us a small wave of goodbye as he left. Violet sighed heavily, drowning herself in her glass of wine and polishing off what little was left before standing.

"I…shall return." She hiccupped.

"I shall not." Brynn chuckled. "It's late."

"Agreed. Go to bed once the meeting's over, Violet. Sleep some of this off. You need the rest anyway." I suggested.

"The rest of what?"

"What? Never mind, just…go to bed when you're done. Bye. Love you." I laughed, Brynn shooting me a supportive look as she helped guide Violet out into the hall.

"Brynn's a sweetheart." Andrea folded her arms, leaning back in her chair. "She'll find her wild side someday."

"I don't know that women like her ever do." I argued, sitting next to Amy. "My sister is a lot like her, albeit with better people skills, and she never went through a wild side." Amy paused, looking over at me.

"From what I hear, your sister did…a lot…of cocaine."

Oh, shit. That's right. My god, I can't believe she had her wild phase without me.

"Yeah, but not for fun. That was for…work. As a stimulant." I protested. Andrea chuckled.

"Coke? Caffeine and a host of other things would have done that. Your sister needed an *escape*. Not a pick-me-up." She rolled her eyes, mocking me. "Dummy."

"Val told me she ended up with a bit of a problem. Took her a few months to come off. She didn't quit as soon as you stabilized, and it started more of their…marital issues. But she quit once he had a high-decibel conversation with her. I'm surprised she didn't say anything to you." Amy ran a hand through her shimmering silver hair.

"Hmm. I guess there's still a lot that I'm missing from the time I was out. And a lot that she never told me. She has her reasons, I suppose. And I trust her." I nodded, knowing that there were certain things she still had trouble talking about.

"We all have to trust her." Andrea groaned, standing up. "She's got the cure. Without Alice, this whole plan falls apart. Whether we win or lose the fight, we need her blessing on that cure." She stretched, yawning and pointing to what little remained of the food. "Thanks again, Raven."

"Thank the chef. I just made a phone call. And some…light threats." Raven replied quietly, turning her head as Andrea left the room.

"Probably could have left out the threats." I advised. "Not everything requires them."

"Nah. Adds flavor. Plus I wanted Brynn's food to be correct. I have no idea what the hell kosher even *is*." She placed a palm on the table, lifting herself off the stool and staring at the refrigerator. "Mind if I grab a syringe for the road? Regular food or not, I'm due for one."

"Yeah, top shelf. I have a whole box, take a few if you need."

"Just need the one to make it down the hall." Raven sighed, opening the refrigerator door and watching the cool mist roll out. "Cravings have been bad recently. Too many long nights."

"Too many Wine and Bitches dance nights." Amy corrected, watching Raven administer her own dose.

"That, too." She agreed, removing the needle from her skin. "Long day tomorrow. We're going to have to deal with a lot of people. Patience will be tested."

"That's because you hate people." Amy replied optimistically. Raven paused, nodding once and tossing the now-capped needle into my stainless steel garbage can.

"Sounds about right. See you then." Her farewell was too casual for thc circumstances and merited a quiet chuckle from both of us.

"I can help you clean up?" Amy offered kindly, gesturing to the leftover seafood and collection of glassware. She smirked, realizing that everyone else had left to stick her with the duty, as they knew she'd be too good-natured to decline. "As…long as we put on some quiet background music." She finished.

"Sure." I was more than happy to oblige, much preferring some music in the background over end-of-party silence while I cleaned. "I can't believe we went this long without any. No one said anything." I turned on one of my playlists, the volume low on the speaker in my kitchen.

"Everyone was having fun. Talking, connecting with one another. I can't complain. It was…nice just to have a night in." She brought an armful of dishes over to the sink as I began rinsing them. "Poor Violet, though."

"I *know*." I sighed, remembering Val's look of disappointment in having to pull her away from enjoying her scant time off. "They've really been dogging her with work recently."

"They definitely need the help, but it still sucks."

"It was bound to be like this." I offered. "She has to have our forces and their assets essentially memorized, and it's changing constantly. That's a rough job." I opened the refrigerator door as she started storing the food. Her black skirt swished around her knees as she walked back and forth, helping me clear the bar quickly.

"Not really her line of talent either. Very methodical, very logical. If she had any sort of medical training, I'd trade spots with her. Though I suppose there's little more room for creativity in what I do." Amy sounded equally as empathetic as I was.

"Yeah…not much room for an artist in wartime, I suppose. And I think she knows it, which is why she's not complaining."

"She wouldn't complain anyway. Not on any serious level. She's happy to be so involved. Hell, that might even be why they gave her that role." I nodded at her suggestion, imagining Eric's decision-making process when assigning tasks before we arrived. My head bobbed to the music gently, suds swirling down the drain one after another until the last of the glasses was rinsed and placed on the drying rack. I shut off the sink and turned around to see Amy wiping down the bar with a wet paper towel. "Plans for tonight?" She asked, smirking as she realized I was staring at her awkwardly.

"Oh. Um…Sleep?" She stopped, looking up at me with a raised eyebrow. "Okay, I'd *like* to sleep. Even the stuff Alice gave me doesn't help anymore. I just…can't get tired. Been up for a week or two now, and my brain could really use a reset."

"Don't say that *too* loudly. You've been eight week seizure-free. Let's keep it that way." Amy warned, brushing by me to throw away the rag.

Anxiety. Contentment. Anticipation.

"Good point. Speaking of…I had a question about that. Something that's been on my mind."

"Shoot." She said, switching positions with me and leaning against the sink while I stood by the bar.

"Why do we have this…thing with your powers and no one else does? Even just now, whenever we come into contact, there are these glimpses. We both get them, but you don't have them with anyone else." She looked at me confusedly.

"You…died? Remember me going into your brain and soul-"

"Yeah, but even that part of it…Kara died, Val died, Raven died, Sonya basically died, and *Jesus Christ* is our group of people screwed up." We both laughed at the absurdity of the statement, shaking our heads. "Regardless, my point stands. Why me?"

"Well…" She pondered, putting her hair in a ponytail with a bright red fabric band. "Kara and Val died, but didn't go *through* death. Their memories were captured from before it happened, and their bodies were essentially brand-new. Sonya doesn't have any memory of what happened, so it's just…gone…and I guess Raven wasn't dead enough. From what she said before, she was given transfusions as soon as her on-site medics got there. Probably a precaution from her father to have them so prepared. But either way, she may not have been close enough to death. Whereas you sat squarely in its lap."

What a hell of a way to phrase it.

"Huh. I guess I never thought of it that way." I mused, looking at the floor. "I'm grateful either way, I just guess it's something that's been nagging at me. Your powers like to act up at weird times."

"It could also be that I'm in love with you." She suggested. I laughed, lifting my head just to feel the humor disappear and my heart drop, her wide-open mirror eyes gazing at me as she bounced on her toes a single time. She smirked bashfully, her cheeks turning pink as my face conversely drained of blood.

She's just messing with you, moron. Calm down.

I sighed quickly, the trace amounts of alcohol in my system having delayed my reaction and convincingly forced the perception that she was serious.

"Don't do that to me." I chuckled, pushing in the remaining bar stools and organizing the remaining pile of napkins. "I haven't had a lot to eat. It took me way too long to catch on-"

Affection. Warmth. Fear. Caring.

I shook my head quickly as her fingertips left my shoulder, freezing me into place and eradicating any hope I had of clear thought. Once again, I felt fear stall my heartbeat as I realized she had, indeed, been deadly serious.

No...no, she would have said something by now. Given you hints or signs-

"You...have had a lot to drink tonight." I suggested. "It's definitely messing with your head." I turned around to see her stand less than a foot away from me, her eyes slightly above mine with our difference in height.

"Sober. Mostly." She said quietly. "Andrea was taking all of my shots. Except my last one. I took that one for courage."

Oh, this is not happening. This is not, in any reality, happening right now.

"I...you can't-...You're not serious." I laughed briefly, at a complete loss for words as her face started to fall into pure despair.

"I am." She said calmly, trying to refrain from saying anything else. "I promise you, I am."

"Amy, there's…there's no *way* you're being sincere. You've only known me for-…I mean, come on…" I tilted my head, fear and anxiety allowing for more aggression in my voice than I had intended.

"My parents fell in love on their first date. On the rooftop of a parking garage." She started slowly, the lower lids of her eyes glistening with gentle tears. "I fell in love with you when I touched your soul and watched you defy death itself." She took a quick breath, sniffing and pushing through her emotions. "I think I qualify as having a valid justification for my feelings."

"This is just…it's a crush, just your hormones-" She clenched her teeth, quickly placing her palm against the side of my neck and closing her eyes.

Passion. Fervor. Dedication. Faith.

"Tell me *that* is just from hormones." She snarled hoarsely.

She released her grip, a single, gentle sob rocking her chest as she continued to stare too deeply into my eyes. I was too stunned to say anything for a moment, my own heart chasing those emotions and realizing that they existed somewhere deep within me.

What if you've been burying them? Suppressing your own feelings? Is that why she makes you so happy?

"Amy-" I started, my own mind racing over too many possibilities, and worse, wondering whether the feelings I had grown to have for her over the last many weeks were in tandem with how she felt. "You're twenty. I'm thirteen *time*s your age."

"I've been an adult for sixteen years. Humans would call me thirty-five. I just look younger, the clock has moved slower." She started, clearing her throat. "It does for all of us. My mother is ten times older than my father. Val a hundred years older than Alice. Time moves differently for us."

That...is a fair point. But the rest of what she's saying, I...I can't. I truly can't.

"Amy, your mother and I-"

"You had an addiction." She protested. "There's nothing remaining of that anymore. You *know* that."

"It's still...weird." I said quietly. She took a step back, scoffing and wiping her eyes.

"So you're going to deny any feelings for me just because it's socially awkward?" She asked in disbelief. "I *know* you're not that heartless."

"No, I-...damn it!" I cursed, sighing heavily. "I don't mean it like that, just-" She leaned forward again, lacing her fingers with mine.

Desire. Joy. Devotion. Trust.

"Please...stop doing that." I begged, opening my hand and letting her fingers fall away from mine.

"Every time you see me, I see you." She breathed, locking eyes with me again. "You're *lying* to me."

I can't do this. It's not going to work.

"I'm not." I insisted. "I swear, I'm not." I started to realize that I was being dishonest with myself, second-guessing what aspects of our friendship I was drawn to.

"It won't work." She said, repeating my own thoughts and mocking the words that rung out over and over in my head. "I can't. This isn't happening. I *feel* what you're thinking, what you're telling yourself." I pulled my hand away as she reached out, glaring at her while she relaxed. "You keep trying to convince yourself. But your thoughts and your feelings are separate."

"They've always *been* separate, Amy. I have an impulse control problem. An addiction problem. If I said yes right now, I would be taking advantage of you. Of your feelings. All just to make me happy for a night or two and end up getting bored of you. It's all that my relationships have ever been." My words caught in my throat, tears finally stinging my eyes. "*That* is why I can't. I can't do that to you. I care about you too much."

"I know you do, Krystal." She sniffed again, clenching her jaw to reveal the gentle pressing of two fangs against her lower lip. "That's my whole point. I know you won't hurt me."

My god, this conversation is familiar. I never thought I'd be on the other side of things. I never thought I'd be the one saying no.

"Amy, you should go." I said finally, looking down at the floor and desperately fighting my hormones and the thought of a possible relationship. "You should think about all of this and we can talk once you've had some time." I heard her sigh defeatedly, a quick exhale of hope leaving her body.

"I've *had* time. I can't leave yet." She said firmly, standing still.

"I'm asking. I'm *asking* you to leave before I have to tell you." I crossed my arms, staring at her as she watched my reaction and shook her head.

"This is so cliché." She mumbled, looking up briefly.

"Well, I'm sorry-"

"Not that." She groaned, clenching her fist and taking a massive stride toward me. "This." For only the briefest moment, I saw the flash of her face and the soft touch of her lips on mine before my thoughts rapidly transformed.

Although I couldn't understand more than a few technical terms in each sentence, I stood in the observation window of the surgical suite and watched Amy's keen hand make a precise set of movements with a suturing line. She delicately and gracefully performed her demonstration, slowly increasing her pace until the nurses looked at each other in shocked admiration at her level of skill. She glanced up briefly, her sparkling silver eyes meeting mine in a moment of happy recognition when she acknowledged I had shown up to see her. I gave her a small wave, watching the joy in her eyes as she suddenly stopped, their entire room swiveling to follow the sound of a newborn infant erupting in shrill cries. What little was visible above her surgical mask turned bright red as her eyes shimmered with happy tears, focusing on the closure of the C-section and the recognition that she had brought life into the world.

Although I was still fighting the smell of alcohol on my lips, I couldn't help but move closer to her body and the fragrance of a saccharine perfume while we yelled through the thick noise of the music around us.

"-to shake that ass on a line and let the ego flow-"

"-to tell a bitch take her time and throw the drinks down slow!" Amy screamed, her face lit up in a sense of peace disconnected from the rest of the world. I laughed, wrapping my arms around her neck as we screamed the lyrics at each other, lost in the intense volume of the nightclub. Every sparkle of glitter on her face erupted in brief flashes of light as the strobes passed us, igniting her smiling expression in a beautiful array of dazzling porcelain. Even in the low light, I followed every curve of her frame as she moved her hips in front of me, dancing for no one, yet putting on a show for me, and me alone. My heart swelled to bask in her ecstasy as she lost any sense of stress in the late hours of a long night.

As I rounded the corner to the kitchen, I watched her place the dishes in the sink and pull back the curtain, performing her daily check on the herb garden outside our kitchen window. I tiptoed quietly, hoping to not disturb her, and watched as the edges of a smile crept onto her cheeks at the sight of a blossoming pepper plant. Of course, I knew that she would bring life to everything she touched, but was joyous at her reaction to something so simple in what had once been our chaotic lives. She turned on the sink, just enough of a disguise for the noise of taking two more steps and wrapping my arms around her waist. Immediately, she slunk backward into my waiting arms and leaned into me, allowing her silver hair to rest against my cheek. I moved my hands to intertwine with hers and took a small breath, brushing my lips against her ear.

"I love you."

Whether it was from the deep quivering in my chest or the completion of her intended act, she pulled away from my lips and stared into my eyes while I avoided eye contact with her. The number of memories and visions in my head was overwhelming, and the realization of each suppressed emotion was infinitely too much to bear.

"You're not afraid of hurting me." She whispered, touching her temple to mine. "You're worried of *being* hurt."

How could I have felt so strongly? My death killed any hope of loving anyone ever again.

"You asked me what I wanted most in life. What would make me happy. What would matter to me after the war." She pressed, the warm air of her breath reminding me of how close I was to someone I wished would never leave my side. "You don't get to ask me that question, then *become* the answer and leave me by myself." I stood as still as I could, shaking and trembling while she continued. "Your death…took the idea of love with it. I've been trying to help you let go of death so you could feel the way you know you want to."

"Amy…" I whispered, barely capable of speaking. "I love you, but I don't know if I can do this. I'm not the kind of person you want to fall for." I hated myself for saying anything that would have taken her away from me, anything that would have distanced her in the moment, but I cared too much for her well-being to speak anything other than the absolute truth. She smiled, the slow crawl of the corner of her mouth a defiant face against the reality I swore I knew.

"I've seen your soul." She breathed. "And I could never imagine loving someone else. Not in a million years. Not with any of a million other souls." She paused, trying to speak clearly through her emotions. "I fell in love with you. And you fell in love with me."

"You warned me so many times." I realized. "You kept telling me I was…repressing something."

"You thought that love hurt you in your past life." Amy furrowed her brow, tracing a single finger along the line of my jaw, somehow without triggering any additional emotions. "You put a wall up for your own protection."

"I know that love didn't hurt me. I…hurt myself. My choices. My actions." I lamented, realizing how poorly I had chosen to live my previous life. "I brought my own death on myself." Amy's hand moved to cup my cheek, caressing my face and comforting me.

"Then you need to ask yourself…what do you want out of your new life?" She paused, her irises encountering my lips briefly before moving back to my eyes. "What would make you happy?"

"Peace." I whispered, feeling my tailbone press against the bar as her hips leaned into mine. She paused for only a brief moment, her hopeful eyes peering into my heart with a raw sense of promise.

"Would you let me be your peace?" Amy's whisper echoed in the empty room, the drifting sounds of quiet music lilting through the air and saturating our space with tranquility.

There's nothing that I want more from my new life than to have peace. But if I had nothing else…I would want her. Because no other, singular thing makes me happier than she does.

I found myself entirely incapable of answering her question, instead brushing off her closeness to me with a sense of haste and taking a deep breath. I walked up to the refrigerator and whipped open the door to grab the remainder of the vodka I had opened.

If you ignored every inhibition, how would you feel? If you could do whatever you wanted with no consequence, what choice would you make?

Hearing a lack of response to my actions, I uncapped the bottle and took several large gulps, gagging at the inherent burn of alcohol against my throat and the unrelenting taste of corrupted, artificial pineapple flavoring. I turned back to Amy, pausing in shame at my immediate response, and answered as truthfully as I could.

"Amy...you've turned my life into something I never could have imagined." I paused, anxious at hearing myself try to talk, and took another long drink from the bottle before replacing it in the refrigerator. "You...you make me happy. You take away my fear. You make me...just infinitely happy. But what if, by taking it any further, we run the risk of damaging that? The risk of destroying our friendship?"

You know damn well that won't happen. She makes you happier than you've ever been.

"I mean...hell, we're going to war." I continued, pacing relentlessly in front of her as she watched with a gentle smile. "What if we don't make it? What if something happens, Amy? I couldn't bear the thought of losing you." I confessed, my anxiety growing as my heart rate accelerated to the pace of a racehorse. "You've become such an important part of my life, and...I just can't-"

"Then don't." She said softly, staying in place. "Just don't."

"Don't what?" I asked, exasperated and starting to lose control of my reactions.

There's so much rattling around in my head and I can't even make sense of it.

"You're saying you *can't.* You can't what, lose me?"

"*Yes.*" I emphasized, turning to look at her. For whatever reason that I could never define, her beauty was suddenly amplified as she stood in place, the perfect features of a young goddess withstanding the storm of my internal conflict.

"Then don't." She chuckled, approaching me from her position at the bar. She put her hands on my hips, looking at me in ways I could never describe. Her smile, her eyes, even the subtleties of her brow all conveyed to me that nothing else in the world was as important as I was in the moment we shared together in the confines of my small kitchen.

No one could ever feel this way about me. It's not possible.

"When we go to war…I'm fighting to see you again, Krystal. I'm fighting for the chance that you'll let me be a part of your future. A chance that you'll let it be our future."

"I've…I saw our future." I admitted. "One of the visions-"

"Our house." She interrupted, her hands tightening their grip on my hips as we swayed slowly to the music. "Our garden. Our life. Our future."

Nothing else matters anymore. Even if it's a small chance, the possibility of spending your life with this woman is worth any risk you could ever imagine. She's perfect.

"What if I don't have a future?" I choked, terrified at letting down the hopeful spirit that gazed at me as if I was the only thing in the world.

She is in love with you.

"Then I'll make us a future." She whispered, her forehead touching mine as we rocked back and forth. "We will survive this war. Love alters not with his brief hours and weeks-"

"But bears it out even to the edge of doom." I finished, finally realizing that every detail of my life, down to my favorite poem, had been memorized and categorized by someone who cared enough to pay attention to me.

She's perfect.

Even in the small talks during our daily duties, in the brief chats between meals, Amy had listened with painstaking precision to ensure that every detail of my life was burned into her mind with the sole purpose of fulfilling a need in my life.

Compassion. Adoration. Sincerity. Reverence.

"You love me." She whispered, confirming what she already knew very well. Her smile persisted even through my turmoil.

"I do." I cried gently, hating the words that escaped from my lips and the risk it posed to my sanity. With every bit of strength I had left, I cradled her face in my hands as if she would suddenly disappear.

"Then if I love you…" She leaned in closer, tilting her head to bring her lips to mine. "…what else matters?" For the first time in my life, I felt my body ignite in a heat I had never felt before, eradicating any trace of my abilities as I was encompassed in the warmth and fervent ardor of the first true kiss of my lifetime.

Never before had I felt as wanted, as needed, and as completed as I did with Amy's arms outstretched across my shoulders while her lips gently rested against my own. In a way I had never experienced, and knew I could never have experienced with anyone else, I was in love beyond all comprehension. Regardless of whether or not I was the only one that perceived it as a battle, I recognized that she had won, and I let everything in my being succumb to the notion that I was entirely hers, and hers alone.

In a singular kiss within a singular moment, the history of my life became meaningless while my future became twisted and folded to include hers within its winding path. There was nothing else in our infinite universe I could have desired, and there was nothing else in any reality that mattered more to me than to stay within her perfect embrace, in her perfect arms, against her perfect lips. Through the past visions we had shared of emotion, of feeling, and of sensation, I had never felt anything more right and more true than knowing my willingness to forfeit myself to her in my entirety.

"The last time I surrendered myself was to death." I whispered, sniffling and trying my hardest to speak clearly. "The time before it was to sorrow. I'm so afraid of letting go again." She placed her palms on the back of my hands, gently nuzzling against me.

"Then don't let me go." She breathed, finally showing the same fear that I did and smiling at me through shuddering tears. "And I'll do everything to make sure we're both surrendering to life, instead."

This is what you came back for…to feel this. To find this. Nothing else matters.

"You love me." I echoed her earlier words, the sound of each syllable reverberating in the room against our soft music and lifting my spirit to a place of pure bliss. I smiled finally, accepting that the moment was real and that my feelings were allowed to be valid. "You love me." I laughed softly, leaning more of my weight into her.

"I love you." She smiled back, her eyes sparkling with a vibrance and energy that she had never shared before. "I love your mind. I love your quirks. I love your sense of humor-" I laughed again, our lips meeting briefly before she persisted, resolute in telling me her motives. "I love your body. I love your eyes."

"Amy-"

"Shut up and let me feel like this." She giggled, cupping my chin with one hand and pulling my waist toward hers with the other.

Her energy was only growing the longer we kissed, our fangs creating a clash of deadly violence in juxtaposition with the restraint she tried to exert with the rest of her body. I could feel her impulse control failing alongside my own, the hand on my waist taking a quick grip on my top and pulling it over my head in a swift motion. Before I could say anything, before I could even breathe again, she took my ribcage in her hands and pulled me into her body against the bar. I couldn't catch my breath, my heartbeat pounding beyond its normal limits and feeding her torrential, affectionate energy. She continued, sliding her palms down to my hips and tugging on my shorts.

Wait.

"Amy." I stopped, pulling back for a moment and clearing my throat, trying to allow a fraction of logical thought into our endeavor. "I, um…" I picked up her hands, placing them higher on my hips and away from the exposed inch of my underwear.

"Did…you want to wait?" She asked innocently, the hope in her eyes warning me that she felt inadequate.

"I-…" I found it difficult to say the words I need to, finally mumbling them in a rush. "You're a virgin. I don't want to be…"

"My first time?" She finished, laughing again with a sparkling expression of happiness in her eyes. "I do. I want that."

"You only get one chance. You've already waited fifteen years of your adult life to find the right person-"

"And I did." She replied quietly, combing her fingers through my hair. I looked down, watching her painted nails leave the tips of my hair and run along the top edge of my bra. "I'll never want anyone else."

"You're going to live a long time-"

"Not anymore." She said quietly, a hint of sadness finally finding its way into a sharp wrinkle on her brow. "We'll be human soon. And…the rest of that short life needs to be with you. It's not possible for me to love anyone else, anymore." She leaned back enough to let her eyes roam over every part of my face as I did the same in return. "I'll never see anyone else's life the way I've seen yours. I'll never know someone as intimately as I already know you. Regardless of how long our lives are from now…" She rested her hand on the base of my neck. "I will always feel like I've known you my whole life."

She wants this more than anything, and you want to give her everything. It's a small price to pay for happiness.

"Are you sure?" I asked for a final time, knowing fully that my own desires were irrelevant in the consequences of her future. "I need you to be sure." Her lips closed, a gentle smile gracing the dimples on her cheeks as she dropped her hands and reached into my pocket. I watched as she lifted my phone, sliding the volume up by a moderate fraction before placing the device on the counter. As her hand intertwined with mine, I could feel her abilities reaching out to my chest and slowing down my heartbeat while she walked backward, leading me into my bedroom and dimming the lights as we walked in.

She looks so beautiful. How does someone like her fall for someone like me?

She stared at me for a long moment, holding me at arms' length and waiting for me to close the distance between us. She chuckled shyly, moving back another foot to sit on the edge of my bed. I moved forward as if I was frozen in time, the air around us permeated in a comforting warmth that chipped away at the nerves continually making their way into my throat. As I stood in front of her, looking down into her waiting eyes, I could see the faint edges of her eyeliner smudged from discreetly wiping her eyes and making the effort to maintain her stately appearance. Despite trying to be patient, she deemed that I was moving too slowly for her comfort and pulled me onto the bed with a strength and swiftness that took me by surprise as I fell on top of her.

Her gentle laughs became exerted breaths against my mouth as I lifted her shirt and pulled it away from her before discarding it at the side of the bed. As I turned back to hold her again, she looked away, one arm draped across her chest to hide the vibrant colors of her bra and the shape of her body underneath.

"What's wrong?" I whispered, immediately stopping and laying at her side. She scoffed, shaking her head and turning to look at me.

"I…know you're not going to judge me. But I don't want you to be disappointed by anything. I want to be good enough for you." The look on her face was torn between anxious and uneasy, which was unwarranted entirely by what she had said. I smiled, gently taking her arm and placing it by her side while I leaned forward and placed several kisses along her collarbone.

"You're beautiful." I whispered, laying one of my legs over hers and running my hand over the faint bands of muscle on her abdomen. She tensed briefly at my touch, sighing quietly and relaxing from her stresses. "Everything I see is you. And everything that's you is perfect." I finished. She ran a hand through my hair as my mouth touched the curves and crevices along the width of her body.

With every inch her fingers moved along my scalp, I felt her abilities keeping my own at bay and wrapping me in a protective shroud of heat from my declining body temperature. As I lifted my head and hooked one of my ankles under her own, she reached behind me to unfasten the strap of my bra and drop it on the near side of the bed after pulling it away from me. I watched her mirror-grey eyes inspect every portion of my exposed skin, basking in the sight with flushed pink cheeks and expanded pupils.

Without breaking eye contact, I moved my hands to her hips and crawled further down on the mattress, pulling the length of her black skirt across her calves as I did so. She laid her head on the pillow and closed her eyes while I picked up one of her legs, running my hands across her smooth skin and continuing to kiss my way from her bright-red painted toes to the inside of her honeyed thighs before laying it down on the bed once more. She sat up slowly, wrapping her hands around my back and sliding her chin into my shoulder while I unhooked her bra and dropped it onto the comforter.

Her nails dug into my back, clawing their way through my skin to show her desire before moaning pleasantly and sinking her fangs into the muscle of my freshly-healed shoulder. I jerked at the sensation, a freezing-cold spike of pleasure washing down the length of my arm and across my stomach while her tongue cleaned up any blood that dripped slowly from the healing wound. Her abilities penetrated my muscle and veins, repairing the damage immediately and demonstrating the care she felt in treating me like her personal goddess.

In the brief pause, I closed my eyes and took in her smell, the floral scent of lilies and warm hint of cinnamon from her perfume cleansing my senses. She pulled away from me and grabbed my shoulders, twisting my legs with her own and planting me on my back so she could tug away my shorts in short bursts of frantic energy.

I could sense her vigor as the look in her eyes became more and more wild, transforming from an innocent and wide-eyed woman to a fanatical lover. Impatient at her own inhibitions, she took the waistband of my satin underwear in her fists and ripped the seams apart to throw the shredded fabric across the room and lay on top of me once more. She moved one of my hands to her hips, indicating that she wanted me to do the same, and I eagerly obliged with a short rip and quiet gasp while her mouth explored the sensitive skin of my neck. Refraining from another bite, she shifted her lips to my own again, lashing out with her tongue as she straddled one of my thighs and growled at the shallow pain of my nails on her waist.

"You…should take the lead." She panted, her hips gently rocking the frame of the bed with subtle movements. "Take charge."

"I don't want to-…hmmm…go too fast for you." I whimpered, one of her hands finding a way to interrupt any semblance of coherent thought I could have conjured. She leaned away, her mouth open with bloodstained fangs and a desirous stare diving straight to my core.

"Teach me. Break me." She growled, locking her knees against my hips and changing positions to lay against the piles of pillows behind us. "I only have a lifetime left with you." She grabbed a handful of my hair and pulled back on it, exponentially lifting my cravings for her touch. I indulged in her wishes eagerly, moving her hands to cup her chest while I smirked and slunk down on the mattress to cover both of us with a deep blue blanket.

***

The space around me mimicked the vastness of an infinite ocean with deep blues and seafoam green colors occasionally distorted by subtle waves and ripples. A loose, white mist sprawled across the landscape and obscured the darkened horizon from view. Even through the mist, I could see the distant light of stars above me in constellations I had never seen. My eyes failed to focus on anything particular, simply roaming the landscape as if I was expecting a visitor. In front of me, the mist swirled and twisted in denser clouds of thought until a figure took shape within its grasp. A woman's body emerged with slow steps, a cleanly-cut mess of cerulean hair obscuring a furrowed brow as she made her way toward me.

She said nothing, but stared at me with a deep intent as her footsteps, bare despite the rest of her simple clothing, incited new ripples with every step that infected the peace of the water and instigated a disturbance in the normal pattern of the infinite ocean. I took a step forward, recognizing the woman as myself and ignoring the impossibility of my previously dead body having appeared in front of me.

"Sup?" She finally asked, waving cockily and curtsying with an aura of blatant disregard for respect. "You look…domesticated. What the hell happened to you?" She asked, a smug and conceited grin across a corrupted mouth.

"Who are you?" I asked, failing to see my own soul in the thing that looked back at me.

"I'm you, sweet cheeks. Or, I was. Now we're both here." She beckoned around us, the space seeming to grow in its boundlessness.

"What do you want?" I was perplexed, sure that it must have been a dream but feeling entirely disconnected from what I knew as reality.

"Same as you. Sex, drugs, loud music." She sighed, shaking her head in awe at whatever she found fascinating in me. "Man. Look at you. No wonder we're dead."

"Dead?" I asked in disbelief, trying to wrap my head around the theory. Memories started to emerge of fire, of pain, and of darkness before she nodded again.

"Yeah. The good news is that one of us can make it out of here. And it needs to be me." She shrugged again. "Even better news is that you have a choice." She paused, chuckling. "I'm the badass that takes the emotional brunt of things and gets the job done. You? You're my shadow. The little voice in my head that tells you to do the right thing. The goody two-shoes." She sneered.

"What choice?" I asked, hearing my own voice echo through the mist and reverberate across the water.

"I can live." She started. "Or you can choose peace in death. Decision's yours. But the clock's running out. Our body doesn't have a whole lot of time left to figure this shit out." I stood in silence, hearing truth in her voice without acknowledging that the devil in front of me could have ever been a part of who I was.

"We want the same things-"

"No." She said forcefully, taking another step toward me and creating swells in the water behind her. "You...wanted to die. So this is your chance. Let me the hell out of here. Give up and go chase after your peace. Let me live, and we'll have a second chance." I mused, mulling over her words in my head and confusedly recognizing them as a lie.

"I want peace. But I don't want to die."

"Not an option. Time's almost up. Make your choice." Her voice grew in strength, but I could see through the façade and identify the edges of fear on her lips.

"I don't want to become you again." I whispered, a thundering crack resonating in the distance as the first sign of an oncoming storm.

"Let me live." She repeated, nervously looking over her shoulder as storm clouds obscured the stars.

"No." I began, tilting my head to inspect her more closely. "I choose peace in death." She took a step back, her lower lip trembling in anger.

"You idiot."

"But not mine." I smiled gently, feeling the first drops of rain patter against my skin. "I can find peace in your death." She recoiled, jumping as a crack of lightning lit the sky overhead.

"You can't do that!" She screamed, lashing out at me. "You can't choose death!"

"No… but you can." I whispered, the rain intensifying and softening the sound of the storm. "You could have made the same choices. But you never did. You left that option to me."

"Traitor." She growled, her eyes wrathful as she stared into my own.

"I only ever betrayed myself." I realized, watching the white mist return and roll its edges against her back.

"Coward. You should have let yourself go." She hissed, fighting against the mist.

"I did. And I found myself here."

"The most perfect you've ever been was without a pulse." I could feel her hold on our indeterminate realm lessening, her outline succumbing to the fog.

"I never found my reason to carry a pulse. Not until now." A face flashed across my memory, a beautiful woman with ruby-red hair that held me while I cried. Another, a strong man with dark hazel eyes that cared for me deeply in moments of despair.

"Go back to your grave, you selfish whore." She snarled, reaching out toward me. As her hand made contact with my face, it disappeared in a swirl of white haze.

"No grave can hold me." A young woman with jet black hair, her deep chocolate eyes peering at me in curiosity. Another woman, older, and of the same appearance with a powerful and caring dignity.

"You've lost love. You've lost friendship. You've lost everything. Go back to the solitude you've always wanted." She continued, her voice becoming more and more distant as the downpour saturated my sense of self.

"My solitude is gone…replaced by those I love. I've lost nothing but my hatred." A blonde woman with caring hands embracing me after too long away from home.

"Return to the prison you made for yourself."

"My prison is what freed me." A perfect soldier, soothing and fatherly in his words.

"Go back to the tomb."

"My tomb is empty." A fallen friend, with words of wisdom from a deep and booming voice.

"Go back to your sorrow." Her last word stalled my thoughts, casting them in a brilliant light before I took a deep breath and watched her bright blue eyes disappear behind a wall of death.

"Sorrow is dead." The clouds vanished, the mist disappeared, and the ocean became still as a familiar sensation crept into my fingertips.

I was…cold.

HOLIDAY

AMY

Her arm twitched reflexively, and in addition to the flickering of her closed eyes, I could tell that she was in the middle of an intense dream. I debated waking her, but I waited for it to pass instead and laid on my side while staring at her sleeping face. Living with my mother and sister, I had grown to know the faces of sleeping women as largely unattractive messes of drool and catastrophic messes of hair. Watching Krystal was an experience entirely separate, her slightly open mouth giving way to pristine white teeth outlined in lips the color of thriving cherry blossoms.

Her skin was radiant, a warm white that silhouetted perfection in every curve along her body. Although she was cradling the spare blanket against her chest, I was able to admire the shapeliness of her slim legs and curvy hips as her breaths started to become longer, slower, and more deliberate. I smiled as her eyes flickered briefly before opening, a slow daze of sleep quickly washed away by the realization of where, and with whom, she lay. I moved one of my hands, sliding it under her pillow and laying it across her fingers.

Anxiety. Fear. Shame. Dread. Dreams of death.

"You're afraid." I verbalized, searching for the reasons in her eyes. The deep blue of her irises was sadder than I had seen in previous weeks, drawing down to look at the sheets.

"I am." She whispered, the raspy voice of the freshly-woken infecting her melodic vocal chords. She cleared her throat, shaking her head. "But not of death."

"Then what?" I asked gently, stroking each of her fingers with my own.

"Of whatever you're going to say next." The mystical flicker of our touch-based sensing faded as I recognized her feelings without the need to use my abilities.

"I still love you." I smiled, closing my fingers around hers. She closed her eyes and sighed, a tear squeezing out from the corner of one eye before they opened again with a brilliant and warming smile.

"And I still love you."

"So what else matters?" I asked, repeating my question from the previous night and finding myself against her lips once more with a plush blanket squished between us. Her normal energy arose quickly, realizing that she was in no danger of being hurt or taken away from her life.

"Just spending Christmas Eve with you, I suppose." She propped herself up on one elbow before moving the blanket and closing the space between us to cuddle.

"How about I take you to dinner?" I teased, our upcoming event lacking in inspiration too much to be considered a date.

"That sounds *lovely*." She sighed, kissing me on the neck. "Ugh, what time is it, anyway? We didn't fall asleep until what, four?"

"Four-thirty." I corrected, rolling over and tapping the screen of my phone. "And it's two o' clock. How anyone hasn't asked us where we are is a miracle." Her face stalled for a moment, becoming blank before her eyes flitted over to mine.

"Speaking of…what happens if someone finds out?" Her nervousness was unwarranted, Krystal being loved by the entirety of the city and its people. I chuckled, placing a finger under her chin.

"Then they find out. So what? Would that bother you?"

"Them knowing? No. The impending discussions and-or-killing me again, yes." I sighed, biting my lip and tucking the extra strands of hair on my temple behind my ear.

"I think you're overthinking it." I started, running my palm along the length of her ribs and waist. "We've been together every day since we came to Vanaheim. I'm pretty sure people already suspect-"

"There's no way." She warned, shaking her head. "No one thinks we're a thing." My hand stopped as I gave her a patronizing look.

"You didn't even pick up on the fact that Emily has been hounding after you for the last month. Do you have *any* idea how much extra work I had to give her to keep her from asking you out?" The look on her face was priceless as she started piecing together what I was saying.

"Wow. You've…been hinting at this for a while."

"You're used to your women being more direct." I shrugged, secretly avoiding the thoughts of Krystal having been with other women. "I didn't want you to feel pressured."

"Until last night." She teased. "Then you decided to throw everything you had at me."

"Hmm…not *everything*." I hinted, raising my eyebrows and leaning in to kiss her again. Her touch was magical, the two of us creating a physical bond that lasted long after we pulled away from each other. "I think I have a little bit left to throw at you." I moved my hips closer to hers, throwing a leg over her left thigh and kissing her shoulder.

"I...*definitely* want to...but we really should get ready." I laughed again at her hesitance and persisted, pressing my luck while she battled the logical notion of being on time for the city's event. She placed a gentle hand on my chest and pushed me away with a caring level of force, looking into my eyes with a devious glare.

"Why don't we save that energy for later?" She had made her decision, and in the most lighthearted of ways, wanted to resume her public appearance of normalcy as soon as possible.

"Okay, fine..." I whined pathetically, hoping I could guilt her into at least a few minutes more. She continued her mischievous stare, squinting at me. "I *guess* I'll get up."

"We do still have to shower." She remarked quickly as I rolled out of bed and reached over to my nightstand to grab the black bathrobe laying across it. "I mean, we can...we still have to shower." Her attempt at recovery was shameless, and she knew it as she broke out in laughter and rolled out of the other side of the bed to swagger into the bathroom.

That's what I love. The cuteness. Putting me first. Not taking anything too seriously.

I made my way into the bathroom, staring at the assorted makeup and cosmetics that were spread across the counter while I re-established a decent ponytail. Krystal stepped into the shower and cranked the hot water lever to maximum, which was indicated by a burst of steam and vapor.

"If you wait for me..." I closed the door to trap the heat inside, discarding the robe onto the floor and swinging open the glass door of the shower. "I can help your body heat so we can *both* enjoy it." I reached back to the counter, grabbing a clean washcloth as I realized she wouldn't have something else for me to use.

I have nothing over here. No clothes, no makeup, nothing.

"You don't like hot showers?" She countered, looking around and grabbing her loofah from the top shelf. She rinsed her hair quickly, the blue mass sticking to her back as the water ran down the length of her body. I tried not to stare too much, stepping in quickly and holding her elbow to use my abilities. She turned the knob down slowly, simultaneously increasing the cold water level until the spray that hit both of us was at a perfect level of warmth.

"*Clearly* I like hot." I smirked, her lips turning up further at my joke. "But your showers must be insane."

"Have to be." She defended, cupping her hands and creating a small block of ice from the water that accumulated. "Most of the time, I do *that* by accident."

"Well…now you have me." I could feel my abilities pulling against her own and maintaining an equilibrium to counter her temperature.

"Indeed, I do." She turned to face me, letting the water fall down her back as I pulled her close and kissed her again. She leaned backward, letting the mist from her showerhead spray us both in warmth and peace as her fangs started to crawl from her gumline.

Yes. Got her.

She growled lightly as she pulled away, turning her head to glare at me again. "Not this time, foul temptress." She mocked, squeezing an exorbitant amount of lavender-scented body wash across her loofah.

Dammit. So close.

She handed me the bottle and we sat in silence for a long moment, cleansing ourselves from the previous night and restoring some sense of hygiene. I refused to wet my hair, not needing it washed again for another day and knowing it would take too long to dry with Krystal needing to utilize her only blow dryer. The moment was peaceful, neither of us feeling the need to break the silence with empty words or small talk, and instead we enjoyed the subtle delights of showering together in the random contact we made against each other and the lovely smell that filled the air. More than once, I leaned against her body to place a small kiss on her shoulder or chest to use my abilities and preserve the heat in our small haven. I grabbed the bottle of shampoo from one of the small shelves and moved my finger in a small circle so she would turn around. She complied happily, letting my fingers work the soap through her hair and massage her scalp. She sighed in contentedness, as if she would fall asleep again, and rolled her neck in small circles.

"I've never had this with anyone, you know." She said unexpectedly, turning around to face me and rinse her hair.

"A shower? You said most-"

"No, *this.*" She shrugged, her eyes pointedly looking around. "The…kindness and…slow stuff…I don't know what to call it."

"Romance?" I suggested quizzically. She exhaled from her nostrils, turning around again so I could apply conditioner.

"Yeah, I guess you're right. I've…never had anyone be…actually in love with me." Her tone fell to a somber, low sadness and I felt for the loss she had experienced over so many attempts to exhibit her emotions over the years. "I never knew how much I was missing until last night."

"Well, get used to it." I chirped happily, slapping her behind lightly and letting her conduct a final rinse across her scalp. "You're mine, now. And you deserve to be treated with all the romance in the world. You name it." I fell for my own emotions, letting the happiness in my heart pretend the world was intact and normal. "Fancy dinners, bedside breakfasts. Rose petals everywhere, of course." She laughed, turning the water off and retrieving two towels from the rack outside the door. She handed one to me and wrapped her hair in the other before grabbing a third.

"That sounds-…actually, that sounds like *torture.*" She giggled, looking at me in dazed confusion. "If *anyone* else had suggested that to me, I'd have thrown up, I swear. But coming from you, listening to you say those words…" Her tone softened as she tied her towel around her midsection and looked back into my eyes. "You make me want those things."

"I was serious." I said sternly, kissing her cheek and walking over to stand in front of the mirror. It was apparently a lavish fixture, as it was entirely fogless and showed my makeup-less face in perfect clarity. "You have to do things with me, you know. Things that let me put on heels and dresses."

"I'm more of a quiet autumn girl, myself." She said, taking her place next to me and plugging in her hair dryer. "Walks in the woods, picking apples to make pies-"

"*Li-ar.*" I sang, tying my towel and turning toward the door. "You're as expensive as they come, you wouldn't be caught dead in flannel." I turned the handle, looking over my shoulder. "Gotta run back to my room, all my crap is there. I'll bring it over to finish getting ready with you. Be back in two seconds."

"Just-…make sure no one sees you." She whipped around, lowering her voice as if it suddenly mattered.

"Everyone's going to be down there already to set up the event or talk to Raven about logistics. We're probably the last ones left from this end of the city. It's fine." I dismissed, briskly walking to her bedroom door and cracking it open to peer down the hall. My room was directly across from Krystal's, and only a span of five feet of concrete lay between me and my destination. Barefooted and dripping wet, I clutched my towel and sprinted the short distance, deftly throwing my door open and closing it behind me.

Okay. Cool. Made it. Ninja-style.

My bedroom was structured similarly to Krystal's, and I was able to walk straight through the door and into my bedroom to enter the en-suite bathroom. Rounding the corner, I jumped backward and yelped at a pale-skinned and mysterious figure, wreathed in black hair, that stood in front of my mirror with cherry-red lips.

"Ah!"

"Ah!" We both screamed, Violet whipping around before leaning back against the vanity in a state of recovery from the near heart-stopping jump scare. She sighed heavily, bowing her head and groaning.

"Ugh. My head…did not like that." She started, looking back at me. "I am *so* hung over."

"Yeah, I…can tell. What…are you doing in my bathroom?" I didn't mean to sound accusatory since we had shared living spaces for more than half our lives, but was confused as to why she had been occupying mine.

"I have a beautiful shower…but no hairspray." She held up the can, doubling over again to lean against her knees. "Just trying to be frizz-free today."

"Let me help you." I chuckled, taking the can from her hand and guiding her back to stand upright as she faced the mirror. "You gonna make it, champ?" I asked lightheartedly.

"Yeah. Forgot to take any medicine before I went to bed. Woke up with a craving so bad I almost drank from my own wrists. And without it, my body couldn't fully process the alcohol." She sighed as I picked up my hairbrush and spritzed her roots. "'Nother hour, cup of coffee, I'll be fine."

"Better be. Long day."

"Yeah, speaking of…why aren't you ready yet? You're usually early to literally everything." I only hesitated for a millisecond, my brain working at overclocked speeds to conjure a solid lie.

"My shower wasn't working. Had to use Krystal's after she was done."

"Oh." She looked down at my vanity, which contained nearly every item I had come to claim and escape with. "You forgot all your stuff. Like…*all* of your stuff."

"Yeah, I-…I woke up late and was in a rush. Panicked when the water didn't work. Ran over, left everything here. Dumb…me." With every word in my defense, she rotated another degree away from the mirror until she was facing me directly, her mouth wide-open in shock and disbelief.

"Holy shit, no way." She started, one corner of her lips creeping upward on her cheekbones.

"What?" I asked innocently, pretending to be confused.

Oh, come on. She's smarter than that. Think! Cover your tracks, hurry up.

"Okay, fine. I spent the night at Krystal's. We got wasted after you guys left and I passed out on the couch, overslept. Broken shower made me even later. So I rushed." I continued to work on her hair in spite of her unchanging expression and believed I had done my due diligence in a suitable defense for my situation. With a quick glance of her eyes, I took notice of my mistake and lunged half a second after she did.

"No, wait-" As I finally managed to wrestle a grip on her shoulders, the arm I didn't have pinned reached up and spun the knob on my shower. My shame poured out with every drop of water that hit the floor of the tub, swirling around the drain while it shook its imaginary head at me in disappointment. "Hey look, it works now." I declared weakly, letting her recover to a standing position in front of me. I remained on the floor, taking a seat and finding comfort in my towel as if it was a shielding blanket.

"Hollllly shit!" Violet squeaked with the quietest of voices. "I *knew* you two would-"

"Not a word, Violet. To anyone." I found my mother's voice in my throat, unfortunately against the ears of someone who shared the same cold blood.

"Okay, okay, but like, I *called* this. I *knew* you two were going somewhere." Violet whispered frantically. "I *knew* you liked her as more than a friend. So this means if you marry her, my best friend will be my sister in law-…Well, half-sister-in-law, but whatever, and-"

"Violet." I interrupted. "Please. Let's tone it down? A bit?"

"Noooo." She squealed again, almost at a whisper. "This is the best day of my life!"

"Okay, but if word gets out that we slept together-"

Oh, you piece of shit, dumb as shit, dumbass piece of shit-

"You WHAT?" She roared, grabbing a washcloth to scream into at the last word. "*Amelia!*" No genuine scolding was being articulated, her eyes sparkling and alight with raw happiness as my own poker face failed and started to show some of my joy at the situation.

"I need to get ready." I laughed awkwardly at the embarrassment, standing up and collecting everything I could grab in one fell swoop, taking an armful of miscellaneous cosmetics and lotions into the bedroom and dropping it next to my pillow. I quickly trotted to the closet, throwing it open and looking for something appropriate for the evening. I tried to pretend as if Violet would disappear, but she floated through the doorway like an ecstatic little ghost that chose to haunt my room, and stared at me with watchful eyes.

"I…cannot…believe you." She started, hearing a broad smile in her low voice. "On the *first date*?"

"It wasn't a-…God, why am I even talking about this with you?" I sighed, pulling out a silver dress and dropping it on the bed while I checked my dresser for suitable undergarments.

"I am your sister, and I swear I will disown you if you don't tell me how it went." She pressed.

"Violet!"

"I don't need to hear the *details*. But like…how did things start, did she say something first, or did you?"

"No, I-…I kind of just went for it." I confessed, chuckling as I searched the bottom of my closet for a specific pair of flats. "I just told her how I felt. And…my abilities helped show her. She felt the same deep down, but she didn't know it at first."

"How did she react, I mean…was she into it?"

"No, not at all." I admitted, finally finding my shoes but deciding to finish the brief conversation with my sister. "But we talked. I helped her discuss her feelings, we used my abilities to bring out her repressed emotions, and…that was that." I finished, shrugging.

"What the hell does that mean?" Violet made a face, puzzled and patronizing. "You spend an evening asking to be more than friends, unburying emotions, and then suddenly you tripped and fell over onto her bed?"

"Ugh…Vi, please stop with that…" I hung my head in shame hearing the words spoken so casually. "No, I-…we felt really strongly. Both of us did. I have, for a long time. And once she…*experienced* my emotions, she knew that she felt the same way. She just…looked at me." I smiled faintly, remembering the way her eyes met mine in her kitchen, quiet music playing in the background with her hands on my hips.

"Holy shit, you are in *deep*. That's the same, exact, specific look our mom had after meeting your dad for the first time." She clapped her hands rapidly, trying to contain herself. "Oh, this is awesome. You two being in love-"

"Again, not a *word*, Violet. I will make Legacy's torture look like a spa day compared to what I'll do to you." Before I could make any further threats, a knock on my door froze us both in place.

"Amy?" Krystal called quietly. "You good?"

"Uh, getting dressed!"

"Come in!" Violet and I had polar opposite answers, the opening of the door ending in a seething glare as I stared Violet down. "What?" She shrugged as Krystal made her way into my bedroom. She was already dressed, an elegant blue gown complimenting a subtle shade of downplayed rosy lipstick and darkened eyeliner. Her hair wasn't yet dry, likely a process interrupted to check on my absence. Instead of her traditional and expensive gold jewelry, she had accompanied her outfit with a silver bracelet and silver earrings alongside a diamond and silver necklace.

Did...she wear that to match me? That's adorable. I gotta wear something blue now.

"She's the other half of this whole issue, anyway." Violet finished with a chuckle. Krystal's head snapped to look at Violet, hoping that she was talking about something else. She was proven wrong immediately, Violet's inability to keep her mouth shut a sign of her rapidly impending murder. "So, Kryyystal...stay toasty last night?"

***

I stalked my way down the hall next to my sister, who I had hoped with everything in me would find something better to do than be my shadow, yet persisted in staying less than a foot away from me at all times. I could hear Krystal's heels in the distance, unnecessarily remaining a distance of a hundred feet behind us as we made our way through the crowd.

"You are one disgusting little perv." I sneered, shaking my head at her in disappointment.

"I just asked-"

"I *heard* what you asked." I hissed, the blush I had applied on my cheeks likely not hiding the increased flushing of anger in my face. "And I have *never* seen Krystal's face get that red. It was *wildly*, inconceivably inappropriate."

"Not for me." She chuckled. "It's not like I judge. Like I said, this is a good thing. Just wanna make sure things...went well."

"Things went well." I replied curtly, trying to keep my words vague against any listening ears. She paused, looking around the cavern and dropping her voice to a sickening level of nonchalance.

"Good. Good. Glad to hear it. So how many times did things *go well?*"

"Stop it!" I growled, my heartbeat pounding against the too-tight lacing of my dress. "Please, Violet, just…shut your never-ending mouth. For five minutes."

"Never." She beamed. "I am happy. I am nosy. I am shameless."

"It shows." I returned coldly, no amount of rudeness in my voice dissuading her from prying into the most intimate details of my life to date.

"Look, I've never had…what you have." She changed her expression quickly to a lower volume as I shot her another glance. "So I have to live it vicariously through you."

"She's your best friend." I whispered, walking past the bistro and approaching the wide set of shallow steps that led into the residential hall. "And I am your sister. Half-sister. Whatever. How is that not gross to think about?"

"I want to make sure you're happy. Well, I want *her* happy, too." She added quickly. "Besides, she's already told me all kinds of details about her previous-"

"Okay, *this* conversation's over. Bye. Love you." I spat frantically, seeing my parents standing behind chairs on the opposite side of the hall.

Ugh. Please don't think about Krystal's exes. One of them tried to kill me.

I lifted my dress a few inches, taking care not to trip over it as I made my way over to them. My mother was, as could be expected, wearing mostly black, but by what was likely my father's request had decided on a grey belt over the dress and some cherry-red lipstick for contrast. My father looked as poised as ever, having decided to shave his beard and replace it with a clean-cut stubble to outline his strong jawline. His suit was sharp and well-pressed, with a deep black jacket matching a brilliant white shirt and grey tie. They both waved at me, my mother showing more excitement than my father in seeing me.

He looks exhausted. Still so confident, dignified, and stately. But I know him better than that. He's preoccupied.

"Hey, princess." My mother reached out and hugged me, tucking her chin into my shoulder. "You look so, so beautiful. You really do."

"Thanks, mom. So do you. Hey, dad." I smirked, giving him a hug and avoiding my powdered face making contact with his suit.

"Hey, angel." He whispered, holding me a second longer than my mother. "Glad you could finally make it, I know you've been working overtime. Holding up okay with war preparations?" He only briefly mentioned my lateness, thankfully not asking any other questions.

"Shaken…but unbroken." He smiled at my response, his full faith in my ability to be resilient.

"Where's Vi? And Krystal?" My mother asked, looking in the direction I came from.

"Uh, Violet got distracted. Think she's on the other side. Not sure about Krystal. I think she's on her way." Although the need to feign indifference was unnecessary, I did my part on avoiding any direct talk regarding the woman I couldn't stop thinking about.

I want to go back to her room. I want to crawl under those sheets again. I want to cuddle with her again and share another glass of wine. I want-

"Hey, you." Val's booming voice was softened to a resonant hum of caring as he placed a palm on my shoulder. He and Alice both approached from behind me, apparently having come from the infirmary close behind us. Alice wore a magnificent scarlet dress emblazoned with yellow and orange stitching around the bottom hem while Val closely resembled a bearded version of my father.

"Hey!" I smiled, turning around to hug them both. "Ready to answer dumb questions from people all day?"

"If the rest of the city is anything like my trainees, I'm going to need more than a cabinet of booze." Val griped. Alice giggled at him quietly, shaking her head.

"It'll be fun. And how many excuses have we had to do something like this as a city?" She asked, my mother turning around as Alice asked the question.

"Never." My mother said quietly, a gentle smile on her face. "Not since our weddings. And I regret never being able to do more of this for Aerael." We all looked over as Raven approached us in much different attire than the rest of us had chosen.

"We ready?" She sighed, half-rolling her eyes and scratching the shaved hair above her ear. "I'd like to get this thing started so we can all go home." Her tight dress was nearly inappropriate for the event, but the embedded crystals under her bust resembled snowmen, and attempted to match the décor that surrounded the immediate area.

"Where's Sonya?" I asked, looking around at our group.

"Helping the residents. Special project." Dad winked at me, suggesting I wait to find out. I was okay with a bit of excitement, having relished Christmases past and hoping this one could be enjoyed with my paramour eventually by my side.

She looked so pretty in that dress. The eyeliner really makes her blue eyes pop. Can't she come over for a few seconds? It's been too long already.

I ignored my inner thoughts and listened to the brief conversation around me.

"Eric?"

"Helping Sonya."

"Rest of us here?"

"I'm sure Vi and Kryssi will come around when we call out to get seated."

"Sounds good. No point in waiting."

"Let's do it."

"Someone better have pie." The last comment was made by Val, who provoked a laugh from the group before Raven pulled a phone from her clutch and swiped several times. She lifted it to her mouth, apparently accessing the PA system for the speakers on either side of the podium at the head of the table.

"If everyone could take their seats." She said coolly, pleasantries clearly not something she was used to. Before I could make my way to the chairs and claim a spot at the table, Raven nudged my side and pointed to the podium in front of our extended table.

"You weren't here when I said it earlier, but a few people are going to speak before we eat. Alice wants you to announce the cure."

"What? That's not my area of expertise, she-" I protested, looking over at an oblivious Alice while she gossiped with a group of her nurses.

"According to her, it is." Raven shrugged, turning her back to me and exposing the colossal and intricate tattoo of a darkly-inked bird across the width of her shoulders.

What a goth power-move. Respect. Bet her father didn't like that one.

The crowd started to disperse evenly, a vast array of smaller tables – some taken from the conference rooms – hastily strewn across the width of the hall and spanning several dozen feet backward. Other citizens retreated to the doorways of their homes, small chairs and stools enough comfort for their liking and providing an adequate view of our places of honor. My mother was seated centrally on the table while my father took the position to her right.

Raven occupied the right-side corner while Violet sat next to Eric as they engaged in deep conversation. I decided to sit next to my mother, leaving an open space for Krystal on my left before she approached and silently took her place.

Took you long enough.

She gave me a quick, impersonal smile as she sat down, her nerves likely on par with my own. She adjusted her bracelet slyly, allowing the glimmering silver charms to indicate that she was thinking of me. I avoided a random smirk and started taking note of the layout around me.

Okay, so it's...empty chair on the far left, then Val and Alice. Krystal and mom are on either side of me, and dad's on the other side of mom...then an empty chair, then Violet, Eric, and Raven.

I went over the seating arrangement in my head, noting the order in case I needed to speak with someone, but I noticed that there was an additional chair at the table. The crowd was now much more organized and I noted that another, smaller table was roughly thirty feet ahead of us to seat Andrea, Dr. Weiss, and an unexpected and visiting Layla, along with Dr. Goodson and a few of Alice's nurses, Eric's techs, and Val's highest-performing officers.

Seats of honor. It's good that they're not mixed in with everyone else. They deserve the privilege.

The noise of the residents making small conversation began to die down as they turned their attention to my father. He stood as quickly as he had been seated, walking around the table to approach the podium and gently sliding one of the switches next to the attached microphone.

"Test. Testing?" He asked quietly, the volume slowly increasing to his liking as the gathering awkwardly watched. "That's better. Uh...welcome, I guess, is the best way of getting started today. I appreciate everyone showing up today and taking part in something great for this city. As a people." His voice was heard down the length of the hall, resulting in a polite and voluminous round of applause and quiet cheers. He paused, taking the noise into account before speaking again. "Food, drinks, and coffee should all be out shortly for each table, but in the meantime, we have one more Christmas miracle to showcase here in Vanaheim. Sonya?"

He stood on his tiptoes, looking over the swarm of people as they all turned their heads. With a dazzling set of flickers and flashes, light emerged from the farthest end of the cavern near the secondary conference room and made itself out in the shape of a Christmas tree as it erected slowly above everyone's heads. Applause rang out again, more enthusiastically than the last time as Sonya emerged from the side of the hall and manipulated her hands to raise the twenty-foot-tall tree. Eric's techs quickly bolted it to a stable base while she held it erect with her telekinetic abilities.

"That tree was the biggest damn thing we could fit down our…weird little path into the city." My father remarked, prompting laughter. "And the best part is…it's completely useless." The crowd rapidly grew silent in confusion before he resumed. Many of them stared at the magnificent piece of foliage, glittering with hundreds, potentially thousands of lights and an iridescent gold star to top it off. Sonya started making her way toward the table, shimmying along the side of the crowd so as not to distract anyone. "That tree has no reason to be here. And that's the entire point. You all have forged such a safety and security in this city, the beautiful and industrious city of Vanaheim, that we can have things like *that*…things that don't belong to war, or to hate. But to something we can celebrate as a community."

My mother helped write this speech and I damn well know it.

I elbowed my mother slightly, a smile emerging on her face while she continued to stare straight ahead and avoid the admission that I was correct.

"As we celebrate Christmas Eve today, and Christmas with our families tomorrow, I'd like to have some of us come up and say a few words regarding topics of interest for the city." He stepped away, nodding to Val as they switched places.

Baristas, servers, and chefs began to trot down the steps from the side of the hall, carrying massive plates of food and platters of bread to each of the tables. Carafes of coffee were planted sporadically, with several of the staff treating our table to a large surplus of food and drink. One of the sommeliers from the Japanese bar delivered a bottle of wine for every other person along with a dazzling set of crystal glasses.

Our plates landed in front of us, steaming hot with mounds of food I couldn't have hoped to gorge myself on during my hungriest of days. Val took a moment to get to the podium, visibly centering his thoughts and trying to avoid staring at his abandoned plate. We all waited to begin eating, recognizing that the food was too hot and we still had speeches left. Val scoffed briefly at the small Santa Claus cutouts surrounding the microphone and looked out at the table of honor in front of us.

"Good afternoon." He started, clearly inexperienced with how to address large numbers of people. "As cool as it would be to have medals or certificates or something, the world above us doesn't have a place right now to put them to use. So instead, I just want to take the time to address a few people. Lieutenant Andrea Scott, Doctor Brynn Weiss, Lieutenant Layla Goss, Doctor Tamara Goodson, and Marcus Olsen, if you could please stand." The collection of named figures stood at their table, slightly surprised and clearly humbled. "All of you have been guiding figures in Vanaheim's new era. As the heads of departments and leaders in their own right, I'd like the city to raise a round of applause, and more importantly, see these individuals as being merited the highest order of integrity and selflessness that we could ask from any of you. The hope we have today is because of you." Val's speech became more eloquent as he spoke from the heart rather than attempting to impress the crowd. "And Dr. Weiss, to you and the other members of our Jewish community in Vanaheim, we'd like to wish you all a Happy Hannukah. Thank you." He acknowledged that they could be seated and took a deep breath. "I'd also like to make a surprise announcement, and recognize one more figure. If you could all please welcome back...Anthony Williams." Val turned around as our table stood up and watched Tony make his way down the other end of the hall toward us, raising a significant volume from echoing praise.

He waved at the crowd before looking at all of us, a slight smile on his face becoming the rarest thing I had ever seen. Val approached him, making his way over and embracing him in a tight hug before Tony took a seat at the empty chair on my far left. He stared at the plate longingly, and I realized that he probably hadn't been eating quality food during his stay at Quantico. Krystal and I both waved at him, his face appearing more hopeful and positive than any of us had ever seen. Val took his seat as well, giving me a brief glance to indicate that my time for making speeches had arrived.

Holy shit, I haven't even been thinking about what I'm going to say. How do I phrase things, how do-

An electric tingle on the back of my neck brought a sharpened awareness to my surroundings, taking notice of Krystal's seated stance changing in my peripheral vision as her legs braced underneath her. Her eyes were savage as they locked onto something within the crowd. Before I could react, her chair flew several feet behind her and her body became a blur of blue energy during a hurricane of movement. She had extended one arm, wrapping the other under my own and spun in a half-circle, embracing me tightly as her hand touched the back of my neck in a bitter bite of cold.

Fear. Panic. Distress. Anguish.

Despite her abilities not penetrating my skin, I remained frozen and could only see the opposite end of the table where Sonya stood behind her chair, her arm extended toward the crowd.

"I've got him." She growled, lifting her other hand and whipping it to the side as metal clattered in the distance.

What the hell just happened?

My ears started ringing in panic as Krystal released her grip and turned around to look behind her. I did the same, a wall of transparent ice having risen three feet off our table in a protective shield. While I could barely make it out from the white cracks that made a crawling pattern across its surface, I was able to see a single bullet lodged in the ice, nearly having penetrated through its thickness. The copper-colored head of the round protruded toward me, and was barely but successfully stopped by Krystal's lightning-fast rescue.

She saved my life. She…she put herself in front of that danger. She wasn't sure if her powers could stop it. She could have been shot…just to save me.

Krystal's eyes met my own in a loving look that we could only share behind the veil of frost for a few seconds, telling each other things that words wouldn't describe. Severing our connection, she angrily smashed the shield with the back of her closed fist, breaking it into several pieces before it shattered on the floor in front of the table. Finally, I was able to see that Sonya had disarmed a pistol from a man at one of the tables, using her powers to immobilize him and drag his levitating body to a halfway point between us and the table of honor. Our entire table was on its feet, some of us impossibly enraged and others still in a mild shock. The silence didn't last long, Kara using her powers to move the microphone from the podium to our table.

"Bold move." She started, staring down the wolf within the clothing of our city's sheep. He was as unassuming as one could expect, and I had never seen him involved in any of the significant war-planning activities in the city. "That came from Schillinger. The order may have been from

Legacy…but that was from Schillinger's playbook." She cocked her head. "It doesn't work twice."

"Unassuming guy in the city with a stolen gun? Didn't even work the first time, if I recall." My father noted, looking at his wife before glancing over at me. I gave him a brief nod that I was okay, my heart still racing in my chest.

Krystal saved my life. So did Sonya. Why…wait…why me?

Their speech was picked up on the microphone and heard by the entire hall, settling some of the citizens who had stood and begun to leave in fear.

"Please. Sit. Everyone." My father asked, looking at the crowd before doing the same to our table. Sonya, Krystal, and myself continued to stand while the others took their seats. Krystal's arm remained behind me in a protective posture without making contact with me. Dad looked at his plate for a long moment, picking up a fork and poking a giant pile of stuffing before glancing at our silent assailant again.

"Why did you try to kill my daughter?" My father asked calmly, spinning the end of his fork in the lump of his food.

"Legacy's orders. She's not needed anymore, and a message has to be sent!" The man roared. Dad nodded slowly, taking in the aroma coming from his plate.

"What's your name?"

"I have no name. I am a part of the Legacy!" He spat again, struggling against Sonya's hold pathetically. Her powers were immeasurably strong and visible in their grip on his body.

"Well…I'm gonna call you Smith. For that Smith and Wesson you tried to pull on my youngest." He paused, finally taking a small helping of stuffing onto his utensil and savoring a massive bite. He groaned quietly, nodding with enthusiasm at my mother. She chuckled, beginning to eat from her own plate. The rest of the table looked at them with bewilderment, Raven beginning to silently question their sanity. "So…Smith." Dad started, putting his food to one side of his mouth to speak. "You suck at your job." The man he called Smith stared at us with frantic eyes, trying to discern what sick joke was being played on him.

"You're just…people!" He barked. "You're not special. None of you are special!" Dad almost choked on his food, a quick laugh interrupting his chewing.

"Yeah, I know. Tell all of *them* that." He pointed at the crowd with his fork, taking a few green beans off his plate and staring at them. "Leave my city." He said calmly, the statement echoing through the PA speakers and across the hall. Smith scrunched his brow, staring at the table for a long moment before responding.

"Wha-…no, never! You'll have to kill me."

"Nope." My father continued to eat, demolishing his vegetables before approaching the slab of ham on his plate. "See…" He swallowed. "I know your type. Martyr. Goes out in a fight, dies knowing he did his duty. Not gonna let that happen. So…you're going to leave." His tone was more than peaceable, almost indifferent to an apparent attack on our city.

Where's he going with this?

Krystal brushed my back briefly with her hand, a soothing gesture that melted my heart in knowing she was still focused on my well-being.

"I won't leave until-"

"We can sedate him." My mother interposed, lifting her eyebrows and looking behind us to glance at Alice. "You have enough drugs, right?"

"Yeah." Alice agreed, shrugging hesitantly.

"So we'll sedate you, drop you off in the parking lot of the hospital, and you can go back on your very merry Christmas way." My mother finished, stopping as a bite of food reached her mouth and frantically using her knife to point at her ham in satisfaction.

"You'll-…I'll just come back!" Smith said, exhausted of whatever sanity he started his mission with. "I'll just do it again!"

"You won't be armed, genius. We're keeping the gun. And for that matter-…God, this is *so* good-" Dad interjected abruptly. "-we'll do it as many times as we need to. Don't think you're a huge risk unarmed. Just my guess." His taunt went unchallenged, Smith visibly lost in the intent of my family's decisions.

"Then I'll go back to Legacy. I'll give him every detail of Vanaheim, every piece of information-"

"Oh, your colleague did that. He's probably halfway home by now." Mom suggested. The crowd became uneasy at her words, but like the regal movements of a queen, she lifted a hand only a few inches and the noise stopped faster than it began. "You wouldn't have come alone. And *you* clearly don't expect to make it out. So someone slipped out and is on their way to Legacy. I hope he tells them all about us."

"You see…" Dad started again, placing his silverware on his plate and wiping his mouth with the crimson napkin from his lap. "We're the deadliest group of supercharged badasses the world has ever seen. We're lethally trained, adequately equipped, and geared up for the sole purpose of killing your allies. Killing Legacy's…Tortured. We have double the manpower you see here, weapons and tactical vehicles galore…and more importantly, we're entrenched. A nuclear bomb would just annoy us with the vibrations at this depth." He pointed to the ceiling. "And make it a bitch to get to my car. There's exactly one way in and out and it's wide enough for three people at a time, which we can barricade and shoot at. So what exactly is the plan here, Smith?" The man's face resolved itself of anger and instead was trying to calculate precisely what his next choice of words would be.

"He could come for Quantico." Smith decided, his words more suggestive than angry, which all of us took note of.

He doesn't know. Which means he's a pawn. My parents are playing him to get information.

"Quantico?" My mother scoffed, an arrogance I had never seen crossing her face. "So he would just change the place of war from Washington, D.C. to Quantico. He would attack where we're established and can easily provide a thousand troops as backup. No…no, he's not going to do that. He wants us to attack him. You're here to provoke us."

"And you *suck*…at your job." Dad emphasized again. "How much Factor Five you got left?" He asked unexpectedly.

"A week. Maybe…maybe less." Smith answered, growing uncomfortable.

"Oof. That's rough, buddy. That withdrawal is going to be something awful, right up until it kills you." He took another bite from his plate, mashed potatoes being his target of choice. "What?" He pointed to the plate, looking at my mother. "How the hell do they get the potatoes like this?"

"They use cream and butter." She prepared for a statement she didn't want to make, knowing his next response.

"I use cream and butter." He defended. "Mine don't come out this good."

"Honey, you-…you have *other* talents…" She placed a hand on his, and I watched my poor father's heart break in front of my eyes. The guarded realization in his eyes was gruesome to witness.

"Aw, man, you-…everyone said they liked my food."

"We said it was unbelievable." Val chimed from the far end of the table.

"Something I had never tasted before." Violet added.

"Unique and unexpected." Sonya included.

"I said it was almost too much to handle." Alice spoke up. Eric started laughing hysterically at the responses, dismaying my father even further as he looked at each of us in despair. Finally, his eyes met mine and I cringed, knowing that I had to supply a response.

"I said it had a lot of character." I mumbled softly, Krystal's arm twitching in a stifled laugh. He sighed heavily, turning back to Smith and ignoring the barrage of long-hidden insults. He had to wait, hearing Raven finally break into a fit of cackling that shattered her typical aura of apathy.

"Smith…I'll make you a deal. You tell us the most important thing you can think of, *one* thing that would help us tremendously, and we'll get you through your withdrawal." I heard Alice's chair creak as she flinched, clearly desiring to object. The room was deadly silent, and Smith's eyes looked around the hall as he contemplated what few options he had left. Sonya's grip held strong, no sign of weakening in her powerful stance.

"You can't do that." Smith decided. "You can't help me. No one can."

"*We* can." My mother stated compellingly. "If anyone can, we can. We have a patient right now, a commander of one of the scout teams we captured, that's undergoing the process. It's hard. But not harder than death." She paused. "And not as hard as the torture that made you this way." Smith's face softened, reflecting on the likelihood that we were being honest.

"Why would you?" He seemed to realize something, almost acknowledge a nonexistent certainty that we were being deceitful.

"Because we're not you." I said quietly, more to myself than anyone else. I meant to voice the thought aloud for those around me, but the microphone picked up the quiet sound of my voice and carried it to his ears. He sat in contemplation for far longer than any of us would have wished, but it culminated in a single word from his mouth.

"Northside." Smith mumbled, speaking up after a pause so we could hear him more easily. "It's what Legacy calls the DMZ north of the White House. It's…not safe anymore. When I got here, when I snuck in with the recruits that were switched last week…he had just started converting them."

"Wait, the civilians-" My mother stopped him, standing up with her voice growing in fury. "-those innocents he let live, the ones in D.C. He's turning them into soldiers?"

"He lost Quantico." Smith defended, his energy waning. "He knew he had to prepare for war. He…he needed more soldiers. He's afraid of you." The last phrase rung out into the hall and changed the look of fear on people's faces into hope. Dad touched her hand lightly, encouraging her to sit down again. She complied, shaking her head as her eyes grew distant and sad.

"You kept your word, we'll keep ours. Doctor Goodson, if you and the three soldiers on your left could escort Mr. Smith to the infirmary, please." He gave an order, sounding much more like a request in all but its force, and began to foster the same look that permeated my mother's eyes.

They looked at each other for only a moment, and in that moment spoke volumes to one another that I unfortunately understood as well as anyone else at the table. Krystal and I decided to forsake the risk of a misunderstood gesture as she laced her fingers with mine behind my back in angst and burden. My father was the braver of my parents to speak, although my mother's words would likely have been an inadequate source of inspiration and rather serve as fuel for a rising fire.

"The last time this happened…Vampyres went to war." He started, forsaking the podium. "And so we must again." To my surprise, there were no quiet array of murmurs or shocked gasps, and instead the civilization in front of us remained engrossed in stillness. "The city of Aerael fell not from time or battle, but from attrition. The lives of *people*, not those of warfighters or hardened soldiers, were unfairly put at risk and deceived of the threat that faced them. In the defense of that city, we provided ourselves as a shield and instead obscured those people from the view of the evil we faced. In turn, we were declared immoral, unjust, and controlling. Titles only so deserved." He took a deep breath as my mother stood to support him, providing her full image to the crowd at his side. "But we do not face that here in Vanaheim. Here, we remain servants of your leaders. Your people. The ones that sit at that table of honor, the ones who brought us our food and our wine. The ones that sit at Quantico at this very moment at risk of air strikes and ground assaults. Those people are who we serve. And an untold number of those people are now at risk of the worst torture that one could never imagine only to fall subject to an army that seeks the destruction of more innocent people. Even in our own home, there's been an attempt on the life of my darling daughter. One of the people I care most about in this world was-" He cleared his throat after pulling the microphone away, trying to stay composed. "-was put at risk. And here we stand. Shaken…but unbroken."

I love you too, Dad.

"Today is for celebration…celebration of all we have done. But for many of us, it will be our last. We have reached the boundaries of the time we fought for and now must execute the most difficult part of training for war: the war itself. I know many of you are light on training and I know many of you feel unprepared for the coming battle. But I can assure you that a week of training with your leaders is better than a dozen years in Legacy's army. Because while he indoctrinates his people, we allow ours to fight for free lives. And we've just proven that his indoctrination can be broken. So please…take tonight to celebrate. Hold those you love close to you." He looked over at Alice briefly. "As of this morning, the work on our cure is finished. So tomorrow…we go to war." He placed the microphone on the table and took my mother's hands in his own, leaning his head gently against her own.

I need that kind of comfort right now. I…we can't be going to war already. We can't. Not yet.

"Hell, yeah!" A voice from the crowd, feminine but harsh, echoed against the otherwise noiseless halls around us. We all watched to see Andrea stand up, facing Layla as she followed suit. "What the hell else have we been waiting for?" She started, looking around as no one else seemed to be in the mood to revel in the face of combat. "You all want to wait while our country dies? You all want to sit here while Legacy's army gathers strength?" She scoffed, nudging Dr. Weiss. "We've been watching our world fall apart and now we have the chance to change it!"

"These animals killed our friends!" Layla joined her. "Our families! They dropped a nuclear bomb on New York and we're gonna sit here? Hell, no! Let's go take our future back and show Legacy what *real* animals look like!" A chorus of voices joined her in audible support, incited further with her follow-up. "We're going to go to D.C. and show those drugged-up assholes what real Vampyres look like!" More voices joined in, some lingering even after her statement.

"We're gonna get in there…" Andrea stood up on a chair, and in doing so I realized that she had consumed a substantial amount of alcohol before showing up to the day's event. "We're going to take back the White House, and we're going to get our goddamned lives back!" This time, the entire hall stood up, throwing their fists in the air and otherwise providing an incoherent chaos throughout the city. I watched as everyone that was spread from one side of the hall to the other screamed and shouted in support, and finally recognized the importance of their role in fighting for their freedom.

"Goddamn Marines." I heard my father chuckle, my parents sharing a brief laugh as they held each other. I turned to say something to Krystal, who was already watching me with eyes full of sad tears and a horrified trembling on her chin.

"Amy…" She started, whispering. She let go of my hand and sniffed hard, trying to catch her breath. I had never seen her composure disappear so quickly, and it terrified me to see her in such a state. "Last time I left…" She couldn't say more than a few words, the vivid blue of her eyes shrouded in a maddening shade of red and a watery shine. "I didn't come back." She finished, sobbing once and exerting every ounce of control not to touch me in any divulging way. My heart fell as I realized the gravity of her situation, having to deal with the memories of her trauma yet another time. "I can't lose you." She whimpered, the hoarse whisper from her throat finally breaking my heart cleanly in half enough that there was cause for me to quickly repair it.

You may not want me to touch you…you may not want anyone to find out about us. Frankly, my dear, I don't give a damn.

My eyes gave away my actions before I could move, my head tilting and arms moving to hold her as quickly as I possibly could. With both arms wrapped behind her neck and cradling the back of her head as gently as I was able, I slowly sank my lips onto her own, decimating any chance she had of continuing her thoughts of tragedy. I tried for a brief moment to care about anyone watching, and I tried to care about the social implications of our relationship being revealed, and struggled to find any reason to damage a moment so implicitly and intrinsically perfect. Her tears were shared now, running across my face as well, as she placed one gentle hand on the side of my head and the other on my waist to stay in our tranquil state of solitude for as long as we wanted.

Nothing is more important than this. Nothing is more important than you.

Her lips parted for the shortest instant, closing again after a short, shuddering breath and the firm belief that she was allowed to be in love with me, and more importantly, was allowed to tell me as much in any way she deemed necessary. In our brief and desperate kiss, I felt the satin of her dress roll against my fingertips as one hand fell to touch her hip while the other gently combed through her magnificent cerulean hair. I smelled the grandeur of her perfume and the loveliness of her lavender soap. I tasted her tears and the gentle sweetness of her mouth in the space between our lips. I heard the melodic rattle of the silver charms on her wrist move and dance behind my ear. Nothing had ever been so perfect, and I was convinced that nothing ever could be again, as I washed away her fears and drowned them in the unrelenting love I had for her.

Only after hearing a set of clicking footsteps uncomfortably close to my body did I pull away from her, even still locking eyes for a moment as she understood my support for what she was going through. Unfortunately, she looked behind me before I did, and I watched her pupils rapidly constrict in a primal, fear-based response of vast proportions. Knowing that only my mother could do that to another being, I turned around slowly to look upward a few inches into her confused, disoriented expression before I grimaced and took Krystal's hand again. I opened my mouth and sheepishly attempted an excuse with the intent of placating the atmosphere between us.

"Damn mistletoe got me again."

***

While my father had taken to pacing with his unwrapped tie draped around his neck, my mother sat on the recliner across from us with the same confused look as before. It was as if she was making every effort to become a marble statue and refused to fidget or show signs that she was breathing. Neither of them had said anything, which was driving Krystal's anxiety through the roof as she clamped down on my hand in a semi-permanent fit of panic. I glimpsed fleetingly at the piano in the corner of my room, wishing that even some music would have broken the unyielding silence.

"I feel like we have more important things at the moment-"

"No. Nope. We do not." My father interrupted, pausing his trek across my room for the hundred-thousandth time before resuming his indoor nature walk.

Really saying something since…we're fighting for our very existence in 24 hours. No pressure.

"Is…is this the part where I say *but mom, I love her*?" My sarcasm was handled poorly, my mother's distant look becoming a weapon of mass destruction as quickly as my father's.

"Just-…let's go from the beginning. How long has this been going on?" He finally asked, leaning against the back of the chair my mother was cemented to.

"Honestly, I've had feelings for her since we got to Vanaheim. A little bit before, even. But I only told her last night."

"Last night? And you two are already…this close? Krystal, I can…assume you've also had…feelings?" He had no desire to finish the sentence, and almost appeared to be growing sick.

"No." Krystal breathed. "She…touched…my soul…" Her word choice was sporadic, and she very clearly wasn't thinking straight.

Ha-ha. Thinking straight. Because we're lesb-

"Touched your…soul? I'm going to *pray* that's not a euphemism."

"Dad!" I neglected to mention that my own thoughts strayed toward humor as well, and instead explained the situation to the best of my ability. "No, she…the issue we had with my powers. I could sense her emotions the way I could sense a normal person's pain. I helped *heal* some of the trauma from her death, and…I just got lost in who she is as a person. I saw so much in who she was, and I…I fell in love with her. I saw her strength, her tenacity, her passion for life and the joys she wants from it. Some of my feelings transferred to her, as well, but we…needed to talk about it, first. She was repressing a lot. From the…trauma." I slowly started to get the feeling that my explanation was simply more sound in the room as my words went unheeded.

"So…you two are…" He started again, having no idea what he even meant, let alone how to finish the sentence. I raised an eyebrow and shrugged, shaking my head so he would try to make some sense. "You both have feelings." He decided, whipping off his tie and wrapping it across one hand and onto the other.

"Yes." I answered simply. "So can we…go now?" My mother's hand twitched at the question, so I sighed and slunk back in the couch another inch. Keeping Krystal's powers under control was a constant task, and I would have been worried for the temperature of the surrounding rooms had I let go of her hand.

"Anytime, hon." He looked at my mother pointedly, waiting for her to finally enter the conversation, but it was to no result, and he returned to his pacing. "Everyone else is prepping for the final briefing, and *we*…are doing *this*…" He whispered, taking off his jacket and laying it on my bed.

"Okay, I'm sorry, but what is this really about? She, what, used to use drugs?" My sharp snap finally caught their full attention, and even Krystal became more animated while trying to slink further away from the center of the room. "Age difference? The addiction-based crush she had on you?" I had to reach out and mentally soothe Krystal's stomach as a massive heave nearly forced her to vomit. It went unnoticed by my parents, so I continued. "Just tell me what the issue is. Didn't want me to be gay? Wanted me to get with a nice guy and have babies and-"

"Amy, it's…it's none of that. Couldn't care less, honestly." He waved his hands gently and sighed, finally making his way to the center of the room and taking a seat. "You're in *love* with someone." I pursed my lips, waiting for an elaboration, but he stared at me as if that was a complete thought.

"Yeah. Yep. That…happens? I couldn't meet a lot of people over the last fifteen years. World's kind of a barren wasteland."

"Yeah, but…" He sighed again, completing his tenth strong exhale over the past minute. "The-…*that*…isn't like…dating." He groaned, looking over at the fragile porcelain decoration on my reclining chair and shook his head. "Look, we expected you to meet people, to date, to…whatever. But you've never been with anyone before, and what we just witnessed was…" He shook his head, a positive light in his eyes at a brief memory in his head. "It's what I felt for your mother. What I still do. Neither of us could have expected that. And out of the blue, and right after you were nearly shot, and right before we go to war-"

"Wait." I interjected. "So this…this isn't about Krystal *specifically*?" I clarified, hoping to get my partner involved in the conversation at some point.

Partner? Lover? Girlfriend? Fiancée? Ooh, bride…wife. Wife has…such a nice ring to it. Wait, yesterday was the first date. Focus.

"Not…not as much, no. I mean, part of it. I'm still…I have a lot of human left in me, so the thought of it is going to take some time. I knew her literally before you were even born. It'll take a second to wrap my head around, but I get the…Vampyre thing. And you're more mature than any twenty *or* thirty-five year old I know. More mature than Krystal was twenty years ago." He ran a hand through his hair, looking directly at me this time. "We've always been terrified of this. Of...accepting someone as being good enough for you."

Oh...Aww. That's sweet.

"And...we went from zero to a hundred in literally seconds. So we're shellshocked, I guess. I just...we don't have time. And we need time. This is very sudden." He finished, offering no solution.

"Maybe it's better that you know her. Especially after she's gotten a lot of her issues worked out. No drugs, no partying, no-"

"I saw those Missy Grey videos. Don't-...don't say *no partying*." He warned.

"Look, from what I heard, that night was pretty mild compared to what she used to be like. Either way, we're getting off track." I looked at Krystal and my mother, both looking at absolutely nothing and completely empty-faced. "The damn women around here, come *on*, guys. All I can say is that I have the ability to sense pain. Always have. I heal things. In her, I sense emotion. And in doing so, I'm better attuned to *my* emotions. Neither one of us is taking this lightly, and I truly cannot describe the seriousness of being with her. I don't know what else you want from this conversation." He nodded, somehow satisfied with my chaotically-thought-up response.

"We're going back to war." My mother finally whispered, the whispering breeze of her voice catching the entire room off-guard. Her eyes flitted over to me with a look I was unfamiliar with. "Love is going to be the first casualty, Amy. Your father lost me to death...I lost you to death...and Krystal lost everything to death. Death spares no one from its pain." Her jaw shifted a fraction of an inch. "Regardless of how you feel, you're not ready for that pain."

"I didn't lose everything." Krystal spoke up, an unusual and surprising strength in her voice. "I lost what I hated. I gained a new life, a *better* life with a reason to live for it."

"And war will not care about your reasons." My mother returned coldly. Krystal was determined in meeting my mother's eyes, a tension between the two of them I couldn't have hoped to understand.

"We will win this war." Krystal said confidently. "We will make it through this. I know we will."

"Easy to say when the fighting hasn't started."

"Easy to say when your *daughter* won't be the one fighting." Krystal's rebuke had an edge of energy that could have cleaved a boulder in half, and my father and I both shared a concerned look.

What…is going on?

"I never wanted her to fight." My mother growled. "Her father and I swore that she would never know that life."

"An oath that's been broken." Krystal seethed. "The fight is here already."

"And she won't be a part of that."

"You can't know that!" They both leapt up from their positions, Krystal's verbal hostility met in the center of the room as they stared each other down. "You are *not* the harbinger of war, Kara, and I know *damn* well how hard you've tried to be." My mother opened her mouth to fight back, but was kept at bay by Krystal's sheer aggression while she pressed harder. "The corrupt, the evil, the Legacies in this world will *always* make decisions that lead far outside the life you would choose for her. The life that would lead to a safe existence for her. But you're not her goddamned *commander!*" Krystal bellowed, forcing my mother to take a step back.

What the literal, actual, verifiable hell is happening right now?

"You're not her squadmate! You're not her sword or her shield! You're her *mother.* And I know damn well that thought *terrifies* you, I know it must keep you awake at night as you fear for her life every time she is out of your sight and I know that because *I* feel that fear!" Krystal's eyes grew teary, glistening drops rolling down her cheeks as my mother stared in awe. "I felt that fear from the first vision and the first time she touched me! I felt that fear when she dove headfirst into the recesses of my mind to rescue me from the memories of my own *death!* I felt that fear when she looked me in the eyes last night and told me that she *loved* me! I felt that fear, Kara. I have felt that fear every day that she's been at my side, even when we couldn't say we were anything more than friends. Because that fear comes from loving someone so much that you believe you will not live without them. And I know that must *terrify* you to believe that someone could be bold enough to say they feel that love for her the way you do. But I do. And there is nothing, there is *no one* that will keep me from holding onto and cherishing that. There is *nothing*, there is *no goddamned army* on this planet that will keep me from believing that this woman is anything but perfect! There is *nothing* that will keep me from knowing, loving, and *fearing* for everything that she is…wholly…and unconditionally." Krystal's voice grew hoarse, sighing as she let the final words leave her lips. I looked up at her in complete reverence as she towered over my mother and confessed everything she could have conjured to describe exactly how I felt for her, as well.

You're everything to me.

I reached over and took her hand, letting my abilities reach out and grasp at any feelings I could sense. Instead, I felt the nerve endings in her hand as I would have with anyone else. I pulled gently, bringing her away from the conflict and back toward the couch I sat on.

You already feel the way that she does. Your powers won't reveal anything new.

My mother gazed emptily at Krystal for another few moments, my father trying to stay as far out of the line of fire as possible.

"I'm sorry." She finally whispered emotionally. "Krystal. I...I'm sorry." I knew Krystal felt guilty for imposing any kind of undue stress on her under the circumstances, and it showed in the bashful silence she took up at my side.

"No, I-...*I'm* sorry." Krystal returned after a moment, squeezing my hand. "To both of you. I shouldn't have gotten defensive. I wouldn't trust me either. Not with someone like her." Her following silence was mournful, an intense inadequacy suddenly gripping her throat.

"Look, maybe it's just me-" Dad started. "But everything you just said goes a long way. There's...there's a right way to love someone. And then there's not truly loving someone. And I guess we know which side you're on."

"I promise you both, I am in love with everything about her. Her intelligence, her wit, her charm, her desire to help others-"

"The perfect ass I carry around with me."

"Don't talk about me like that. I'm a bitch, not an ass." A brief but awkward chuckle between us helped the situation, with Krystal and I perfectly ricocheting our comedic timing off one another.

"I just want you to be happy." Dad looked directly at me, leaving Krystal out of the equation for a brief moment. "That's all."

"I *am* happy. The kind of person I felt, that I saw in her most raw form, is something I will always be happy with. I know I'm not making a light decision, and I know I'm not being rash. This is something deeper than I can even explain. But I promise I'm happy." He nodded slowly, thinking about my words.

"Well...that's about it, then. Can't beat a dead horse. Lot to do. Lot going on. We should get back to it." My father mumbled. "Eric called Yuri. They're gearing up at Quantico. We have about twelve hours until they're ready. At that point, I'll get us all together and we'll do our final briefing." He stood up, taking my mother's hand and squeezing it lightly. "I'll uh…preface *this*…with everyone else beforehand. Just so it's not as awkward later when we're all in the same room." They started to leave, stopping as my mother paused and turned to face the two of us.

"I love both of you." She started, looking back and forth between us slowly. "I want us to make it through. But if we don't, well…take it from me. Better to have loved and lost." She gave Krystal a small smile, the equivalent of a blessing, and left through my front door alongside my father. Krystal sighed and turned to me, immediately gushing a mess of words at me.

"I'm so sorry for causing all of this. I didn't mean to start that fight with Kara, and I definitely di-…mmm…" I interrupted her with another heartfelt kiss, this time to shut her up rather than to indulge myself. I pulled away after taking several moments to savor the occasion.

"We got through it. Uncomfortable, melancholy, sure. But meaningful. And…I think it's exactly what they needed to hear. I know it's what I needed to hear." I reassured.

"I don't even know how the things I'm saying are possible. I've lived a long, full life. And this is…it's so new to me. So foreign." I took her hand as she spoke and walked her over to my bedroom, patting the bed as I hopped into it and laid across the blanket in my gown. She hesitated, slowly sitting down and unlacing her heels.

"I mean…well, I haven't lived as long as you. But it's new to me, too. We'll figure it out. That's part of the fun, right?" I smirked. She smiled for a moment before it was taken away by negative thoughts.

"I'm afraid." She laid down next to me, clasping one of my hands in both of hers and kissing my knuckles. "For us. For our future. For your parents, for my sister. For everyone."

"Everyone is afraid for everyone." I explained, stroking her hair. "And that makes for too much fear. All we have to do is our job. We follow our leaders, our planners, and our experts, and we'll be okay."

"Seen too many wars to know that's not always the case." She sighed, tilting her head. "But I trust the people we'll have at our backs. Our family. Our friends."

"Our…girlfriends?" I questioned. "Partners, or…?"

"I-…look, I have no idea. I'm just going to call you my personal nerd."

"Huh. I'm cool with having a personal Ice Queen."

"Queen? If we're going with *royal* titles, then I have the entire world's princess in my arms." She raised her eyebrows, prompting another quick kiss before I rolled over and slid backward against her body. Reaching behind me, I grabbed one of her arms and draped it over my chest to touch each of her fingers with my own.

"I'm afraid, too. For the same reasons you are. But I want to be strong for you."

We're going to war. You could lose everything. Everyone. You could lose her.

"Be strong for *yourself*, my love. If I know you're okay, then I'll be okay." I smiled at her consideration, laying my head on the mattress.

"Call me *love* again." I whispered, playing with the charms on her bracelet.

"Anything for you, my love." She tucked her chin behind my ear, playfully biting it.

She saved your life today. Show the woman some gratitude.

"Holy shit, you saved my life today." I whipped around as she giggled, rolling onto her back and laughing. "I forgot. Somehow." I confessed, the events of the past twenty-four hours having happened in such a blur. She smiled at me, beaming her perfect white teeth. "I…feel like I owe you. Like I need to do something, I don't know." She stared at me for a moment, her eyes still alight with happiness.

"You can hold me." She whispered finally, still smiling and letting me roll onto her arm as I laid at her side. "You can hold me like there won't be a tomorrow." I snuggled into a comfortable position next to her, feeling the slow rise and fall of her chest as she breathed peacefully in her perfect gown. I kissed her cheek again, closing my eyes and responding to her request.

"Anything for you…my love."

KEYSTONE

KARA

My hands and feet still seemed numb from the exchange, but I tried to shake the feeling by letting go of my husband's hand and asking him an honest question.

"Am…I wrong to feel vigilant?" I sighed, leaning against the wall outside Amy's door and trying to clear my thoughts.

She looked so happy. So content with the world in spite of its madness.

"If you're wrong, I'm wrong, too. I…that was a bit much. It's all a bit much." He agreed, taking a spot next to me and wrapping his arm around my waist. "If I had known they were going in that direction, I would have said something. Maybe. Or at least been prepared, I don't know." He winced, shaking his head. "I don't know."

"Neither do I. I mean, Krystal's been nothing but kind to her-"

"No, yeah, she's been great. It's just…" He agreed with my sentiment, but was trying to voice the same words I couldn't.

I can't let her get hurt. Above all else, I can't let her get hurt.

"Is this just how love works?" I chuckled, the thought of our first date rattling around in my head. "Just unexpected bursts of emotion out of nowhere?"

"Pretty much." He nodded slowly. "That's how it was with you. Saw you in the bar and knew you were made of something different. And as soon as you pulled up to the restaurant and I saw you in that dress…" A light smile graced his handsome face as he quietly reminisced. "Yeah. Sometimes it's out of nowhere."

"She's our daughter, though, Jalix. I just-…I can't help but worry." I tried arguing a point I couldn't even make. Krystal's words started to shake my confidence again, second-guessing how much I needed to stress over the situation.

"If she had kissed anyone else in front of the whole city, would you feel any different?"

Damn. He's right. In fact, I might have been harder on someone else. Anyone else, really.

"I *want* it to bother me that it's Krystal, too." I looked over at him, who nodded slowly without returning eye contact. "I mean…for so long she-…but she's a whole new person now. The same way I was after my own death, and I have no idea how to handle that. I have memories of her, images of her that are going to mess with my head when I think about her with Amy."

"Amy's a grown, independent, and amazing adult. You haven't seen Krystal in twenty years, and…let's be honest." He shrugged. "Amy knows her better than you ever will. They've spent all this time together and had what was apparently a pretty intense experience with her powers."

Maybe I just need to get to know Krystal as who she is now. As a new person.

"Maybe you're right." I exhaled.

"That being said, if she breaks Amy's heart, I will kill-"

"Be nice. No death threats on the eve of war." I chuckled. He smirked, gesturing to Alice's door.

"Think we can go bother them? We're not the only couple that's stressed. Might be nice to talk this through with someone else."

"Oh, God. We're old." I laughed, taking a step toward Alice's door. "Kids growing up, we have to lean on our other friends for support. Starting to feel like we just aged a lot."

"Says…you?" He laughed, turning to me. "Kara, I'm fifty. You're-"

"Forty-eight." I denied his accusations of being nearly four centuries old and quietly rapped on Alice's door. While I wouldn't have expected her to leap toward the door or call out with no warning, there was a long pause before any noise came from the room, and it was in the form of Val's low voice speaking to Alice. We leaned away from the door, awaiting a response, and could only hear the faint buzz of their voices as they went back and forth for a moment. Even without hearing the words, the tone of the conversation was tense and forlorn, and I couldn't have imagined what the topic would have been. A heavy set of footsteps shuffled toward the door before it opened, Val's arm reaching out to give me a brief hug.

"Hey, sis." He rested his chin atop my head for a moment, clearly in need of comforting more than I was. "Hey, Jalix."

"Val. What's up? You guys alright?" Being the observant person he was, Jalix spoke only loud enough for Val to hear, since Alice was still nowhere to be seen. Val grimaced, starting to nod but stopping and beckoning toward the hallway. We stepped back, letting him mostly close the door before running his hand across his face. On the edges of his eye socket, I made out the faintest traces of a healing bruise.

A black eye? Did she…hit him?

"We, um...we're just working some things out right now." In the darkened terracotta of his eyes, I watched a sadness fill his mind and heart.

"Old arguments or new ones?" I wanted to help, but didn't want to press him for any unwarranted details. He didn't answer right away, looking away and gritting his teeth together.

He's on the verge of tears...what the hell is going on? This isn't like him. Either of them.

"Val..." I tried again.

"I just wanted one last night with her." He lost his battle, looking away to hide his tears. "Just *one* last goddamn night." He finished his sentence in a whisper, his throat clearly tightening.

"What's going on, man? Talk to us, we're here to help." Jalix offered his support.

"Not much anyone can do." Val replied, his back to us. He lifted an arm, wiping his eyes. "You or me or Kara. Not Krystal. Not Violet."

"Val, we can-"

"I can't *touch* her." He said hoarsely, turning slowly and leaning against the doorframe. "She's...every time I'm behind her, she jumps in fear. Every time I touch her, she slinks away. She keeps having panic attacks and flashbacks-"

"Hey, it's alright." I put a hand on his shoulder to slow him down. "Take your time and talk with us, we're not going anywhere."

"They tore a piece of her soul out. They-...they *destroyed* her innocence, her sense of peace. She can't forget what they did to her." He sniffed, gritting his teeth again as he became frustrated with showing any sign of emotion.

"The Tortured...when they kidnapped the women." Jalix sighed, starting to see the problem. "I know *nothing* about what she went through, at least from a personal perspective. But I know PTSD. In and out, left and right, I've seen guys after deployments break down exactly like she is. Their wives scare the shit out of them and they get arrested for swinging or reacting when they were just…genuinely frightened. Doesn't excuse the disgusting pieces of shit that did it on purpose, but…my point is, she's not alone."

"She wants to be alone. That's the problem." Val sighed, crossing his arms. "She wants to be buried in her work or-" His head turned to the end of the hallway, watching Sonya round the corner and stop suddenly at the sight of our – very obviously private – conversation.

"Whoop. Sorry." She held up her hands in apology, but approached anyway. "Don't mean to intrude, I-…she texted me. Another panic attack, she said."

"Yeah." Val whispered, nodding. Sonya stared at him for a moment, seeing the remains of his injury and sighed. "Oh, no. Val…"

"*I'm* fine. She's not." He said firmly. "She can swing all she needs to if it gets this shit out of her system."

"It's-…Val, it doesn't work like that." Sonya tilted her head, empathetic beyond her usual sense of general compassion. "It's sweet that you don't blame her, but we can't let you be a punching bag for her emotional expression. It's not *her* that's doing this. It's the panic, and that's not something you need subjected to."

"I'm alright, Sonya. I promise. And I know, I just…I don't know what to do other than let her get everything out."

"What exactly happened?" Jalix asked gently. Val took a moment, letting Sonya into our small circle.

"I, um…thought I'd be romantic. She was making coffee, didn't hear me come out of the bathroom. Distracted, I guess. Came up behind her and went to give her a hug. Caught a coffee mug to the temple and our kitchen is…we're going to need a few things replaced. Need some scorch marks painted over." His eyes roamed, trying to avoid any more tears. "Her reaction was so fast, before and after. She felt *horrible.* Like she had tried to kill me or something. Kept saying I needed to get away from her, that she can't have me around-" He stopped, his voice too tight to continue speaking.

"This is why she texts me. I've been trying to help her with these panic attacks in private, but that's not cutting it anymore." Sonya added. "She didn't want anyone to know how badly she was suffering."

"She should have told *me.*" Val's voice was earnest, enough that Jalix took a step back and turned away for a moment. My own eyes welled with tears at the thought of Alice's current condition. Val started to recognize the similarities between my changes after the violence Schillinger imposed on me and Alice's situation, drawing parallels in his mind.

I know what she's been through. Maybe I'm the only one that truly knows. But I shut down and she kept going…God, the strength it must have taken these past months…

"You were the one person she couldn't tell, Val." I started, clearing my throat. "Think about it. She loves you more than anything. You're the one thing she can't lose. So she's going to do *everything* to maintain the image that she's what you fell in love with. Even if she's a mess on the inside. That's why she's pushing you away. She doesn't want to put her pain on you." He shook his head, almost in denial that she was distancing herself again. "Let me go talk to her." I finished.

"Why didn't we hear any of the fight? We were just barely down the hall." Jalix wondered.

"It happened more than an hour ago. Right after the dinner. You guys were…talking to Amy and Krystal out in the main hall, I think. I heard you come down, but it was already said and done by then. She's been…she's just been silent. She laid down on the bed and wouldn't talk to me." Sonya went to say something, but Val pressed his lips together and held up his hand, shaking his head and leaving our group to briskly walk toward the end of the hall. Jalix nodded to me once, following him while Sonya touched my shoulder lightly.

"You mind if I come with? Alice had asked me to come down, it's why I'm here."

"Please. I think you're the only other one she'll entertain right now." I bit my lip, pushing open the door and becoming woefully unprepared for the conversation at hand.

What the hell do I say to her? It took me…decades to try and recover. Even now, I-…I still have my nightmares. I still have my scars and my reminders. How do I help someone when I haven't fully helped myself?

I made my entrance known, putting a light force into my footsteps so we wouldn't alert her and cause further stress. Their quarters were laid out differently than ours, the bedroom being around the left corner from the main door and tucked away to the side. While she was no longer laying down, Alice sat on the bed in front of a stack of pillows, her eyes reddened from prolonged irritation. Before we could cross the threshold into her room, she tilted her head and apologized to us.

"I'm sorry." Her bright green eyes were even more vivid against the redness behind them. "I didn't mean to start something or-"

"Alice…we're here because we love you. Not because anyone is upset with you."

"Don't even *tell* me that." She cried, pointing to the door and arguing with me. "Val doesn't even think I love him anymore." She was barely able to speak the words, grabbing a tissue from a nearly exhausted box and blowing her nose. She kept her eyes closed, weeping into her knees as she pressed them into her chest. She wasn't distraught in a conventional manner, the way we so often dealt with in heartbreak and chaos. Her brutal shaking and suffocating sobs were entirely different, and was something that shook me to my core in watching.

"Alice-"

"I don't need pity." She whispered, sighing deeply before lifting her head and looking past the two of us. "I just want to be left alone."

"No. We're not doing that." Sonya blurted bluntly, remaining the voice of reason so I could remain the more empathetic of the two of us. "I need you to recognize that your well-being is too important for us to ignore. We're here for you, and we're going to continue to be here. Okay?" Alice nodded slowly, finally exhaling.

"I don't need this." She started, shaking her head. "I've *helped* trauma survivors. I know the rules, I know the methods, the protocols. And mine-…I didn't have it as badly as others did." She glanced at me knowingly, shaking her head.

"Hey, don't do that." I protested. "You can't compare situations and say that one of us had it *worse* than another. The fact is-"

"The *fact* is that it was different." Alice sniffed, trying to shake herself away from her more intense emotions and revert to the appearance of normality. "What *almost* happened to me is not the same as what *actually* happened to you." She paused, frowning before looking back at her bedspread. "Almost…is only a victory in the imagination."

She's still trying to hide from it all, trying to downplay it and internalize it.

"Alice." Sonya said firmly. "There was no *almost.* You were assaulted. Hurt. Threatened. And so was your family. That was real, regardless of anything else. And you can't push that away in light of the fact that we were able to stop things from getting worse. You're *allowed* to feel like it's the worst thing that's ever happened to you. Don't compare your situation to anyone else's, especially Kara's."

"She's right. I don't want that." I continued, trying to hide the subtle shaking in my hands by sliding them under my thighs. "I don't want to be used as an example or a lesson. You don't think I've heard the hushed discussions over the years? Don't want to *end up like Kara* or *go through what Kara did.* It's exhausting to have people use your trauma as some...emblem of terror, especially when they didn't know what the trauma was. To have your name paraded around as the pinnacle of tragedy. I'm a person, and I'm here, and I'm whole. Schillinger couldn't take away who I am. I didn't let him, and I know damn well that you're not about to let Legacy do the same to you."

"He already has." She returned in a quiet whisper, starting to tear up again. "I didn't mean to hit Val. I swear-"

"Alice. No one, not even Val, is blaming you for that. He just told us that he'd *rather* see you hitting him than to feel this way. He's willing to withstand that for your well-being. What does that tell you about how much he loves you?" Sonya softened her voice, hoping that firmness wouldn't be needed.

"It tells me he deserves better." Alice whispered, lifting her hand to look at her wedding ring. "He deserves someone that isn't broken. Someone he doesn't have to babysit."

"Am *I* broken?" I asked plainly. She shook her head, raising an eyebrow. "And you both stood by my side for so many years. Why do you deserve less?"

"Because I'm not *like* you, Kara. I'm not like either of you. I'm not some great leader, I'm not an all-powerful force of good. I'm a doctor. I might seem special to people who aren't, but do you have any idea how insignificant I am in the grand scheme of things?"

"Yeah, it was super insignificant that you came up with the cure for the world's deadliest and most virulent mutant virus. Not at all important that you single-handedly made sure we had hope for a globally-integrated future. We could have done without it, honestly." Sonya's sarcasm was aggressive to prove a point, inciting a quiet sigh from Alice.

"It's just research. Lab work. Anyone could have-"

"Alright, we're going to nip this conversation in the bud. Lemme ask you a question." I was appreciative of Sonya's ability to retain control of the situation, remaining far more objective than I could have been. "If you were me, sitting here and trying to help, right? Except Violet was sitting where you are, instead. What things would you be saying to her right now?" Alice sat for a moment, a long stare into her bedspread a contemplative silence.

"I don't know. She's…so much more innocent than I am. She hasn't killed people like I have-"

"Whoa, wha-….nope, not having any of that." I interrupted, grabbing her hand tightly in spite of its boiling heat. I shifted my head to her eye level, staring at her with a degree of intensity. "If you're somehow about to say that you *deserved* this, *I'm* going to hit you. Look, I-"

"Okay, easy, girl." Sonya chuckled, patting my shoulder. "What Kara's trying to say is that you're taking the pain and trying to justify it. But this time, it doesn't have a reason. You can take a stubbed toe or a bumped head and blame yourself for that pain. Not paying attention, not watching where you were going, whatever. But this was outside of your control. That's scary. It's terrifying to have something happen that you can't stop, that you can't control. And you're going to find every excuse to make it your fault, because then it's easier to deal with. You'd have a logical train leading up to the trauma. But that's not how it happened. The first thing you need to accept is that it was the fault of those Tortured – who are all dead, by the way – and there was nothing that anyone could have done to prevent it. Can you agree with me on that?"

She's as good as Amy at talking to people. I hate the circumstances, but I know she's doing what she does best right now.

"Yeah, I know…" Alice nodded. "Sorry."

"Don't be." I added, releasing her hand and trying to discreetly cool my palm against the skin of my forearm. "You've been so buried in work that you haven't had time to deal with any of this properly. One conversation isn't going to fix this. One talk isn't going to make everything go away. But it'll make things better. Thought by thought, discussion by discussion, things will get better. And maybe you'll never get back to the way you were before, but one day you'll realize you've conquered it. And it'll be a scar instead of a bleeding wound."

"I'm a doctor." She chuckled sniffling. "I'm supposed to fix the wounds, not have them. And I'm certainly not supposed to *make* them. God, Val…"

"Val!" I called over my shoulder, hoping he and Jalix were close enough to hear me.

"Kara, no. Please, I am *not* ready to talk to him yet."

"Yes, you are. Val!"

"Kara!" She squeaked, grabbing my arm. "Please. Not yet."

"I'm not doing it for you." I said coolly, staring into her despairing eyes. "If you want to treat a wound, then your husband needs to be your first patient."

"She's right." Sonya agreed. "You need to learn to trust him with these things. He should be your go-to guy, your rock in all the hard places. We'll always be here for you, but your husband made vows to love you no matter what. He needs a chance to live up to them. Besides, he settles the oldest argument you've ever had." Alice looked at Sonya briefly in confusion. "You and Krystal? No chance. Val? *He's* always been the hot one." She winked at Alice as the three of us looked toward the door, two sets of footsteps stopping outside the entryway.

"Can I come in?" Val asked, his voice quiet and kind. I looked at Alice, wanting her independent response instead of forcing my involvement. She shuddered, choking up and nodding quickly.

"Yes." She coughed, hugging her knees tighter. The door opened slowly, my brother replacing Sonya at the foot of the bed while he stared at her in shock and helplessness. They sat in silence for a moment, Alice's crying continuing in spite of their eye contact.

"I love you." Val mumbled hoarsely, reaching out to place his fingers next to hers. "Always have. Always will."

"I l-love you, too." She whispered back, hiccupping once. "I'm so sorry."

"No…you can't be sorry for what isn't your fault, Ally. Just…just don't give up on me. Okay?" He exhaled, moving closer to her. "Don't give up on me."

"I'm not." She cried quietly, tilting her head. "I love you. I'm with you." She withdrew her hands into her sleeve to protect him, but wrapped her covered fingers around his palm and held it tightly. Val's attempts at remaining calm were failing, but it was helping Alice realize his own sense of pain.

"I love you. I'm with you." He repeated. "Now and forever. I'm not about to lose you to memories." He forsook the distance between them and moved to cradle her body against his own, stroking her hair slowly as they rocked back and forth. I wiped away my own tears, standing up quickly to escape the room with Jalix and Sonya. As we left, I took Jalix's hand and laced my fingers in his. He closed the door behind us, moving several steps down the hallway before speaking.

"They're a mess." He sighed, looking at the door. "I love them. But I care about them too much to say they're remotely close to fine. I-…I'm trying to stay objective through all of this, you know? And our war is coming. I can't ask them-"

"You can't ask them to fight, but you won't be able to stop them, either." Sonya added. "This war? It's their ultimate redemption. Everything that's broken them over the last twenty years can be fixed in one battle. Nothing you can say is going to stop them from fighting for each other." She ran a hand over her face before teasing it through her length of hair and gathering the blonde mess behind her shoulders. "God, it's…these talks with her have been *so* rough."

"You must have been the only one she told. I never knew it was this bad." I admitted.

"She didn't want anyone else knowing. She's been masking it. And like you said, she stayed focused on the cure. That was her coping mechanism. Even gave her some moments of peace knowing that she was making progress. But it's going to take a long time to get her back to her own normal."

"We don't have that time." Jalix added gently. "That's my point." Sonya exhaled, smirking.

"None of us do, Jalix. Nobody going into this war is intact. Not Alice, not Val, not Krystal. I can't think of a single person who has their shit together right now. But we just need to be okay enough to focus on the fight. Fixing everything else and finding peace? That's for *after* the war. And it's a damn good motivation to stay alive." She turned to walk away and leave the two of us alone, but Jalix stopped her with a brief question.

"What about you?" He asked, prompting her to turn her head. "What's your motivation?" For the first time in days, I saw a familiar twinkle in her eye as she stared back at Jalix.

"What it's always been. Kicking ass." The gentle smile stuck with her as she turned the corner, likely making her way to the civilian residences.

"Let's hope everyone feels that way." Jalix sighed, kissing my temple. "I heard the crowd earlier, but…there was still a lot of reservation. They might be motivated by the idea, but as soon as they're handed weapons and seated in the convoy…"

"You think people will have doubts?" I asked, reaching over to open our own door. "Everyone has a stake in this. They know that. It's why everyone has colossal issues right now. Tensions are high." I took a step into the room, giving Jalix a moment to hang his jacket on the coat hooks inside the door.

"Back in my SF training, we learned how to use a local population to fight a war. Convince them that their only way to freedom was fighting for it, which for the most part was true. But we were also taught to expect them to act like rational people. Not soldiers. Those who seek war are often those who don't fight in them. I don't know what I'm waiting for, but I feel like some of them are going to want out." He admitted, reaching to close the door. As it swung shut, a quiet voice called out and quickly diminished.

"Can I-…nope, o-…kay." Jalix tilted his head, hearing the distinct sound of Violet's voice trail away as the door shut. He cracked it open once more, peering out into the hall at her half-turned figure as I chuckled. He stared for a moment before speaking.

"You got issues, too?" He asked.

"Oh, plenty." Violet responded sunnily.

"Come on down." He opened the door again, letting Violet make her way into our room. She still looked marvelous from her time at the dinner, our short-lived event having finally put all three of my daughters in one place with formal evening wear. Her similarities to my own features were drastically more apparent as she moved through the room, her physique extraordinarily similar to mine.

I hope she's not ashamed to be my daughter. I hid it for so long…

"Thanks for letting me crash the party." She added, looking around at our living space. "Damn. Do you guys ever clean up around here?"

"Yeah, whenever we have an hour of free time." Jalix playfully fired back. "Come here to critique our apartment or to talk?"

"Eh. Both." She shrugged nonchalantly, clearly avoidant of whatever issues she wanted to discuss. She finally looked over at me, nodding once.

"Hey. Mom."

"You can just call me Kara if-"

"Nah, I used to call you mom anyway. Just not when you were around." She looked around again, enjoying that we had hung a few of our paintings on the sage-green walls of our living room. "No point in being pissy just because it's truer than I thought."

She used to call me mom? Do I look like a mom, or was it because she lived with us and Amy?

Jalix remained silent, enjoying the small victory.

"Nerves?" I asked, indicating that she could sit down. "Everyone's a bit tense at the moment."

"Yes, they are. We're walking into a bloodbath tomorrow. It's going to be a slaughterhouse, and there's a chance none of us will make it out alive. Anything else even need said? Something about saving the world or a greater sacrifice?" She chuckled. "I don't need a pep talk, but I know how dire our stakes are, and they scare the shit out of me."

"Us, too." Jalix nodded. "None of us want this. If I had it my way, I'd have tried anything else. Andrea and I talked through so many different plans." He sighed, taking a seat next to me on the cream-colored couch and sprawling out in a moment of relaxation. "Dropping the virus canisters from the air would trigger the anti-air platforms and those canisters wouldn't make it to the ground. Disperse the cure somewhere else, we still have the White House problem and nuclear bombs if Legacy finds out. We ran through every scenario we could, even a small-scale suicide run at D.C., and nothing panned out within the realm of possibility. So…here we are. All-out warfare."

"Yeah, so how about Amy and Krystal?" Violet asked, crossing her legs. Jalix and I both stared at her for a moment, the topic change giving us whiplash. "Told you I didn't need a pep talk. I'd rather avoid the war 'til we get there. So…daughter. Dating Krystal. What are the odds you guys poison Krystal's coffee?"

"Low."

"*Zero.*" I retorted, shooting Jalix a warning glance. "We both trust Krystal, and I've never seen Amy like this. Or Krystal, for that matter. They…I think they have a good thing going. Their personalities match up pretty well, all things considered. If they…love…each other…" I tried to get the words out smoothly, and failed as I stumbled at the discomfort of the statement. "…then it'll work out for them both. They have our support, at least."

"Damn. That's great." Violet responded, smiling gently. "I'm happy for them, too. I was worried you guys would turn on Krystal, but I probably should have known you're both smarter than that."

"I was with Krystal before she died. I watched her leave an old life behind, and she didn't expect to get a new one. I'm okay with putting faith in her that she'll stick to her new ways. She's happier." Jalix suggested.

"Happiness is something she never had during her addiction." I added. "She had moments of enjoyment and laughter, but she wasn't content deep down. Amy fulfills something in her that she's never had. Better than any drug, better than any deep-seated need for attention. I'll take it. It means she's going to treat Amy well for years to come."

"She's been a bit of a buzzkill at our parties since she drinks less, but I'm okay with the sense of responsibility she has now." Violet ran a hand through her hair, unadorned and straightened without additional tampering. "She'll be fun enough to keep Amy excited, and Amy will keep her on the straight and narrow. I hope you guys actually understand *how* lucky you got." She chuckled. "Amy could have wound up with one of the random infantry dudes or one of Eric's techs or something. She'd have gotten bored within a few years. Krystal is going to keep her engaged for a lifetime."

As long as they make it through this, otherwise, they won't have a lifetime. Even if we do, it'll be a shorter one.

"Yeah. I agree." I replied, trying to keep my thoughts to myself. I looked over as Jalix's phone buzzed, lighting up as he pulled it out of his pocket and unlocked the screen. I waited patiently, watching him slowly sit up and prepare to relay the information from the message.

"Um…Yuri dispatched most of the vehicles. They're on their way to us, along with everyone who isn't in Yuri's air assault unit. They're obviously staying behind to come into D.C. by helicopter. Quantico is almost emptied. Once the drivers and passengers get here, we'll give everyone a short break, give the vehicles some fuel, and load everyone else up to leave. The…jets are fueled and armed, ready to fly. Andrea and Layla just need to get there." Jalix looked up briefly, reminding me that they had only left for Quantico an hour ago. "Blackhawks are getting set up, but they're not anticipating any issues. Mine is already on the way with the ground vehicles. And…oh, no way." He smirked. "Hamilton, my pilot friend at Nellis, finally responded. Yuri says he's already airborne. He's going to land at Quantico for fuel, then join Layla and Andrea. We're definitely moving."

"I guess the war's in full swing for Yuri." Violet remarked. "All the prep work he's doing on his own, it's crazy."

"He's used to crazy." Jalix chuckled. "He's got it handled. I'm just glad to see we-"

Noise from the main hall, near the entrance to the city. Was it something from the training room?

Jalix and I both snapped to look at the door, hearing the same, singular noise and reacting equally. Violet stood slowly, taking a step forward.

"Guys. Relax. Probably people letting out steam in the cage-" We jumped back as the sound repeated, this time in tenfold magnitude and in a clear, rapid enfilade of suppressed gunfire.

Oh, no. No, no, no…not here.

"Hide in the bathroom." I turned quickly, pushing Violet toward the door with my abilities. I held back the concept of panic, although my heart leapt toward my breastbone in pounding thumps of anxiety. "Don't come out unless-" I buckled suddenly, an impact in my back forcing me to fall to the ground in a sudden rush of weakness. Jalix fell on top of me as the sound erupted again, closer to our small hallway.

My back-…no…my chest. Oh, God. I'm bleeding. This is too much blood.

Jalix rolled away from me, continuing to lay on the ground as our room was torn to pieces by a hail of bullets ripping straight through the door and annihilating our living space. I felt Jalix's firm hand on my shoulder as he turned me, inciting a cough as I craned my head to look at the damage. A steady stream of blood, pouring in ounces rather than drops, gushed from a small hole on the left side of my chest. Jalix immediately pressed on the wound, his fearful eyes moving to my own.

I focused on Jalix's face, breathing as regularly as I was able and saving any energy rather than vocalizing my concerns of an imminent death.

Not here. Don't let me be killed at home, and most of all, don't let this be from our own people.

"Kara, we-…I have to get Amy." He shuddered, staring at me with an intensity and apprehension I hadn't seen before in his face. No matter the dangers we had faced, Jalix was always the most steady when it came to decisions, but his eyes told me under no uncertain terms that he was imminently afraid for my life.

"No." I groaned, tension building in my chest and increasing the pain. "Jalix, let go."

"No, you need pressure-"

"Let go!" I roared, pushing him back a few feet with my abilities and sliding his kneeling figure across the floor. I took a deep breath, the pressure relieved as the wound started gushing blood again. "No pressure. Blood creating too much force on my heart. Need Alice. And blood. Real blood." I muttered quickly, trying to avoid the futility of my situation.

"Kara!" Violet cried loudly from our bathroom, having peeked at my situation and being unable to do anything. Another, significantly louder series of gunshots blasted the hallway from the left side of our door, implying that either Amy or Krystal had retrieved their handgun and started shooting back. After a pause in her shots, the rounds stopped flying into our room despite the noise still reverberating from the main hall. Through the chewed-up hole in our door, I was able to see that Krystal had erected a wall of ice at the end of the hall to provide cover.

I feel…lightheaded. I'm losing too much blood.

"Krystal, send Amy! Now!" Jalix yelled, reaching up quickly to pull open the door. Krystal's face was visible, peeking out of Amy's door and holding her sidearm. She nodded once, able to see the situation in full view and understanding that time was of the essence. A second wave of lightheadedness made me dizzy and tired, my head rolling back and being caught by Jalix.

"Hey, stay with me." He warned, fear taking hold of his face as he failed to continue his normal sense of calm. He shook violently, the trauma of my previous death already enough for one lifetime.

"I am." I whispered, fighting to stay awake. Thankfully, I received a jolt of energy at Amy sliding into place by my side and immediately placing her hands on my chest. I felt the electric tingle of her abilities penetrate straight downward, stopping at my heart and lingering.

"Mom, you've…the bullet ricocheted. A fragment lodged in your pulmonary artery. It's in your heart. I can't heal it until the piece is removed." She mumbled, turning to her father. "This is advanced cardiac surgery. We don't have time, even if Alice was standing *right* here."

"Then what do we do?" He deferred to her expertise, realizing that time was running out. She shook her head before pausing suddenly and tilting her head.

"You're going to have to trust me." She whispered, looking into my eyes. I nodded, smiling the best I could.

"I trust you, my darling girl." I mumbled, finding oxygen much more of a precious resource than before.

I love her so much. I love both of them…

"I'm going to agitate the area around the bullet so you can feel where it is. But I need you to use *your* powers to pull it out. We don't have time for anything fancy, and we can't do surgery in time to save you. Just rip it out, straight outward from your chest. Breathe out all the way when you do it so we can avoid damage to your lung. Once it's out, I can heal all the damage. Ready?" I didn't have much time to prepare, but couldn't have been any more productive with more warning.

"Amy, this could easily kill her, is there-"

"No other option." Amy exhaled, reacting to Jalix's question quickly. "Ready?" She asked me again. I nodded, closing my eyes so I could concentrate on the sensations in my chest. The pain was negligible in comparison to what I had been through in my lifetime, but the penetrating wound in my back and the small exit wound seemed to tear a singular cavity through my torso. I was further distracted by the sound of continuing gunfire and the smashing of large pieces of ice against the ground as Krystal held our sacred barrier at bay. Frenzied screaming from a distance proved the identity of our assailants, clearly Tortured from their frantic and shrieking voices.

The war arrived early. And I might not live to see the rest of it…

The sensation of a mild electric shock started again, this time growing in magnitude and encircling a small area near the center of my chest. I could almost feel the metal fragment vibrating against the tissue around it.

It's…I can't focus. It's small. Centered on the…pain. But I can't…

I exhaled, opening my eyes and letting a final wave of thoughts bless my body with the gift of adrenaline in a moment of defiance.

Three inches from the rib, and an inch back. Get up so you can save your family.

I screamed, placing a palm on my chest before throwing my hand to the sky and letting a second traumatizing wound tear through the skin of my chest. The fragment bounced lightly off the ceiling and fell, landing next to my ear with a quiet thump. It took almost all of my energy to stay awake, so I focused on Amy's actions and closed my eyes once more. She placed a hand on each wound, closing her eyes and sighing. The tightness I felt around my heart surged exponentially for a brief moment before subsiding and turning into a more sore, shooting pain down my left arm. I groaned, making a grave mistake as it suddenly became almost impossible to breathe.

"Don't panic. I have to stop your heart for a second." Amy muttered, continuing her work.

"Are you serious? Amy, we-"

"Shut up." She returned, unwilling to deal with Jalix's sense of concern. "Get your gun. Shoot back." She commanded quickly, needing to focus on my body and be less concerned with the attack. After another sharp pain, I felt my heart roar to life in a smattering of racing beats, pounding against the unmistakably intact wall of my chest. She lifted her hands from my wounds, the skin still not fully healed, and grabbed my arms to drag me behind the concrete wall next to the doorway. "You're alright, mom. Deep breaths. You lost a lot of blood. Get some oxygen back." She lifted me slightly, letting me rest upright against the wall as my sense of self began to return to a lower magnitude than before the shooting began.

"What the hell's going on out there?" I asked, licking my dry lips and placing a hand over the skin-deep wounds that oozed blood.

"No idea. Krystal and I heard shots in the distance, then your door got annihilated. You're the only door facing the end of the hall, so everyone else is safe right now. As long as they can't get into the hall, they can't shoot through anyone else's door." At the end of her statement, Violet darted out of the bathroom and slid next to us, leaning in to talk. Jalix had apparently found his pistol and stood next to the doorway in preparedness.

"Jesus, are you okay?" She asked, her eyes filled with concern as she stared at my injuries.

"I'm…good. Need a blood transfusion. Powers are going to be useless without." I tried to keep my sentences short, still catching my breath.

"I'll get you some med-"

"Our medicine will be useless, too." Amy stopped her sister from running toward our kitchen. "She needs Factor Five and a unit or two of blood." She looked over at the floor where I had lain, correcting herself as she basked in sight of the crimson ocean in our living room. "Make that three units. But you're not gonna die, at least. Just stay here and catch your breath-…dad!" Amy looked up at her father, quickly sprinting across the doorway and moving to slide her hands under the back of his shirt. "You jackass." She scolded.

"Your mother…needed the help more." Jalix groaned, cooperating as Amy forcibly turned his back to face us and expose three crimson blossoms against the white of his undershirt.

"Fine, she's fixed. Now let me take care of *your* shit." She replied, leaning him against the wall while she used her abilities. Violet looked at me again, confirming that I was recovering before sitting next to me in a state of terrified uselessness.

"Guys, I can't hold this thing forever! We need a plan!" Krystal called.

"No plan!" Violet called back. "They're both hurt! Get Alice and Val!"

"We're here!" Alice's voice was more distant, but still audible. Krystal's shield kept a reasonable barrier against the high-decibel noise from its opposite side. "I can't burn them! I don't know where they're positioned in the hall! As soon as she drops that barrier, we're done!" Alice called out.

"No pressure, Alice!" Krystal roared in irritation. "Do you have any idea how *dense* this needs to be to make it bulletproof? Very!"

"Call Sonya." I said to Violet, nodding to Jalix and indicating that she use his phone. Jalix overheard the conversation and tossed it to her, caught deftly before being confronted by his lock screen.

"What's the password?" She asked, shaking the phone in her hands.

"Five, two, seven, two." She typed in the PIN and quickly dialed Sonya, hunkering by my side for protection. She lifted the device from her ear and put it on speaker so I could also hear.

"Sonya's Rescue Service." The voice on the other end said cheerily.

"We're pinned at the hallway to our quarters! Krystal is keeping them blocked off, but she won't last much longer." I spat in a rush. Sonya chuckled, much to the confusion of Violet and I, and responded quickly.

"Neither will they." She paused. "We had just started issuing weapons in the residential area. There's a good fight going, and the Tortured are losing like hell."

"Doesn't sound like it!" Violet returned.

"We're losing, too!" I tried to yell, which came out as a high-volume whisper. I coughed, losing my vision for a moment as black spots rolled across my eyes. Violet put a reassuring hand on my shoulder as Sonya's positive tenor continued.

"They had made it halfway across the main hall. We've already pushed them back past the infirmary to the bistro. We're almost there, just hang on a bit longer. Vishnu!" She called to someone in the background, moving the phone from her ear. I could hear the results of our people as the pattern of gunshots increased to a constant rolling patter of earsplitting pops that grew closer and closer. The weapons Sonya had been issuing apparently weren't suppressed, and gave a good indication of how close our own army had approached. "Give the phone to Alice." Sonya demanded, provoking a fast response from Violet. She stood up quickly, peering around our door and shouting.

"Alice! Catch!" She tossed the phone into the hall, the results of which I couldn't see from my position on the floor.

Come on. Muster some kind of energy. They need you.

I planted a hand on the ground, starting to push as Violet once again knelt next to me and put her hands on my shoulders. Behind her, I watched Amy dart across the hall to join Krystal, escaping from the room.

"Stay down. We'll handle this. It'll all be okay." She breathed, locking eyes with me. I saw for the first time a perfect reflection of the mysterious aspect of my personality that demanded respect and admiration from those under my charge. Within the deep chocolate-brown of her irises, I saw a power and confidence that settled my heart and invoked a love for her I had tried for so long to keep hidden.

"I love you." I whispered, my sense of calm disappearing with a single tear that fell down my cheek. Her lips spread into a gentle smile, kissing me on the forehead and replying quietly.

"I love you, too." I could barely hear her over the chaos, but it was enough to ease any sense of burden and lift away the fears I held.

Jalix leapt back from the door, reacting to something that Alice had shouted into the hall. With a horrified stare, he watched the hallway before diving toward us and covering thc two of us with his body.

What the hell is coming?

With only fractions of a second to react, I lifted my head away from his embrace and looked at the door, seeing a brilliant burst of yellow light rush toward the entrance to our apartment.

Alice.

I inhaled quickly and pushed my arm outward, breaking half of my body free from the safety of my husband's arms in the hope of keeping my daughter and partner safe from the incoming danger. As the first wave of fire rolled through the doorway, I concentrated and pushed outward with a sense of touch I hadn't attempted before.

Ignore the fire, ignore the flames, ignore the heat. Air…soft, whipping through my fingers as it rushes past my hand. Cool breezes and warm winds through my hair.

The struggle increased as the fires fought against me, a blazing rage tearing through the air toward us and stopping at an invisible wall held with the last fragment of my concentration.

The feeling of wind on my face during a fast drive in Krystal's convertible. The first bursts of clouds and harsh weather before a bad storm.

The fires circled and danced only a few feet from us, wrapping around itself and twirling in the air as it faded to a neon orange, then a cool red before disappearing entirely. I dropped my hand, lowering my head as a wave of smoke and ash overwhelmed the air around us and saturated our breathing with an impossible heat. We stayed in our huddle during the ensuing silence, a ringing in our ears keeping everything muffled but the hiss of burning embers from the carnage around our bodies. Jalix was the first to lift his head, looking behind him and realizing what I had done.

I feel…tired. So tired.

"Come on." He groaned, coughing several times as he helped Violet lift me from the ground and hastily make our way into the hall. I was incapable of moving, my arms and legs feeling miles away as I held onto the faintest tips of consciousness. With an arm around each of their shoulders, they moved me through the hall as quickly as possible while trying to ignore the searing radiance of the hallway's heat. The concrete had trapped the temperature, holding onto it and battled only by Krystal's efforts to cool down our path as she followed behind us. My head bobbed several times with the risk of passing out. I was only able to see the journey into the main hall in flashes and mental snapshots during my battle to stay awake.

"Alice." I heard Jalix say quietly, her figure close enough to speak at a normal volume. Alice was gasping for air, and I was able to capture a brief view of her body leaning heavily against the wall. Krystal stood next to her, slowly running her hands up and down Alice's body. Her clothes were partially melted, the remains of her dress a series of fabric strips and a few surviving layers underneath. She nodded once, staring at me and recognizing my condition.

"What…happened?" She coughed, looking over my shoulder.

"Shot. Round went into her back and through her chest." Amy's voice was strong and confident as she exited the short hallway and made her way to my front. "Fragment caught in her pulmonary artery. We fixed it, but she lost a lot of blood. She needs a transfusion. We need to get to the infirmary *now.*" Amy stroked my hair gently, giving me something else to focus on as Jalix and Violet started dragging me quickly through the main hall. We bypassed the arboretum, its small trees and shapely hedges having been incinerated in a blast of immense power. Jalix's dress shoes trampled over smoking piles of ash and cinders while my head hung, staring downward at our apocalyptic pathway. More than once, I spotted a burn-covered body smoking with the sizzling effect of melted polyester sinking through their skin.

"Go prep an ICU. Grab-…Sonya!" Alice gave someone a command, evidently my brother by the way he sprinted past us, and called out to Sonya. "Help Val. ICU number three, and prep four units of O negative." My hearing starting to return, I heard the sound of running boots stop a few dozen feet from us as she responded.

"Got it. I'll have Factor Five ready, too." She added, racing to join Val. I tried lifting my head again to look around, and regretted making the attempt. While I wasn't able to perceive the full vista of death that surrounded us, my thin band of vision took in the sight of dozens of bodies fallen and burned with no hope of survival. Charred marks stained the concrete with swaths of black soot and indicated an explosion, or several, of some sort.

My body jerked forward as the crowd around me stopped moving, held in place by a forceful scream of desperation. It resonated twice, the first a cry of surprise, followed quickly by an unrelenting howl of pain and agony. The voice was masculine, and familiar in tone, but never having heard it in such pain was unsure who it belonged to until my husband confirmed their identity.

"Tony! What's wrong?" He called, almost dropping me in the desire to run toward his friend. Tony's voice was far from us, to the left of the infirmary we were so close to and at the end of the main hall toward the conference room. Without a response, Amy and Krystal broke out into a sprint while Violet used her other hand to cover her mouth in horrified realization.

"Raven…" She cried quietly, sobbing into the back of her hand before gasping once more in shock and buckling, releasing my care to Jalix entirely. My eyes opened wider, watching her stare at the end of the hall and wail in grief. I felt him shudder, pulling me close and whispering another name before I slipped fully into a deep sleep.

"And *Eric*…not Eric…"

SALVO

JALIX

My emotional capacity was nearly empty, and I didn't think my grief could fall into a lower depth of horrified acceptance until the woman on the other end of the phone confirmed the unsettling fact once more.

"I'm so sorry, Jalix-"

"Don't. Just don't." I sighed, watching the steady and occasional change to Kara's heart rate on the monitor next to me. "I-…sorry. Thank you for telling me." It tested my patience to try and remain neutral to Layla, but I knew nothing that happened at Quantico was her fault.

"We're still intact. Pilots are okay, all sixteen of us. But we need to know who's next in the chain of command." She paused, taking a deep breath. "Marcus has his own job at the head of Val's assault. He can't take over for Yuri and it would take him hours to get here."

"I know." I mumbled, shaking my head in disbelief.

How the hell did this happen? How were we so blind to the possibility of attack? Were we so arrogant?

"Taylor. Put Taylor in charge. She was the lead officer for all the urban ops training. She can handle it." I confirmed.

"I'll let her know." Layla's response was short, and she knew the last thing I needed was to deal with any further complications. "Jalix, we're okay here. We only lost a handful."

"I lost a friend." I argued, not willing to accept her downplaying of the situation. "Yuri was an ally, and a strong one. And everyone here…Quantico wasn't the only place that just got attacked-"

"I-…I'm sorry, I didn't mean-"

"I know." I repeated. I turned around, making my way across the dim room to Kara's side. Each step reminded me of the pain in my back from Alice having removed three bullets from the muscle and tissue. While I was in mild pain, I was healing quickly and concerned myself much more with the state of my wife.

Alice's handiwork was impeccable, restoring Kara to her normal color, as pale as it was in its natural state. She had bandaged Kara's wounds with perfectly wrapped dressing and minimized her connected IV lines to two. Despite the electronics that kept track of her physical state, she seemed to be as close to life and normalcy as I could ask for.

It's been three hours…and she hasn't woken up. We need you, my darling wife. Now more than ever.

"Mourn the dead, and leave a contingent of people behind to bury them. Ten or so. Quantico has a cemetery on the north end. They deserve to be buried with the other soldiers." I paused, reflecting on the memories of my fallen teammates from nearly a lifetime ago. "And restart the air operations. We need you airborne in two hours."

"Two hours-…Jalix, we can't-"

"I have a parking lot full of armored vehicles over my head that remains a standing target as long as they sit there. You have an airfield of vulnerable helicopters, and we *both* have losses to mourn. I'm not waiting for Legacy's next wave. We move in two hours. Prep Taylor and get my Blackhawk here as soon as possible." I knelt down, running my fingers through Kara's ponytail, fashioned by Alice and only sported due to the ease of keeping it from tangling into a thousand other objects during her care. It was a rare sight, and didn't seem to help convincing me that she was back to normal. "That's an order." I finished. I could hear the pause as her mission settled into her mind.

"Yes, sir." She ended the call, leaving me alone with my wife in a moment of consuming silence.

Sonya leaned away from the far wall of the room, shaking her head slowly at Kara's sleeping figure. I could tell she was waiting, wanting to say something and finding the words impossible to say in the horror and tragedy that had befallen our city.

"Must've been what it was like." She mumbled, apparently to herself. I looked up at her, raising an eyebrow to elicit an explanation. "When I…when I was hurt. This must have been what it was like watching over me. Knowing that she'd be okay. Having that faith…but having the doubt, too. The fear." I nodded slowly, running a finger along Kara's arm.

"Kara passed on a piece of wisdom from Eric. Years ago. He said that love is just…the fear of losing a person. In moments like these, you know how accurate that statement really is." I paused, taking a quick breath and trying to change the topic. "Thanks, by the way. Your response to the attack was-"

"The people knew what needed done. They weren't about to lie down during the Tortured's incursion, I'll tell you that much." She chuckled lightly. "They didn't stand a chance."

"Speaking of, how did you…what happened between you and Alice? Everything from the conference room to the Counsel apartments is a scorch mark. What kind of plan did you guys – quite literally – cook up?" She chuckled at my pun, glancing down at my wife.

"Vishnu, the waiter…I had him grab the propane tanks from the kitchen he worked in. Start chucking them into the hall. Got our people to retreat and Alice did her thing." She raised her eyebrows briefly. "Boom." I pulled my hand away from Kara and took a final look at her body, finally recognizing that there was nothing to do but wait. Sonya shared my sentiment, taking a seat next to Kara's bed and nodding once at me.

Knowing that I was unable to assist with anything else, and was merely waiting for her to wake up again, I left her in a sleeping and stable condition to wander across the hall into Raven's care room. There was a stark contrast between the two intensive care units, with nurses and technicians nearly occupying the full space as they connected, disconnected, and adjusted intricate pieces of equipment to her body. As Raven lay on the bed, Amy crouched at her side, a swath of bandages obscured everything above her eyes with additional dressing across her nose. Alice was among the staff and turned to speak with me quietly as I entered.

"It's not looking good." She started, whispering. "The EEG is picking up distortions. She's not brain-dead, but she's only holding on to life by a thread. I…don't expect her to pull through, if we're being honest. If we can buy her some time…I don't know. Maybe." She stared at me as if I was to provide some form of intellectual response, but my words failed and came out in the form of recent memory.

"Yuri is dead." I said simply, watching her mouth fall open. "Quantico was attacked, too. A few minutes after we were. Sonya was smart to call and warn them. They had time to mount a brief defense, but…"

"My God…" Alice exhaled, horrified and overwhelmed. "Did they-…how bad was it?"

"Not as bad as it could have been. Yuri led the defense. Him and a team were killed in an explosion. A grenade, they said. Everyone else saw and pushed the Tortured with everything they had. We lost about thirty. No pilots injured."

"At least we can-" I took a step forward, an instinct kicking in as I saw a train of thought behind my daughter's eyes. "Amy." I said, strongly enough that everyone but Alice stopped moving entirely. Amy froze for a moment, looking at Raven with a confidence I was uncomfortable with.

"Eric is alive." She started without looking over at me. "He has a long recovery, might not walk without crutches again, but he's alive. Raven…she's the one we need to save."

"I know she's your sister-"

"Then what else needs said?" Amy fired back at Alice, snapping her head back to Raven in a moment of defiance before I could push through the nurses.

"Amy, no!" I yelled, reaching out to stop her hand from making contact with Raven's arm. I was too late, too far away to beat her reflexes, and pulled back sharply so as not to be caught in the chaos that her abilities could have presented. Her body reacted in two stages: at first, she seemed to be in pain as her brow furrowed and her teeth clenched, but her mother's pale complexion tumbled into pallor as she fell backward against the ground, eyes wide open, and remained immobile.

Not you…not my baby girl.

I moved with Alice to crouch over my daughter's body and elevated her head while Alice checked for a pulse. I could see Alice's fingernails blossom with white as more pressure was applied to try and find some kind of heartbeat, but she leapt back and started making demands of the nurses within moments.

"I need a crash cart and a bed, *STAT!* Prep room six, *now*!" She quickly lifted Amy's body while I watched in horrorstruck realization and started to make sense of what had happened.

Amy feels and experiences injuries. But if Raven's brain isn't functional anymore…

"Shit!" I hissed, my eyes brimming with tears before I could harden myself to the wave of emotion.

My wife. My daughter. My friends. I'm not doing this, not before I've had a chance to kill the bastard in charge.

Every person in the room abandoned Raven's care and poured through the doorway ahead of Alice to prepare the next phase of emergency response. I watched Amy's head fall backward in Alice's arms, her eyes still open and hair dangling loosely to the ground.

"Alice-"

"Jalix, not now. We'll save her, just-…go away." Alice deserted her position of pleasantness to convey her message's urgency, which told me more than I needed to know.

She's scared, too. What if Amy doesn't make it?

My fingers curled into a fist of frustration watching Alice abscond with my daughter's body in a move of desperation. I looked at Raven briefly, wanting to blame her for what had happened, but knew Amy would have me understand her intentions.

But there is someone to blame. Someone nearby. Someone I can…speak to.

I turned the corner, walking past the intensive care rooms as Krystal and Violet rushed out of Eric's presence to descend on Alice. Krystal wept loudly, demanding to know what happened as Violet offered her support, but I continued to the end of the hall and looked into the more secure room used for Rachel's detox. Tamara was speaking with the man I previously identified as Smith, maintaining some kind of casual conversation with respect to his trembling and sweating. He was clearly itching for another dose of Factor Five, and the look in his eyes screamed it in the way I had seen others feel before. The scar tissue on

Tamara's face immobilized some of the muscle, and I wasn't able to make out what she was saying to him. Pushing open the door quietly, the conversation halted.

"Don't stop on my account." I spoke calmly and fought the tremors that rolled down each of my arms. Smith was strapped to a bed for security, layers of leather and synthetic material binding his wrists and ankles to reinforced parts of the hospital bed. They remained silent as I paced at the foot of the bed, thinking to myself.

"Jalix." Tamara acknowledged coolly.

"Dr. Goodson. Tamara, sorry. How's our patient?" Smith looked at me for only a moment as I spoke, the rage in my eyes more obvious than necessary.

"Starting withdrawal. It's faster than we expected, but about the same results we saw in Rachel." I looked over at the other bed, Rachel laying on her side in a deep sleep.

"Looks like her survival odds are pretty high." I suggested, beckoning to Rachel.

"Indeed. Alice's course of treatments were effective. It wasn't without pain, but that was…expected. She's recovering nicely." I nodded at her response, pausing near Smith's right foot.

"I expect Smith is going to have a harder time with the injuries he suffered." I furrowed my brow, nodding.

"Injuries?" Tamara enquired. "I-…" She stopped her rebuttal, quickly realizing why I was present. "Ah." She whispered, setting his patient file on the small table to her left. "Should I leave?"

"I'd like you to help." I said honestly. "But I won't ask you to do anything you're not comfortable with." I paused. "See, my wife and two of her children are…currently down the hall. Each bordering on death. So is a close friend of mine in the room next to theirs, while another friend is dead entirely. All because *you* decided to be on the wrong side, Smith. Why not tell me about the imminent attacks?" I paused, curious as to his answer.

"I didn't know about them." He shuddered, a bead of the sweat from his brow trickling down the side of his face. "Legacy must have been using me as a trigger to start it all."

"Must have been." I replied, too distant to pay too much attention to his words. "Must have been an innocent pawn, right?" He nodded, inhaling sharply at a spasm in his side. "See, I don't believe you, Smith. I think you *knew* what was about to happen. But when you thought you could get on our good side, you took advantage. You weren't going to give us the information that would make us even angrier, right? And if Legacy and his boys had won the day here in Vanaheim…well, you'd have been a hero. Taking on the city, a lone wolf." I rolled my neck before leaning forward and resting my hands across his covered ankle. "It's smart. I won't lie to you."

"I have to…I had to save m-myself." He mumbled, shaking his head. He was already suffering minor tremors from the withdrawal, a layer of shine on his brow from cold sweat.

"Oh, but I thought you didn't expect to make it out. I thought you planned on dying. In fact, you *asked* me to kill you. Almost like that would have been the cue for them to move in. But…plans foiled, they got impatient, and they rushed in without knowing how much of a fight they'd encounter. Irrelevant now." I sighed, looking at Dr. Goodson. "Let him go or keep him with us?" I asked with a note of positivity. "We could send him back to Legacy, maybe in more pieces than expected." She stared at Smith for a moment, looking back at me with her ruling.

"He would probably be of more use here." She decided. Smith's attention turned back to me while Tamara rifled through one of the drawers in the cabinet to her left.

"Hmm. I accept your judgment. You'll stay here." I smirked at Smith, patting his leg. He raised an eyebrow, tilting his head.

"So I can…detox?" He asked.

"Dr. Goodson seems to think that detoxing from Factor Five is painful. Now, I've been through it, and it's no bed of roses. Mine wasn't as bad, wasn't as much an addiction as most people developed. Stopped once they realized they couldn't break me. But I remember it being painful. So maybe we'll help distract you from that pain. How about another dose? Just a small one. To taper off." I shrugged, reaching out to grab the IV bag that Tamara was handing me. I turned and quickly hung the bag without connecting it to a line of tubing.

"You would do that?" He sighed gratefully.

"I certainly would. *But* I also know what Factor Five is for, and that's for repairing cellular damage. So we have to give it a purpose before we can inject it." I patted his leg again, this time using one hand to push down on his knee while the other pulled upward on his ankle. With little effort, the joint popped loudly and displaced a mess of cartilage and tissue in the area surrounding his knee. His head shook violently as he screamed, thrashing against his bonds.

"Jalix-"

"If you want to leave, leave." I returned sternly, looking at Tamara as she began speaking.

"No, I was *going* to say…we need to ensure we're causing injuries that don't cause internal bleeding. It'll keep him alive longer."

We? Good girl; she's joining the game.

"What would you recommend?" My question was interrupted by Smith, who sat forward to the best of his ability and pleaded with me.

"What else do you want to know?" He spat in a rush. "I'll tell you everything. Please, I can't go through this again."

One of the heart monitors started beeping as an indicator of his rising pulse, but was silenced by the deft touch of my colleague.

"There's nothing you can tell me anymore. I'm not here for information, I'm here for vengeance." I dropped his leg as she pointed to his arm. I took a step back and gave her a sweeping beckon to allow her the honor of doing it herself. Without much hesitation, she moved around the bed to my side. "Smith, you put yourself in a bit of a tough spot. The last people to put my family in danger got themselves killed. I'm not making the mistake of going too quickly this time." Tamara wrapped her hands around his forearm, squeezing tightly until the bones started to crack and splinter under the skin. He screamed again, breathing heavily and triggering several of the other monitors. We ignored the beeping sounds, watching the pain contort his face while he sucked in oxygen.

"You messed up." He exhaled quickly. "Your mistakes. Should have…gone into hiding. Not…prepared for war."

"*War* is the only thing that's going to kill Legacy." I looked over my shoulder as Rachel started to stir, reminding me that she was present. She had clearly been in a drug-induced sleep, the noise not bothering her until the most recent series of shrieks disrupted her deep rest.

"He c-can't be killed. P-people have tried." Smith argued between breaths.

"They weren't me." I retorted, raising my eyebrows. "Any other sage wisdom for me? Any words of advice or pieces of valuable intelligence?"

"Unless you let me go, I'm not telling you *anything*." Smith growled in defiance, grimacing at the pain that wracked one side of his body.

"Alright." I reached to the small of my back and withdrew the black handgun from my belt, briefly pressing the barrel to his forehead before pulling the trigger and dealing with the shock of ringing eardrums. The action was fast enough that Tamara hadn't anticipated my seriousness and flinched, taking a step back and avoiding staring at the body.

Go to hell. And stay there.

Alice darted into the room, confused as to the source of the gunshot and slumped her shoulders as she looked down to see the pistol in my hand.

"Jalix-"

"If my daughter's not back, then I don't know why you're here." I snarled, tucking the weapon back into the safety of my belt, this time in the front. She gritted her teeth for a moment, her jaw clenching as she stared into my eyes.

"She's back." Alice hissed.

Oh, thank God...

"Get out of my hospital." She continued, pointing to the hallway. I hesitated at the boldness of her request, wondering if she had forgotten that half my family was contained within the surrounding rooms.

"No." I started, my knuckles starting to ache from the tightness in my fist. "Not until they're better. At least Kara and Amy-"

"It wasn't a request." She said firmly, taking another step forward. Val stepped out from behind her, his arms crossed while he avoided making eye contact with me. He stared at the floor, trying to avoid reality. I scoffed, approaching her while speaking.

"I just killed one of our enemies. I'm not sorry about that. And now I need to go do it again a thousand times over. I can't do that until-"

"Take Krystal and Violet. Get everyone together for a meeting. Our...final meeting. Or take Val and get in the boxing ring, I don't care. Go do *something*, but get the hell out of my hospital." Her words came from a place of sadness, and I started to feel remorse that the war had come to find a home on her doorstep. "*If* they're ready in time, I'll send them to you."

"I-…" I struggled with what to say, finally looking at Val. "Are you needed here?" His eyes flitted upward to look at me, his head shaking briefly.

"No. I want to wait for Kara, but…we don't have time. And I know that." He already knew the totality of our circumstances and the precious time we had left to act if we were to survive.

"Alright. Get changed. Take Krystal and Violet to the conference room. Call over to Quantico and get a video chat set up. Amy and I will be right behind you."

"So will I." Alice interjected. "Tamara." She said over my shoulder. "You're going to be in charge while I'm gone. I'm leaving ten nurses. Should be enough for Eric and Raven. Kara's stable and Rachel just needs to stay sedated so she can recover. Amy's not going anywhere until I talk to her." She stated firmly, waving me into the hall. I rounded the corner, leaving Tamara behind with Rachel and the corpse. "I said Amy was *back*. Not ready for war." Alice prompted.

"Val, go ahead. Alice and I need to talk, if you don't mind." I said quietly, stopping in the hallway.

"Alright. We'll have the meeting prepped. I'll have to convince Tony to leave Eric's side." He sighed, looking at both of us before nodding.

"Thank you. And take Sonya, she's in Kara's room. Have her and a few of the infantry guys bring our combat gear straight to the meeting. Mine's already there, but have her gather everyone else's. We're leaving as soon as everyone's briefed." Val stared at me for a long, uncomfortable moment, finally responding with a painful question.

"This is it, isn't it?" His low tone was unusually somber. "I thought we had more time."

We all did. And now we're paying the price for it.

"We'll have our time after the fight's over." I decided. "This is a scar in our history. Not the end of it. We'll get through this." He looked away for a moment before turning and making his way down the hall of the intensive care wing. Alice turned to me almost immediately, before Val was out of earshot.

"Amy shouldn't go." She started. "Not only is her health questionable, but so are her decisions. What she did was stupid, and could have gotten her killed. She's lucky it was as mild as it was."

"What happened?" I asked, fending off the defense of my daughter's decisions until I was aware of the facts. "She touched Raven for…seconds. Less."

"Her heart stopped. Beyond that…" She looked at her white sneakers, thrown on in haste during a brief pause between surgeries. "The brain is impossibly complex. Billions of transactions per second, and Amy's was disrupted because her body thought there was a hole going through it. Whatever she went through…Jalix, it *should* have killed her. And if she tries again, it will. Being alive after that is…trillion-to-one odds. Are you willing to take that risk?"

"No." I replied immediately. "But neither is she. She knows-"

"She knew damn well she shouldn't have even tried!" Alice hissed in an intense whisper, her voice low to avoid yelling. "All the years we spent experimenting with her capabilities were more than enough to tell her not to try something so risky. And she did anyway. I can't have her on the battlefield with Vampyres dying left and right while she tries to save every single one."

"Oh, like *you* did in New York?" She paused at my question, shame falling over her face. "Krystal told me about your little detour. Jumping into radiation, into rubble. You want to tell me that she's the only one that takes risks?"

"No, Jalix. I'm telling you that she's the only one we can't afford to lose." Her words had intensity, but were gentle. "We need her more than anything. She's…the best we have. As a leader, as the future of our species. If we fail…she's going to be the one that leads the next generation of us to victory. We…we can't risk that. Amy shouldn't go." She repeated. I mulled over her words, accepting them as truth but knowing that it wouldn't be as simple as explaining it to my daughter.

"I don't have a choice, Alice." I smirked, looking at the room Amy was in. "She's coming along whether I want her to or not. Nothing that any of us says is going to change that." I went to say more, but was stopped as Amy rounded the corner and looked toward us while donning a hooded sweatshirt.

"Damn straight. Dad knows me too well."

She's okay.

She smiled at me, dark circles surrounding her eyes in a ghastly reminder of the trauma she had just been through.

"I'm alright. Looks worse than it is. Factor Five and a defibrillator goes a long way." She concluded.

"Amy, you-…why did you do that?" I asked in gentle exasperation. Amy paused, crossing her arms and looking over her shoulder.

"She'd have done the same for me. I had to try. If I hadn't…I would have spent too long wondering if I could have changed the outcome. The way I saw it, I didn't have a choice. I'm sorry. She's…if she's not going to make it, then that's the way it is. But I did my best."

I'm proud of you. Just…don't ever do that again.

"I need to run some tests on you before you're-"

"No time." Amy interrupted Alice's request. "Dad's right. We need to move. The sooner Legacy thinks the city is empty, the sooner we remove the risk that he attacks it. I think we all know this was just a test. One probing assault isn't going to be his last, and it already cost us…too much. I'm going to check on mom. You guys can…finish talking." She took several steps across the hall, vanishing into her mother's care room. I sighed, rubbing my brow.

That's who you're putting in the line of fire. Who you're willing to let die. Is it worth it?

"Jalix, I-…" She snorted, cocking her head. "We don't even have time to debate these things anymore, do we?"

"No." I answered honestly. "And I wish we did. I wish I could be convinced in thirty seconds or less that she needs to stay behind. I wish I could be convinced that there was another way. I want to talk about the plan, hear its flaws, be ridiculed by Kara for missing something…but our time is up. And it's do or die."

"I prefer doing over dying." She tensed her lips, looking over at me. "I'll meet you down there. Go see your wife. Your daughter. Just don't be too long." I looked over her shoulder, smirking as Amy left the room with her mother closely in tow. Kara's proud figure stood tall against the gloom of her environment and removed any sense of hopelessness with a unique smile across an unblemished face.

"I'll see you there."

***

The mumblings that filled the air of the conference room reminded me most of a coffee shop. No single conversation was more prominent than another, but the quiet chattering between groups created a calm buzz and the illusion of peace. The quiet discussion between Krystal and Kara, who had included me in their talk, was the only thing I could clearly make out.

"I'm sorry." Krystal concluded. "I just wasn't sure who else I could talk about it with."

"I don't want Amy going, either." Kara agreed. "But we need her to come along. If Legacy does anything out of line, we'll need her to reassure international leadership as soon as possible. The few hours it would take to get her to the White House might be detrimental otherwise."

"I know." Krystal sighed, looking over her shoulder at Amy. As if the glance was audible, my daughter returned the look with a gentle smile and happy eyes. "I just don't know what I'd do if something happens to her. What happened with her and Raven was bad enough. I'm tired of thinking I could lose her."

"She's going to be the most protected thing on the battlefield." I reassured. "I know we have our mission, but this can't be a suicide run. And if anyone makes it, it needs to be her. She'll have the best of the best watching her back." I touched her shoulder to indicate that I was talking about her presence, as well as ours. Krystal smirked blushingly, drawing in a deep breath and exhaling before looking at Kara.

"I'm sure you feel right at home." She remarked, my wife being confused by her comment.

"What do you mean?" Kara asked. "The war?"

"No, just…being a leader again. A warrior. Being the best that Sorrow was." Kara nodded, understanding what Krystal meant.

"You know, I never believed in the title. Not until Sonya had her accident. And then I thought…I felt like I was alone. Like Val didn't need me, like my people were independent. I felt like a burden had lifted and I could do what needed done. But I was wrong." She paused, her eyes flashing away in remembrance. "After my death…I learned that Sorrow doesn't come from loss, like I thought it had. Loss leaves us with memories, with a story. Loss gives us feeling, it doesn't take something away from us. Sorrow came from being in love with an idea or a person and…not being able to reach them because the pain of fear keeps us at a distance. The torment of not being able to act on what our personal truth is. Being paralyzed because of despair. I realized it with Violet, with Sonya…even with myself." She paused, lightly taking Krystal's hand. "And as much as I did, you learned those same lessons. Those same truths." Krystal's face collapsed into a teary gaze of respect and awe.

"I was a mistake." Krystal denied. "I was wrong, *always* wrong. And I knew that."

"You acted on what you believed in, and you did that for yourself. You were honest, and that's what hurt. You didn't have the lies that made you feel better the way I did. Going through that pain…it's something I know all too well. It's the reason I could never have loved you." Krystal sniffed, looking around briefly to confirm that no one else was watching. It hurt to see her so upset, but the amount of care and honesty Kara was putting into her centuries-long friend was more than I could have ever given. Krystal took a quick breath, attempting to steel herself.

"I…thought your spark, your fire was going to melt the cold in my heart. And it didn't. It just burned away everything else about me while giving me enough light to watch it happen. And then I was alone. Cold ashes in the dark."

"I was just as afraid as you were." Kara replied quietly. "But when I looked at you…I saw Sorrow more than I saw Krystal. And I could never have fallen in love with her. And now Sorrow is dead. I can love Jalix, and you can love Amy, and we can be who we were always meant to be."

"Yeah." Krystal breathed. "But there's more to who I was meant to be. I *know* there is. And I want to get through this to find more of myself."

"Then get through this." I affirmed. "For you and Amy, and not for anyone else. Not for anything else. Everyone has their reason today. Hold yours close." She smiled, nodding and pulling us both in for a brief hug.

Take care of her, Krystal. Please.

The moment we had been waiting for, Tony pushed the front doors open and triggered an intense silence throughout the room. He propped each one open to allow a medium-sized cart through the doors, which carried two olive-green boxes made of plastic and metal. Each was roughly the size of a washing machine, but behaved as though they weighed a fraction of the weight as they bounced with the cart over the conference room's threshold. I pulled back, glancing as the room's eyes descended on me.

"It's time." I said grimly, forcing everyone to purposefully scatter to their seats. What had been a social moment of conversation before an impending doom rapidly transformed into a solemn professionalism. Tony wheeled the cart to the front of the room as I stepped toward the projector and enabled the connected team on the other end of our line to appear on its screen. "Sound check. Taylor, can you hear us alright?"

"Yeah, we're good." Taylor replied, her image that of a soldier outfitted for battle. She was already equipped with her flight suit, the helmet sitting on her lap becoming an object with which to fidget nervously.

"Alright, good." Sonya and a few members of the ground-based combat team followed a few seconds after Tony, bringing in duffel bags and setting them in the corner of the room. I took two steps to the side, standing next to a small table covered in equipment. "Everyone grab a bag as they start to make their way in. Don't be shy. Alice and Amy, you're obviously an exception. You guys have your stuff?" They didn't say anything, but pulled out smaller backpacks from under their seats and placed them on their respective laps. Sonya was kind enough to start passing the bags around so the majority of the room could remain seated. "Cool.

So…I'm going to run through the packing list really quick. If it's in your bag, good. If it's not, make some noise so we can fix the problem. First and foremost should be a ballistic vest. Sizes should be pretty damn close. Attached are going to be two pouches, and each pouch should have six magazines. Yes?" I looked around the room, watching as quiet counting preceded a series of nods. "Perfect. There should also be a small medical pack on the back, near the side opening. In it, you'll find two tourniquets, six doses of Vampyre medicine, one bag of Factor Five, and a bottle of painkillers. Krystal, yours is going to look a little different." She looked up at me with a soft smirk, appreciative that I respected her sobriety. Again, the room remained silent but indicated that everything was present. "Next…the majority of you have standard rifles like we've always used in the past. Exceptions for Amy and Alice since they'll need both their hands available, but everyone *also* has a standard sidearm. Nine millimeter handgun. Guns themselves might vary in design, but magazines are compatible if you need to grab some off a body." There was a hesitant pause in the room's movement as I made reference to the dead, but I attempted to cover it up with a brief backtrack. "I mean an enemy's body, obviously. We're all using the same gear. Grab ammo when you can. It goes quicker than you'd think."

"The trucks also have spare ammo crates, so if you're closer to a vehicle, that's your safest bet." Val added.

"Thank you, Val. Um…last but not least, you'll find a handheld radio. When you get your vest on, clip it to the shoulder. There's an earpiece included with each one, but…they can be a bit on the fragile side. If it breaks or stops working, disconnect, discard, and use the radio's speaker. Don't try and fix the stuff. Everyone good?" Once again, a silent and unanimous nod throughout the room.

"My vehicle is going to be third from the front." Marcus started, sitting closest to Val. "We have spare everything.

Three full kits. Like Jalix said, if something is broken, don't try to fix it. Call for a new kit and we'll get it to you. Jalix, I believe the lead assault Blackhawk also has spares?"

"Correct. Thanks, Marcus. Both assault teams are covered; we had more than enough from Quantico and we're bringing everything to the fight that we can make fit. Any questions *whatsoever* on the gear?" I looked around, seeing Val lift his head to speak.

"What radio frequency?" He asked.

"Channel three, band C is going to be used for the Operators. That's everyone in this room plus Marcus' team and Tony's team. Channel two on that same band is the air assault team and channel one is the ground team. So don't use bands A or B at all. You two should stay on channel three with the Operators since you both have team members that can handle basic comms for your teams."

"Got it." Val acknowledged, replacing the device in his bag. I waited for any other questions, and hearing none, grabbed the clicker from the desk next to me to turn on the presentation.

"We've had to make some adjustments due to…the recent events in Vanaheim. So bear with me." I warned, starting with an overlay of Washington, D.C. "The original plan is essentially the same, but I'm going to run through it in detail one last time, and I'm going to make it as simple as possible. As we speak, Vanaheim is emptying. We've evacuated all the civilians to the safe parts of New York and the soldiers are loading up into the combat vehicles. The only people staying behind are Doctor Goodson and her team of nurses, plus those currently under their care. They'll have a small contingent for security, but Legacy doesn't want the city. There's no reason for the Tortured to attack again, and they'd have to get through the convoy to do so." I took a quick breath, using the laser pointer to draw a line along one of the highways. "Val's ground assault team is going to make up the bulk of our forces. His vehicles will take a path around the city in a wide loop before arriving at the south end of the National Mall. As *soon* as the lead vehicle gets off the exit, Andrea and Layla will be overhead and delivering an explosive payload on the two anti-air platforms to blow them up. Afterward, they're going to become an air patrol for any of Legacy's own aircraft and engage as needed. The missile platforms are currently located on either side of the Washington Monument and waiting to shoot down any of our jets or helicopters. If either of our payloads miss, Val's team is going to push forward and take those out so the Blackhawks can come in. Any questions so far?"

"Yeah, actually." Taylor interjected. "Since we have Hamilton now and his F-22, could we have him try another run if Layla or Andrea miss those launchers?"

"No." I said firmly, looking up at the screen. "He's not equipped with the defenses you guys have. He comes in *only* after those things are junked. A downed aircraft could smash into our own forces and cause more damage or plow through the civilians on the north end. We don't need that kind of collateral."

"Understood." She replied, nodding.

"Okay. So after the platforms are scrapped, Val's team is going to push forward to get Marcus and his raid team to the White House South Lawn, securing a setup zone for our own launcher. At the same time, Taylor's Blackhawks are going to get the green-light to move in. They'll be just under radar coverage on the eastern outskirts of the city. Once they receive the word, she's going to fly in and start taking out the garrisoned Tortured on the east side. This will keep them occupied and let Val and Marcus focus on the heavy defenses along the southern route. It'll also keep us clear of their rooftop defenses, if they have any. When the Blackhawks have an opening, they can start picking up the wounded and taking them to Quantico to get patched up.

During this time, Sonya and Kara are going to be escorting Alice and Amy *around* the Tortured buildings on the east side, flanking to the north. They're going to move east to west and rescue as many civilians as they can. When Tony and Doctor Weiss get the launcher working, we're going to have the civilians evacuate even further north, away from the battle, and to whatever safety they can find. As this happens, the launcher will fire the cure, infecting those civilians as well as all the combatants on the battlefield. Everyone following so far?" I paused, looking at Violet as she appeared confused.

"Uh…" She started. "Okay. Airstrike to take out Legacy's anti-air, then Val gets to the White House from the south, Taylor wipes out the buildings to the east, and everyone else except Krystal and I escort the innocents to the north."

"Correct. You and Krystal will have…a unique job." I moved to the side, allowing Tony to pull the cart up to where I stood and open one of the green boxes. A rolling white mist emanated from its inside, revealing a silver canister roughly the size of a five-gallon water jug. At its center, a translucent piece of blue glass allowed us to see that there was a liquid contained inside.

"This is our cure." Tony said quietly, holding up the canister for everyone to see. "This is the last relic of our species. Everything, regardless of the fighting, regardless of killing Legacy, requires that these be kept safe. They also need refrigerated. These cases do exactly that, but they only have about three hours of battery life. Jalix will have one, which will get plugged into his Blackhawk. Krystal and Violet will have another near the rear of Val's convoy. When Val's team secures the launcher site and Marcus moves in to secure the White House, Krystal is going to deliver this to Doctor Weiss and I so we can load and charge the munitions for launch. The reason there are two…" He paused. "…is in case one of them is damaged or lost."

"In case Jalix's helicopter goes down or Violet and I get killed." Krystal recapped. "Pleasant."

"In a word, yes. But you're unique. If something happens and the Relic is at risk, you can move it wherever you need to. Your abilities will let you handle this thing without the carrying case. As long as it stays *cold*, we're okay. So…if this battle is a chess game, your piece is the queen. You move where you want, when you want in order to keep this safe."

"As if her ego needed to hear that." Alice mumbled, smirking. A quiet chuckle alleviated the seriousness of the situation before I took over again.

"Krystal, you're in charge of your Relic. Mine is backup only. Yours doesn't require a landing zone and wouldn't become a huge target for landing next to a defensive perimeter like mine would. Violet is going to be there to watch your back and take over in case anything happens. No matter what, this thing *needs* to arrive as soon as Tony's ready with Doctor Weiss. Until then…just keep it safe." They both nodded, Violet clearly proud to have such a critical task bestowed upon her.

I think…that's it.

"Obviously, Eric and Raven were supposed to be overhead with drones and satellites to give guidance and help fix any major issues. As much as I want to be on the front line, my aircraft and I are going to take on that role. I'll be airborne the entire time, circling the battlefield. I won't be much help in firefights, but I'm going to keep everything moving forward and keep eyes on everything. This is it, guys." I realized quickly that I was running out of things to say, already having reviewed this plan a hundred times over with most of the group. "We kill Legacy, release the cure, and Amy reassures the world that there's a chance. No speech this time. We just need to get this last part done."

"What happens if Legacy escapes Marcus and his team?" Sonya asked, looking over at Kara. "If we get enough warning before he moves in, Kara and I can be on standby for any cleanup duty."

"I should have clarified. Marcus and his team are leading the raid, but Val has about forty other soldiers going in behind him. There are secret ways in and out of the White House, but as long as the cure is dispersed, Legacy is irrelevant. As much as I hate to say it...killing him is secondary."

"The hell it is." Kara countered aggressively. "We made this mistake before. Killing Schillinger, Kilkovf, Raven, all without finishing off the organization. We have to dismantle him or-"

"I know." I interrupted. "But we can do that afterward. Once the cure is out, we can have the entire country look for him. Hell, we can ask for foreign aid in tracking him down. Dozens of specialized police forces, military units, anyone and everyone that has eyes can scour the globe until he's found. But that *has* to come last. Look..." I stepped away from the projector and approached the family, sitting on the edge of the conference table. "The goals that we *want* to accomplish and the ones we *need* to accomplish are different right now. After this, the only thing we'll ever need to do is whatever we want. So for now, all of you...keep the emotions as low as necessary. If everyone is willing to make a sacrifice, then none of us may come home." Dr. Weiss wiped her eyes, nodding as Val leaned forward and spoke up.

"Twenty years ago, I jumped out of a moving car onto a bobsled to buy us another sixty seconds of time. If I hadn't, Schillinger might have been able to make his first plans work. With this, we have the chance to buy all the time of our lives. Human or not, I'm gonna want that time. And if Legacy thinks for even a *second* that he's going to take that away from us, he's wrong."

"Then let's get going." Amy stood, wrestling the minimalistic ballistic vest over her head. "The civilians in the north district don't have much time."

"And the longer we wait, the more of a target our convoy becomes." Alice agreed, shouldering her bag.

"We can get geared up in the vehicles." Krystal added, picking up her duffel bag.

"Agreed. Taylor, get airborne." I slid off the table, avoiding any thoughts of my climbing heart rate and trying as hard as possible to focus on the next few moments.

Bag is under the chair. Vest in the bag. Radio in the bag. Rifle gets slung-

My distracting thoughts were interrupted by a gentle touch on my shoulder that turned me around as I watched my wife stand in front of me. The screen to her right turned off, Taylor having disconnected her call. Even in the dim light, Kara's eyes almost glowed with a radiant silver. Her irises were outlined with a ring of pitch black, but the redness that crept toward it only grew the longer she stared.

"I love you." She sighed, the rest of the group hurrying out of the conference room and chattering nervously to one another. She grabbed both of my hands, hers much more motionless than my own as I labored to avoid shaking.

"And I love you, Kara." I whispered back, forsaking a romantic kiss for an opportunity to wrap my arms around her and lean into her body once more. Her embrace was more comforting than anything else could have been, wrapping me in a pause within time I wished I could have held onto.

"We're going to be right here. This time tomorrow." She whispered, sniffling tearily and looking up at me.

"Yeah." I breathed, smiling as I cupped her cheek. "I'll be human again."

"And I'll know what humanity is like." She sighed quietly, lachrymose as her apprehension for the future finally overwhelmed her.

"I'll show you." I reassured, stroking her palm. "I'll show you exactly what it's like to be human. And I'll show you how to enjoy every year we have together. Every decade we have left."

"I'd like that." She smiled, looking down. "I'd like that very much. I want to spend every day with my husband. With the man I married. With my beautiful daughters."

"You will." I rested my chin atop her head as she fell into me, suppressing her sobs and holding onto my shoulders as if I were the last being alive. "But we need to go earn that time. And if nothing else, buy that time for our girls." She pulled away, nodding. "And the rest of our family."

"We will." She sniffed once more, turning away to grab her bag. "We will." I slung the equipment over my back, the rifle smacking against my shoulder blade as I took her hand and left the conference room. We turned right, neither one of us wanting to bask in a final sight of the city in its current state. For the first few feet in front of us, the concrete was charred and marked with melted bits of plastic before the ash and ember of the arboretum's remains began. Only the first portion was harmed, as the flowers and trees closer to the bistro were alive and well, but the scar reminded me too much of nearly losing everyone.

"Thank you." Kara said quietly as we started our way up the staircase to the first floor of the hospital. "I…needed a moment before we left."

"Everyone did." I reassured. "You're not alone in feeling this way." We made our way upward, floor by floor and stair by stair, until she spoke again.

"It doesn't seem like you do. You're…calm. I don't know how." I chuckled, shaking my head as we reached the top of the steps.

"I'm not calm. I'm terrified, Kara. But I have to accept that we have no other option. And I have to accept that we're going to succeed. If I start mourning a loss we have yet to encounter, no one is going to benefit from it." She smirked at my sentiment, raising her eyebrows.

"This is why I married you."

I love you so, so much.

I could already make out the chaotic noise of the hospital's parking lot as we exited the stairwell doors and entered the far side of the facility's ground floor. The earth itself seemed to shake under my feet at the dozens and dozens of vehicle engines that idled outside of the building. The rushing beat of helicopter blades was also distinct, closer than I had expected and awaiting my arrival. Both of us remained defiantly silent in the long walk through the lobby, her hand finally stopping me as we reached the glass and metal doors.

Without making another comment on her fears or relaying another explanation regarding our impending warfare, she pulled the front of my shirt gently and ensured that she was able to receive one more kiss before we left. I could feel the front of her fangs against her mouth, frustrated and saddened that she would have to depart my side and eager to show one last sign of affection. I returned the gesture, dropping the bag to hold her waist as we challenged the nature of the evil we faced and shared a moment of pure love for one another. I pulled away, looking into her eyes a final time before turning to walk through the doors.

I'm going to see you again.

A man greeted me almost immediately, having been apparently waiting for my arrival. He wore an aviation helmet, distinct from the other combat helmets worn among the throngs of soldiers that swarmed the vehicles of the parking lot.

"Good to see you, sir!" He shouted through his helmet, leaning toward me. "Name's Jack!"

"Nice to meet you, Jack!" I returned, needing to increase my volume as we neared the aircraft.

Although it had been decades since I had been aboard one, I had nothing but boundless respect for the piece of advanced technology that was willing to carry me into the fight. Jack jogged in front of me, ducking down to avoid the furious winds of the rotors, and extended a hand to help me aboard. I took it gratefully, stepping up with confidence before he handed me a headset. Very willing to block out the deafening sound, I donned it and tapped the microphone. After a moment, Jack's voice came in a much calmer tone through the speakers that covered my ears.

"Welcome to the fight, sir."

"Good to be back in one." I responded, dropping my duffel bag and beginning to rifle through it.

"I'm the crew chief for the flight, but you're not gonna see me back here once we lift off." He explained, reaching over to grab a tether. I was familiar with the coming steps and ripped the ballistic vest from my bag so I could put it on as rapidly as possible. "I'm going to monitor all that fancy equipment your friend installed. Pilot's gonna have his hands full. His name's John if you need him."

"Hi, John." I introduced myself through the microphone as I strapped the last buckle of my vest closed and felt a tug at the nape of my neck. Jack tested my safety tether with a brief pull before John responded.

"Good to meet you, sir. We're lifting off in three."

"Three minutes?" I asked, grabbing the gloves from my bag and pulling them on.

"Two…" John continued humorously.

"Oh." I said to myself, standing quickly to grab one of the supports with my free hand. I looped my ankle through the strap of the duffel so it wouldn't move and braced my legs as the engine's noise grew. Although the winter weather was already a bitter sting, the winds around me only made the situation worse. I was glad to have anticipated it with multiple layers of undergarments to maintain my body heat. We rocked gently as the Blackhawk hovered only a few feet off the ground, starting to climb after maintaining several seconds of steadiness. "You one of the new pilots or their instructor?" I asked warily.

"Pilot?" John remarked. "Someone left the keys in here and I thought it would be fun." I finally let myself smile, the jokes of a veteran making themselves apparent.

"That answers that." I remarked, watching as the mass of vehicles became a smaller, more cluttered mess of greenish-gray and desert tan below. We climbed slowly, moving in a straight line upward from the ground.

Few passengers remained in view since most had mounted their respective trucks, and the ground force's readiness was indicated by the lead troop carrier slowly making its way onto the road. The pattern of visual consistency was broken with the occasional passenger bus: the only way we could transport large numbers of soldiers at once. We hovered a few hundred feet above them, watching as the first wave of forty-some vehicles of various types followed in each other's tracks along the highway. The second group lingered, knowing they would wait to depart until the first group was several minutes ahead. I could still spot Tony's missile launcher, now a canister launcher, solidly in the center of the immobile second group.

The aircraft lurched slightly, tilting to move forward only enough that we could move parallel to the convoy and watch for any movement ahead of them. We were stable, and the only movement in the helicopter was the gentle rocking of an object gliding smoothly through the air. I reached down, secured from falling out via the safety tether, and scrounged for my radio. I clipped it to the front of my vest and snuck the earpiece under the left side of the headset.

"I have to communicate with our fixed-wing pilots." I explained to Jack and John. "If you guys hear me talking, it's probably not to you."

"Not much to say anyway, sir. We'll take it from here. You deal with the fast-movers." Jack reassured my confidence as I switched on the radio and made contact.

"Andrea, you online?"

"Online and moving quick." Her response was both immediate and excited, the opportunity to fly again likely a thrill for someone whose career had once depended on it.

"Two's company." Layla chimed in.

"And three's crowd. How the hell are you, Kane?" I heard the old, familiar voice of a friend and was nearly taken aback at how similar he sounded to our last interaction.

"Hamilton. God damn, dude. Here to save my ass again, huh? How was Colorado?"

"Got boring. You know I wouldn't miss a party like this. How've you been, Kane? Heard Fallujah kicked your ass a little bit."

"Fallujah wasn't bad, it was Kandahar that decided to bite back." Our conversation felt familiar and comfortable, our pilots being more confident than I could have expected. "How far out are you guys?"

"About thirty miles to the west. Holding just under thirty thousand feet at six hundred knots. Flew below radar level 'til Ocean City to stay out of sight, then burned north toward you guys." Layla responded.

"Any trouble?" I asked, knowing they would have mentioned something already if that had been the case.

"None yet, and you'd better hope we don't have any." Andrea responded. "Layla and I each have two AIM-one-twenties and Hamilton has four, but we need to make them count. I don't know what we're going to encounter once we hit D.C. Can't burn all our air-to-air missiles over a few of Legacy's helicopters or something."

"We'll be alright." I sighed, praying that we still had the element of surprise. "Glad to have you on overwatch."

Looking behind us, I could see the snakelike trail of the next convoy finally leave the hospital. It was a dozen miles behind us, and if I were human, wouldn't have been able to see it happen at all. The scene unfolding was one of an early victory, and one I hadn't dared hope to see so easily. Even the weather, although freezing, gave us a clear sky and a ground free of snow so typical for this time of year. I watched the first convoy barrel down the highway for several minutes, counting the vehicles to take note of which ones contained members of my family. It was a painful sight in spite of our success, and reminded me too heavily of what was at stake.

You made the right choice. We couldn't stay in Vanaheim. We couldn't run. All that was left was the fight.

I tried repeatedly distracting myself throughout the flight, alternating between the stunning views below, the distant aerial dance of the jets, and the meandering course of our brave fighters, and only barely managed to shake away the fear that stemmed from the scale of our impending task. Time seemed to have no meaning; although I checked my watch every few minutes, each precious second seemed to pass with little regard to my sense of how long ago we had left Vanaheim. The radio was nearly silent during the entirety of the journey. While there was an occasional check-in and the crackling sound of someone pressing their call button by accident, no conversation or noble speech was issued as we barreled toward our objective. After too short of a time, John spoke up as the aircraft began to descend.

"Sir, we're going to set down atop this hill crest over here. It's the only good landing zone I can spot and we're nearly within range of the missile launchers' radar."

"No, wait." I argued. "We have the defenses onboard. We should stay airborne. They won't be able to get a lock-"

"It's untested, sir." Jack argued. "As much as I want to have faith in the tech, let's save using it for emergencies. We can take off as soon as the fast-movers confirm we're clear."

I sighed, realizing they were right, and remained silent. As much as I had confidence in my decisions, I knew better than to argue with the best in the profession and allowed my life to rest in the hands of those who knew better than I did.

"Anyone else catch that?" Hamilton quipped, the first time any of the pilots had spoken in more than half an hour. "Got a blip."

"No. Heading?" Layla asked, occupied with something in the background but concerned at his inquiry. There wasn't a response, and I was able to see them overhead several miles behind us casting wide, loose circles over the second convoy. "Hamilton. What heading was-"

"Climb. You and Andrea, set your ceiling at four-five thousand. Now." As if my nerves weren't fatigued enough, hearing his voice in a panic sent my stress through the roof once more.

My aircraft kissed the ground, hardly a bump as we landed, and I leaned out to get a better view of the combat aircraft. Two of them started to rapidly ascend, forsaking their defensive posture for a higher altitude. Had I not known exactly where they were via the radar in the cockpit, I would never have been able to spot the miniscule specks speeding through the air. Although the weather was still clear, a few stringy clouds obscured them for intermittent moments and forced me to lose sight of them for a couple seconds at a time.

What the hell's going on?

"I see it on radar." Andrea confirmed. "Other side of D.C. Good catch. Our sensors aren't great at looking above our altitude, and they're…it's gone again." She said confusedly. "What the hell-"

"Adjust heading one-five and increase speed to eight-five-zero. We have guests." Hamilton said confidently, his craft starting to charge the region ahead of the first convoy. It zipped past our forces, the other two pilots having to make wider turns to catch up. "It's another stealth craft. They have the same technology you guys do, just without Tony and Eric's missile defenses. Radar's only going to catch them if they're banking and creating a profile wide enough to hit. If we can't see them, they're either coming right at us or heading away. And I doubt it's the latter." He explained, sending data to the interface in front of Jack. I could hear it beep faintly in the cockpit, lighting up with a new interface and sharing the radar data from his jet. I watched the three pilots zoom past us and continue north for a ways before turning and circling back to us.

Was it a false alarm?

"I don't want to get too close to those launchers downtown. If it was a craft, it must have been heading away from us, I don't see any-" Layla started.

"Shit!" Andrea hissed, the pitch of her voice rising. "Behind us. You guys have incoming from the east."

"Who, us?" I asked, looking over at Jack as he gave a thumbs-up that our anti-radar equipment was working.

"No, the...Val..." Her voice fell into a whisper at the same moment I turned to face the winding set of highways and streets to our east, listening to a much closer, much louder set of two combat jets scream over my head toward the convoy before sharply banking to the north.

I know what an attack run looks like. And that...was one of them.

It didn't matter what I or the other pilots had said in the few scant seconds that we were able to catch the maneuvers above our own formation. At the speed their missiles were deployed, there wasn't even enough time to take a breath before they made impact and ripped a hole through the center of the row of vehicles. Four simultaneous explosions covered more than half of the trucks, troop carriers, and armored vehicles with jagged bursts of concrete dust and flame that obstructed my view and rapped against the hull of my Blackhawk with shockwaves. I continued to stare, already feeling tears fall down my face as our pilots valiantly tried to salvage the situation by engaging them as quickly as possible.

"Two bandits heading one-seven-zero. Good lock for AMRAAM one, fox three." Hamilton's composure was professional, but his voice was broken by the shock of how suddenly our mission had diminished in hope.

Who…just…died? How many?

My throat still too tight to speak, I croaked incoherent syllables into my radio in the hopes of reaching Val and gave up, trying to compose myself. The dust refused to settle, metal shrapnel and ignited fuel cascading through the middle of the highway.

"He threw flares and chaff. Shot trashed. I'm on the other one. Wait…" Andrea paused, taking a quick breath as she struggled against the forces the aircraft put on her chest and lungs. "Lock, fox three."

"Trashed. Shit!" Layla echoed Andrea. "I'm diving, we need to get closer. We can't keep wasting ordnance."

"Watch your back, they're coming around."

"Banking, descending to one-five thousand. We need to nail these bastards."

I listened to their radio chatter, composing myself enough to push the air in my lungs through my throat with a hoarse, harsh command.

"No." I cleared my throat, shaking my head. "Push the objective. Andrea, Layla, prep the AGMs for drop on Legacy's launchers. Hamilton, you need to keep Legacy's fighters busy. We can't afford to lose the attack runs on those missile launchers. We need our helicopters to get there and assault the east buildings."

"Jalix, he can't handle-"

"He's right." Hamilton groaned, breathing heavily. I watched his jet rotate, flipping onto its side to allow Legacy's jets to get behind Andrea and Layla. "Radar lock, fox three." His explanation was interrupted with another air-to-air missile, invisible to my eyes until a clear explosion above my head indicated its detonation. "Goddamn it. He threw chaff, shot trashed. You girls go. Little brother needs a chance to play, too. They can't outmaneuver me in a straight fight. I can buy you time."

"Hamil-"

"Layla, we don't have time to argue. Engaging burners." Andrea sided with me, a short spout of flame erupting from her turbines.

"Burning." Layla sounded despondent, but the two of them began to race away from the engagement and headed toward the city. I could see the outline of white mist roll through both of them as they broke the sound barrier.

"Taylor, what's your status?" I spat, realizing how little time we had left before we would be in the thick of the fight.

If they hit those launchers, she has a chance. If not...this may end more quickly than we expected.

"We're green. We're east of your position in a small valley, safe from radar coverage. Give the word and we'll be there in under a minute." She responded.

"Val?" I finally asked, leaning against the doorway. "You there?"

"Yeah!" He roared immediately. "Didn't want to interrupt! Third vehicle!" He yelled, prompting me to look and follow what he was trying to indicate. Kara and Sonya were leaned against one another from what looked like exhaustion more than injury. Val was rallying his troops, redirecting them and signaling to the drivers. "First convoy's alright." He continued, still loud but lowering his voice as he moved away from the chaos to check on Kara and Sonya.

"Alright?" I shook my head, staring at one of the few vehicles visible through the dust as it belched waves of flame. "What-"

"Ask your wife. And Sonya. Superhero powers, man. They saved us. Redirected the missiles and suppressed the explosions into the concrete. Two vehicles are fried and four are hit pretty bad from the one direct hit that snagged us. Casualties look minimal overall." He was breathing heavily and I could see his figure leaning over to yell at people in between sentences. "We're moving the passengers. Amy's making her way up to provide medical-"

"No!" I bellowed, making my point clear. "Legacy *wants* her vulnerable! Amy, keep your ass exactly where you are!"

"Damn, I haven't heard the *grounded* voice in years." She quipped. "Understood, staying put."

"Val, get the convoy moving, now! We're a sitting target!" I demanded, watching him usher people back into the intact vehicles.

"Andrea, I'm locked. Sync your-"

"Syncing, lock is three seconds out."

"Val, I need to go. Handle your people." I reacted quickly to Layla and Andrea getting closer to their targets, returning the focus of my attention to the air.

Whatever is out there...whoever is listening...please get us through this.

"I'm locked. Birds affirm."

"Birds away."

This is it.

I held my breath as both of them veered away after a brief dive toward the city's center, the seconds passing creating a furious palpation in my chest that threatened to kill me before the shooting started. A synchronous explosion resonated through the distant air, only interrupted with the tight battle raging overhead between Hamilton and Legacy's two aircraft.

"Confirming…ten seconds." Andrea said quietly. As Layla sped toward us again to help Hamilton, Andrea made a wide arc to fly over the city and scan for a confirmation that they hit their targets. "We hit!" She screamed, a girlish excitement dominating the previous professionalism she was able to so proudly wear. "Hope it hurt, you son of a bitch! Merry goddamn Christmas, asshole!" She roared, cackling in a moment of euphoria. I exhaled, hunching over before I realized my work was far from done and my reaction time would shape the coming fight.

"Taylor, you're green! East side of the city's yours."

"Won't let you down, Kane. Godspeed."

"Godspeed." I echoed, watching a formation of darkly-painted helicopters lift from the ground in an expertly tight formation and start to shift toward me, roaring overhead and thundering toward their target in a deadly mass.

"Layla, I need help!" Hamilton shouted. "Flares out!" I looked to the west, to the far side of the convoy, and watched as Hamilton's smaller jet spun through the air with a shadow of fiery sparks flying out from the rear of his craft. The trail of a missile narrowly missed him, jerking to the side before it would have impacted and leaving an explosion too close for comfort. "Status Winchester, I need to bug out."

Winchester…shit, he's out of anti-air missiles. He's useless right now.

"Hamilton, bugout approved. Get back to Quantico." I confirmed, looking over to see Val's convoy start moving forward again.

"Good luck, girls." He called, turning south and drastically increasing in speed. "Burning to Mach two. Hamilton out." Our adversaries gave no pause to Layla and Andrea, pursuing them relentlessly with maneuvers that would have been impossible for human bodies to handle.

"Layla, on your tail!"

"I'm out of flares!"

"Get in the weeds! Turn left, now!"

They're hardly off the ground anymore.

The fight had continued to descend in altitude, playing to the strength of the women's specialized training. All four jets were highly visible and following one another in an elaborate dance of death at speeds faster than sound.

Without warning, the chassis of Layla's aircraft showed its belly and started to rotate, spinning in mid-air as it moved in a direction opposite of the way it faced. A maneuver I was sure would have sheared the wings off the plane provided her an unparalleled braking system that allowed Andrea a clear shot at one of Legacy's pilots without the risk of collateral damage.

"I'm locked, fox three." Andrea called, angled perfectly toward one of the two enemies. Short moments after the call, a massive explosion engulfed her opponent in fire and decimated any prospect of survival. "Good hit!" Andrea yelled excitedly.

From my vantage point, it seemed like Layla took far too long to regain control of herself, slowed too much to avoid the second pilot from taking advantage of the opportunity. She floated toward the ground, picking up speed too gradually to avoid a massive decline in altitude and giving her no chance to avoid her adversary's attempt at slaying her. A missile was launched from the jet behind her, hurtling toward Layla at incredible speeds before it suddenly skyrocketed and exploded hundreds of feet away from her. Finally able to regain some form of control, the nose of her aircraft turned upward from the ground.

Tony's system worked.

"Come get me, you son of a bitch." Layla growled, the blazing glow of her afterburners meriting a screaming pass over my head as the other two jets in the sky followed.

"Layla, I'm out of munitions, but he doesn't know that. Break left, I'll let him chase me for a bit. You're gonna have to go in for the kill."

Snap out of it. There's nothing else you can do. Get to the front line.

"John, get us off the ground." I took a step back, gripping one of the handholds for support as he obliged. We rocked gently, hovering a few dozen feet before moving forward and clearing the hill we sat on for so long.

"Jalix?" Violet's voice came through my earpiece, a surprising entry to the radio chatter from someone who had yet to make contact with me.

"Violet? You okay?"

"Yeah, it's…" She paused, her speech clearly tainted with distress. "It's Legacy."

"What do you mean?" I returned almost immediately.

"He…called my phone. He wants to speak with you."

He must have been trying to reach me. I wouldn't have had cell signal on the flight here.

"Do you have a comms guy in your vehicle? Have him get the call onto this radio channel. I want all of you to hear this." I was infuriated that he had the nerve to try and talk to us when he should have been running for his life, but I was curious to hear what he wanted.

Though I knew it wasn't an announcement of defeat by any means, his attempt at contact as my Blackhawk began circling the National Mall and its surrounding buildings gave me the first rise of confidence I could have conjured since we left Vanaheim. Taylor's forces were landing on various rooftops, the rotors of helicopter blades slowing as elite soldiers poured from them and began preparations for their individual assaults. Some were lucky enough to have easy access to the interior of their buildings and spilled down sets of stairs to disappear from view.

I looked to my left, watching the convoy arrive at the highway's exit and blow through the first layer of the city's outer defenses. While the entry control points and makeshift watchtowers poured gunfire onto my allies, none impacted with any effect and bounced off the armored plating on each of the lead vehicles. The first two trucks acted as bulldozers, massive grates and steel plows crushing obstacles and moving concrete barriers aside with ease. I took in the view for almost a full minute before finally hearing a steely voice resound in my ear.

"Jalix Nicholas Kane. Ultimate soldier and fearless leader."

"Legacy. Want to resign yet? Hard being the guy in charge, isn't it?" He chuckled, no single indication of fear in any part of his confident voice.

"You act as though I didn't know you were coming. Fourteen Blackhawk helicopters, each carrying sixteen soldiers. Two stealth combat aircraft and another last-generation fighter from Nellis Air Force base, who has already retreated. A hundred and seven combat vehicles of various grade and quality, each loaded with passengers of their own. And you. Alone."

"Hey, you can count. Puts you head and shoulders above Kilkovf." I heard Krystal chuckle in the background at my comment, reminding me that the leaders of the battle could hear the conversation.

"You are not special, Mr. Kane. You were chosen because your wife was too weak to pick up the mantle of leadership after her…previous failures." I gritted my teeth, but said nothing to maintain the image that he wasn't affecting me. It was a cheap tactic, but any mention of Kara or my family was sore with the risks below only increasing in scale as time went on. "Your forces are outnumbered two to one, and outmatched in strength and endurance. I want to give you a final chance to retreat before you and your family are decimated."

"Legacy, I-"

"But you won't. So I am going to kill you. I am going to torture your wife and her daughters into submission, no matter the *great* effort and time that may take, and I will take personal satisfaction in doing so. Then I am going to find every ally you have in this battleground and skin them alive to set an example." He paused, an unsettling rumble within the intent behind his voice. "I have tracked everything your pathetic army has done since the moment you tried convincing me that Kara fled your alliance. I've given you time to prepare your army so I could kill all of you in one, singular battle. The Tortured do not feel fear, and neither do I. You…are not special, Mr. Kane. And you will die here, today."

I'm going to rip out his throat personally for bringing my daughters into this.

"Legacy…you're making the same mistake that your predecessor did. You and Schillinger both seemed to think that fear is some kind of weakness. But your troops are going to fall to stupid mistakes today while mine fight for their families. Their loved ones. You're going to watch your army collapse, because despite your abilities, despite your military and your defenses, *you* are incomplete. So was Schillinger. He pursued Kara because she had something he could never find. Something you'll never have. You want to know what makes us special? Violet, tell your comms guy to put me on wide-band. I want every radio, every speaker we have online." I took a moment for myself, closing my eyes and breathing deeply. A quick crackle and brief feedback forced me to pull the earpiece from its place and speak into the microphone attached to my aviator's headset.

This ends today.

"Today is not an easy day." I started, watching as the convoy continued to plow through Legacy's defenses and approach its destination south of the Washington Monument. "Today, for many of you, came too soon. I know you expected to spend Christmas with your families, and here you are instead fighting to save their lives. Today you said your goodbyes, made your peace, and went off to war. A war you might never return from. But one thing that we have each borne in mind through the winter is that today we would do battle with the enemy that threatens the world. Many of you have become comfortable with your training, and some of you have made the idea of war your home. But in this war…this war is only home to death." As if I was speaking directly to Kara, I watched her vehicle buck and jump over a curb as it swerved to avoid the crushing fire of a machine gun. "Today we knock on the door of that home with the full might of our forces, bringing to bear the training and preparation you've achieved against an enemy that outmatches us in every way imaginable. But this enemy is afraid of us. They don't fear us because we're invincible, they fear us because we *can* be killed, and we have had the strength to defy that fact and do battle in the face of impossible odds. They fear us because time and time again, they have tried to kill us and we have pushed them back at every turn. So today, you face this war. You face this war to be free from oppression. From persecution and terror. You face this war to bring the spirit of Vanaheim and Aerael to the world in ways it has never seen before. Long ago, humans called us the undead…the undying. The world wanted to call us monsters. I want you to show these Tortured why we earned those names. Legacy wants his troops to break you the same way he was able to break them. But your leaders stand before you unbroken. We have fought this war, some of us for centuries, against this enemy and we have earned being called the Unbroken. This world belongs to the Unbroken, and as long as one of us draws breath…it always will. Legacy wants to take this life away from you." I placed my hand on the microphone's switch, ready to end the transmission. "Go take it back." Andrea's jet screamed over the conflict within the city, now engaging in hellish warfare, and was chased by Legacy's pilot with Layla pulling up the rear of the fight. They charged past only a hundred yards from me and marked the end of the aerial battle with a roaring rush of wings and fury.

"Andrea, break now. I have a lock."

"Breaking off. Nail the bastard."

"Firing. Fox three, fox three."

BATTLEGROUND

VALTERIUS

I bowed my head, listening to the pounding of fists against the towering doors of the chapel and ignoring it to the best of my ability. Violet made her way from the front to where I was seated behind the podium, shaking her head.

"They're pissed off, Val. I don't know what else to tell them."

"Tell them not to be pissed off." I replied, shrugging. "I…I don't know either, Vi. They're angry about something outside of our control. Something lost to the mistakes in our history. It's not like we can snap our fingers and correct what's going on." I heard the familiar sound of Amy's mouth open, half a breath taken in before she closed it again and decided to remain neutral.

"You gotta stop doing that." Violet chuckled, shaking her head at her adopted sister. I turned to look at my niece, a fresh-faced young adult with distinctive silver hair and eyes to match.

"We're listening. Nothing you say is ever dumb." I assured, gesturing to the doors. "Especially right now."

"It's just…why don't we talk to them? I mean, I know we've talked to them a lot, but why can't we sit down and have a discourse about these things?" Her naiveté was at its most prominent in the innocence of her gaze, watching for my reaction. Knowing she absorbed every detail of

body language and took sarcasm as an insult to her intellect, I sighed and leaned forward in my chair.

"People don't always want to hear the truth. Right now, the truth is that nothing can change. This infection, our virus, is now out there in the world. No one wants that, especially with the way it's infecting people. But they're looking for someone to blame. And the truth is…the people to blame are all dead. So they feel powerless. And that's the truth they don't want to hear." Amy nodded her head slowly, her eyes roaming in front of her as she processed the information. After a brief pause, she looked up again.

"Why don't they take power in the ways they can? The ways that help? They could be volunteering at the hospitals or the morgues. There's so much else they could be doing to make things better." Violet and I shared a silent, painful pang at her innocent yet truthful words.

"You're right." I decided. "But I want you to listen to them closely." I waited, watching her eyes scan the doors as the thumping raps against the wood echoed through the room and filled the empty pews with frustration. The voices outside weren't screaming or furious, but demanded explanation and remained steadfast in their beliefs. "Do you believe that they're ready to accept what you're saying?" A young queen, she understood the situation and nodded once, maturing before my eyes with a robust understanding of painful societal trauma.

"It'll be alright, Amy. People…cool off. I've seen stuff like this before, and it just takes a little bit of time before they come to their senses. Then we can-" Violet stopped as a cracking noise interrupted her insight.

The latch broken by the throng of individuals on the other side, the doors opened without much resistance and swung to allow the crowd inside. Although they only numbered a few dozen, the anger in their faces multiplied the apparent size of the confrontational group. I stood immediately, placing a protective arm in front of Amy before gesturing that the two girls should follow me through the mass of protesting Vampyres. I ignored the questions shouted at us, some of them echoes of others, and gently pressed my way through the thick of the crowd.

"-told us decades ago about this-"

"-with Kara and Jalix screwing around with the government-"

"-worse than you have any idea-"

"-killing people by the thousands every day-"

Some words bruised my heart more than others, but I was dedicated to getting the two young women out of the room and to someplace they could expect a modicum of privacy. Although I knew the crowd would continue to follow me until I confronted them, it was a problem I endeavored to delay for as long as possible. After a short struggle, we were able to breathe cooler air away from the group and start to hastily make our way down the main hall. Aerael's arboretum was littered with watching eyes, knowing and hopefully opposing the group that followed too closely behind us.

"Alright, I need both of you to head to Kara's room. I don't want you in the residential areas until I-" I slowed my walking pace, holding my arms outward to push the girls back as a man made his way from a bench near the bistro and stood in front of me. I paused, assessing the situation to the best of my ability before things could get out of hand.

His red hair was a mess, an oily texture indicating that he had been sweating profusely, likely for several days. In spite of the neutral weather, he wore a tan windbreaker and had one hand shoved too deeply into one of its pockets. While he had confronted me directly, he avoided eye contact and viciously stared at the ground in front of my feet.

"You don't need that gun, kid. But don't try and pretend like you don't have it." I spoke as calmly as possible, and even the crowd behind me started to disperse to avoid whatever situation was brewing.

"I'm not a kid. I'm thirty-two." He spat.

"Hey. Me, too." Violet said quietly, trying to play to a sense of peace and light humor to defuse the state of affairs. His eyes remained locked on the ground, a furious glare of rage that he refused to direct toward any of us.

"You're a kid." I replied peacefully. "I'm three hundred and fifty-seven years old. Everyone's a kid to me. Don't take it personally."

"I don't care. It doesn't matter." He mumbled, shaking with a violent tremor. I was questioning the possibility of drug use, but knew better from seeing some of Alice's psychiatric patients.

"Who are you angry with?" I probed, hoping the answer was myself rather than either of the innocent women behind me.

"All of you." He hissed, glancing up at me. "You. Your sister. Even that Jalix asshole. Your precious family." He finally pulled the gun from his jacket, holding it at his side rather than pointing it at me. I watched out of the corner of my eye as several armed residents discreetly drew their weapons. Out of respect, they knew not to do anything rash unless I, or the girls behind me, were at imminent risk. Looking over his shoulder, I could see two more younger residents, likely in their early twenties, approach from the same direction and stand behind him with their own handguns. "This is my brother Scott. My sister Natalie. You-…you probably don't even know who we are." He continued. His anger didn't seem to fade, something buried deeply continuing to feed the fire in his eyes.

"I don't." I responded. "But I would like to."

"Oh, I bet you would. I bet you said that to my cousin, too. And her parents, who were basically our parents until your sister got them killed. You must've said that to every family that your bitch of a sister put in danger."

"If Kara-"

"Her name was Maddie!" He roared, lifting the gun and aiming it at me roughly. I lifted one of my hands and directed a glance at the armed onlookers, begging them not to shoot as they snapped into defensive poses. "She was like a little sister to me!"

"I knew Maddie." Violet said quietly, moving one of my arms to speak with him. "Kara had nothing to do with her death, it was Kilkovf that-"

"It was Kilkovf that would have returned her if Kara had just gone with them! You think she hasn't told the story? You think she hasn't sat in front of that church and put on a show for everyone? Crying and weeping and talking about how hard it was to deal with…Do you know how I know she's lying? Because she doesn't even have the memories. She can't even care! And the disrespect-"

"She may not remember it happening…" I interrupted him. "But she felt the consequences of it. We all did."

"This is exactly the bullshit we're talking about." The girl he called Natalie vocalized from behind the young man. "You're full of shit. 'Felt' the consequences? We still feel them! It's not in the past tense!"

"Kilkovf was a sadistic bastard that tried to kill everything Kara loved. As soon as she surrendered herself, he would have killed your family anyway." I defended.

"Better Kara than an innocent, eleven-year-old little girl." He moved forward, angling the gun at my head. He briefly pointed it at Violet, but snapped it back toward my temple as I snorted loudly and took a step toward him. "You all deserved to die."

"No one deserved what Schillinger and his followers did. It's what we're fighting against."

"It's what you lost against!" Scott shouted. The young man in front of me chuckled, shaking his head.

"At least one of you had the decency to actually stay dead." He sneered. I tried to control my breathing, rapidly spiraling out of control as the stimulation around me forced my body into a state I struggled to avoid. In conscious thinking, I knew I could still try to salvage the conversation, but the reality of three armed people in front of me and the two young women behind me were enough to warrant a protective kill switch tethered to a hair trigger.

"Jared was a good man." My calm was quickly fading, replaced with an unintentional darkness in my voice. "He didn't deserve to die."

"A good man?" He scoffed, his lips curled in anger. "None of you are good people. He betrayed us and lied just as much as any one of Kara's bullshit counsel. Maybe more, considering how useless he was in the city."

"Kid, don't." I warned, feeling my abilities swell the veins in my arms beneath the suit jacket I was wearing. "Don't go there."

"And a pastor teaching elementary school? I bet he touched kid-" My right arm swept in an arc in front of me, catching the side of his face and bringing it into the concrete wall to my left with an impact that left nothing resembling the remains of a human head.

Everything upward of his neck clung to the wall in gory pieces while the rest of his body slumped downward and gushed blood onto the floor.

I turned to see Violet covering Amy's eyes in an act of protection, a moment lasting a fraction of a second before the distinct sound of two gunshots rang out from the direction where he had been standing. While I felt the pain of both rounds, it was distant enough to ignore entirely as I advanced on both shooters. The girl tried to duck before taking off in a sprint, but a snap of her elbow allowed me access to her handgun and the quick end to her life. The remaining man, Scott, got another shot off that pierced straight through my shoulder as he crawled backward toward the wall. The back of my right hand hit the steel of his pistol and knocked it from his grasp so I could lift him by the neck with my left and pin him to the wall in a fluid movement.

"You think I betrayed this city?" I growled, watching his eyes dart hopelessly in fear as he started to run out of air. "You think I killed that little girl?" I roared, turning my chest and throwing Scott's body halfway across the main hall. My legs were ready to sprint to the spot where he landed, his head bouncing off the floor and knocking him unconscious, but I was stopped by the delicate touch of a fragile young woman and her bright silver eyes that filled to the brim with tears.

"Val..." She sniffled. "Please stop. This isn't you."

"Amy, move-"

"This is the truth you need to hear right now." She begged, locking me in place with my own words and destroying the previous haze of red that had occupied my vision. "Even if you don't want to." I looked down, choking on the tightness in my throat as she pulled her hand away from my shoulder and looked at the blood that covered it.

"Goddamn it..." I whispered, looking behind her at the disgusted bystanders that stared at me with loathing and revulsion. "I'm so sorry." I tried to increase my volume, and only managed a whisper from the depths of my throat.

"I forgive you." She whispered back, looking over her shoulder at the spectators as they started to usher each other away in fear and shock. She swallowed hard, placing a gentle hand on my neck so her healing powers could take effect. "But I don't know if they ever will."

***

"Fox three, fox three." I closed my eyes, paying more attention to my radio than I was the muffled gunfire that shrouded the immediate area. My vehicle came to a sudden stop, lurching me to the side as I tried to stay in place within the cramped cabin. I felt the watchful eyes of my radio assistant stare at me awkwardly in her place across from my seat, listening to her own radio channel and waiting for me to need her assistance.

"Grandslam, all enemy aircraft down. We're RTB. Burning to Quantico. Good luck, guys." Layla's call marked the end of any risk from Legacy's fighter jets and gave me a hopeful breath of air at the sound of both pilots being alive and well.

"Good jobs, ladies. RTB approved. Leave the porch light on when you get home." Jalix complimented, the faint click in my ear an indication that the pilots had tuned out of our station.

"Ryan, what's going on?" I turned to my driver, watching the tracking system on his touchscreen with ferocious intensity.

"Blockade one is getting established, sir. But they're encountering problems. It looks like the Tortured have-" His sentence was cut short by an explosion that rocked our heavy vehicle off its tires on the left side before slamming back into the ground. All of the passengers were thrown violently, my helmet protecting me from the fierce impact my head encountered against the cabin wall. Ryan took a moment, exhaling and turning back to me. "Grenade launchers." He finished. "Possibly rockets, but we can't confirm that one yet."

"Marcus." I moved the switch on my earpiece, enabling its microphone. "I need your team on sniper support to take out these grenadiers."

"We're too close to give you sniper support." Marcus argued, clearly engaged in an active and intense firefight.

"We'll focus our fire, but eight-four should have a marksman squad." I turned to my radio operator as she scratched the short, blonde hair on the back of her head in response to the previous turmoil.

"Felix, get eight-four to-"

"Yeah, I got it." She already knew what I was going to say, calling to the eighty-fourth truck in the convoy to request the help we needed.

You'd be more help out there. You're a soldier just like them. You should be fighting, not sitting in the damn truck.

"Eight-four is dismounted and engaging." She paused, tilting her head to listen. "Blockade one just called. They're established."

"Showtime." I sighed, turning to face the rear of the vehicle and watching as the ramp lowered to the ground.

The sounds from outside immediately penetrated the peace, shattering any sense of security we had from being inside and proving a brief reminder of the hazards that surrounded us. Felix was diligent in her duty, staying less than an arm's reach away as I climbed out and ducked down to make my way forward. Rounds screamed overhead, whistling and buzzing as they whipped past and found a target in whatever they could. The row of twenty vehicles ahead of us provided shelter from being visible directly from the front, but didn't help in blocking the occasional grenades that were fired in blind arcs above them, nor any bullets fired from raised enemy positions.

"All Operators, this is Alice. We're clearing the first buildings. We're just northwest of Taylor's position." Alice's voice almost caused my knees to collapse under me, a fatal reminder of what I had to lose and couldn't protect anymore. "These civilians…they're in rough shape. God…" She paused. "Val, I need the buses to get them all out before the fighting gets here. They'll need armed escort, too." Her voice was relatively quiet, an indication that Sonya and Kara were dealing with the Tortured without gunfire. I nodded to Felix, letting her relay the command to the back of our second convoy. I couldn't even hear her speaking over the resounding gunfire, but she nodded to me that the request was completed.

I pointed to our destination and we sprinted forward, most of the explosions around us being dozens of yards away, and finally found a solid stopping point behind one of the centermost trucks. One of the men there, a medic by the identifying patch on his chest, turned to me after standing up to fire several rounds through the limited space between the vehicles. His actions mirrored the fifty other soldiers that dotted the rows next to me.

"Thought you'd be in your truck, sir!" He yelled, ducking as a plume of dirt erupted and covered us in grass and soil. I could see one of our fighters collapse a few yards to my left, holding his face as it started to gush blood before one of the other medics slid into place at his side and began first aid.

"No fun back there! What's the holdup with blockade two?" I asked, unslinging my own rifle and peering through the tight space to look at the enemy's territory for the first time.

My question was answered, the sheer size of Legacy's forces tearing through me in astonishment. The terrain was relatively flat, mostly grass or dirt speckled with trees barren from the biting winter weather. A few sidewalks and small buildings provided landmarks for our forces to assemble, but everything was slowly being annihilated in the results of our intense warfare.

Every hundred yards between us and our target, a line of makeshift bunkers kept more than a dozen machine guns protected and reinforced while riflemen crouched behind concrete barriers or crates filled with piles of sandbags. The White House was easily visible in the background, but seemed miles away from us against the sparkling image of hundreds of muzzle flashes.

We can get there.

"They're taking out the wheels and tracks of the vehicles, sir!" The medic bellowed, screaming to overpower the noise of the machine gun above his head rattling off a belt of rounds. "We need the explosions to stop!"

"I need the whole *war* to stop, man! We need to push through it!" I tapped Felix on the shoulder, looking down into her waiting eyes. I leaned into her ear so I wouldn't ruin my vocal cords in the first few minutes of the fight. "Get the dozers up here. Tell them to make us a path." I pulled away, watching her reaction as she turned her head and looked at me in doubt.

"That's suicide, sir. They won't make it halfway." She leaned in the same way I had, her brow furrowed in confusion and angst. I didn't respond aloud, giving her a small shrug and a frown as the realities of sacrifice began to become apparent. She nodded once, leaning away and giving the command. I stared behind us at the mass of stopped trucks, most of them returning fire with mounted weapons, and watched as the two vehicles that previously led the convoy made their way to the front once more.

No hesitation. They know what needs done.

I could make out the sound of their diesel engines revving while they accelerated, blowing past the blockade and enthusiastically engaging the enemies with five tons of steel moving in excess of thirty miles an hour. As fearless as the Tortured claimed to be, the thought of being maimed by the front end of a steel plow was enough motivation to abandon their bunkers and sprint toward the rear of their formation as fast as their legs could carry them. I turned to give my next command, but Felix was already on her radio requesting that the second blockade make their way forward. During the retreat, the gunfire diminished by a small degree and gave me a rise in confidence.

Like a well-oiled machine, a dozen tan troop carriers drove around each side of the blockade and advanced to create the next barrier against enemy gunfire. Waves of infantry followed, using the armor plating as a shield while taking well-placed shots at the hundreds of Tortured that fired back at them. Another explosion sent a gust of air across the field, one lucky rocket blowing a Humvee to pieces and shredding the personnel that surrounded it.

"Op-operators, this is-…this is Taylor." Her voice was almost too quiet to hear, quivering in fear and nearly whimpering. "My….team is down. Too many of them-" She fell silent after a quick gasp and I listened closely to try and follow what was happening. "They-…they've got me pinned. I'm hurt."

"Taylor, we can send reinforcements-"

"No." Jalix's offer of support was rejected almost immediately. "I'm not going to make it. I'm bleeding. Almost out of ammo." She continued tearily. "There's not many left here. The rest…they escaped to the streets a few minutes ago. Dozens of them. I don't know where they're going."

"I'm on the west side over the Potomac. We're circling to you now." Jalix proposed.

"I think they're heading south. They-…no, please!" Taylor screamed, a barrage of noise and vicious voices from her end of the transmission. "Stop!" I could hear her struggling, and I quickly realized how demoralizing it was to listen to the events unfold as my family was forced to do the same. "Stop it!" She shrieked pleadingly, her survival and resistance to whatever was occurring meaning there was more to the intent of the Tortured than sheer violence. I sat paralyzed as I listened to her shout screaming sobs, protesting with as much ferocity as she could conjure before an earsplitting gunshot preceded a melancholy silence. A few moments passed, each of us considering speaking before we could hear the Tortured through her microphone.

"She's still warm."

"Pretty one, too."

"Jack, kill her transmission." Jalix quickly intervened, only a few other mumbles from the Tortured audible before the line went silent again. "And I want the closest air assault team to go reclaim her body with extreme prejudice. Take down the whole goddamn building if you have to." Jalix's nerves were clearly shaken, as were all of ours in the impossibly despondent way her life had ended.

No one on this Earth deserves an end like that.

I looked out at the battlefield again, our second blockade firmly in place and Felix staring at me in curiosity. I shook my head, indicating that she didn't want to know what had transpired before I gripped my rifle again and ran across the line of vehicles in front of me.

I hope we kill every last one of them. Marcus had better take his time ending Legacy's life.

"Marcus, how do we look?" I called, breathing heavily as I stopped at the corner of the first blockade.

"Ready for number three. Might as well start moving the launcher forward. Legacy's forces are at about half strength." His response was immediate, his radio crackling slightly

"Half?" I asked in disbelief. "We've made that much of a dent?"

"You should see it up here, man." He chuckled, firing off a burst of rounds. "We're slaughtering them. We don't have much to go, but we need more firepower up here. They're keeping our heads down."

"Can we push the advantage?" I asked quickly, looking at the remaining vehicles behind me. As the trucks for the third blockade departed, I could see Tony's vehicle and the launcher behind it creep forward. Another explosive munition impacted a few yards ahead of it, but managed to do nothing more than cover it with rocks and soil.

"That's your call, Val. You want my advice?" He paused. "We have the momentum. If we go now-" I grabbed the radio from Felix, holding it to my mouth before Marcus could finish his sentence.

"All available ground units, advance to the frontline and secure the White House lawn. I want every soldier, every technician, and every medic supporting Marcus and his team." I hesitated, knowing what I was asking of them.

What would Jalix say?

"This is it." I continued, watching the remaining vehicles pick up speed and roll past me. "We have the opportunity to win, but only if we push with everything we have. The Tortured are at half strength and we have yet to hit the one-hundred casualty mark. We're winning. Go finish the fight." I tossed the radio back to Felix, watching as Tony's vehicle stopped next to me and opened its door so he could get out and make his way to my side. He reached out, clasping my arm and patting my back briefly. The gunfire had grown increasingly distant as the front of the fight advanced, and he was able to speak just above normal volume.

"How long until we're secured?" He asked, tucking his hands under the chestpiece of his ballistic vest for warmth.

"Minutes. As soon as Marcus calls that he's breaching the White House, I want you up there as fast as possible." Tony nodded, looking up at his machine with reverence. "Last couple minutes as a Vampyre, then." He chuckled. "Got anything else heavy you wanna lift before those abilities go away?" I scoffed, changing out my partially depleted magazine for one that was fully loaded.

"As *if* these muscles are going anywhere. You think-"

"Val!" Krystal's screech was panicked and unwarranted, forcing Tony and I to both look to the rear of the formation.

While I couldn't see the last few vehicles, no radio calls had indicated that they were in trouble.

"Krystal? What's-"

"God!" She screamed, breathing heavily. A long wait kept me in suspense before she spoke again. "We've been trying to reach you for five minutes!" Her breaths were shaky and her voice was intermittently broken with emotion. "We got attacked! Violet and I, we-…we're on the run. The Tortured from Taylor's building, they-…they swarmed us."

"What?" I demanded, leaving Tony behind and dashing to the rear of the battleground. As I ran, medics tended to wounded soldiers and our few, precious religious staff gave last rites to those who were dead or dying. More were being carried to safety by either their squadmates or spare medics.

"Something happened to our radio, we couldn't reach you. They ambushed us. They had suppressed weapons. We were screaming, but the noise-…no one could hear us."

"Krystal, I need to know *exactly* where you and Violet are." Jalix chimed in, trying to track them from his view in the sky. I could see his helicopter above us, moving toward the east side of the city.

"I-…I don't know." Her voice cracked, fear starting to dominate her senses. "I have the Relic. Violet's with me, but we just…ran. We're hiding in one of the abandoned buildings. We're both okay, but they were *right* behind us. Maybe ten of them."

"Which building? I need to know, Krystal."

"I don't fucking know, Val!" She screamed, sniffling as she cried. "We just *ran*…"

"It's okay. You're alright. Stay where you are." I said firmly. "Hide wherever you can. Find a closet, find a door that locks, do whatever you need to. I'm *going* to find you. Marcus, are you hearing this?"

"Yes!" He called, breathing heavily. "Go! I've got the front!"

"I'll take over perimeter defenses, Val. Dr. Weiss can set up the launcher. Go find them." Tony offered his support as I turned my focus back to Krystal. I faced the nearest set of buildings, looking up at the stone masonry of each one and trying to judge a path from the abandoned vehicles to the group of structures. Looking at her point of origin, I saw the massacre that prevented any call for help, throats having been ripped out by vicious fangs and others shot multiple times in the head.

Focus. You need to track them. Avenues of approach, obstacles, terrain. Look at your variables.

"Krystal. When you left the back of your vehicle, did you turn left?" I tried to keep the questions as simple as possible to avoid confusion.

"Yes." She breathed, sniffling again. "We went left."

"Okay. How far did you travel?" I looked up as one of our helicopters lifted from the roof of a building and began its journey south to begin transporting the casualties back to Quantico for treatment.

"I…don't know. I-…" She paused. "Vi says a couple of blocks. We stopped a few times. Couldn't lose them."

"Look around the room you're in. What does it look like?" I ran around the closest building, knowing they wouldn't have stopped their journey so soon if they were being pursued.

"There's…desks, offices. Wait…here." She cleared her throat, reading from something. "From the office of the Mayor of the District of Columbia."

The Wilson building.

"I know where you are!" I imparted eagerly, holding my rifle at the ready and scanning the street for any sign of lingering enemies. One unlucky member of Legacy's army ran across the road and, failing to see me, caught a bullet to his temple. "Okay. Get to the ground floor, and I-" A thundering explosion shook the air over my head, a lucky rocket fired by one of the Tortured having hit the Blackhawk that was taking off from the rooftop to my left. I sprinted across the street, avoiding some of the falling debris and looking up as the helicopter tumbled through the air before slamming into the side of a building just to the north of where I stood.

Some of the debris was lucky enough to find its way to my watching face, a fist-sized ball of metal and Kevlar smacking me with enough force to knock me to the ground and create a ripping pain through the right half of my skull. The only thing I was able to do was lay still for the first full minute after the devastating blow, the pain in my head and neck unbearable for too many long seconds. I pressed my hands against the sidewalk, my vision still blurry and distant, and forced myself into an upright position. Staring downward, I could see a small pool of blood from where I had lain and could hear the droplets from my face smacking into the cement. I took several stumbling steps onto the road, staring for a moment as the shock hit me before I took off in a dead sprint.

No. No, no. Please. Not the building they're hiding in.

The stone and mortar crumbled under the impact of the aircraft's weight, a mangled set of helicopter blades barely identifying what had struck the building. No fire had broken out, but the dust that spewed onto the street was enough to make it difficult to breathe a block away.

"Krystal!" I shouted, leaving the microphone on so I could speak as I ran. "Violet! Either of you, please say something!" I became more desperate, throwing my rifle aside as I approached the decimated face of the building and glowered at the remains. My eyesight was still severely hampered, a concussion noticeable and already affecting my thought patterns.

I'll die a hundred times over before either of them gets hurt.

"Krys-" I realized my voice was slightly off, and I put my hand to my mouth before feeling that my lips were wet with blood and clearly disfigured on the right side. "Krystal…" I rasped, looking for an opening in the side of the building before climbing through.

"Val…" Jalix started. "I'm sending backup to help-" Intense coughing from a feminine voice permeated his gesture, my spine nearly collapsing under the wave of relief that one or both of the ladies were alive.

"Krystal?" I asked again, making my way to the inside of the building. I had to climb the wreckage, entering the building on its second floor. The rubble was still shifting and sliding, the interior a decimated scene of antiquated furniture and crushed rock.

"Vi?" Krystal croaked, her coughing still audible over the radio, but not heard in my immediate surroundings. "Vi, are you okay?" I listened to Violet mumble a few words, enough of a reason to take a pause for myself. The pain in my skull was relentless, shooting across my right eye socket and down my jaw.

"Tony, we're at the doors. Securing a perimeter now." Marcus called, his transmission more important than any other that could have been made. "We've locked down a lane for you straight down the middle, but they're still firing at us from either side."

"We have escorts." Tony assured. "We're on the move. Arrival in sixty seconds." I had to inhale through my nose, my mouth repeatedly filling with blood.

"Krystal." I repeated.

"Val. We're here. We're trapped. But alive. My…I think my leg's broken, but it's not too bad. Vi's okay." I shook my head, trying to make sense of her words.

I can't…think straight. My head…

"Where are you?" I mumbled, struggling to amble down the nearest hallway.

"We're right below-…wait, go back! I think I just saw you!" The tenor of her voice rose to a panicked happiness, and I spun around to look for some sign of her presence. "Below you." She repeated. I looked at the floor under my feet, seeing an opening where the Blackhawk's cockpit had sheared through the flooring.

Krystal's vibrant blue hair was visible in the gap, barely a foot wide, and gave me enough reason to fall to my knees. She covered her mouth with her hand, crying quietly as I looked down at her. Violet was leaning against her shoulder, both of them seated in the narrow corner of a room and covered in dirt. Krystal's right leg was pinned by a large piece of stone, but they appeared otherwise unharmed. The Relic was out of its case, Krystal's other hand keeping it protected and cold.

Damn the Relic. I need to get them out of there.

"It's okay, Krystal." I tried comforting her. "I'm going to help-"

"What the hell happened?" She asked, removing her hand from her mouth and tilting her head as she stared at me in distress.

"Rocket. Hit one of the…Blackhawks. It crashed-"

"No, Val-…what happened to *you*?" Violet lifted her head at Krystal's question, tired eyes immediately shooting open and brimming with shocked tears.

"Oh, my God…" She whispered, looking at Krystal.

"I got hit by some debris. I'm okay." I tried to downplay the roaring pain in my head and the mental fog that diminished my competence.

"Val, you're *not* okay. Jesus. Have-…do you know what you look like?" Krystal asked, lifting her hand off the Relic to pull the cell phone from her pocket.

"Handsome." I joked, the only humor I could muster.

Krystal turned on her front-facing camera and held out her phone, showing me the image of my own, unrecognizable face. The right side had almost no skin left on it, burns cauterizing some of the flesh while the rest bled openly. My right mandible was exposed, the stark yellow-white bone of my jaw being a steep contrast against the blackened burns around it. My right eye was gone entirely, a hole of black and crimson left in its stead as I tried to mentally deal with the severity and permanence of my injuries.

You'll...you'll be okay. Alice will take care of you. Amy can heal you, at least enough to live.

"I...need to get you out-"

"All Operators, this is Marcus. We're breaching the White House now. We need confirmation of Relic One or we're going to have to find a landing zone for Relic Two." I stared at Krystal for a long moment, her happy blue eyes gazing at me while she slowly lifted the cylinder to the opening.

"Take it." She whispered, smiling through her tears. "We'll be okay."

"I'm *not* leaving you here." I murmured, spitting blood off to the side and realizing that even my ability to spit was a tremendous struggle. "You're my family." She shuddered, the dirt on her face washing away in a waterfall of tears that met her brilliant smile.

"Go save the day, handsome." She swallowed hard, kissing Violet on the top of her head as it rested on her shoulder again. "Jalix." She said into her radio with a shuddering breath. "Val has the Relic. He's on his way. And...Violet and I would *really* like a rescue team." I exhaled, laughing the best I could as I took the Relic into my gloved hands, staring into the blue glass indicator.

"I'll see you soon." The remains of my face contorted as I cried, locking eyes with one of my best friends as I made a promise I wasn't sure I could keep. She nodded, biting her lip silently.

"Krystal, I'm sending a team as soon as I have an opening. Hang in there." Jalix's voice was too calm, unaware of how difficult the situation on the ground had become. I took a few steps toward the obliterated opening to the outside world, stepping onto the pile of rubble and immediately falling. I slid down the piles of jagged rocks as I clutched the Relic to my chest in protection. My head hit the ground as I reached the bottom, the final insult in a long line of pain.

"Val, I think I see where you are. Head directly west. I'm going to have a handoff team pick up the Relic. Watch for Felix, she's going to meet you."

"Right…" I groaned, moving to stand before a shooting pain in my left leg forced me back to the ground.

What the hell happened now?

I ran my hand down my left leg, feeling intact bone and skin under my cargo pants until I reached my ankle. Clearly broken, the bone and cartilage punished my foot with waves of dull pain as I stared at the empty road ahead of me and trudged forward to the best of my ability. Each step was a labor in its own right, consciousness starting to slip as I had moments of stalled thought.

"Val, we have a problem!" Marcus roared.

"I'm…coming." I gurgled, more blood dripping down my throat. The open fields of the main battleground were devastated by violence and seemed too distant to ever reach.

Just keep…walking.

"It's Legacy!" He returned, his ferocity increased as the result of pure adrenaline. "Some kind of aircraft just came in from the north!"

"That's not possible." Jalix said calmly. "Marcus, I have nothing on sensors and can't see-"

"Jalix, I'm staring right at it! Lafayette Park, it's landing now!" I spun around, unable to see anything in the sky past the dead trees.

"Oh, no…" Sonya entered the conversation. "The stealth craft that Hamilton picked up. The one that caught their radar's attention before the convoy was attacked. It was in the north part of the city."

"It's a VTOL!" Marcus had to continue shouting over the sounds of withering machine gun fire. "Takes off like a helicopter, flies like a jet! It must have landed between buildings to hide, that's why it vanished from their radar and didn't show on yours!"

Lafayette Park…it's north of the White house. Blocked from view, shielded from gunfire. We can't get there in time.

"What the hell do we do?" Tony asked, likely looking to Jalix for guidance.

"Focus on the cure." Jalix's reply was curt, but I knew he was biting his tongue. "That's all that matters."

"He needs to pay!" Violet had apparently taken Krystal's radio, finding a sudden energy in the face of Legacy's escape. "Legacy *needs* to die!"

"There's nothing anyone can do, Vi."

"Sanchez, go scour the bodies for a launcher!"

"Sonya, with me."

"Kara, leave him!"

"I'm not letting him get away with this!"

"Kara, no!" I croaked desperately. The radio channel descended into pandemonium, all sense of order being lost. The only significance I could make was Kara requesting Sonya's presence, and it was something I knew stemmed from the two of them being physically closest to Legacy.

Sis…don't sacrifice yourself. Not again.

"We stay airborne. I don't care *what* kind of weapons it might have." Jalix was arguing with his pilot as I found a clearing, finally able to see the sky above the White House as Legacy's transportation made its way into my view. The aircraft had a set of thrusters pointed downward, lifting it vertically off the ground and rising just above the roof of the building he had just abandoned.

Just keep walking. Just keep moving forward.

"Kara, get off that roof, please!" Jalix begged.

"My team's pinned!" Marcus roared. "We can't fire at him!"

"I need a medic, now!" Tony shouted in anguish. "Brynn's down! Get me a medic!" My vision started to blur, a haze of monochromatic disruption keeping me from being functional in the panic of the moment.

Just...keep moving. Walk. Don't listen. Just...walk...

I was useless, even as I found myself standing on the battlefield less than a hundred yards from my goal. Tony's launcher was in place, surrounded by technicians as they worked diligently to get it operational. Some of them faltered as distant and scattered Tortured took shots of opportunity in a failed attempt at a resurgence. More than one bullet came dangerously close to me, but I was likely invisible as an unmoving object among the chaos. I was physically unable to walk any further, either shock or pain keeping me immobile as I stood alone among a sea of corpses and watched as everything we had worked for began to fall apart.

Demolished vehicles – piles of unidentifiable scrap to the unknowing – spewed clouds of black smoke into the air around me and filled my nostrils with a putrid and burning fume. I became an observer, desperately holding onto consciousness as I clutched the frigid canister to my chest and stared into the sky. Legacy's jet began to slowly move in my direction, clearly bound for a destination to the east, and its thrusters started to fold upward as it picked up speed.

If I live...I'm going to find you after all of this. I'm going to track you down and I'm going to make you pay for every crime you've committed. And I'm going to take half of your face as payment.

The aircraft lurched forward as the thrusters engaged, and as if grasped by the hand of a deity, became completely frozen in its place hundreds of feet above the ground. Short, white-orange flames still erupted from its turbines, but it sat entirely still in its spot against the blue winter sky. A brief second passed, its engines firing with more ferocity and trying desperately to escape its invisible hold. I stared in confused awe, wondering whether I was hallucinating from pain or my concussion before I heard a brief, whimpering grunt through the radio.

No…that's not possible…

Another short gasp for air signaled an incomprehensible struggle, followed by a bloodcurdling scream that I could hear without the need for my radio's earpiece. The left wing of the aircraft exploded in a violent shockwave of pure force, shearing it from the body and throwing them in separate directions. In a move of primal reaction, I dove out of the way as the massive metal wing plummeted toward me and missed my body by only a few short feet. I quickly crawled backward against a defective vehicle, avoiding the growing flames from igniting jet fuel, and stared at the sky as Legacy's only hope at escape spun out of control like the last leaf from an autumn tree. It spiraled backward through the air, partially thrown by the initial shockwave, and disappeared behind one of the buildings to the northeast in a rumbling series of collisions.

We did it. He…he's dead.

"Val!" Tony called. "We need the Relic now!" I breathed heavily, trying to let my throat form words and managing only to hiss occasional breaths.

Tony…always the professional.

"Val, I lost you. What's your status?" Jalix asked, his own sense of concern growing. "Val?"

You were a good friend, man. Glad you married my sister.

"I see him." Felix had tuned into our radio station to relay my whereabouts, my fading vision picking up her face as she fell to her knees in front of me and whipped off her helmet. The Relic sat on my lap, my hands wrapped around it as she watched me with growing realization. "Oh, shit…" She whispered, staring at my face before looking down at the object in my hands. With all the energy I had left, I poured my strength into the Relic, the canister moving an inch off my legs before falling again, my arms quickly growing numb and distant.

I…can't lift it…

Felix inhaled sharply, ripping it from my grasp and kicking off in a sprint back toward her allies.

Congrats, kid…you just won us the war.

I let the left half of my face curl into as much of a smile as I could while feeling my head fall limply onto my shoulder and drifting off into the deepest, darkest sleep of my long life.

'Til death…do us part. I'll always love you, Alice.

BATTLEGROUND

SONYA

Raven sighed, taking a step back from the door and lightly scuffing her shoe into the concrete. Despite the obvious, I tried my luck anyway and pulled on the metal handle of the door as if our efforts would yield different results.

"It's locked, genius." She rolled her eyes, shaking her head in disbelief.

"I'm the wrong one to get snippy with." I warned, briefly glaring at her. "I know it's locked, but my question is whether or not it's worth breaking." She shrugged, caring far less than I did about speaking with Violet.

"Grown woman. Her decision. She wants to stay locked in an unfinished nightclub, I say let her. She's got shit to deal with."

"And shouldn't deal with it alone. This how you treat all your friends?" I was bewildered at her lack of empathy before I remembered her upbringing.

"Yep. All two of them." She retorted.

"Well, she's apparently your family. Not an acquaintance. She deserves more than that." I paused, Raven suddenly growing more concerned as the muffled wail of Violet's mournful weeping could be heard even through the thick metal doors. "And if you have any hope in

hell of this city working, you need to think of the rest of them as family, too. Related or not."

"The rest of them? What, you're not interested?" Her words tried to return to their former iciness, but failed at the sounds of Violet's anguish so close to us.

"I just know better than to have expectations of the emotionally numb. Seen it in Kara, seen it in Krystal, and I know what you're made of. I'm not interested in the empathy of a dead woman. I'll be around when you find a soul." She stepped away from the door at my comment, turning toward me aggressively, yet with no intent of attempting violence.

"You're one to talk. You act so sweet in front of everyone else. Sonya, the enlightened spirit of Vampyres. The savior of Sorrow. And here you are, as toxic as any of them." She sneered. I raised my eyebrows, forsaking Violet for a moment and knowing that Raven needed dealt with before she could be allowed anywhere near her twin sister.

"There is a stark difference between knowing who deserves my time, love, and energy, and being a toxic person. Everyone is given a chance, multiple chances, even. But you eroded any trust I could have had long before we met. Some of my first memories after my recovery are rescuing Kara and Val from your clutches, stopping Krystal's suicide because Kara was taken from her, and then losing her to death anyway. After that, it was a lot of apocalypse with some mourning mixed in, all because of your Project Catalyst." I paused, letting my words sink in. "You need to earn anything that I have to give. Unlike everyone else I care for, you're not starting off as an innocent person with a fresh start."

"Oh, this isn't enough?" She gestured around her, indicating that she was referring to the city.

"Not even close." I chuckled. "You'd have done all of this anyway. The fact that we're here, and alive, is a convenient coincidence. Your manipulation over Eric is transparent, and your personality made him a darker person. You think you've-"

"I've paid for my crimes." She said huskily, her voice drawn in a darker tone. "What you and Kara rescued me from – the same thing

Alice went through – that's something worse than I deserved. Dying was worse than I deserved. And yet-"

"And yet you act like right here, right now, is about you." I pressed my lips together, gesturing toward the door. She cleared her throat, looking at her shoes briefly.

"I need you on my side if I'm going to talk to Violet." She started. "Not for my sake. But for hers. If I go in there as my father's progeny…that's all she's going to see of herself. It's going to destroy her. I'm her twin sister. I'm a look in the mirror at what she could have been." I stared at her in stunned silence as her statement sharply contrasted everything I had expected from her personality. "It's the same reason I changed my appearance before I came into your lives. The doll makeup, the Viking hair. Even keeping up with my damn tan. I didn't need this side of things revealed, and I didn't want it to be, but here we are. Look, I don't need to earn your trust, Sonya. I'll do that through my actions in the coming war. But right now…I need to borrow it." She tilted her head, the left side of her hair shaved down while the top and right side of her head boasted a clear family trait of Kara's lineage.

"For Violet's sake, I will play nice." I touched the door, quickly whipping the deadbolt open with my mind and accidentally stripping the lock. "The way she perceives herself may depend on your words." I pushed one door open just wide enough for us to enter. "Choose wisely."

"Sup, bitch?" Raven immediately shattered any sense of peace with her casual and inappropriate entry to the dark space ahead of us. I reached to the left of the door and felt around for light switches, finding only one and turning it on. Rather than a flood of lights above our heads, a gentle glow of blue luminescence came from recessed lighting around the upper edges of the room. The stools at the bar were upturned, siting off the ground and neatly stored with one exception. One of them held a heartbroken, dark-haired young woman who leaned into the surface heavily and ignored our presence entirely.

"Vi." I started, closing the door behind me. "It's just Raven and I. We're here to check on you. Not to lecture." She stifled a heaving sob in her chest, sniffling and nodding while her back was turned to us. We

approached, crossing a few feet of the entryway and turning right to descend into the lowered bar area. Raven grabbed two stools, setting them next to Violet but keeping a respectful distance.

"Thanks." Violet finally managed to whisper, turning her head slightly. "But that's my line." Raven laughed quietly, nodding.

"I know. But we're all bitches here. Said it yourself." I was surprised that Raven was able to break into conversation with her so quickly. "Do you want us here?" The question surprised us both, a blunt and obvious subject already sensitive. Violet didn't answer right away, several attempts to compose herself slipping from her grasp.

"Yeah." She whispered finally. "But you might not like what I have to say." She coughed, sniffling several times and wiping her eyes on the sleeve of her shirt.

"Won't be anything I haven't said myself." Raven returned. I took a seat next to her and tried observing rather than inserting myself into the conversation. "When I found out Kara was my mother…to say I was pissed off is an understatement. But I had other reasons." I grabbed Raven's arm, hissing into her ear.

"It's not about you." I growled quietly. She shook my arm away, shooting me a frustrated glare before she continued.

"I never saw the evil in my father. I only saw his effort to create this…empire of peace. A world where humans weren't warring with each other, weren't shooting each other in the streets. A world where basic human rights weren't being stripped away and personal security wasn't needed. So to me, Kara had abandoned me. Never wanted me, never came for me. He talked about her efforts, everything she was doing to his empire. And sure, I knew that maybe my father was going about his prospects the wrong way. I wasn't blind. But to me, Kara was destroying everything he was working for in an attempt to wipe out everything he built. And…that included me. I always thought she'd be the one to kill me. Ironic that the thing that killed her wasn't her firstborn daughter, but her third."

"Don't talk about Amy like that." Violet said quietly, turning her head.

"Didn't mean it that way." Raven defended. "Only a statement of fact. Either way, I just meant I always thought Kara was going to come after me and wipe me off the map like she wanted with my father. In fact, he told me I'd be a target. I lived my whole life hating Kara. Hating you." Violet's head snapped upward at the statement, staring at Raven in curiosity. Her tears still fell, but weren't controlled by the heaving sobs in her stomach that dominated her body when we first entered the room.

"Me? Why me?" She asked simply.

"You were wanted. Loved. Kara rescued you from-"

"Rescued?" Violet shouted incredulously. Much more animated than before, she stood up from her spot at the bar and took a step back, folding her arms. "You have no idea what I went through in the foster system!" Raven remained silent, letting Violet vent her lungs into the waiting air. "I've been beaten, burned, told I was useless, used for government checks, abandoned in malls and grocery stores, and that was just from one set of foster parents! Kara could have prevented all of that by keeping me from the start instead of throwing me away like the rest of them did!"

"Vi, you didn't hear the story. Kara didn't put you into the foster system." I sighed, bracing for the consequences. "I did." She stared at me for a long moment, too long, and looked across the dim room with an unwavering stare.

"What? You?"

"Kara was-…keep in mind, I don't remember any of this, okay? Kara was catatonic when Alice and I broke out of Schillinger's prison. I had you in my arms, Alice had Kara. Your mother-"

"Don't call her that." Violet growled forcefully. In a way only Kara had ever managed with her voice, the hair on the back of my neck stood up in dread.

"Fine. Kara was mentally absent for months. Staring at the wall, saying nothing, not eating or drinking. The trauma was too much for her mind to handle, so it shut down. I knew that if I…if you were introduced to her in any way, you would be a symbol of that trauma. So I hid you back in the US while Alice and I kept tabs on you.

Kara…never really knew you existed at first. Only that she had given birth, and her daughter was gone. Everything else was repressed."

"Sorry to interrupt-" Raven began. *"-but that part is important. And you need to understand how much depth there is to your escape from what might have happened. You being around Kara while she recovered, while she tried to find herself…you really think you would have been loved any more than being rescued as a teenager?"* Violet turned around, leaning against the wall to hide her face from us.

"Vi…when we told her, after she started to become a person again, she cried for days. Days. She couldn't handle the thought of another person being like her, being at risk of the same things she was. Of being targeted. But we found out about what was happening to you too late. The reports from Child Services were private, and we had no idea to look for them. Kara had nothing to do with you being abandoned. It…was me." I held back the lump in my throat, knowing there was nothing Alice and I could have done at the time. Regardless, an unwavering guilt kept me from any feelings of positive progress in helping Violet feel any better.

"It's a lot to take in." Raven added. *"But there's no one person to blame for what you went through. The bottom line is that you were loved from the moment you were born. If not by Kara until later in your life, then by Sonya and Alice from the very beginning."*

"It explains so much…and I hate that." Violet sniffled, turning to face us again. *"It shouldn't make sense, and it does. I need to hear this in her words, and I can't-…I don't want to talk to her."* The exhaustion from crying too much had started to take form, letting a slump overtake her shoulders and her eyes to diminish to a reddened anguish.

"Your…presence-" I tried to choose my words carefully. *"Triggered one of Kara's biggest changes. When she visited you, finally adopted you and brought you to the city, she started to feel again. Slowly. She started to lose who Sorrow was and become Kara again. And Jalix…she saw him as someone who could share that life with both of you. Amy was the turning point. Kara's death was the final stake in Sorrow's heart. When she came back to life-"*

"Sorrow." Violet mumbled. "Was…that was because of me, wasn't it? Because of us?" She asked the question to Raven, who glanced at me briefly before answering.

"According to Alice, it was the word Kara first responded to." Raven looked away from Violet for a moment. "Alice asked Kara how she felt, trying to get her to speak, to say…anything. And she tried to offer emotions. Sadness, anger, shock…when Alice said the word sorrow, Kara finally looked over at her and nodded. After that, Alice used it as a codename while trying to get herself and Kara out of Russia and back home. The name stuck, I guess."

"Not many people in the city knew Kara anyway. She was gone a lot, and when she was present, she was virtually a ghost. I was the friendly one, she was the huntress. After you were born, that codename became a whisper. A rumor, then a legend. The woman who faced down Schillinger in person and lived. Sorrow. The icon of defiance in the face of despair." I recounted the events from Alice's explanations.

"I never knew." Violet mumbled, shaking her head. "She never…even Val never really told me. Just that it was an old codename that stuck."

"Because he never knew. No one knew. Only Alice and I. And then after my injury…only Alice."

"Even I never got the whole story. My father never fully explained it. Maybe he never knew or-"

"Our father." Violet quietly corrected Raven. "Not just yours."

"No." Raven stood, approaching Violet and picking up her hand to hold it gently. "My father. And mine alone. You're the product of a different environment. You don't have the evil inside you that I do."

"You're admitting you're still the evil bitch of the group?" Violet asked, half-chuckling.

"Yes." Raven replied honestly. "I can't take back what I've done. And I'll always live with that. But you don't have the ghosts that I do. You don't have the skeletons in your closet that I do. You have a chance. And that…that's more than I ever had. You have love, the love of everyone around you."

"I need time." Violet pulled her hand away, taking several steps away from us. "Alone. I can't-"

"You can have your time." I smiled at her, nodding. "But you'll never be alone. Never again."

***

"Fox three, fox three." The armored vehicle's hull roared as bullets ricocheted away from its body and protected us from a violent and early death. Kara smirked at me, gesturing around us.

"Wish you remembered some of our earlier adventures." She tapped her helmet. "This isn't our first time in this situation."

"First time we've had to worry about airstrikes, I'll bet." I returned.

"Not anymore. Sounds like Layla nailed the bastard." I let her brief statement of victory become a pause in our back-and-forth, appreciating that we had conquered one of many important facets of the battle. I tried to ignore the noise through the radio, thinking about Amy and Alice in the vehicles behind us. I could feel the slight turn as we changed paths and broke away from the rest of Val's forces, the helicopters that thundered overhead becoming a good indicator of our location.

We're getting close.

"You okay?" Kara asked, reaching out to touch my hand. I nodded, sighing as I looked around us.

"Yeah, sorry. Just thinking. Preparing." We were alone in our vehicle, the driver being the only other occupant and allowing us some peace without watching eyes.

"Alice, you hear me?" Kara asked, leaning back in her seat and touching her earpiece. I couldn't hear her voice through my own, and started checking the electronics to ensure I had set everything up correctly. Looking over at her vest, I realized that she had two radios, and had one earpiece hidden behind the hair covering her left ear.

"Private conversation?" I teased, gesturing to her setup.

"Channel A-two. For the boss ladies only." She winked, smiling as I adjusted the channel. Alice's voice started to come through as I clipped the device to my chest again.

"-ming up on our first building. Looks like they're signaling that it's clear…" Her voice sounded mystified, almost confused that her security didn't see any of the Tortured in the building they were checking first.

"Thought Jalix said not to use any other channels." I suggested, implying that he should be kept in the loop.

"*Jalix* also doesn't want to hear his wife's charming wit for the next few hours. If we have anything relevant, I'll call it out, but you and I are largely on our own, anyway. We're here for Alice and the civilians, not for Val's side of the battle."

"Oh, I'm glad to hear that Alice has your support, *mom*." Amy chimed in over the radio, clearly teasing Kara about being left out. "Looks like you guys are almost here. Alice and I will be inside." We slowed down, our weight shifting toward the cockpit and rocking us as we came to a halt. Kara went to stand and paused, listening to something on the main channel. She leaned toward the driver, tapping him on the shoulder and giving him a thumbs-up.

"Alice just asked for the transport buses and some armed security." She tapped my back as we made our way out of the truck and looked at our surroundings. "She said the civilians are in rough shape." I nodded, but her words had less weight than the pandemonium that I struggled to make sense of. We were far enough to the north that a wide street separated us from the east buildings under Taylor's responsibility, but close enough to hear the roar of gunfire from the main arena between Val and the White House.

We're behind the enemy. If we could just sneak up…

"Sonya." Kara said quietly, touching my shoulder. I spun, facing her as I was jerked away from my daze.

"Yeah, sorry. I'm good. Let's go." Our transports created a semi-circle of protective cover, keeping us out of sight from watching eyes and shielding us from stray bullets as we approached the front doors of our objective. Soldiers, some that I even recognized from many hours of training, stood watch and provided safe passage to Amy and Alice. Neither of them had made it far into the building, as the interior was a reeking disgrace of wasting corpses and mostly-dead Vampyres.

"What the hell-" Kara started.

"We need more medics." Alice determined, shaking her head as Amy connected a bag of Factor Five to the arm of a man whose legs were missing. It was an unfortunately common sight, the floor's surface bearing a thin coating of dried blood across the massive width of the large hall we stood in and hosting an uncountable number of dead and dying across the length of its walls. Quiet groans of pain could be heard echoing toward us, while other cries for help were more dominant against the soundscape.

This must be what hell looks like.

There was no justification for the manner in which the people had been handled, some of the dead being mutilated and torn into unidentifiable piles of discarded organs while others were thrown against the piles of dead just to live out their remaining moments. It was clear that the Tortured had earned their name, as nothing could have broken a person more than being subjected to the environment that surrounded us. Even those who still clung to life were bleeding openly, covered in burns, or missing pieces of their body. The smell was almost too horrifying to bear for more than a few moments, and it was definitely one that was unrecognizable even in comparison to other foul odors.

Mostly men…these must have been a rush to manufacture soldiers for the fight.

"God, I didn't think it would be this bad." Amy sighed, pushing away from her patient and looking around the room. "So many are just…dead. What-" She snorted, her fist curling into a ball of knuckles. "What *good* does that even do them? How does it help their numbers to kill these people?"

Gold stars. Red flags and black lines. Winter nights and weary eyes. Death. Dismay.

"This…seems familiar, almost." I looked at Kara in confusion, reaching out once again to memories that didn't exist. "I swear, it's like we've been here before. I know that's a horrible thing to say-"

"No, you're right." Kara realized, looking around. The windows had been shuttered, only sparse rays of light casting a grim view onto the scene. "Dachau. Nazi Germany. We've been here…just not for a rescue."

"Not a mistake I'm making twice." Alice grunted, pulling a young man away from a stack of the deceased Vampyres and watching him struggle for air. "Amy, collapsed lung, right side. Shattered ribcage…and he's jaundiced. Some kind of liver damage."

"I'm on it." Amy whispered, shaking herself out of the terror and committing to her own sense of goodwill. "How the hell are we going to get through this many on our own?" Alice looked around at Amy's observation, watching the dozen nurses she brought hastily pick through the masses of dead to find the living.

"Legacy's gonna pay for this." Kara assured, taking several more steps toward the center of the hall. The environment resembled a museum, but one stripped of its artifacts and left as an empty space. "This is more evil than even Schillinger managed to conjure."

"This evil *is* Schillinger." My reminder didn't seem to help her growing fury, but reminded her that the very core of the fight stemmed from a longstanding war. "This is what he looks like without his shackles."

"Alice, I need more Factor Five!" Amy gasped suddenly, turning to look at her colleague.

"What? He'll be fine, we have more pressing patients-"

"He's trying to talk to us. To…Kara, I think." We all turned, seeing the young man's eyes locked onto Kara and flicker with the remnants of his alertness. "He needs to tell us something, but he's fading fast."

"Alright, hold on." Alice stepped away from her own patient, who had seemingly died only moments ago, and dropped her bag next to Amy. As they went to work, Kara leaned in to speak quietly.

"Most of them are too bad to be treated at Quantico. I know that's our evac point for casualties, but they're not set up to handle this much." She paused, leaning back to look into my eyes. "Can they make the drive to Vanaheim?"

"Why drive?" I returned. "The Blackhawks-"

"Are the reason Quantico is already going to be stressed to its limits. Those helos are going to be full to capacity with fallen soldiers and the attending medics. Alice trained them well, but they're not nurses or doctors. Vanaheim's the only place-"

"That we can't have revealed right now." I argued. "Sending a convoy of wounded back to the city is only going to expose where we've been hiding."

"Legacy attacked us, Sonya. *In* Vanaheim. That ship sailed."

"Then why are you even asking me? You seem to have your mind made up." The stress antagonized my tone, but I was trying not to sound angry with her. She closed her eyes, taking in a deep breath before looking at me again.

"I want to know if I'd be making a bad call." She emphasized. "I want your input."

She trusts me. I've done this before. I forget that I used to keep her in check. That I was…the same leader that she is today.

"It's the right thing to do." I decided. "Plus it takes them further north like we planned. If we load the buses and have all the windows down, the cure can-"

"The cure will kill them." Kara warned. "Whoever isn't stable…Sonya, our virus is the only thing keeping some of them alive. Factor Five is almost useless in humans."

"We don't have a choice. The cure…it's the whole reason we're here. If we can't save those too far gone, that's not our fault. We came here to do everything we could, Kara. And we have."

"*We* haven't." She sighed, looking around as she realized how useless the two of us were in the grand scheme of things. "Alice, use the security to start hauling anyone stable out to the buses. Keep the windows rolled down and tell the drivers to head to Vanaheim the moment the cure is released."

"Yeah, got it." Alice mumbled, speaking into her second radio as she darted away to rescue another doomed patient.

Kara leaned away from me suddenly, holding up a single finger and listening to the shared radio channel of Jalix's commanders. I waited for a long minute, desiring to hear what was going on and quickly coming to terms with the fact that I wanted nothing to do with whatever Kara was listening to. Her face contorted briefly, horrified sadness forcing her to shed more than a few tears before she ripped out the earpiece in frustrated anguish and let it dangle from her shoulder.

"Taylor." She whispered, tilting her head and staring at me tearily. "She…didn't make it. I'll spare you the details."

"Oh, no." I sighed, closing my eyes and praying that she had, at the very least, found a quick death in whatever fate fell upon her.

"Mom. Sonya." Amy waved us over, watching us as she sat her patient upright and cracked a vial of smelling salts under his nose. As his head dipped, the odor registered in his brain and he shot upright with his eyes wide. "Hey. You were trying to talk. What's going on?" Amy asked.

"Y-you…" He pointed at Kara. "You." He whispered, shaking violently.

"Me, yes. Kara. I'm here to help you." Kara wiped her eyes, trying to regain her sense of control.

"No, they…*you*…" His lips curled, attempting to prevent tears. "He k-knew you were coming. T-tried to kill…us…" He looked around, overtaken by the horrors of his environment. "Didn't want us saved." He paused, taking a few deep breaths. "He gave orders to kill everyone. The Tortured…killed some. Fed on some. Others had it even worse."

"*Fed?*" Kara asked incredulously. "They drained some of you?"

"We had real blood, mixed with the Factor Five in our systems." He nodded. "It was the best drug they ever had. Legacy never knew. Apparently they've been doing it for a while. They would keep some of us alive, the strong-willed ones, just to feed on."

Absolute monsters.

"They're not going to hurt you anymore." Amy tried calming him. "We're fighting them-"

"Not all of them. That-that's what I had to tell you!" He exclaimed, suddenly realizing that he had wanted to speak with us for a specific purpose. "There's more. More than just on the battlefield. The Tortured that weren't under Legacy's control took one of the-"

"Wait, the *what?*" I demanded. "What do you mean the ones that *weren't* in his control?"

"You…didn't know?" He asked innocently. "I heard so many of them talking, they wouldn't shut up about it. A bunch of them di-didn't agree with Legacy. Didn't think anyone should rule over them. They may have been broken, but…they developed their own willpower over time. They're waiting until the battle brings attrition to both sides, diminishes the numbers, then they want to come in and finish the job. Take the White House and the cure for themselves."

"Disobeying Legacy's orders." Kara mumbled, shaking her head.

"The rogue team that took Alice and the girls. The one we rescued them from, that Rachel was in charge of. They were proof, how did we not see it?" I realized.

"They were supposed to deliver us and had their own ideas." Amy agreed with me. "Proof that Legacy can't control his own army."

"All I know is they operate out of a building not far from here." The young man gestured. "Maybe two hundred of them, could be even more. And they're waiting."

"Not for long." Kara growled, standing up with me. "Amy, I need you and Alice working overtime. We need *everyone* on those buses. Even if they're on the brink of death, they need to be ready. You guys can fix them on the way."

"I…won't be able to save some of them. Not on the trip back to Vanaheim." Amy grimaced, looking into her mother's eyes.

She'll be human. She won't have her powers anymore. Her and Alice will have to resort to surgical options.

"Right." Kara whispered. "Do what you can, as fast as you can. Sonya and I are going to take out those Tortured before they can reinforce the main group. If we don't get to them, Tony, Val, and Marcus don't stand a chance."

"Go, I'll tell Alice. I love you both. Be careful."

"Hey, which building? We need to know what it looks like." I asked Amy's patient, grabbing Kara before she ran off.

"The tallest one just northwest of here. It's gotta be fifteen, twenty stories high. It's for a bank or a tech company or something."

"Got it." I nodded once, watching the tips of Amy's lustrous silver hair stain red with blood as she laid him down to rest and recover. "Back doors." I pointed, indicating to Kara what our best route would be. I looked around as we jogged, trying to ignore the death and torment that surrounded us. "Where'd Alice go?"

"Not our focus right now." Kara breathed, throwing open the doors and exposing us to the louder noise of the warzone. It was far enough from us to lack a warrant for immediate concern, but thinking of Val and the others was a torture in its own right. "That must be the building. We need to stay out of sight." Kara pointed, a towering structure dominating the shorter buildings around it.

"How the hell are we going to kill them all? We need backup, some of Val's-"

"Val needs every soldier he has. This one's ours." She returned, analyzing the space around us for a vantage point or avenue of approach.

"Kara." I paused, touching her shoulder. "How the *hell* are we going to kill them all? If he's right, we can't take out two hundred-"

"We don't have a choice, Sonya. Val can't spare the soldiers, Marcus needs to hit Legacy, and Taylor's teams have to watch the streets once their own areas are cleaned up. We're alone."

"Alone or not, we *can't* do it. It's too many." Kara stared upward for a moment, the slightest smirk creeping across her lips.

"Then we don't fight *them*. We fight the building."

This is such an overestimation of our powers. Even combined, that's a hell of a feat.

"How do you fight a *building*?" I asked, half of me being sarcastic and the other half looking for answers.

"One brick at a time, babe. Come on, I have an idea." She patted my arm briefly before she led the way along the westbound street to our left. I watched the skyscraper nervously as we ran, paranoid that someone was watching through the windows and was capable of seeing our efforts to get closer. "This way." She stopped suddenly in front of another building, bringing her elbow sharply into the door and shattering the glass so we could walk through. "You take this one. Hit the roof. I'll be next door." I made my way inside, the unlit interior exposing a lack of use in spite of its potential as an office space. Looking around, I was able to find the doors to the stairwell tucked into the corner of the bottom floor and made my way toward it.

"Got any more details on this plan?" I tapped my earpiece to speak with her, pushing the doors open and climbing floor after floor.

"Not particularly. But if we start with a corner of that skyscraper and keep pulling chunks away from the bottom, it'll eventually reach a breaking point." She returned.

"Oh. Like that, uh…the damn…game with the blocks. Alice and I played it during my recovery. It was a fine-motor skills thing. The hell was it called…?" I paused in the stairwell, furrowing my brow and trying to remember the name of the often rage-inducing game we had shared.

"Alice, not a word." Kara quipped, reminding me that she was a part of our private channel.

"Busy." Alice returned briefly, apparently requesting that she be left out of the conversation.

"Oh, come on. Kara, I *know* you know what I'm talking about." I sighed, continuing my path across the last few sets of winding stairs.

"Yep." She agreed gleefully, sending my brain into a spiraling overdrive.

This is so, so rude. Okay, it's a game of stacked blocks. Or do you…stack the blocks? No, they start stacked. And you yell something at the end. Jamba? Jinkies? What the hell is it?

I threw open the door of my building's roof access, watching Kara do the same a few dozen yards to my left and expose a much greater view of our target. The building did, indeed, belong to a banking company, and had the potential to hide the hundreds of Tortured that their victim had mentioned.

"It's not called Jackpot, is it?"

"Nope. How's your view of the objective?"

"Damn it. And I can see it just fine." I returned, chuckling. "Oh, Jigsaw, right? Maybe?"

"Not even close." She waited for a moment as we both readied ourselves, the nearest corner of the building the only one we could see from the section of the city we occupied. "Ready?"

"You can go first." I exhaled, crouching to stare at the building's construction and start assembling the mixed sensations in my mind.

Concrete. Looks poured. Smooth, but porous. Strong and cohesive. Might be reinforced with rebar. Cold and hard, but flexible under enough force. Steel beams for support and structure. Supporting thousands of pounds.

I watched Kara stare at the building across the distance between us, raising her hand and holding a steady position before pulling back her fist and letting the unrelenting forces of her abilities tear a massive chunk from the corner of the structure. In an explosive surge, the building materials I had correctly guessed flooded the street in a dusty, violent wave of energy.

"Your turn." She groaned, taking a moment to recover.

"Jingle!" I asserted. "It's Jingle." I lifted my hand, envisioning my grasp on the nearest wall before letting it fill with a surge of explosive energy. It crumbled with the same result as Kara's efforts, but to a lesser scale.

"Nope, good guess. Focus on the *ceiling* of the first floor, too. Those rafters." She suggested, mirroring her first set of actions with another, powerful tug and the ripping of the building's bottom corner into decimated pieces.

Pieces of the steel reinforcements started to shear, accompanying the cement and rubble that cascaded onto the road. I was already feeling the effects from the first pull, and knew that even Kara would have been feeling the physical impact after both explosions. Regardless, I mustered my strength, standing and reaching out to the structure once more.

Crushing, unimaginable weight. Letting the steel beams succumb to the forces above them. Freeing them, pulling them away from their bolts.

"Jiggle!" I roared, ripping away the largest section yet and almost collapsing under the fatigue that surged up from the base of my spine and infected my eyes with a dim set of spots. I ended up sitting down for a moment, trying to recover before the next effort.

"We're talking about a child's game, not your ass." Her words were humorous but labored as she breathed as heavily as I did.

"Watching my ass, are you?" I quipped, gulping air and listening to Kara's next set of results. I glanced up, seeing the building itself begin to exhibit signs of stress. The windows on the bottom several floors had shattered, the tiniest degree of a lean overtaking the precise straightness it had before we began. I could see Tortured within the building start to panic, the fleeting images of bodies that sprinted past the windows giving me hope that we could take them out before they could escape. I knelt, starting to get back into position and watching Kara fall to her knees unintentionally. "Hey. Hang in there." I added.

"I am. I'm alright." She nodded, gesturing to me. "Your turn." It was hard to see her face, but I could tell that another effort would likely force her to pass out.

This isn't just another struggle. This is to save everyone down there fighting.

I bowed my head for a moment, closing my eyes and letting the thoughts of my family give me the confidence and energy I needed to finish our task. I glowered at the building, watching each and every corner, every structural anomaly and sign of weakness guide me to the perfect spot. I lifted my hand, reaching out before I paused, starting to laugh.

"You okay?" Kara asked, her voice audible to my left but louder and close in my earpiece.

"Yeah." I sighed, closing my fist and letting my adrenaline nourish my abilities with merciless power. "*Jenga!*" I roared, pulling back and watching the support column in the center of the bottom floor disintegrate into crumbs of useless dirt and dust.

Gravity didn't hesitate to take control, a thundering collapse shattering the building as it was brought to the ground in waves of earsplitting noise. Although the towering building leaned away from us, the top floors started to slide on the layers of material underneath and make their way toward us in a terrifying tsunami of unstoppable force. Kara quickly looked at me, and without saying anything, we both began a ripping sprint across the next several rooftops, leaping across the gaps between them and earning every inch of distance we could from the impending doom that chased us.

As Kara stopped and spun around, I could feel the ground under my feet wash away as my boot left its surface. She reached out quickly, snatching me away from an unforgiving fall, and used her powers to lift me the last few feet and across the final gap. Leaning against one another, we turned around to see the results of our destruction and stared in awe at the river of carnage that now separated us from Alice and Amy's position. The remains of the skyscraper had crushed a small building adjacent to where the medical staff had been working, but left their temporary headquarters thankfully untouched.

"Take a break?" Kara suggested quietly, lowering herself to the ground and pulling the medical kit from her lower back. I did the same, my body roaring in pain from the craving that pained my stomach. I pulled out the contents of the kit, staring at them for a moment before glancing at Kara.

"The fight's not over yet. Taking out those two hundred Tortured isn't gonna do much." I looked to our south and nodded to the battlefield, hidden behind a row of buildings. "We could go help."

"Or we could go after Legacy." Kara pointed to our right, the White House now a reasonable distance from us. We both still breathed heavily, sucking in gulps of air. "I can't see what kind of defenses he has in front, but…we might be able to take him."

"Not without help." I picked up the bag of Factor Five and shook it lightly. "Worth it?" She looked away for a moment, staring at her own dosage before nodding.

"That took a lot out of me. And if we get hurt, having it hooked up already will help. Yeah, let's do it." We started to prepare the bags, connecting IV lines and stashing the medicine itself on the pouches near our shoulder blades.

"I should…get back on the radio." Kara paused as she slid a needle into her arm, withdrawing the metallic component and leaving the flexible plastic port in place. I reached over and placed a piece of tape over it for extra support before she continued. "Jalix might be able to tell us where we need the most help."

"Agreed." I sighed, feeling the brief euphoria and rush of energy as the medicine ripped through my arm and across my chest. I tossed the needle off the edge of the building and tuned my radio back into the shared channel. Immediately, a calamity of voices erupted and flooded both of us with information.

"All Operators, this is Marcus. We're breaching the White House now. We need confirmation of Relic One or we're going to have to find a landing zone for Relic Two." The familiar voice of our raid forces' commander incited an elated smile between the two of us.

"They reached the doors. They made it. Val made it!" Kara giggled, collapsing into me with a forceful hug. I shared her embrace, laughing as tears made their way down my face in sheer happiness. We spent a long moment holding one another, the centuries-long battle for our freedom coming to an end with a success we couldn't have imagined.

"Val, I think I see where you are. Head directly west. I'm going to have a handoff team pick up the Relic. Watch for Felix, she's going to meet you." Jalix's proud voice was stressed, but composed.

"Right…" Val grunted, struggling with something.

"He made it." I echoed, squeezing her torso gently. "Not over yet, though." I pulled away, letting out a long sigh. "We have work to do. We can-" We both noticed the same sound, a glaring contrast from the noises of battle, and spun to face the direction it came from. Kara stood slowly, watching in horror as a low-flying aircraft began to lower itself onto the area just north of the White House.

"No…" Kara whispered, her fist curling into a mass of infuriated knuckles.

"Val, we have a problem!" Marcus roared.

"I'm…coming." Val's voice was distant and distorted as if something had damaged his microphone.

"It's Legacy!" Marcus began to audibly panic. "Some kind of aircraft just came in from the north!"

"That's not possible." Jalix returned. "Marcus, I have nothing on sensors and can't see-"

"Jalix, I'm staring right at it! Lafayette Park, it's landing now!"

How did we not see this coming? How couldn't Jalix detect it?

"Oh, no…" I mumbled, pressing the tip of my finger against my earpiece while looking at Kara. "The stealth craft that Hamilton picked up. The one that caught their radar's attention before the convoy was attacked. It was in the north part of the city-" I jumped, my sentence ending without further explanation as gunfire rang out from the direction of the aircraft. Clearly, the area had been heavily fortified with a defensive position.

"It's a VTOL!" Marcus screamed over the sound of his team returning fire. "Takes off like a helicopter, flies like a jet! It must have landed between buildings to hide, that's why it vanished from their radar and didn't show on yours!"

We can make it.

"Kara, we could go." I started, grabbing her arm so she would focus her attention on me. "We could make it." She stared at me, her mouth open as the risk of Legacy's escape washed over her mind. She pressed against her earpiece, turning on her microphone but unable to say anything.

"What the hell do we do?" Tony demanded, unable to assist with his current duties.

"Focus on the cure." Jalix replied after a short pause. "That's all that matters."

"He needs to pay!" Violet roared. "Legacy *needs* to die!"

"There's nothing anyone can do, Vi."

"Sanchez, go scour the bodies for a launcher!" As the transmissions between Operators became more panicked, Kara's eyes fell into a cooler sense of calm and nodded once.

"Sonya, with me." She took off in a sprint, pointing to a building across the street as our unspoken language started to become our primary form of communication.

Sprint to the edge and jump. Let her powers take you the rest of the way across the street.

In the same way I had before, I let the full strength of my legs carry me over the edge of the building before I felt gravity shift and change to throw my body across the gap.

"Kara, leave him!" Jalix roared, his voice ringing in my ear as I hit the rooftop. I spun around immediately, watching Kara take the same leap of faith.

"I'm *not* letting him get away with this!" She yelled, jumping as I reached out to catch her.

"Kara, no!" Val's voice was the most desperate of them all, pleading with his sister to keep her safe. Standing together, we were able to see the body of the aircraft as it began to rise, apparently having rescued a waiting Legacy from his fortress before we could arrive.

"We stay airborne. I don't care *what* kind of weapons it might have." Jalix paused, arguing with the crew of his Blackhawk. "Kara, get off that roof, please!" Kara and I looked up, watching Jalix make a sweeping pass a hundred feet over our heads. Once more, Kara pulled out her earpiece slowly, her head falling to stare at her feet for a long moment.

"My team's pinned! We can't fire at him!"

"I need a medic, now! Brynn's down! Get me a medic!" Marcus and Tony's voices continued to rattle off in my ear, signs of sudden and fatal setbacks sweeping over the outcome of our fight. I placed my hand on Kara's shoulder, kissing her on the cheek as Legacy's aircraft hovered above the ground and prepared for higher speeds.

"I love you." I whispered, placing my temple against hers. She reached over to hold my hand for a moment, letting my fingers fall between hers after too brief of a time.

"I love you, too." She met my gaze with glimmering eyes, an unyielding love and friendship never having been broken by time or distance in her mind. We looked at the sky, reaching out with the extent our abilities would let us, and finally let pure hatred reign over us for the last time.

This is for everything that I lost along with my memories.

Legacy's own power prevented any kind of tangible senses from returning to me, but I felt Kara's abilities working in tandem with my own to gain some form of control.

This is for taking away my friends. My family. For destroying our peace and endangering our people.

As the aircraft began to shift, the physical exertion against my mind and body increased tenfold. The resistance to my grasp was of unimaginable strength, and only as my nose began to bleed with my blood pressure and heart rate rising could I see a foothold slip into my reach.

This is for the innocent people you slayed in New York. The innocent people you slayed just below us.

My eyes shot open, the sensation of smooth metal and a screaming heat from the turbines ripping through my brain in an anarchic frenzy of bodily sensations. I gasped, pain shooting through my body as the traditionally negligible sense of distant touch became an overwhelmingly powerful sense of physical contact.

This is for Jared. This is for Krystal. For Kara. Dead or alive, for everyone you've ever hurt.

With a quiet whimper, I felt Kara's body collapse, her head brushing against my leg before hitting the ground. While it pulled me away for the briefest moment, I watched as the engines fired with more force and ignited my body with the agonizing perception of burning alive. I screamed, rejecting any form of distraction from reaching my goal as I gazed at the wings of the aircraft and imagined them snapping off like tree branches.

You know what? This one's for me, you sadistic asshole.

I fell backwards, thrown by the lack of connection between myself and Legacy as an explosion resonated through the air and gave me the remarkable sight of success. I stayed upright the best I could, watching the wing fall straight downward and the rest of the vehicle spin through the air. I tried reaching out again to inflict more damage, but was entirely depleted of my capacity to use my abilities. In spite of my hindrances, Legacy spiraled out of control and crashed just beyond the wave of rubble that Kara and I created. I closed my eyes for a moment, letting a single blissful tear fall down my face in light of his destruction.

No more. That evil is finally dead.

"Val!" Tony called over the radio, breaking the brief silence. "We need the Relic now!"

"Val, I lost you. What's your status?" Jalix paused, Val apparently having been lost to the chaos of battle. "Val?" Jalix asked again, trying desperately to reach his friend. I kept my eyes closed, breathing deeply and fighting the unconsciousness that threatened me.

"I see him. Oh, shit…" An unknown woman's voice confirmed that she was able to spot him, but my eyes opened as I caught onto her mournful tone. "I have the Relic, but he-…he needs medical attention."

"All Operators, this is Jalix." Jalix's voice was unnerved, a growling tone working its way into his throat. "I have visual confirmation that Legacy…he survived the crash."

"The hell he did!" I roared, lurching forward and screaming at the air.

"He just crawled away from the aircraft. I'm descending to land and I'll go after him. Everyone else, focus on the cure-"

"No! I've got it!" Violet called, her grunts an indication of exertion as she started to run.

"Violet, no!" Amy bellowed. "Stay the hell away from him!"

"I'm right behind her." Krystal's breathing was heavier, and it clearly sounded like she was in pain. "Trying to…stop her." My legs felt numb, and the distance between myself and the wreckage forced the realization that there was nothing I would be able to do in the situation.

"Kara." I mumbled, rolling over to lay at her side. I shook her shoulder, her length of jet-black hair covering most of her face. "Kara, come on. Wake up." I groaned, rolling her onto her back and moving the hair from her face. The rosy color of her lips was gone, replaced with a pallid tone that matched the rest of her face. Her eyes were open, the silver irises she bore in renowned fashion glossed over as they blankly stared at the sky in an unmoving gaze. There was no mistaking the absence of life in her face, no misunderstanding of how impossibly limp she had become. "Kara!" I panicked, screaming in her face and shaking her shoulders.

Stay calm. She has Factor Five in her system. Figure out what's wrong.

I pressed a shaky set of two fingers to her neck, watching her chest as the natural rise and fall of her breath was gone completely from the empty body that lay in front of me. No pulse thumped against my fingertips, and no other sign of life pervaded her still frame.

"Jalix!" I screeched, tears completely blocking my vision as I repeatedly pressed downward against her chest in an effort to start her heart. "It's…Kara!" My throat grew so tight that I could barely say anything else. "Please. Come get her." I cried, pressing my lips to hers and trying to breathe life into her lungs.

"What? I…I'm on my way." Jalix's voice was understandably baffled, but responded immediately and gave up any prospect of chasing down Legacy. "Everyone stay away from Legacy. Please. He's…he's not worth it." Jalix pled into the radio, his helicopter turning sharply away from the wreckage and moving toward us.

"Jalix, he can't get to his nuclear arsenal! He'll kill all of us!" Violet insisted, still exerting herself.

I looked down at Kara again, resting my hands against her chest to feel for her heart.

"Come on…" I sobbed, shaking my head. "Amy needs you. Violet and Jalix." I whimpered, trembling ferociously. "I need you, too. I need you."

Ribcage. Sternum. Lungs…heart. Gently. Gently.

I placed my other hand on my own heart, trying to match the beating and rhythm, and knew I was failing in the lack of response her body gave me. I stopped for a moment, coughing hoarse sobs at her and finally resorting to cradling her body against my chest.

"You're my best friend." I pleaded, holding her as closely as I could. "Please, don't. Please!" I screamed, hoping somewhere in her mind she could still hear me. "Please, Kara!"

I'll give anything. I'll give my own life if I have to, but please don't let her die.

I lifted her further, pressing the side of her face against my own as I wept and howled at the empty air around us. My own voice became harder to distinguish as the rotors of Jalix's Blackhawk grew closer to land on our rooftop and washed away any other sounds. I screamed louder, knowing I couldn't be heard anymore, and bled my anguish into the biting winter air.

SPEARHEAD

DR. TAMARA GOODSON
FIFTEEN YEARS EARLIER

Nothing could have annoyed me more than the insistence my sunglasses made on sliding further down the bridge of my nose as I walked briskly across the campus. I nudged them back toward my eyes, making at least the slightest effort to obscure my face as much as I was able. Regardless, people would always stare as I passed them, the burns and scar tissue across my head and face enough to permanently ensure I would never blend in. I brushed my fingertips against one of my wireless headphones, un-muting the call and taking a short moment to enjoy the memories of my hair in the texture of my wig.

"I'm here." I said curtly, tucking away some of my temporary hair and revealing the earbud to make it obvious that I was on a phone call. My purse sagged on my shoulder, heavier than normal with its unique inventory and additional decoy items.

"Good. The rest of us are ready. Just call out what you need." I kept my pace as my colleague responded, his voice infinitely more nervous than mine.

"What I *need* is a professional team." I seethed. "Get your shit together. You sound like you're about to run screaming back to your mother." I glowered at the walls of the hospital, the easternmost of them under construction to hang its newest change of name while other healthcare professionals scurried through its front door during the change of shift. They each carried the impossibly straight posture and awareness that our virus brought, making it apparent that the entire staff consisted of Vampyres.

Smart. Using humans puts the staff at risk of infection and shortages from being sick during conversion.

"I'm sorry, ma'am. But what we're about to do-"

"I don't recall asking for your opinion." I replied coolly, hoping that he would return to silence as I made my way through the entrance. The lobby inside the front doors was largely pandemonium, only a few areas open enough to walk through and none wide enough to move any further unnoticed. I sighed, flicking the badge on my blazer as I walked through the metal detectors and started to look up at the second floor. The lifted walkway that spanned the perimeter of the atrium was aglow with natural sunlight from the skylights and gave me more than enough vision to find the room I was looking for. "I see it. Ready in three." I muttered, pushing past throngs of family members and hunched-over humans that vomited from the intensity of their oncoming conversion to Vampyrism. Nurses were scrambling to find doctors, doctors scrambling to find patients, and I knew I stood out somehow as the only collected person within the entire building.

The stairwell wasn't something reached easily, more than enough hospital staff raising their eyebrows with curious surprise as their gaze met my marred skin in silent glances of judgment.

They'll forget about you in a few hours. Keep walking.

I encountered the stairwell I intended to use, the shortest route to my destination, but the construction teams that performed the hospital's renovations had its access blocked. Immediately to the right was an elevator, and I waited impatiently behind another small crowd of people for an available opening. The hospital's PA system chimed again with its automated, friendly female voice amidst the sounds of pained chaos. I rolled my eyes, another elevator car filling up without an available spot for me to join.

"*Thank you for choosing Kane-Hudson as your primary point of treatment! We welcome all patients and will do our best to find you and your family an opening with our caring VMP staff as quickly as possible. If you or someone you know has a possible infection, please remember to keep at least six feet apart, and visit our website for the symptoms and management of new conversions. Our goal is-*"

I scoffed at the transparency of the robotic statement, finally finding an opening in a small group that made their way forward. I strode inside, pressing the button for the second floor as I did so, and hid the best I could at the back of the group.

"Ready?" The voice in my ear asked as I stood silently, waiting for the car to finish its ascent. I cleared my throat discreetly, unable to speak without drawing attention to myself.

Idiots, every one of them. If I fail because of these morons-

The bell chimed, myself and one other person strolling out onto the walkway that overlooked the lobby. I stood for a moment, seeing the crawling of ants below me from a better vantage than I had before, and spoke once the other person was far enough away.

"Don't ask me if I'm ready. I will *tell* you." I hissed. "Don't be trigger-happy."

"Sorry." The voice replied, audibly grimacing.

"If this goes sideways, you won't be sorry." I paused, making my way down the ramp and toward my intended room. "You'll be dead."

"Y'know, that's not necessary." Another voice replied. "We already know that-"

"Shut up." I groaned, exhausted of all patience. "Thirty seconds. Don't screw anything up." I unzipped the outside pocket of my purse and removed the lone key that lay inside, keeping it curled within my fingers and firmly pressed against my palm. I passed room after room, some belonging to patients with rooms full of medical students while others had their doors closed for the privacy of the doctors working within their offices. I reached the end of the hall, turning to my left and facing the electronic combination lock and badge scanner next to the final door. I stared at it for a brief moment before the hospital suddenly flushed with a brief silence, the lights on the electronic lock disappearing and voices becoming much more clear as their panicked tones clashed against one another.

"Power's off. Go."

I can see that, imbecile.

I placed one hand on the door's handle and pressed the key into the physical slot just above it, rotating the handle in a jerk of success and disappearing inside. As soon as the door clicked shut, I could hear the emergency generators kick on, illuminating the light inside the room and outlining the shelves that surrounded me.

Made it. Barely, but that's good enough.

"I'm ready at the generators. Just say when." The second voice called. I ignored it, once again recognizing that standing orders had been useless and my employees needed to be walked through every step of the way instead. I opened my purse, withdrawing the first of several items before I decided to empty them all onto the empty space of an unused shelf. Starting with the aerosol spray, I rotated the nozzle and unleashed its contents onto the pile of bed linens, towels, and pillowcases that took up a majority of the space inside. It took longer than anticipated to empty the container, having more of a charge than I expected. Finally empty, I placed it back into my purse and picked up the first of several syringes, gazing at the small stack of bottled water.

I uncapped the needle and picked up one of the bottles, guiding the instrument into the plastic between its safety seal and the threads of the cap. I let five droplets fall into the liquid itself, withdrawing the gleaming steel and moving to the next of many bottles.

"I need a distraction." I mumbled quietly, hoping not to be heard by anyone passing by. "This is taking longer than I thought."

"I'm on it." A third voice said confidently, a short time elapsing before I heard a man's bloodcurdling scream from the atrium.

"Oh, God! My stomach! Someone *please* help me!" He roared, audible even through the thick door I stood behind. I paused, sighing briefly before continuing my work. I shook my head as I went through each of the dozens of bottles, working as quickly as I could. His artificial screams of pain continued, capturing the attention of everyone below me.

Overselling it much? If you get caught, you'll be dead before you can rat me out.

I finished the last of the syringes, placing the orange safety cap back on each and shouldering my purse once again.

"Chris, hit the generators." I placed my hand on the door handle again, preparing to use my key. With only a moment of suspension, the power went out once more and allowed me an escape from the room without the digital fingerprint of using my badge or leaving any trace that I had ever been present. "I'm clear. Pull the car around. Everyone's payment is in the hotel room. Head there. I'll meet you." I mumbled, staring straight ahead as students, doctors, and technicians scrambled to take action during the loss of their backup power. I went largely ignored, making my way toward the stairwell next to the elevator. The construction crews had already made room for people to walk, understanding that the elevators were now out of commission.

"The roundabout is full. I can't get close to the front doors."

"It's fine, I can walk to you. How far back?" I heard muttering as he counted under his breath.

"Eleventh car. Navy blue luxury sedan with chrome trim." I nodded to myself and hung up the phone call as I cleared the bottom of the steps and tried to control my pace through the atrium once more. Every square inch of the lobby was packed during my brief absence, people pouring inside to ask questions about the loss of power and patients' families enquiring about the safety of their loved ones. I was the only one heading toward the exit, and was able to push my way through the crowd with little resistance. The hair on the back of my neck stood up, something in the corner of my vision catching my attention and stalling my progress toward victory. I turned my head, a volume of shimmering red hair accompanying a fair face and peaceful demeanor while she addressed the crowd.

It's her. She's here.

My heart leapt in my chest, a lump in my throat increasing at the growing rage that I felt encompassing my rising pulse and heavier breathing. I could smell how close I was to her, her vanilla perfume pervading the air in light of the real doctors that surrounded her refusing such superficial frivolities. I stared at her, wondering whether my life had any other purpose now that my calculated task had been completed. Looking at the way she spoke and her relaxed tone of voice, I could almost recall the smell of my own burning flesh and the incomprehensible sensation of searing flame that ripped away at the inside of my throat.

If you kill her now…this will all have been pointless. A quick, violent death is better than she deserves.

I spun around and hurried toward the door to arrive without further impediment, breathing a discreet sigh of relief that my presence during the event was trivial. I took a moment to berate myself for hesitating, but my self-control was something I knew I would appreciate over the coming years.

The hard part's over. Now to close the deal.

I didn't count the cars, seeing only a few dozen feet away the sedan that awaited me and climbed in as soon as I reached it. Sliding into the backseat, I withdrew the suspicious contents of my purse and started to stuff them in the black backpack that was left for the purpose of their disposal. My driver turned the wheel and made his way around the line, shifting into the second lane and taking us away from the hospital. Immediately after zipping the bag shut and ridding myself of the evidence, my phone rang, and I answered without pause.

"Doctor Goodson. I hope all is well." The low voice on the other end was the only thing about the day's events that unnerved me, but I refused him any satisfaction from it.

"Indeed. I'm done. We're heading to you now." I shifted to look around the passenger seat, peering through the windshield as we travelled along the highway.

"I look forward to it. My car is only a short distance from you. Your driver has the address." He paused, his statements a matter of cool fact with no air of concern or hesitance. "I trust that your presence was unnoticed."

"It was. I can assume you've held up your commitment toward my…discretion?" He chuckled at my question, a moment of silence between us afterward.

"My men are at the hotel already. Your employees won't be a loose thread by the end of the day. You have no cause for concern." I breathed a silent sigh of relief, half-expecting his betrayal once the task was completed. Our car started to slow down, taking an exit and nearing the parking lot of a nearly-abandoned shopping mall. The line in my ear went dead and the call ended without further conversation. Our destination was adjacent to a similar vehicle, a black luxury sedan parked in a spot with no other vehicles surrounding it. I was able to see its occupants as I neared, a driver accompanying two well-dressed men with inconspicuous earpieces as well as my contact. My car came to a stop, both vehicles' doors opening to allow its passengers outside.

"No tail, no one following?" One of the security members asked my driver as he stretched next to his door.

"Nope, not a chance. We-" I slid into the backseat of the other vehicle as a silenced gunshot caught me by surprise and forced me to look back. The driver's limp body was grabbed before it hit the ground and was shoved into the backseat of his car. The shooter jammed the weapon into her blazer pocket and got behind the wheel, driving away with every last piece of evidence from the crime.

"The unfortunate ways of the world, come full circle. The cycle of death to begin something greater." The man next to me muttered, his brow furrowed at the retreating vehicle. The remaining guard took a few steps away from the vehicle, lighting a cigarette without smoking it and joining the driver in a façade of casual conversation.

"I could have killed her." I retorted, still bitter. "She was right there, just inside the lobby. Talking to people, convincing them there was nothing wrong. That they'd be okay." I paused, refusing to look at him and instead staring through my window. "The same thing she said to me before my cell caught on fire."

"Those who portray themselves as saviors often lie to maintain their false identity. None of them are superior to those they protect, and fewer still are worthy of protecting them." He continued. I scoffed quietly, accepting his word as truth but growing tired of the conversation.

"I didn't come here for pithy words of wisdom. My end is done. Now it's your turn." I finally looked over at him, a neutral expression on his face as he responded in kind.

"Understandable. You'll see proof of your efforts within the week. There won't be any need to contact me again to obtain it. The nightly news will suffice."

"You think this virus killing a few people in a hospital is going to make news these days?" I ridiculed. "I want *proof*-"

"Doctor Goodson, I have told you everything you need to know. Your proof will be visible in the coming days and your efforts will be noted in the history of our nation." I paused, knowing that he was a deliberate speaker and always chose his words carefully.

"This is going to kill outside of the hospital, isn't it? You used something…infectious. Something more volatile-"

"I provided you with the strain necessary to do as you asked and seek revenge on Allison. Fulfilling my own goals is an aside to you, and should be none of your consideration." He looked over at me, a hollow and unnerving lack of humanity behind his eyes. "Your work is appreciated, Doctor Goodson. But your services are no longer necessary."

"Services." I chuckled. "I didn't do this for *you*."

"No. Of course not." He nodded, a light smile on his face. "You did this for revenge. And you have succeeded. Allison will be broken by the cascade of events to follow. You've set things in motion for a larger stratagem. It's why you'll walk free today. You should be proud."

"I lost my pride five years ago, along with everything else." I snapped. "I'll settle for satisfaction. For retribution."

"I suggest you leave the area, doctor. Perhaps find a…larger city to settle into." His baritone voice had the aura of a threat without the words required of one. "I believe our agreement included relocation. Your next opportunity for life lies in New York. Jamal here will provide you with everything you need to seize that opportunity."

"While you, what, climb the ladder of politics?" I pressed, trying to glean the consequences of my actions further than I initially had foreseen. He smirked, nodding slowly.

"Events have been set in motion." He repeated. "But we will not meet again. *This* is a parting gift." He reached between his feet and handed me a leather satchel that looked like it had come from centuries ago. It was closed with a single strip of thin leather, tied in a gentle knot to keep its contents secure. As I took it from him, I could tell that it contained a book of some kind, and the satchel was for its protection. "This is not meant for your eyes. You will know who to give this to. And when. Until then, it is yours for safekeeping and eventual delivery."

As if given a command, the remaining guard opened the door and made his way to my own, opening it and beckoning for me to leave. I waited for a moment, looking back to provide my own words of wisdom.

"You can't beat them." I started quietly. "You may break some of them, you may kill some of them. But you can't win. Not as a president or as a Legacy. You're going to lose your war." He contemplated my words, tilting his head to the side.

"I don't need to win, Doctor Goodson. In the end, there is no…*winning.* Victory is a concept shared by lesser beings fighting lesser evils." He paused, his gaze returning to me with a hollow and piercing stare of malice. "My crusade is waged against reality itself. And every sentient being will hear the war drums of a greater Legacy."

***

I climbed the final set of stairs, the rumble of my footsteps rattling the shaky concrete and metal poles under my shoes. Fumbling with my keys in the dark, I scolded myself for not leaving my front door's light on before I left, and for having to once again rely on the surrounding light from the city's nighttime glow to find the key to my apartment. Victorious, I finally swung the door open and dropped the keys on the small table next to my entryway. The plastic bags I carried dug into my arms and encouraged a swift journey to the kitchen where I set them on the counter to relieve the pressure against my skin. Flicking the light on, I started to realize that I had failed to find enough groceries to last more than a week.

"Goddamn federal purchase limits." I grunted, throwing open the door of my refrigerator and stuffing the cold food into the empty space. "Lulu." I called, moving my head to find my cat. "Dinner time, hon." I finished with the cold items, closing my refrigerator door and deciding to leave everything else for a later time. "Lulu." I repeated, her pattering footsteps usually milliseconds ahead of calling her name. I raised an eyebrow, looking around my kitchen to find her mysteriously absent.

She usually greets me at the door. The hell's going on with her?

"Lulu…" I tried sweetly, turning the corner to peek into my small bedroom. The bed was empty, the small blanket dedicated to her sleeping spot abandoned. "What the hell, cat…?" I whispered, deciding to look in the living room. I raised the dial on the dimmer switch and froze, seeing a figure seated in my recliner with my cat comfortably draped across her lap. Faintly, I could hear the sound of Lulu's purring as the stranger gently stroked her fur.

"Cool-ass cat. Hate most of these damn things." The woman smiled quietly, her voice gravelly and rough with an impossibly lilting edge to its tenor. "Piss everywhere, they're antisocial." Lulu sat up and stretched, arching her back and enjoying the stranger's scratches placed tactically behind her ear. "Not this one. This one's a little badass."

"Her name is Lulu. What's yours?" I asked coolly, trying to maintain my composure without showing weakness.

"You know my name. We've met, worked together. Just give it a second, it'll come to you." She suggested, no sign of an imminent threat apparent through the smoky haze of her voice. I stared at her, paying more attention to the half of her hair that was present rather than the shaved-down side in the fashion of a Viking wife.

It-…couldn't be. But if I survived…

"Raven." I said the answer with confidence, although the impossibility still pervaded me.

"Hello, Doctor Goodson. It's good to see you again." She said sweetly, ushering Lulu off her lap with a gentle sweep. She came running to my legs, brushing against my shins as if to say that she approved of her new friend.

"Lulu hates strangers." I warned. "You got lucky."

"I *feel* lucky. My whole view on pet animals has forever changed." She smirked, the half-sarcastic bite of her words familiar to me. "And I get to catch up with an old colleague. Very lucky today."

"Prisoner." I corrected. "Under threat of death or worse."

"Worse, by the look of it." Raven chuckled, beckoning to the obvious scars that ran down both of my arms and across my head and neck. "*But* you survived. Thrived, even. Enough to go back and get revenge." I remained frozen in spite of the instinct to run, wondering how the hell she could have known what I had done half a decade ago.

"That was five years ago." I warned. "I had no idea what kind of destruction that virus would have wrought-"

"Oh, I know. We all know. In fact, there are a *lot* of things we know about you. Including your dealings with a certain…Legacy. Those five years ago."

"Dealings is all they were." I insisted, recoiling a fraction as she stood and swept the cat hair from an expensive pair of slacks. "I never worked *for* him. Then or ever. I don't even know where he is or-"

"I do." She quipped, raising her eyebrows. "He's not a friend. Doesn't know I exist, either. So we're going to keep it that way, if that's alright with you." I remained silent, Raven perceiving the act as compliance. "I have a question, and then I have an offer. But the question depends on the offer you get. So answer truthfully, if you could." I swallowed hard, nodding and wondering what lurked outside in the shadows that she brought for her own protection.

She wouldn't have come alone. Not in a million years.

"What's the question?" I challenged her sense of dominance with my own.

"Will you kill me?" She spread her arms, unmoving from where she stood. "I recruited you. My father locked you in that lab. And world's saviors caused your…injuries. Two of those problems are dealt with." She paused. "Do you hate me enough to kill me?"

I wouldn't be in this situation if she hadn't put me there. She helped her father build their damn empire, build the prison that I was kept in. Manufactured the collar that I tore off my neck after three days of being trapped.

"I hate you enough to kill you." I answered truthfully, accepting my fate regardless of her impending judgment. "But I won't. I've…killed enough. I've killed too much."

"You're right on that one, sweet cheeks. You've damn near killed everyone." She chuckled, lowering her arms and looking around my living room. "A hundred and fifty million dead so far with no sign of stopping. All for revenge. And the woman you wanted to torment has been successfully beaten back down to a state of depressed workaholism. I hear even her husband has broken away from her social circles. You've won. Albeit through holocaust."

"I never meant for this to happen." I growled, pointing at Raven as tears started to creep into my eyes. "I had no reason to do this. I was told-"

"Oh, you *know* what you were told, dear. You knew he was vague, and you didn't care. Blinded by vengeance. The thing that gets you killed." She tilted her head, beckoning to a grotesque half-moon of scars on her neck. "I know the feeling. We both went too far. But my offer is to give you a chance to fix it."

"Fix it?" I scoffed. "It just broke the border to Mexico. Rumors have an outbreak in Canada. The world is going to die, Raven. There's no stopping it."

"Project Catalyst." She affirmed. "You know how much potential we unlocked."

"The data from Catalyst was used to *create* this monstrosity. There's no-"

"VZH-three." She interjected. "Mean anything to you?"

"Yeah, it was what I worked on. My specialty." I thought back to my work on our virus from over a decade ago. "The blocker protein-"

"Right, nerdy stuff. Yes, yes. Hypothetically, what would happen if we applied it to an earlier point in the genetic sequence? Used the protein higher in its process?"

"Why? What would be the point?" I wrinkled my nose, understanding what she was trying to say but confused as to why it would matter.

"Because if we can override the current strain with the new one, force a mutation-"

"It would act as a preventive from future infection. You're…talking about a live-virus vaccine, but…an active one. An infection to keep others out."

"A gatekeeper." She summarized. I started to pace, considering her words.

"It would take years-"

"We've already started. That's why I'm here." Raven said pointedly. "*That* is my offer." I laughed genuinely, shaking my head in shock.

"Because this worked out *so* well last time. Come work for you, make lots of money, get collared-"

"They're free." She said quietly. I paused, waiting for her to elaborate. "Our...location. Free Vampyres to come and go as they please. Including the researchers. No tags, no threats. Just a society that understands you."

"*No one* understands me." I warned.

"No one understands you *better* than we do, Tamara. No one else was let down by Kara and her Counsel more than we were. No one else was betrayed by my father more than we were. And no one wants to control this virus more than we do, before it spirals out of control. But you're special. You...worked on a critical piece. Adding that would be monumental to our efforts."

"And if I say no?" I prompted, more interested in hearing hypocrisy from her answer than details regarding an acceptance.

"I leave. And yes, you'll be monitored to ensure my identity remains a secret. Should you betray me to Legacy, you'd be killed before you reach him. That kind of thing. But...you have a chance to rectify this apocalypse. To make up for the millions of deaths by saving *billions* of human lives from the very virus you released." She smirked. "I think you want that chance." I paused, bowing my head and considering her offer.

I...want to believe that she's lying. But the way she'd do it would be different. Is she only giving me the illusion of choice? I suppose she could have kidnapped me if she wanted to. I...could undo things, though. Try and make something better. Not be known as the world's worst mass-murderer.

"I *could* do this." I began, looking up at her. "But it would come with conditions."

"Name your price." She offered quickly.

"Wherever you're holed up, I want to work somewhere nearby. Somewhere different, where I'm not looking over my shoulder and expecting a knife in the back." Raven chuckled at my request.

"That's a convenient condition. Hmm…" She looked around again, inspecting the space and almost appearing to mentally measure the walls and windows. "We're nearby. Close enough, anyway. We can bring what you'd need right here. Connect you to my people digitally to share data. If you want an assistant, I'll provide one. But you will, as we get closer to the end, have to finish the project onsite. Is that a fair request?"

She's asking. Making counteroffers. This is an actual negotiation.

"I can accept those terms." I nodded.

"Perfect. Look at us ugly bitches, making the world go round." She moved past me with haste and opened the door to leave my apartment, looking back at Lulu for a moment.

"I'm not doing this for you. I'm doing it for myself." I asserted.

"When I have my people deliver the equipment, I'll throw in some treats for the little one. Hope it makes up for the messed-up face." She closed the door with a degree too much force, leaving Lulu and I alone in our apartment once more. The howl of ambulances, as they were on most nights, ran rampant as they shuttled the dead and dying across the city.

"Hear that, Lu?" I knelt down, picking her up to hold in my arms. "We have *real* work to do."

BATTLEGROUND

ALICE

I struggled to remember the nurse's name as she handed me the small plastic cup containing my requested pills, more distracted by the violent pounding in my chest than anything else.

"Thanks." I mumbled, looking around for my vanilla protein shake and using it to swallow the medicine. I finished the drink, knowing it had been more than a day since I had taken in any form of responsible nutrients, and tossed the bottle in the garbage before looking back at my computer monitor. Val spoke up as the nurse's footsteps fell out of earshot.

"And those were…" My husband's voice was filled with stern disapproval, a near edge of anger on his voice.

"Amphetamines." I responded curtly, wondering whether he had a purpose in standing around near my desk. "And a few other things. Why?"

"Why?" He scoffed, leaning away from the frame of the door. "Because that's your third dose since I showed up this morning. You've taken more pills than you have spoken words to me."

"Do you want my sister dead or do you want her to get better?" I snapped, turning my chair to point to Krystal. Her bed was recently adorned with yet another painting from Violet, her coping mechanism

dominating the walls of the intensive care room. "Because if I'm tired and I miss something, if my attention span has any kind of a gap-"

"Alice, she's been in that coma for three months. You already made sure her odds-"

"Her odds should be a hundred percent, and they're not. I'm not willing to take the remaining risk." I turned back toward my computer, opening the file I received while the two of us spoke.

"Allison…" He started, placing a hand on my shoulder. "The best and brightest you have are all focusing on her. You can take a break for a day. A few hours, even."

"My best and brightest aren't me." I mumbled, scanning over the details of my most recent project. "They can't come up with the ideas I do, they don't have the experience that I do." He scoffed again, removing his hand.

"Okay, well what experience do you have with-"

"I did it for Sonya, I can do it for Krystal." I growled, pausing. "I helped put Sonya together from pieces. My sister is intact, I just can't figure out why the hell she's asleep."

"She died." Val emphasized, taking a step away from me. "You're still holding onto this…idea that she'll come out of this okay. If Sonya hadn't been lucky-" I pushed myself away from the desk, realizing that dealing with his provocation quickly was the best way to stop being distracted.

"Sonya wasn't lucky, she lost her memories! Hundreds of years, gone. I can't let that happen to Krystal. I refuse to." I shook my head, staring at my sister's bed and trying to let the ideas in my head formulate into something meaningful.

"Alice, Christ…you might not have a choice, that's my point. You're killing yourself over what might end up being a body." I turned my head slowly to look at him, his face unchanging as he tried to convey a point I didn't believe in.

"Krystal is there, somewhere. If you don't believe that, get the hell out of my hospital and don't come back." I hissed, taking a deep breath as my fangs started to creep from my gumline. Val took a step back, staring at me as if I were something to be disgusted at.

"What's left of you anymore, Ally?" He whispered, looking over my body. "You are killing yourself." He repeated.

"Okay, don't be dramat-" He whipped his arm toward my waist, pulling the drawstring on my scrub pants and letting the waistband start to fall past my hips. I grabbed the seam quickly, scowling at him as I tied the drawstring back together. "Excuse me!"

"You've lost weight. About twenty pounds, from the look of it. Your pants barely fit."

"Oh, I'm sorry, do I not have time to be a model wife?" I mocked. "If you've lost interest, go screw my sister when she wakes up. You might not be her flavor, but I bet she'd love holding it over my head."

"I'm talking about your health." His voice increased in volume and desperation. "I don't give a damn what you look like, I care about what's going on in your body. You're doing the same thing Krystal did with her own drugs, you're escaping-"

"Oh yeah, keep talking medicine. I love hearing about pharmacodynamics and its psychological impact from someone who has no idea what the hell they're talking about." I fired back, gesturing to the door. "Seriously, you're making me lose time. Go find something, or someone, else to do. My trials with Factor Four-"

"Would you stop?" He asked quietly. "With those references. I'm not going to start seeing someone else. I've been with you for…almost three hundred years. Why the hell would I leave you now?"

"Sounds like you want to. Sounds like I'm the screw-up Krystal was, the same drug addict, the same-"

"Stop."

"-thing you hated seeing in her. I'm never home, I'm never around you? Why wouldn't you want to find someone else? It's not like I plan on stopping until Krystal's awake and-"

"Alice!" He shouted, his fist curling into a ball at his side while he glowered at me. I didn't back down, staring at him the same way he did to me. "I love you. But you're losing yourself to this crazy shit. You are trying to do the impossible. If you're going to keep trying, then at least take a break."

"You know what? Why is it that I have to stop doing what I'm doing? How about a little help once in a while? From any of you?" I threw my hands in the air. "It's not like any of you are useful, but I see one of you every day come by and stare at her like it'll magically wake her up."

"You're saying we can't visit our family? My own sister-in-law?"

"Oh now she's your sister-in-law? Now that she's hurt, the poor thing. Until then, it was always that she was your friend." Val took a deep breath, relaxing his posture and closing his eyes for a moment.

"You're very stressed. And you're taking that out by arguing with me. And I understand-"

"Don't try the psychological shit on me, I know the rule book better than anyone."

"I know, which is why you ignore it-" He paused as another of my nurses entered the room, hesitating at the sight of our obvious conflict before moving to Krystal's bedside and starting to swap out the empty IV bags for fresh ones.

"Don't stop on her account." I retorted. "Say what you need to say. Not like she listens to any goddamn word that comes out of my mouth anyway." The nurse stopped, turning to look at me with a glance of distress and angst.

"Ma'am, I did every-"

"-thing wrong." I finished. "I can see from across the room that you're hooking up saline. I updated her chart ten minutes ago that she's supposed to get Lactated Ringer's to prep her perfusion rates for the Factor Four experiment and get the sodium lactate in her system-"

"Ma'am, I checked the chart half an hour ago. I missed the update, I'm sorry." She apologized hastily.

"Oh, it's fine. Just make sure to mention that at her real funeral. I'll even let you give the eulogy as the nurse that filled her with useless bullshit while her body died." She whipped the tray away from the bed, running out of the room as she burst into tears. "See? They're not just stupid, they're lazy." I finished, sighing and taking a mental note that Krystal's fluids were delayed.

"You are making impossible demands of the people around you." He *asserted. "And you're treating everyone like they're dogs."*

"I'll stop treating them like dogs when they start acting like semi-intelligent people. Unless I fire them first." I rolled my eyes, sitting back into my chair and waiting for Val to say something else. "Are we done here?"

"Not really." He *mumbled. "Not until you stop acting like this."*

"Then be my guest at changing things." I gestured to where Krystal laid. "Want me to be the cute little plaything you drag around with you, wake her up. I'll celebrating by eating cake so my ass is as big as you prefer."

"You're not yourself." He *raised his eyebrows, chuckling. "Those words aren't even yours. This, all of this, has nothing to do with me, and you're-"*

"Nothing to do with you?" I started. "She went on that mission, she killed herself, because of a chance to rescue your sister. You're the one that fed into her bullshit all those years, put it into her head that if she changed her ways, she could be a hero. Congrats. She's comatose and slipping further from normality every day." Val took a step back, averting his gaze and staring at the empty plastic cup on my desk.

"You're...blaming me for what happened?"

"I'm blaming everyone. Myself included. She should have been tied down and forcibly detoxed decades ago. And no one had the balls to do anything about it." I spun around to face my computer, hoping he would leave. "I'm not taking the nice girl route anymore. I'm fixing her at all costs."

"What if I'm one of those costs-"

"Then so be it. I don't care anymore." The words left my tongue faster than I had expected, overtaking my mouth faster than my brain could filter the response and I spun immediately to look at Val. His face was in awe, completely unaware that I was even capable of saying what I did. "I didn't mean that." I backpedaled. "I just meant-"

"No, I know what you meant." Val grimaced, his eyes glistening. "I'm not a priority. Not a consideration right now."

"Val-"

"No, it's fine. Go save your sister. I'll...I'll be here whenever you're done. 'Til death do us part." He turned toward the door and left, one word mumbled under his breath before he was gone. "Again." I gritted my teeth, my eyes unable to focus on the vast sprawl of information in front of me as his words ran through my head again and again. I hated him for bringing up his own death, and the devastation from repeatedly losing him was a scar I didn't need.

"You son of a bitch." I whispered tearily, shaking my head and staring at the collection of folders, pencil cups, and neatly-organized files that sat on the surface of my desk. The overwhelming hatred for Val's words finally got the better of me, an uncontrollable rage at the thought that he left, that he didn't fight me any harder.

"You son of a bitch!" I roared, sweeping the piles off the desk and scattering them across the room. I ripped the monitor from its mount and hurled it into the hallway, feeling the skin under my scrubs flicker and spark with heat. "Come back here and fight me!" I bellowed, screaming at the open door as my fingertips danced with flame. "Come back and hate me the way I know you do!"

I stared into the hallway, realizing that it was completely empty and had been likely abandoned the same time Val and I started fighting. I knew I was volatile, and with Krystal being the only patient in the infirmary, I knew that for however long, I would be alone. As I stared, I felt tears try to make their way onto my face and evaporate before they had the chance. I glanced over at Krystal, her peaceful face undisturbed by my outburst and immune to the knowledge of what her sister had turned into. I inhaled quickly, trying to clear my mind while making my way to the medicine cabinet, throwing open the door and leafing through its contents.

"Alright, sis. You win." I wept, snatching one of the bottles and dropping two tablets of morphine into my hand. "If I need to get inside your brain..." I threw them into my mouth and ground them down into a chalky paste before swallowing. "I need to know how it worked." I shook my head, the heat that radiated from my body dying down to a calmer temperature as I neared the winter air surrounding her bedside. I took her hand in my own, her limp fingers unable to curl around mine,

and felt the biting chill that writhed against my palm. "I saved you from death once. He hasn't earned a second shot at you yet." I stared at her blank face, few signs within it that indicated she was even still alive. "But why did you do this?" I shuddered, crying as I squeezed her hand. "Why?" Her closed eyes gave no response, no change in her heart rate or brainwaves indicating that she could even hear me. "Why?" I cried louder, unable to hold myself back from the anger of her suicide. "Why?"

***

"Fox three, fox three." As I left the safety of my vehicle, I looked up at the sky to watch Andrea and Layla chase a flaming fireball over our heads and signal a confirmation that we had gained an advantage.

I focused on my immediate surroundings, feeling Amy lean against me as she did the same. We were protected from danger by means of any path behind us due to the vehicle we had just exited, and the soldiers to our front seemed to have arrived with enough time to kill the Tortured that guarded our first target building, establishing a protective force at its entrance. One of them waved us over, so I switched my radio channel to the one Kara and I had agreed upon before ducking to sprint across the road.

"Alice, you hear me?" Kara's voice buzzed unpleasantly in my earpiece, which had apparently already started to malfunction.

"Yeah." I replied, turning on its microphone. "We're coming up on our first building. Looks like they're signaling that it's clear." I hesitated with the words, seeing only a few bodies on the outside, and many of the security that had entered the building exited in a frenzy to vomit next to the door rather than establish a fight inside. Amy said something in the radio as one of our security team members leaned in to speak with me.

"It's…gruesome, ma'am. Just be ready. We'll need a pretty comprehensive evac." He gestured to the door, and at a brief glance I already knew what he was talking about. In a manner I had only ever seen in Nazi prison camps and slaughterhouses, the dead and dying were combined into a horrific series of masses that were pushed against the walls within a darkened building. I took a step inside and changed my radio back to the main station for a moment, lowering my voice so I wouldn't cause alarm to the Tortured civilians.

"All Operators, this is Alice. We're clearing the first buildings. We're just northwest of Taylor's position. These civilians…" I stared at a man whose legs were missing as he scrambled to reattach a tourniquet that had slipped off from the slick blood that pooled against his clothing. "They're in rough shape. God…Val, I need the buses to get them all out before the fighting gets here. They'll need armed escort, too." I decided, trying to use our resources wisely while rescuing as many as possible. Amy squeezed past me, making her way into the building and starting care for those closest to the door. My trauma teams and medics were all hard at work, but the looks on their faces proved that training wasn't enough.

"This is Felix. Evac with escort is on its way. Ten minutes or so, they're going to loop behind Taylor's position and take the long route." I nodded to myself at the reply over the radio, spinning around and trying to find a victim I could treat. Amy ran over to the double amputee and started treatment before I could claim him as my own patient.

High-volume blood loss. Transfusions would use too many resources and they'll die as soon as the cure hits. They're gone. She's jaundiced, badly. Bruised, that means liver damage. She's too far gone. Give me someone, anyone.

Kara's footsteps came faster than I had assumed they would, appearing behind me as she and Sonya made their way inside.

"What the hell-"

"We need more medics." I interrupted, gesturing to Amy's patient.

"God, I didn't think it would be this bad." Amy exhaled after finishing up with a bag of Factor Five, backing up a few feet and examining the collection of victims. "So many are just…dead. What-…what *good* does that even do them? How does it help their numbers to kill these people?" She was visibly angry, her cheeks starting to flush.

"This…seems familiar, almost." Sonya said to Kara, breaking her silence "I swear, it's like we've been here before. I know that's a horrible thing to say-"

"No, you're right." Kara confirmed. "Dachau. Nazi Germany. We've been here…just not for a rescue."

"Not a mistake I'm making twice." I struggled to tug a young man away from a pile of bodies, realizing that he was trying to breathe. "Amy, collapsed lung, right side. Shattered ribcage…and he's jaundiced. Some kind of liver damage."

Liver damage could be from one of the ribs. Either way, he'll be one of the lucky ones if he can pull through.

"I'm on it." Amy mumbled, jerking another pre-sealed bag of supplies from her satchel. She beckoned to the room as she started healing his collapsed lung. "How the hell are we going to get through this many on our own?" Her closed eyes held a sense of dismay, overwhelmed at those she wouldn't have time to heal. Kara stepped away for a moment as I nervously watched the nurses drag more and more nearly-dead bodies out of their mass graves. One of them was placed by my side without explanation, a middle-aged man in hypovolemic shock that seemed to be rapidly approaching death.

The medics are just pulling anyone left alive, they're not just picking the ones that have a fighting chance.

"Alice, I need more Factor Five!" Amy said quickly, turning to look up at me.

"What? He'll be fine, we have more pressing patients-"

"He's trying to talk to us. To…Kara, I think." Surely enough, his eyes were transfixed on Kara as she spoke to Sonya about something a few feet away. "He needs to tell us something, but he's fading fast."

"Alright, hold on." I sighed, watching my recently-delivered patient's last breath leave his body.

As if I'm expected to save any of these people. They've been dying for days. Infected with bacteria, septic, in shock from blood loss and psychological trauma. We're just here to watch the end of it all. My nurses are delivering me impossible situations just because I have Amy here.

I set my bag on the ground next to Amy, analyzing him as she used her abilities.

"Vocal cords are shredded." Amy paused, looking over at me. "He must have been intubated by some jackass that didn't know how to do it properly. I can't heal what's not there, he's literally missing fibers. Let's hope that Factor Five can help restore enough functionality to talk."

"It will. They're quick to heal." I established a port in his forearm, starting with a quick injection of Vampyre medicine before connecting a bag of Factor Five and hanging it from a decorative stud in the wall. "That'll have to work. What else does he have going on?"

"His…immune system is under stress. Risk of septicemia, but he's not there yet. I'm working on his liver. Rib fragment pierced it. Start a note." I pulled out a wad of paper tags, each with an attached string and whipped the pen out of my pocket so she could start speaking. "He has three inches of rib piercing his liver, directly adjacent to the hepatic artery. My healing is going to create a ring of scar tissue to stabilize the bone, but if there's pressure put on his abdomen, he could hemorrhage-"

-special transport precautions: supine only; special notes: do not apply pressure to stomach-

"-his diaphragm is going to be screwed for a bit, so we'll need to watch for hiccups that move the rib piece-"

-drugs recommended: IV antibiotic re: compat w/ pt hx, paracetamol, gabapentin, fentanyl patch PRN-

"-and he'll need extensive surgery for the rest of his chest." I was writing as fast as I was able, trying to keep in time with her diagnoses before signing the slip and wrapping the string around his wrist. I looked into his eyes, placing the paper between his fingers.

"These are instructions for the doctor. It tells them what is wrong with you. If they have this, they can help you. Understand?" I tried to speak clearly and in short sentences, knowing he was still suffering from a lot of confusion in the midst of everything. "Hold that paper with your life." I warned, turning around to see Kara and Sonya approach again.

"We don't have a choice. The cure…it's the whole reason we're here. If we can't save those too far gone, that's not our fault. We came here to do everything we could, Kara. And we have." Sonya's sentiments echoed my own, and as much as I wanted to rescue more before the day was over, my hope was dwindling.

"*We* haven't." Kara sighed in discontent. "Alice, use the security to start hauling anyone stable out to the buses. Keep the windows rolled down and tell the drivers to head to Vanaheim the moment the cure is released."

"Yeah, got it." I mumbled, standing up as my radio channel started to explode in a frenzy of announcements. I took a few steps away, trying to make out what was said, but my uncooperative earpiece made it nearly impossible to understand. I tuned the station to Kara and Sonya's private channel and unplugged the earpiece, dialing up the volume in case I needed to use it during patient care.

"Shannon." I tapped one of the nurses as she stood, backing away from a stabilized victim. "Where am I needed most?" I shrugged, gesturing. "I feel useless." She pointed to a group of medics at the farthest end of the hall, all huddled together in a depressed-looking group of hopelessness. I nodded, making my way toward them and getting their attention as I approached.

"Hey! People to save, why are we standing around? Just because you're not getting shot at-"

"Ma'am…the next building over…" The male that spoke to me looked as if he had just graduated high school, and his innocence was marred with some form of disturbed shock.

"What about it? More victims?" I dropped my drill-sergeant tone, realizing they were no longer recruits and had a genuine concern.

"You could say that." One of the women coughed, trying not to vomit. "We need specialized teams, what we have isn't enough."

"We can make it work." I encouraged. "Come on." I opened the side door they stood in front of, peeking out to see two armed security nod to us and usher us across the alleyway. In a brief moment, I could see our allies' vehicles creating layered blockades and span nearly half the width of the field. They were nearing the White House faster than anyone expected, and Val had clearly been inventive with his methods of dealing with the Tortured. Two trucks with massive plows barreled through piles of sandbags and crushed abandoned machine guns under their tracks as even grenade explosions hardly put a dent in their armor.

"That's my babe. Get 'em, Val." I smiled, continuing the quick trip toward the next building, pushing through its doors and strolling inside. While we didn't have a formal security presence, the soldiers from the previous door followed closely behind us and dedicated their purpose to the defense of our group.

"-we start with a corner of that skyscraper and keep pulling chunks away from the bottom, it'll eventually reach a breaking point." Kara's voice crackled through my radio.

"Oh. Like that, uh…the damn…game with the blocks. Alice and I played it during my recovery. It was a fine-motor skills thing. The hell was it called…?" Sonya responded.

"Alice, not a word." Kara added cheekily, as if I agreed to play a game with them.

"Busy." I said quietly, turning the radio off for the time being. "Where were they?"

"This way." One of the three medics took the lead, glass windows leaving our image largely exposed to our left, but ignored in the face of greater threats. The battle was still more than a hundred yards away, and we were northeast of the main endeavor. Little threat from that front struck us with fear, but our right side housed a collection of doors, each with a small room behind them

"This one." One of them pointed to a set of open double doors, a large presentation room inside with a stage at the far end. The space was devoted to an expansive array of beds with roughly six feet between each of them, and they spanned the length of the chamber. The purpose for the room didn't become clear until I started to make my way through the area and witness the only thing worse than the bloody massacre I had abandoned only minutes prior.

This building isn't a breeding ground for soldiers. This one is just…a breeding ground.

Half of the women that laid across the beds were dead, having passed away during labor, but no medical help had remained with them after the fight had started. Some were completely drained from the birthing process the way Kara had been with Amy, and others were clinging to life as delicately as they were their children. The children were a worse sight, some newborn infants struggling to breathe in the arms of their dead mothers and others having fallen next to the beds and dying of abandonment.

"Disgusting goddamn animals." I growled, stalking my way between the aisles and looking at the horrific carnage that permeated the room. "Pieces of Tortured *shit*!" I kicked an empty bed, the metal frame clanging loudly and causing a few shrill cries to pierce the air. "Find the ones that are still breathing!" I pointed to the other medics, realizing that my accidental genius would help us identify those with our best survival odds.

"What do you want us to do with the mothers? Some are alive, and some…they're bad." One of them said, looking down at a deceased parent holding their grey child.

"Use a permanent marker." I spoke frantically, dropping my bag and rifling through it. "Go in order of these rows, front to back and left to right, and mark every parent and child with matching letters of the alphabet, A through Z. It'll help us match them when we get back to the city since they'll be separated for care. Do it for the deceased, too. They'll get funerals eventually." I sighed, reluctantly stepping up to my role and starting to pace between the aisles.

The horrific things these women must have been through. I can't imagine. This might not even be the first time some of them have given birth like this.

"Alice, live pair here. They look okay." My head snapped to one of the trio, finally prompting a question.

"What are your names?"

"Erin."

"Phoenix."

"Devon."

"Okay. Erin, take care of that mother and child and get them ready to move. Once they're capable of being walked a few hundred feet, go deliver them *straight* to Amy and tell her what's going on. Have her send reinforcements over." I tried to follow the cries, quickly realizing that there weren't enough among the corpses to have a positive outlook, but were still too many to keep track of. "Phoenix, mark the crying babies and their mothers. If they can both move, send them behind Erin. If the infant is on its own, cut the umbilical cord and get them to Amy. Devon, I need you to do the hard part." I paused, looking over at him. "Find the mothers that are still breathing. If they'll survive the trip, cut the cord and leave the child in the bed. We're coming back for them." He stared at me in shocked confusion for a moment while I checked the pulse of one of the mothers.

"You're denying them…their infant child's body? How can you be so cruel-"

"*This* is cruel, Devon!" I screamed, an unintentional flicker of fire thrown over his head as I pointed outside. "*They* are cruel! What I am doing is a mercy for them!" I lowered my tone to pleading, hoping he would understand. "Look at these women. I…I know what they go through. Okay? I *know* what they go through." I gritted my teeth, my fangs appearing at the same time as my tears. "God willing, Devon…most of them will forget they ever gave birth. But we need to save the living before we do anything else. Do you understand me?" He nodded quickly, a grim frown on his face as he started to realize that we had to act the best we could under the terrible circumstances we were given. I shook my head at the pair I had been attending to, realizing that neither mother nor child were alive or revivable.

I'm allowed to say it this time. What happened to me is nothing compared to these women. And I'm alive to help them. This is my purpose.

"Here…" A dry whisper came from several rows to my right, behind me before I turned to approach the voice. One of the mothers still had half-decent coloring in her face and held a burbling, colorful infant child. I looked down at the sheets of the bed, noticing the considerable tide of red that had stained the area between her legs.

"Hey, I'm here." I started. "My name is Alice. I need you to hold that baby close to your chest, okay? I'm going to take a look at something to see why you're bleeding."

"I'm bleeding?" She whispered, her lips cracked and dry. "I feel…fine." Her eyelids were half-closed, an overwhelming fatigue overtaking her awareness.

"I'm going to take a look, okay? I'm not going to hurt you." I put up both of my hands in a show of peace, kneeling down to look at the source of the blood.

No. No, that's too much damage. They tried to fix this and didn't know how. Idiots. She could have survived…such a simple procedure…

I stood slowly, looking her in the eyes and realizing that time was short on delivering the first of many pieces of bad news to those who yet lived in this room.

"What happened before we arrived?" I asked gently, hoping for some context.

"They have us on a…cycle. They…" She bit her lip, a sob without tears coming from her open mouth. "They *breed* us. And we give birth around the same time. They say it saves time since the doctors are all in the same room. It's…more *efficient.*" She whispered, whimpering. "The doctor was trying to fix something before they all left, I-…I don't know what-" She stammered, shaking her head.

"They were trying to fix something called *placenta accreta.* A…piece of the placenta, the afterbirth, is attached to your uterus. They…tried to remove it and tore the wall of your uterus. If I try to move you, you're going to die. Even if I don't move you…you don't have long."

"No." She moaned, holding her child tighter. "No, this is…this is the first baby of mine I can save. That I can have as my own. They've taken so many."

God, she still wants the child. That's incredible after what she's been through. How lucid she is.

"I can save your baby." I said quietly, a lump in my throat making it harder to speak. "But I can't save *you*." I shook my head, exhaling and watching our supporting medics rush in.

Erin was explaining my process to them, and a total of eight medics and nurses started to mark whoever they could reach and begin basic exams. I allowed the poor woman to cry for a moment, knowing that at some point, I would have to take her newborn daughter. With each sob, I could see another bloody set of droplets gush onto the sheets, the pressure in her abdomen too high for even sobbing to be an acceptable activity. "I'm going to cut the cord real quick, okay? Hold her nice and tight. I won't let her go anywhere." I pulled a pair of scissors from my bag, wiping them down with an alcohol pad before snipping the umbilical cord. As it started to bleed, I applied a small hemostat to clamp down the wound temporarily. "What do you want to name her?" I asked, trying to look at her through my tears. Devon tapped my shoulder, pulling my ear closer to him.

"Amy says she needs to see you immediately."

"It can wait." I argued, shaking my head.

"No. It can't." He insisted, his eyes telling me that something was gravely wrong.

"I want to name her after you." The woman finally whispered, the color in her face nearly drained. "What…was your name again?"

I can't…I can't accept something like that.

"Lily." I lied, believing that my favorite flower was suitable for the tiny girl in front of me.

"Lily…I love it." The mother smiled in awe, staring at her little girl.

"What's *your* name?" I asked, my head snapping to the side as I heard a thundering explosion on the opposite end of the city.

"May." She croaked, lifting the child toward me. "My name is May."

"Then her name is Lily May." I decided, looking over at Devon. He was just as emotional as I was, the scene unbearable for any rational person to have to witness.

"I'm taking her to Amy, I'll go talk to her. Give…give May two nasal sprays of fentanyl and a dissolving tablet in her cheek." He stared at me for a moment, and he knew that I couldn't justify in front of the patient why I was ordering him to provide what would be a lethal dose of painkiller. He nodded once, and allowed me to hastily walk through the aisles, pushing past the nurses and medics, clutching the small child against the warmth of my bulletproof vest.

Nothing like this should ever happen. No evil like this should ever exist.

I moved through the hallway quickly, stopping as I saw our infantry's front line fully advanced and swarming the White House. The launcher was almost entirely assembled, but held at bay by the few Tortured that pestered the perimeter of the battlefield. Shots of opportunity wounded some of the technicians, but none appeared to be fatal, and our heavy truck-mounted guns obliterated the sources of the lingering attacks.

We're close. We're so close.

I held onto the child and sprinted through the exit door, seeing Amy standing in the doorway of the building across from me and waiting for my arrival. She reached out as I got close, guiding me inside and speaking in a flurry of words I could barely understand.

"Alice, we have a foothold, but it's slim. Your sister is trapped in the mayor's building just southeast of us. I need you to go find her and Violet-" She was interrupted at the sound of another explosion, the same direction as the last, and in a confusingly different direction than the rest of the battle. I looked at the four-lane street between our set of buildings and the line of parks that led to the White House, but was only able to confirm that it came from behind us, further north.

"Kara?" I asked, looking at Amy.

"I don't know what that could have-" We both retreated backward quickly as the deafening roar of some destructive wave barreled outside, just past the door we had entered moments ago, and covered the outside view in pieces of rubble. Sheared metal beams, powdered glass, and random bits of large plastic struts from a building's sign poured onto the four-lane street and settled without reaching the other side. I recovered to a standing position after protecting the infant with my body, taking too many long moments to let the horror wash over me.

Everyone in that building is dead.

"No, no, no." I whimpered, looking around desperately and handing the child to the closest medic. "No, please-" I opened the exit door and made it three steps toward the other building before coming to terms with the fact that evidence of its existence had been annihilated.

The remains of a skyscraper had toppled and fallen to crush the lives of too many, and of the last I would ever try to save. My mouth quivered and convulsed in ways it shouldn't have, a horrid sobbing resonating into the still-shifting debris.

Running across rubble, trying to look for life. Searing heat, dust everywhere. New York. No one was saved in New York, either. This is the tragedy that genocide brings.

I coughed, leaning toward the building's remains and trying to listen for signs that medics were trapped inside or that a crying infant was still allowed a fight for a life it deserved. Distant gunfire was my only answer, the pile of rock in front of me establishing its dominance as a tomb for the poor souls under its weight.

"Legacy…"

Amy tapped my shoulder, crying with me, and pointed toward the sky. An aircraft began its ascent off the ground, igniting its thrusters as it slowly made its way toward the east side of the area. It started to pick up speed, but was impossibly stopped by an invisible force halfway through its acceleration. The engines whined with a deafening volume as they tried to escape the grasp of whatever powerful being managed to stop the aircraft. I glowered at the sight of our enemy's imminent escape and found my opportunity to finally make up for the lives I couldn't save.

Not today, you depraved lunatic. This one's for the women.

Extending an arm, I stared at the searing-hot trail of flame that hissed from the turbines and let the full might of my abilities channel into the engine. The ripping heat from the combusting jet fuel intensified, and in the instant my abilities let loose, detonated with a thundering shockwave that sheared the wing from the plane itself. I watched with satisfaction as the wing fell and crashed into the ground below while the body of the aircraft spun and tumbled over our heads. I could hear a low rumble as it crashed into the buildings just northeast of us.

He's dead. Schillinger's Legacy is finally dead.

I still cried mournful tears, unmoving as I watched the collapsed building sit in silent anguish and cover the futures of children that would never see life.

"You saved some of them. You were quick enough to save those few." Amy offered, sniffling and leaning her head into mine. "That *has* to be enough." I sighed, nodding against her head before she snapped upright, placing her hand against her earpiece. "Oh, my God…" She muttered, looking down at my radio. "Alice, Val's hurt. He's hurt badly, and-"

"What do you mean he's hurt? Hurt how?" I started to panic, impatient as she listened to further communication. Her head bowed, looking back at me with anger rather than sadness.

"And Legacy is alive. He made it through the crash." She hissed.

"*I'll* handle him." I growled, sprinting to the opposite end of the room to leave through the front doors of the building. Amy followed closely, gripping me with a heavy dominance and spinning my shoulder around.

"Your *husband* is hurt!" She yelled, looking away quickly in fear as someone else spoke on the radio. "Violet, no!" Amy roared. "Stay the hell away from him!" She looked at me quickly, shaking her head. "I have to go stop them. It's Violet and Krystal, they're trying to get to Legacy."

"Good!" I raged. "I'm joining them. Get the hell out of my way-"

"Allison!" She screamed, standing an inch from my face. It stopped me in my tracks, her eyes piercing my own with sheer willpower. "Legacy has abilities that rival ours. If those girls get there, they're dead. Go save your husband. Leave Legacy to me." Her eyes held a cool confidence I had only ever seen in her mother, and I knew there was no way, no matter what choices I made, to keep her from protecting her sister and her devoted love.

"Right, okay. Shit, I need to hurry." I realized, my thoughts shifting to Val immediately.

I almost let Val die…for revenge…

"Where is he?" I asked as her hand met the door handle.

"Somewhere on the battlefield. Go. You'll find him." Her words of encouragement gave me few feelings of confidence as I turned, looking at the last few of our remaining medics standing in awe and shock.

No more living bodies were tended to, and no hasty attempt at lifesaving efforts motivated them to do anything other than stare out of the window and mourn the dead, marvel at the missile launcher that would save our future, and allow the successes and failures of their hard work sink into their recovering minds. I ambled my way through the building, making my way toward the entrance through which we had first secured early in the battle.

I threw the door open and walked outside, seeing the vehicles that were previously provided for cover now repositioned elsewhere and leaving the side of the building enormously exposed. I glanced at my surroundings, but focused on the battlefield sitting to my southwest. It was close enough that I could run, but the sprint would highlight me as an easy target to the distant Tortured that were still taking shots at whatever they could find.

Behind you.

I spun around, my hearing and instincts keeping me from being ambushed as a lone Tortured jogged across the street with a rifle in his hands, stopping as he saw me.

"Hey, you!" He shouted, raising the rifle. I put both of my hands up, my abilities not faster than a trigger pull.

"Doctor. Not here to hurt anyone." I explained quickly, looking over my shoulder. "Need to-"

"I recognize you. Legacy said to look out for you guys. You're one of the special ones." He claimed, inspecting me from head to toe.

"My husband calls me that, yes." I agreed. "Look, I do have abilities. My virus gave me gifts. But in a few minutes, none of that will matter. So please, let me go save my husband."

"No, he said you all needed to die." He insisted, shouldering his rifle. "And I can't have any witnesses tell Legacy that I ran off from the fight."

"*Legacy?* Legacy is dea-"

His gunshot interrupted the remainder of my sentence, ripping a hole through the center of my skull.

BATTLEGROUND

AMY

I released my hold on the strap of Alice's armor plating, relaxing my face from the angry glare I held against her.

"Go save your husband. Leave Legacy to me." I stressed, watching the sanity finally wash over her eyes. I could see the realization of the mistake she nearly made, her focus quickly switching to the proper way of thinking.

"Right. Okay. Shit, I need to hurry. Where is he?" I shook my head at her and shrugged, only having heard the brief call over the radio that he was in dire need of help.

"Somewhere on the battlefield. Go. You'll find him." I offered, knowing that once she was able to get close, she would be able to easily identify him among the other injured.

Unable to waste any time, I ripped the door open without further guidance and turned to my right. The street was littered with scattered debris from one of our helicopters, having crashed into a building just over a block away from where I stood. I looked around for the scene of another crash, knowing it was somewhere beyond the layers of metropolis at my front. Deep black smoke poured into the sky in a neat column, and while the source was hidden behind the next few blocks of the city, was a clear identifier of Legacy's crash.

Get there. Now.

I dug my heel into the pavement and sprinted, ripping off my bulletproof vest as I ran. Throwing it to the side as I made my way down the empty main street, I was able to lighten my weight and provide a greater degree of comfort while I moved.

Breathe.

I crossed four asphalt lanes of stone dust and twisted metal, making it to the other side within seconds and forcing a quick decision on the fastest way to approach. I ducked into a slim alley between a bank and a retail store, rushing past empty dumpsters and neatly-kept fire escapes. My feet pounded relentlessly against the ground, stressing the leather of my boots to a point far beyond their intended design.

Breathe.

Turning to the right as I exited the alleyway, a magnificent and familiar face met my own in a remarkably shocked look of gratefulness and gratifying surprise. Krystal's length of blue hair was greyed with the same dust that was smeared across her face in smudges of darker mud where it had mixed with sweat and tears. Her chest was covered in blood, but not of her own from an apparent lack of open wounds.

I rushed toward her, noticing that as she did the same, her left leg was favored and her right was held together with a piece of steel rebar and torn pieces of fabric. Rather than touching her leg as I conventionally would have done to heal it, I ambushed her mouth with my own and let my abilities heal her while we shared a blissful kiss in the midst of a raging battle.

Femur snapped clean in half. She's in ripping pain, I can feel it. Both pieces are mated well because of her splint. I can fuse them together for a decent repair. She's afraid.

"Violet." I exclaimed quickly, pulling away from her as the bones in her leg solidified back into one piece. "Where is she?" Her face held a visible sense of relief, but dipped quickly into panic as she pointed behind her.

"I tried chasing her." She gulped, still breathing heavily. "Couldn't move fast enough. She's just ahead, going for Legacy."

"Come on." I patted her arm, watching her tear the splint away from her leg as we ran together. The maze of buildings were a massive obstacle, no direct path seeming to have any preference over which way we would reach Violet any faster.

Breathe.

After two blocks, we reached a T-shaped intersection that diverted traffic away from a massive building that spanned a thousand feet wide and blocked a direct route toward the smoke that plumed from behind it.

"You go right." I decided quickly, unwilling to waste any time in deciding which way Violet would have gone.

Krystal took off without any delay, leaving me with a clear direction to my left while I crossed the concrete pad that marked a large plaza in front of what seemed to be a major government building. I tried to avoid any thoughts of what would happen if Violet had arrived, but hoped that she was smart enough to wait for the two of us to arrive before doing anything rash. Jalix had indicated that he saw Legacy moving away from the wreckage, so I nearly hoped that his escape meant her safety. I rounded the back corner of the structure and turned the corner, revealing another small street and one more building that hid the scene of the impact.

Breathe.

The smell of the aircraft's smoke was acrid, burning my nostrils with the scent of harsh chemicals and scorched materials not meant to be combusted. Alongside my sense of smell, my hearing started to put my senses into overdrive as I neared the corner of the final building, hearing a horrid, wailing scream of pain and anguish that battered against my ears and incited an adrenaline rush unparalleled by any other. Time seemed to slow further and further as the seconds ticked in my head, but I felt further and further away from control over my own actions.

I stopped in my tracks as the scene in front of me unfolded into an unworldly terror. The love of my life and eternal soulmate stood across from me, entering the parking lot much the same way I had. Her open mouth, alongside its screeching howl of agony, held a set of fangs that managed to erupt in a violent display of power at the scene her eyes were fixed onto. The fiery remains of the aircraft were a crumpled mess of metal and fragmented materials that protruded from the hole it created in the diner it had crashed into. Spilled fuel ignited the space around us as waves of harsh flame licked at everything it could reach.

Breathe.

Legacy was laid in front of the wreckage, his body seared and singed to a nearly unrecognizable state. He held a pistol in his outstretched arm, which had started to fall limp due to the stalagmite of solid ice that erupted from the ground and penetrated his skull with a frozen burst of violent gore. His target, it seemed, was my resplendent sister, who stood only a dozen feet in front of him in the center of the empty lot. In the fraction of a second I took to absorb the image into my eyes, I made the decision to continue moving faster than what my body would allow and barrel toward Violet at a breakneck speed.

I was staring at her in the same way Krystal was, keeping my eyes locked tightly on her figure as it started to tip backward in the early throes of death. I tried to ignore the spurt of blood that erupted from the back of her skull, along with the bullet's shockwave and the shattered pieces of bone, and took in a massive breath before encountering her.

"AMY!" Krystal's pained screams changed to a dire plea in the moments before I met Violet's figure. Her fear was warranted, and I didn't have the time to explain the reasoning behind my desperate attempt at saving my sister's life. I knew that every past experience with healing a damaged brain ended in a near-fatal incident, but I couldn't change my course of action in the moments of pure love I felt for the dark-haired woman in front of me.

I love you, Krystal. I'm sorry.

I let my legs buckle beneath me, sliding onto my knees to catch Violet before she hit the ground and placing my right palm on the hole in her skull.

Breathe.

DREAMSCAPE

AMY

Like any child, there was a moment in which I gained a sense of consciousness unlike awakening from sleep. As if I knew I had lived, yet was unable to independently retain any memory of it, I realized my own existence in a wonderous moment of disbelief. My senses seemed to have meaning that surpassed pure survival, instead giving me the ability to think and experience things in a way I never had before.

In that moment, I was able to finally retain a sense of self and observe my surroundings with true purpose. My body, whether real or imagined, was now a part of who I was instead of a machine that operated independently of me, and my eyes – overwhelmed with the sight in front of me – were captivated with the sight of my surroundings.

The sky above, filled with stars and glowing galaxies beyond count, was blackened in vague darkness between its points of light, but emitted a beautiful glow of purples and indigos unspoken of in color palettes known to mankind. The colors streaked across the sky in wide bands of distant stardust, igniting the air around me in a gentle illumination and comforting light. The horizon, which I could see as a defined line between the ground and the sky, confronted the stretched, flat space under my feet. It was distant beyond human measurement, but still visible in spite of the light fog that encompassed it.

The haze across the horizon, although transparent and sparse in its existence, was a spectacular lavender color. It felt lovely just to exist in the space, but a disturbance somewhere in my mind kept me from feeling any form of pleasure. Immediately in front of me, a darker cloud – the shade of ripe plum – touched the ground and sprawled out in the gentle waves of an impact against the intangible surface beneath my feet. As if produced by the dark cloud itself, a young woman with hair the color of onyx stepped out with a broad smile across her face. I knew the woman well, but not in any way I felt familiar with. It was a strange sensation, having an immediate emotional connection and deeply loving bond without a memory of her existence within my lifespan.

"Hi, Amy." The woman said quietly, her face soft with the same love I felt in my own heart. "I can't find the words for how happy I am to see you." I paused, searching my mind for the name of the woman, letting a natural reaction settle onto my lips and tongue.

"Violet." I said quietly, tilting my head. "Sister."

"Yes." She beamed, her shimmering hair tucked behind her ears and exposing an assortment of silver piercings. "Of course it's me. I'm so glad you're here."

Something…

I shook my head, an odd combination of speech and images taking over my mind for the briefest moment. The singular instant seemed to stall the rest of my senses, taking place behind my eyes somewhere and hailing a sense beyond sight, sound, and touch. As I gazed at Violet's patiently waiting face, I felt the sensation again, stronger this time, and outlying from any feeling of self-control.

Something…is wrong.

"Something…is wrong." I voiced aloud the sensation under my scalp, making the phenomenon as real as I could through my own physical actions.

"Yes. Something is wrong." Violet agreed, her calm smile only persisting in light of the statement. "Take a moment to gather yourself. It's okay. I have all the time in the world."

"Gather myself." I repeated, realizing that the phenomenon occurring in my mind was in fact conscious thought, and hadn't existed in the brief moments that I gained awareness.

Something is wrong. You're not supposed to be here.

"I'm not supposed to be here." I vocalized, watching for Violet's response.

"No. But that's okay. You're here now, and that's all that matters." She closed her mouth, hiding her teeth but allowing her rosy pink lips to soothingly confirm that I was safe in this breathtaking prison of thought.

The dark cloud that spawned her existence retreated by a few dozen feet, but remained a source of unknowing darkness while it rolled in waves of smoky mist across the ground. In brief glimpses, it seemed to have its own glow as streaks of tiny lightning bolts connected various wisps in flitters of luminescence. It felt wrong, as if it was out of place from the calming environment we stood within. Violet turned her head slowly, lifting a hand as the smoke followed her movement. The left side of the cloud roiled in waves as it lifted off the ground, but settled as she lowered her hand after a few moments.

Violet is in control here. She is all that matters.

"This is yours. All of it. You're all that matters." I whispered, my thoughts becoming more clear without memories to accompany them. "I…love you." I recognized. She laughed gently, the action spurring a moment of joy in my own heart.

"I love you too, my darling sister." She closed her eyes for a moment, taking in a slow, deep breath and letting the cloud behind her gently surge in a show of power. It threatened to touch her, creeping forward and reaching toward the sky in a menacing flash. "You know why you're here." She whispered, opening her eyes. Her face didn't show any fear, the alabaster of her skin highlighting a deep set of chestnut-brown eyes and a caring regard.

You're dying.

"I'm dying." I breathed, the simple statement causing the wine-red haze to surround us quickly and roll in violent waves between us. At Violet's behest, her hands ushered the cloud behind her once again and calmed it to a tranquil state from a reasonable distance away.

"We're both dying." She confirmed quietly. "You're here…in my mind. But you can't stay. I'm…damaged." She imparted quietly, her eyes darting away for a moment.

She's damaged. That's why you're here.

"That's why I'm here. I want to fix you." I repeated.

The smell of smoke. Waves of fire and flame and fury at your side. Your true love, fearing for your life. The woman of your dreams made of pure courage and defiance in the face of evil. A moment of horror. A moment of sorrow. Wake up, Amy.

"I want to fix you." I repeated, my eyes roaming as a new sense of self started to develop. Waves of memories nearly forced my knees to fail under me in spite of the physical sensation being nonexistent in the world we existed within. My eyes widened, looking at Violet with renewed purpose. "I'm here to fix you!" I laughed, doubling over in relief. "I can fix you." I whispered, taking a step toward her. Finally, and after too many moments of her reassuring expression, her smile faded with the small step she took backward.

"No, Amy…" Violet whispered, her voice resonating softly across the vast emptiness around us. "I'm damaged. That's why you're here. But the *reason* you're here doesn't matter. What matters now is what you and I do. And that…can't include fixing me." Her voice was mournful, and I shared her grief with flashes of her shared emotion, but I raised my voice and defied her.

"I can fix you!" I shouted, recoiling as the fog behind her swelled with fury.

"No, Amy." Her smile returned, along with her heartening demeanor. "But I…can fix *you.*"

You're dying.

"I'm dying." I repeated again, confused at our situation and how the dualities of our deaths played a role in our impossible atmosphere.

"Yes." She smiled wider, her brow raised with happiness. "And I can fix you."

"How?" I murmured, trying to recall any sense of my healing abilities. As if they had never existed, I simply felt human in design while my arms and legs uselessly remained attached without any significant purpose in our collective dream. She lifted her hand momentarily, staring at the coffin-shaped black nails she proudly maintained, and smirked.

"This is my domain." She gestured around us, her eyes moving to take in the sight of the flawless night sky in its seemingly permanent state. "This is my mind. My thoughts, my feelings. My memories."

"That's impossible." I asserted. "This…all of this is *impossible.*"

"But you're here." Violet said again. "And you are all that matters."

"That was my thought." I pondered, looking at her quizzically. "It's what I said to you."

"Our thoughts are the same here." She giggled, her happiness felt in my own soul as she expressed it in her laughter. "We're together in ways I can't explain. I feel you. I know you. And we're sharing this moment."

"This moment." I echoed. "What is time here? There's…an *outside* to this place. There's more beyond this."

"Yes. There is." She confirmed, her posture straightening at my statement. She seemed to become more herself, more composed and relaxed as I gained further awareness. "But right now, we're here. You're here. And I need to fix you."

"I need to fix *you*." I protested gently, fearing the wrath of the lightning-filled cloud behind her. "I can't leave without making you better. Healing you. You said you're damaged, I can *fix* damaged." She chuckled softly, shaking her head.

"You've mistaken something your whole life, my loving sister." She looked at the sky once again as it transformed. The scenic view of a forgiving universe rolled in circles and waves as it reformed into much the same scene, but with the stars in different places than they were previously. The galaxies bore new shapes, some now having spiral arms in graceful curves while others remained orbs of pinpointed light. "The brain can be healed. But the mind is something different. Consciousness, soul, the combination of things that make us a person…that's for something greater than us to heal."

"No…" I said softly. "I healed Krystal. Her trauma-"

"She healed *herself*, Amy." Violet interrupted, grinning cheerfully. "With your help. You exposed her to death while she was alive. You let her process things. That was all Krystal's doing. The same you're doing for me, now. You may be able to manipulate the brain when your gifts allow you…but the mind is handled by its possessor. And you're giving me the chance to show you mine."

"This is your mind." I marveled, staring up at the sky once more. "It's beautiful, Violet. More than I could have imagined."

Something's wrong.

I hesitated, something distantly causing a unique and new phenomenon in my right arm. It was unpleasant, enough that the light around us dimmed and flickered with a sensation of unwanted touch.

Pain. It's called pain.

"I'm in pain." I thought aloud to Violet, who nodded gently.

"You're dying. We're on borrowed time. And I need to make the most of it. You needed to feel pain for what comes next."

"And what comes next?" The darkness abandoned its purpose, the pain in my arm fading slightly.

"I need you to see how I'm going to fix you." She beamed, raising her hands and letting the fog at her back slowly creep several trivial tendrils into the space between us.

Touch it.

Violet reached out and placed her hand within the wisps of the dark haze, waiting for me to do the same. I did, only my left arm having enough strength to lift and move to make contact with a tiny streak of lightning that darted between the gaps in the fog.

***

Jared opened the door for me, letting me walk into the room at my own pace while I struggled to move my stalling feet.

No way this is all mine.

I let out an elated gasp as I moved further into the room and looked around at the space I had always dreamed of. It was calm, and while others would have said it was too small for their taste, I knew it was going to be mine. That was enough to justify happiness. The kitchen was modest, basic cabinetry and an open access to the living room giving the scene a spacious feel. A brand new easel, with white canvasses of every size and shape lay quietly in the living room against a small television set and a pair of speakers.

"Now remember-" He started again, gesturing to the space while I stood in my heavenly trance. "You'll have neighbors. Apartment upstairs, and people to your left and right. Walls are concrete, so don't worry about noise, but be considerate. I don't want to see you avoiding them." He warned, patting my back lightly. His massive hand almost spanned the distance between my shoulder blades, my thin frame hardly having grown in spite of the food I had eaten over the last several days.

"Th-th…thank y-you…Ja-ared." I smiled, remaining tear-free and powering through my stutter long enough to thank him properly. "I-I'll s-s-say hi. To them." I furrowed my brow, looking up at him in somber curiosity. "What if th-they j-j-…" I stopped speaking, clenching my teeth while he waited patiently, leaning his body against the doorframe and averting his kind eyes so as not to stare at me awkwardly. "J…judge m-me?" He returned his gaze, leaning forward and putting his arm around my shoulders.

"Then I beat 'em up." He chuckled, prompting a laugh from me. "No one's gonna judge you, Vi." He looked down at me, nearly a foot taller than I was. "I thought people was gonna judge me, too. I got here, no one else with me. No education, ain't shit to my name. But *Kara*…" He paused, looking at the empty doorway. "She saved me. Alice found me, bit me, all that. But Kara took one look at me. Said I was made of somethin' different. Now I'm doin' school during the daytime, gettin' an education. Sittin' in the same room while she does her planning and shit with Sonya. You got a stutter, girl. Ain't nothin else about it." He laughed, distressing me until he elaborated. "But I wanna talk and act like Kara. Stand proud like her, use the words she uses to influence people. We *all* gotta change. We *all* got shit wrong with us. But we…*we're* gonna get better at being who we want to be." I could tell he put stress on his words, trying to speak more eloquently to prove his point.

I'm not the only one who wants to change. But I have to. He just…wants to.

"You d-don't need to-o change, Jared." I wanted him to know that he was amazing just the way he was, and that I was accepting of him without needing to change. "I l-like the way you-ou talk. It s-sounds tou-ough. You do-on't use extra w-words. Like h-how I talk." He smirked, nodding.

"I appreciate that, Vi. Means something to me. But *I* wanna change. No one else can make me. But *I* can make me. I wanna be better than my family, be better than a Philly crack-slinger. I wanna sound different than all them back home. And then I wanna teach other people. Wanna go back and tell 'em they got another option. Teach 'em they can be better." I looked around again, still basking in the disbelief that I would have my own living space in the comfort of the community that surrounded me.

You'll be just like everyone else. You'll finally blend in.

"J-ared?" I asked, prompting his eyebrows to lift momentarily. "I d-don't want to be b-boring. If m-my stutter is gone…I still w-want to be u-u-nique." He laughed, closing the door and gesturing to the couch.

"I've seen your art, Vi. You are *never* gonna be boring. You think I don't feel like that? Another uneducated Black man from Philly. You think I mean shit to anyone?" He sighed, letting me sit down while he stood in front of me. "News barely even cover me when I got shot. They don't care about me up there. No one does. You got people that are racist, people sexist, homophobic. People are bad, Vi. But *you* are good. You stay good, you can change those people. Show 'em how wrong they can be. How messed up they are."

"I d-don't see that down h-here." I pointed out, reminding him how receptive everyone was of my arrival. "V-Vampyres are k-kind. They kn-know better." He nodded, gesturing to me.

"Exactly. *No one* is gonna judge you, Vi. Not until you get famous with one of those drawings." I laughed, shaking my head. "I'm serious!" He continued, smiling. "Get that shit up for sale, you'd bring in real money. You got talent."

"No one is g-gonna take an a-artist that stu-utters, Jared." I cautioned. He sat down next to me on the couch, throwing his arm over my shoulder and kicking his gargantuan feet up on the coffee table.

"And no one's gonna take in a retired drug dealer. But Kara did. This city did." He smirked, looking deeply into my eyes. "You stay here, you do what you do…the world's gonna know who you are. And they're gonna love you like we do."

***

I blinked, realizing how quickly I had delved into another reality and lived Violet's experiences as my own. As impossible as it may have been, the experience of sitting next to Jared and sharing a heartfelt moment was now my own, a memory from her perspective and mind somehow joining my own collective of memories.

"How did you do that?" I whispered, watching the cloud return to its position a short distance away. As I looked around, I realized that the lavender haze that blurred the edge of the horizon had grown significantly closer and more dense, shrinking the visible area around us to a circle of a few hundred feet. "What…happened?"

"I shared my mind with you. My memories." She knelt down, taking a deep breath and apparently recovering from the experience. I, on the other hand, felt energized and happy at the new memory.

"How?" I questioned. "How? And why?"

"I'm dying." She murmured, standing up again and tilting her head. "And you can't fix me."

"Let me *try*." I insisted, the two of us sharing a horrendously hopeless moment of melancholy.

"There's no trying here. No healing. No gifts. Just…thoughts. Memories." She inspected her hand again, my own right arm shooting with a ripping pain once more. "We have to hurry." She whispered. I finally grabbed my right shoulder, an immeasurable agony decimating the upper part of my arm and numbing the rest down to my fingertips. Violet swayed her hands, throwing them forward and sending the wisps of the burgundy cloud to embrace my chest in warmth.

***

My soul still felt hollow, especially in my state of intoxication, but I was able to feel the warm sting of happiness against my misery while I stared at Amy's tiny, burbling body. Alice sat next to me, staring in much the same way without having said much in the previous minutes of our companionship. Breaking the silence, she turned to me with a brief question.

"Do you still love her?" She mumbled, her eyes reddened with tears long shed and depleted from her own mourning.

"Love who?" I asked, the word *love* being a curse on my lips.

"Krystal." She took in a quivering breath, sighing and speaking quietly. "I…heard you two. Fighting. Do you still love her?" I hesitated for far longer than I should have, staring at Amy with an intense curiosity and a profound confusion within my emotional state.

"I love her." I started, sniffling at the threat of new tears. "But that isn't her. It hasn't *been* her. I don't just love her. I miss her." I looked at Alice in desperation, knowing that she was the only one to have a better handle on her sister's life than I did. Alice nodded, pressing her lips together and letting her head drop.

"I do, too." She whispered, letting out a single sob before she forcibly composed herself. "I miss everyone." She gritted her teeth. "I miss Sonya…even though she's here. Krystal, even though she's here. I miss Jared and Val-" She finally broke at the mention of her husband, saving his name for last because of her inability to function with the thought of him.

I still…can't believe all of this. It can't possibly be the end of us.

I put my hand on her back, the only attempt I could make at being reassuring in my current state. I needed the same, and had no one to provide it for me now that Krystal was solidly in the mindset of fulfilling her impulsive, addictive needs.

"You still have Krystal." I said quietly, looking over at her. "And I know she's not herself right now, but one day…she will be. Again. We'll have her back with us."

"Now that Kara's gone?" Alice asked, doubtful at my statement.

"One day…not soon, but one day, she'll heal. And we'll be here to help her heal. From her addiction, from Kara, from everyone's loss…from all of it. We'll *all* heal."

"I don't think I ever will, Vi." Alice moaned, sinking her face into her hands. "My whole world just fell apart."

"And we'll put it back together." I kissed the side of her head and looked over at Amy again, feeling as much love as my body would allow for the final triumph of Kara's life. "Not today. Not tomorrow. But one day we'll put things back together with what we have." I looked out into the hall as Krystal and Sonya hastily made their way through the main hall. "And for those that died…we'll make sure their legacy survives."

***

"Legacy!" I exclaimed, the thought jerking me away from the memory and back into our mutually-shared atmosphere. My sense of independence returned quickly, but was soured by the continuing numbness in my right arm, everything below my elbow now useless and my shoulder in excruciating pain. As I looked around, I recognized that the constricting fog of our world's border was only a few feet from us, leaving no room to see anything but a small sliver of the night sky.

"You heard that word…you were afraid." Violet observed, now sitting on the ground with an unpleasant expression on her face.

You're both dying.

"I've been afraid since I heard it. Since I knew who he was." I agreed, the lingering memories of his death and Krystal's outstretched hand my only solace in the final moments before our dream. "I…feel like myself again." I observed. "My thoughts are clearer, less…distant. I feel normal."

"Good." She smiled gently, looking up at me. "It's working. But we're…out of time, I think." She gestured to our border, which pressed against the crimson vapor and forced it to take solace above our heads like a bloodthirsty storm cloud.

"Violet…let me *try* to save you. Come on, I know this is-"

"You feel more normal, Amy. And so do I. We're…more in sync. Kinda…like we're just talking outside of this place." She chuckled, shaking her head. "But there's nothing you can do for me."

"There *has* to be something!" I cried, Violet's neutrality fighting the terrible sadness in my heart. I wanted to cry, but it was as if tears were impossible in our small world. "Violet, there *has* to be."

"You can't fix me, Amy." She sighed, tired of repeating the same words. "I know that's why you're here, but you can't. I'm damaged beyond repair. Broken and fading. So what we do here…it has to be for your sake."

"Let me give you my life." I insisted. "There has to be a way to trade. You've had so much more time with everyone, you have so much history with our family."

"I have." She smiled again. "So much time. The good…the bad. The evil. The justice. I've seen so much, Amy. But…it's your turn, now."

Fight back.

While I wasn't allowed to cry, rage was still something that made its way into my body by way of my more emotional thoughts. I used my left arm to swing at the lavender mist, which pushed it back by several feet. With excitement, I started walking in a circle around Violet's body, swinging violently and forcing the haze to cower a dozen feet at a time. I was exhausted after only moments of the effort, making a single trip around the perimeter before kneeling to recover my energy. Watching closely, I could make out a slow creep as it approached us once more.

"There's no fighting this one, Amy." Violet established. "I'm dying."

"You *can't* die!" I roared, approaching her and sitting in front of her. She had leaned back slightly so I wouldn't touch her, but didn't move from her spot on the ground.

"Krystal fought death. That's why you believe I can do the same." She nodded slowly, realizing my logic.

"Yes. You just have to fight back. Not…sit here and wait." I insisted. As if she were a parent explaining something I wouldn't understand until I was older and wiser, she parted her lips and spoke again.

"I won't face death." She breathed, her smile slowly returning. "Don't you see?"

"No, I don't." I pleaded. "Help me understand." She took a deep breath, a tiredness in her eyes.

"You're here with me. Death…won't come. You've taken over my final thoughts, my final moments. When I die, when my body dies…I'll just stop existing. No process, no struggle. You've given me peace in my death. That's…why I feel so happy. There's no void waiting, there's no darkness. I'm here. And then I won't be. I am happy with that."

"How aren't you terrified?" I felt as if I was begging her to feel something other than happiness, but I continued. "I…can't cry because you feel so at peace. Your emotions are keeping me from feeling the sadness I want to. Why aren't you afraid of death?"

"It's the next big adventure." She suggested. "I get to find out if there's an afterlife. If there's a God. I get to become part of the earth, or ashes in the breeze that end up exploring all the corners of the world. Ashes that become atoms that will *always* exist. My death is okay. And I need *you* to be okay with it."

"No." I refused immediately. "I can't let-"

"For me." She interrupted. "It's my last wish. Just to…know I'm not gone. To be there and keep me in your memories."

"Violet, please-"

"We're out of time, Amy." It was the first thing she had said with any sort of alarm, but it came across as a direct statement rather than panic. "Please. Agree to do this for me. Keep me in your memories and don't let me be forgotten. You can't break down because of my death. I *need* you to agree with that." The typical stillness of the lavender mist was now punctuated with periodic spurts of energy, small sections lunging toward us without being able to reach our bodies.

"Okay." I whispered, nodding. "I-…of course I'll never forget you. I can be strong for you. I can…keep you in my memories." Violet's smile widened, an energy returning as she stood up. I followed closely, the vapors constricting the space until we only had room to stand in front of one another. Her porcelain skin showed no signs of distress, instead depicting the image of someone whose life had been entirely fulfilled.

"Then that's my gift to you. My…parting gift." She chuckled, lifting her hands and indicating that I hold them. I stared for too long, waiting for her to explain further. "Jalix once said to our mother that love is a gift. That love wasn't a feeling, but an action. This…is my gift to you. It's everything I am, and everything I would be. You deserve nothing less for the love I bear in my heart for you. The love I'll *always* have for you."

Scream. Cry. Run. Do something. Don't let her do this. Don't let your sister die like this.

Hesitantly, I reached up and placed my hands on hers, squeezing them lightly as a moment permeated the space around us. It was insignificant, only a trace of telltale emotion escaping into the air, but it allowed each of us a single tear as we looked into each other's eyes.

She smirked, the Violet I knew standing in front of me with the presence I had grown up with. Finally, she was fully herself within our dream, and wasn't affected by anything else in our surroundings. "Take care of me, sis." She winked at me, her contentment unwavering. "Go save the world." She dropped her hands, closing her eyes as the thick haze of the lavender clouds finally claimed her, swarming her body with its color and dissipating at infinitely fast speeds toward the horizon.

I was left alone, the sky slowly darkening as each star began to lose its light. The galaxies dimmed, flickering as the process of their decay sped up while they vanished into the everlasting night. I was engrossed in an unfaltering darkness with nothing and no one to hear me. There was no light or sound, and only an empty nothingness surrounding me in every imperceivable direction. No emotional influence constrained my actions, so in spite of my promise, I screamed into the black night with a silent voice.

I had yet to go back to the real world, where my promise would actually matter, and for eons, what felt like millennia, I screamed and cried at the pure essence of absence in the hope that she could still hear me. I wailed at the fading reality of all of life's existence, condemning it for allowing such a beautiful spirit to vanish from the world. Nothing held me back, and I mourned violently at the abyss until my own existence began to fade.

No longer did I have a voice to express my despair, and only my thoughts kept the same wretched thoughts churning through the concept of everything I was. For a moment, I understood what it was to become Sorrow, and in its infinite grief I had a moment of pause. For one moment, I was purified of emotion and left with a hollow blankness that existed in the absence of soul. With a throat I didn't have and ears long vanished within the decay of pure oblivion, a voice somehow resonated through the air with a single, breathy command.

Breathe.

AFTERSHOCK

AMY

I first woke to the sensation of a tear leaving the corner of my eye, which seemed to be the only thing I was able to feel until long moments later. Unfortunately, the physical discovery of my being was delayed by someone who had been watching for signs of life, and they immediately rejoiced.

"Oh, God. Amy…"

"Amy, baby? Can you hear us?" Both of my parents were somewhere to my left, mere voices as I still couldn't quite fully open my eyes. I tried to mumble something, or even groan, but it came out as a sigh, instead. The muscles in my throat couldn't quite control my vocal cords yet.

"Amy? If you can hear us, can you do that again?" Dad asked while my mother cried quietly in joy. I tried again, taking in a breath and managing to apply the smallest amount of intonation to the exhale.

"Mmm……" At my reply, even my father, the hardened veteran he was and survivor of Legacy's infamous torturing process, broke down into tears next to my mother.

They're alive. They made it. We…made it. Right?

As my thoughts started to collect into a rational series of questions, I became aware of how many troublesome thoughts I truly had.

Wait. Where are we? Am I okay, am I paralyzed? Did we get the cure out? Am I human right now?

My stress level started to rise, and it gave a degree more of awareness within the rest of my body. I felt myself squirm for a moment, a test of my ability to move, which was successful aside from my right arm. It felt attached to something, like my arm had been sunken into a cement wall up to the elbow. I couldn't move it, but I knew it was there. I heard footsteps, presumably my father's by their weight, move across an odd-sounding floor and call out into a room.

"She's awake." While echoing footsteps indicated that there were more people in wait for my recovery, one voice echoed with the muffled sound of wailing sobs.

Krystal…my love…

Her reaction delayed any other movement, and I could hear her crying alone while everyone else surrounded me. I placed every ounce of energy into opening my eyes, and with a great effort, a blurry mess opened in front of me. The colors of surfaces were almost too bright, too vibrant for my brain to handle, and I struggled to make out basic patterns. Faces were certainly beyond my grasp, a level of detail needing to provide focus before I could discern anything else. The group was relatively quiet, although a few indistinguishable murmurs identified that they were familiar.

"Hey, sweetie. It's Sonya. You don't have to talk or anything, but…just know that I'm here, okay? I'm so happy you're okay. You're safe. We're safe. Just take your time recovering, alright?" She was unsure of what to say, especially since I couldn't say anything back, and retreated to allow the next person in line to speak their mind.

"Hey, kid. We, uh…we made it. You did great."

Tony.

"We're proud of you, you know? You did some…impossible things. Saved the day. Made sure Legacy was dead. So…thank you. I'll, uh…be here when you're up and around."

And Eric. He's alive! I must be back in Vanaheim.

The positivity of that thought spurred my heart and sharpened my vision with a degree more of clarity. My head, although it felt heavier than a block of lead and moved with the same amount of ease, was able to shift to my left to see my visitors. There was a long pause, no one else around to walk inside.

Wait…that was Krystal crying, right? Not someone else? Why isn't she here?

"Amy, we're giving you a little bit of Factor Five, okay? It should give you some energy and more control. Just take it very, very slow, okay?" My father warned. I couldn't nod in return, but I laid my head back and waited for its effects to take hold. The IV line in my left arm was already pushing fluid into my veins, but its effects changed after a few seconds, and I started to feel my body come alive as the chemicals travelled through my blood vessels.

Left arm. Good movement, fingertips have sensation. Abdominal muscles, I can flex. Same with glutes and legs. Toes have sensation. Oh, my face…I can move my mouth. My tongue, my lips. They're so dry…wait. My fangs. They're still here. Did the Tortured stop the cure? Hang on. My right arm. I can't move it. The lower part I can't even feel.

Taking the wise advice of my father, I lifted my head slowly to finally take in my surroundings with substantial detail. My immediate environment was a homebrewed surgical suite, various pieces of complex equipment having been hooked up wherever they could fit in the small room. I laid on a regular mattress rather than a hospital bed, which surprised me. The room was part of a log cabin, the warm wood interior trapping the heat of a wood-fed fireplace. My parents sat next to it, watching me with wonder.

The entry to the next room was to my left, but my entire right-side view was obscured by a medical-grade privacy curtain that hid everything on the other side of the room. My arm, which I now realized was bound in a cast, was placed through a hole in the curtain and attached to something on the other side. I could hear quiet movement, but it was ignored as a new person, my favorite person, entered and stared at me with her oceanic eyes.

"Amy…" Krystal sobbed happily, making her way to my bedside. I had enough energy to reach for her chin as she sat down, grateful that she was kind enough to allow me a short-lived kiss for my own gratification.

"K…Krystal." I rasped, cleaning my throat several times and coughing.

"No, it's okay. Relax. You've…been through a lot, Amy."

"Where-" I tried to ask one of my many questions, but it was blocked by the partial closure of my throat once more. I felt the odd tingling of my own abilities going to work, finally restoring my body after a period of dormancy. "Oh…" I whispered, the brief pains and aches of newly-restored tissue populating in places across my body. They stopped at the edge of my cast, not allowing for my powers to travel any further.

What the hell happened to my arm? Even my powers won't touch it.

"We'll explain." Krystal offered, seeing my eyes dart to the blue-wrapped plaster cast. I looked back at her, staring for a moment as we examined each other. Her eyes were still red, stung with sadness, but looked at me in curiosity rather than relief. "Your eyes…can you see okay?"

"Eyes? Yeah, I can…see okay." I was able to respond, but had to clear my throat first. "Why?"

"It...doesn't matter right now." She exhaled, staring at me as if I were the most precious thing in the world. "I'm so glad you're back with us."

"You're so strong, Amy." My mother spoke up, reminding me that my parents were present. "I can't tell you how happy we are that you're okay."

"What happened?" I returned quickly, placing a hand on my forehead as a headache started to form behind my eyes. The room was silent for a long moment, no one daring to shatter the peace. Before they could respond, another set of footsteps lumbered heavily outside the door and made its way into my recovery room.

He was one of the largest men I knew, requiring him to kneel at my side. Although I recognized his body and some of his features, the right side of his face was badly mangled and only partially repaired. He wore an eye patch over the socket, and I somehow knew he had lost it during the fight. Krystal stepped away to let the two of us reunite, retreating to the other room as she started to choke up again.

"Hey, you." Val's voice hit me like a train, forcing a hard swallow and more than a few tears as I stared at him. "Not one for long speeches. That's, uh...Jalix's job. So I'll let your dad give you all the long words." He gestured with his head. "But me, I'm glad you're still kicking. Tough. Just like your uncle." He chuckled lightly at his own joke, touching my left shoulder for a moment. "I love you. I'll see you when you're up and around."

"Wait." I protested, sitting up slightly and regretting it due to the nausea that rolled through my body. "Can't you stay?" I laid my head back down, breathing deeply and moving the silver locks of hair that fell in front of my eyes. Val was quiet for a minute, deliberating my request.

"You want me to?" He clarified.

"Yeah, of course." I reassured. "Why wouldn't I?" He paused again.

"I'm…I don't want you to be reminded of things just by being here. By seeing…me." Still unable to sit up fully, I rolled slightly onto my side to peer at him. The source of his injuries would have inflicted severe pain, and I was sure that he was still struggling with it. Regardless of where they came from, I felt more pity for his situation than I did remembrance over the fleeting memories of the battle.

"I want to be reminded I still *have* you." I said softly. "Stay." His left eye had the slight gloss of early tears at hearing my remarks, taking a seat on the floor next to my bed.

"I'm glad you're okay, Amy." He whispered emotionally. I braced myself for the hardest question, knowing full well that I wasn't prepared for the answers.

"I know what I'm about to ask. But…where is everyone else? Raven and Alice, Violet, Brynn and the pilots…I don't see any of them." I kept my tone even and steady, but my heart raced at the unanswered questions in my head.

"Pilots are at Quantico. Holding down the fort, literally. Brynn…didn't make it. Right after you…I guess passed out, there was a second wave of Tortured. Right before we went to launch the cure." My father started.

Oh, no…we couldn't have lost.

"Brynn was killed by a sniper round. No suffering, but no way to save her. The techs already had the launcher assembled, so they helped stage a counteroffensive. We slaughtered nearly every Tortured left on that field. None of them made it within a hundred feet of our perimeter." He paused, his eyes cast in dark shadows against the ground. "We had to put the cure on hold until we could evacuate the wounded. Give them time to heal…as Vampyres. But it worked. We won. Even the remaining Tortured just…fell apart. Got sick, started de-converting on the battlefield. Factor Five didn't help them. The cure worked. Most everyone is back at Vanaheim, dealing with the process of becoming human again. Our medical staff is busy, I'll put it that way."

Thank God…we did it. The cure was effective.

"What about the others?" I asked, looking at my mother. She hesitated, looking at the other side of the privacy curtain and frowning deeply.

"Raven disappeared sometime during the fight. No trace of her in Vanaheim. No one saw her leave, and she didn't take anything. She was comatose, then gone. No note, no reason. Dr. Goodson thinks she had a psychotic break of some kind. Brain trauma from getting shot. She left without clothes, without *anything* from the city. We thought maybe she was betraying us, picking up pieces of Legacy's plan. But…they checked the labs, the computers, the paper files. Nothing was taken. She just…disappeared last week." She furrowed her brow.

"Last week?" I countered immediately. "How long was-"

"Two weeks. Relax." Val said from below me. "Not that long, grand scheme of things. We've…waited longer for people we care about."

Okay. Okay, that's not too bad. Still so many questions.

"Okay, yeah, and the others? What happened to Alice and Violet?" I pressed.

"Alice is right here." Her familiar, comforting voice accompanied a much shorter stature as she made her way out from behind the privacy curtain, struggling to move her wheelchair in the confined space. "Doing what she always does." She smiled at me, placing her hand on my blanketed leg. She had a small scar on her forehead, indicating some kind of injury.

"The wheelchair, is that…permanent?" I hesitated even asking, but everyone else was accustomed to the group's dynamic and I needed to know sooner rather than later. She frowned, looking over at me after a moment.

"I hope not." Her answer was simple, but told me everything I needed to know. "But that'll depend on whether you're able to help with your abilities. When you're feeling better, of course."

"Where's Violet?" I finally demanded, fearing that the long dream I had endured was more in truth than it was my imagination. My mother's head bowed, and both Jalix and Alice looked unsettled at the concept of mentioning my sister's name.

"Amy, that…information should wait until you've been awake a bit longer. Your heart rate is already-"

"Tell me, please." I begged, pleading with Alice directly. "If she's dead, I *need* to know, please-"

"It's…not that simple." Alice warned, sighing. "Amy, I mean it. This is heavy. I need you, if you're going to insist on this, to be ready for some pretty horrible things."

Horrible things? It would have been a quick death, a painless one. If something else happened, something worse…how?

"I need the truth." I swallowed my reservations and set my face into a firm stare before Alice finally surrendered to the pressure. She waved to Jalix and Kara, who stood up and made their way out of the room without a moment's hesitation. Val stood up, held my hand, and shakily took in a large breath of air.

"Your parents don't need to see this." Alice said quietly, gesturing to the door. "I'm sorry that they needed to leave. They know already."

"Know *what?*" I asked again, watching as Alice worked her way through the complicated process of taking down the privacy curtain. There was a seam in the middle, held together with clips, that led to where my arm had been bound. As the clips were taken off so the rest of the curtain could be removed, I realized that my cast was actually much longer than I had thought, and continued in a straight line along someone else's arm.

"When we found you-" Alice started, waiting to explain the situation before she removed the barrier. "You were holding Violet and trying to heal her. No one wanted to touch you in case we would have set something off. You were breathing, and had a heartbeat, but she didn't. We didn't want to sever the connection until we knew what was going on. Especially with you trying to heal a brain. Jalix's personal Blackhawk evacuated all of us immediately. Kara was dead, I was dead, Val was dead…lotta death." Her words kept a light bounce to them, but she was struggling to keep calm. "Val and Kara were easy repairs. Medics started Kara's heart right up. Had stopped because of the bullet she took earlier that day. Too much stress. Started Val's again too, but we added a few units of blood. Me…I got lucky." She nodded to Val. "I was…shot. In the head. My staff knew enough from their training that there was a…certain way to handle my injury. They did everything right. Dr. Goodson did some surgery and I was okay, minus…the legs. Not sure why they're not working."

"Ally's so smart, she had brains to spare." Val joked quietly. Alice chuckled, nodding.

"I guess I do. The shot missed *most* of the important stuff. Kara had the idea to bring us here. It's a…remote set of cabins called the Lynn Woods Reservation. You were born…not even a quarter mile from here. It's away from everyone that has the cure. Secluded. Kara figured that being Vampyres for a bit longer would help our recovery. And then, once I was awake…I worked on you two. You and Violet. Out of the fear you would lose your connection to her, I…bonded you two with a cast. Constant skin-to-skin contact. But…she wasn't making it, Amy."

Oh, no. It was real.

"Yeah, your body kept exerting itself more and more to try and keep her brain active." Val picked up the explanation. "Worked for a little while. But her body was dead. Decaying.

Nothing that any of us could do to stop it. Her brain function stopped. Yours…went haywire. Trying to make a connection that wasn't there, I guess."

"Violet died two weeks ago, Amy. But for your sake…we couldn't disconnect you, not until your brainwaves normalized. It was your only hope at staying alive. I'm so sorry." Alice offered quietly.

No, no, no…

Alice pulled down the curtain, draping it carefully over the deceased body of my sister and only revealing the part of her arm connected to the cast. From her shoulder to her elbow, the skin was blackened from rot and peeling in layers of dead flesh I could already smell from across the room.

No, not Violet…

I couldn't help myself, doubling over in painful sobs as my stomach tightened in spasms beyond my control. I felt sickened, horrified, and dismayed that her life had ended in nothing but a dream and her body had been left to rot just to save my own life.

"It's alright." Val knelt down, resting the side of his head against mine. He was crying as much as I was, but was able to keep his composure while doing so. Alice seemed to be the only one mostly free of tears in watching the two of us.

"Amy…" Alice started. "I'm not done." I shook my head, unwilling to look back at the partially hidden ghastliness that marked my sister's body. "Your arm…you two have been connected for two weeks. Your healing did something it shouldn't have. I-…here, I've…covered everything else up." With another rustle of fabric, I let my eyes peek briefly at the casts, Violet's arm now hidden underneath a towel. "Look here." Alice put the tip of her finger against a hole in the plaster nearly an inch below my elbow. In the opening, I could see that my own skin looked much the same: black and swollen with no hope of restoring function.

I couldn't care less about my goddamned arm. Violet's right there, dead!

"I c-can't right now." I shook my head and waved my left hand, clenching my eyes shut at another wave of quiet crying. Val continued to hold me while Alice gave me another moment of silence before speaking again.

"Amy, this can't wait. I need to talk to you about this."

"About *what*?" I wept, looking at her as a well of tears met my blankets without slowing.

"Amy, I have to take that arm. Today." Alice explained, retrieving a box from under my bed. "I waited as long as I could, and I was going to operate today anyway and take our chances. I'm just glad you woke up before I could. This way, I know you're alive." She held up the box, about two feet long, and set it on my lap.

For DARPA-approved facilities only: LUKE III biomechanical upper limb appliance.

"Your healing abilities kept out infection, and kept the necrosis at bay, but you're fighting a losing battle. If we don't amputate that arm, the bacteria from the dead flesh are going to kill you."

Violet…no. You were there when she let herself go. When she said she…gave you her gift. Whatever that means. She told you she died…why are you surprised? And even more, why are you breaking your promise? You told her you'd keep it together. That you wouldn't break down.

"What's this?" I gestured, sniffling briefly and trying to ignore the intrusive thoughts about my sister.

"It's an advanced project, run by the government when it was still active. Prosthetic, one that trains itself to your nerve impulses and responds similarly to a real hand. This one's the most advanced model. Designed to be attached during the surgery, not after. It provides feedback, too, so you'll have a…*kind of* sense of touch." She winced, trying not to convey the false sense that things would be normal again.

"It's called the Luke arm." Val smiled at me, wiping away his own tears. "If there's ever one thing the government did right, it's work on a bionic arm and actually name it after something badass."

"Yeah." I smirked, looking at the box. "How soon do we need to do the surgery?"

"Soon." Her reply was curt, and I understood from her seriousness that time truly was of the essence. "As soon as you're ready. I can't put you under anesthesia. So I'll have to use locals and some painkillers. I can give you a series of nerve blocks, too. But you have to be conscious." I nodded, understanding the grim task at hand.

This is going to be hard. Not just the pain, but the concept of it all.

"Can I have Krystal in here?" I asked, hoping it wouldn't be an issue.

"Of course. Kryssi?" Alice called, her blue-haired sister appearing within milliseconds of being summoned. Her eyes were still red and inflamed, likely having heard my reaction to the news of Violet's cruel fate. "Amy's going to do the surgery now. She asked if you could stay with her."

"Of course." Krystal returned without hesitance. "I'll stay here the whole time. Right by your side." She knelt quickly, Val letting her be the closer of the two of them and take my free hand. Although she was freezing at our first touch, my powers were still able to raise her temperature to a normal level of comfort. She sighed, smiling at me gently.

"You have no idea how long I've waited to finally feel warm again." Seeing no reason to hold back, she nuzzled her face against my own, kissing my cheek and resting her forehead against my shoulder. "I love you."

"I love you, too." I whispered, looking into her eyes. "We made it. Through the war."

"Yeah." She whispered, her eyes briefly darting to the covered body across the room. "Most of us did."

Damn, she looks sad. Half-expected her to throw a party once I was out of her hair.

"What?"

"What?" Krystal and I exchanged a brief moment of confusion, joined by Val and Alice both staring at us.

"Nothing, sorry. Just…had a moment." I clarified, somehow feeling that the thought came from Violet herself. Alice turned on a nearby sink to scrub her hands, and having prepared the tools and medicines she would need, gestured for Val to leave the room and close the door behind him.

"Tell me stories about her." I held Krystal's hand tighter, wanting to test a theory that fleetingly presented itself at the forefront of my thoughts. "We're going to have some time on our hands."

"Our hands? Can't tell if that was a joke or not." She gestured to the box on my lap. "How do you feel about this?"

"I don't care, Krystal. I really don't." I couldn't stress enough that I was thankful to have my life, and to see most of my family alive and well. "It's an arm. Now *this* one can hold your hand no matter how cold you get." Her look was one of pure reverence at my remark. "Seriously, I…need something to get me though this. A good story about her. Something happy."

"About Violet?" She asked, smiling yet mournful. "Happy stories with Violet." She nodded, trying to think of a quality tale and slowly losing her composure. I let her take the time she needed, feeling Alice insert the first needle of many under my right armpit.

"Oh." Krystal realized quietly, smirking. "There was the time we took apart Kara's furniture while she was asleep."

Oh, my God that was soooo much fun. She beat our asses at chess and Krystal and I wanted to prove a point. Not…sure what the point was, but it was a good time.

Not so much in pure language did the thought occur, but I felt happy at the recall of the memory, seeing through Violet's eyes the two of them stealthily crawling along my mother's kitchen floor and unscrewing the doors of cabinets.

"You…had a red-handled screwdriver. And Violet had a blue one. Before you went in, you asked to trade and she said no. It drove you nuts." I remembered, explaining the memory to Krystal and her shocked expression.

"She told you this story? In *that* much detail?"

"No. When we were connected, she…I can't explain it. She gave a part of herself to me. Her memories. Right before she died, she gave me her whole life. And I think I can *hear* her reactions to things. As momentary thoughts, not as an actual voice."

"Wait, she's in your head somewhere?" Krystal's eyes widened.

"Not…quite. It's like…they're *my* thoughts, *my* memories, but with her influence and point of view. Memories about *her* opinion on something, but applied to the present. It's hard to explain." I shook my head, trying to force the thoughts from Violet's personality to appear again. As much as I wanted, I was only aware of my own. "It's not a whole consciousness. Just brief moments."

"That's something I need to look into. Make sure you're okay." Alice suggested, another injection going into my arm. "That's a lot of synaptic activity. I want to make sure you won't have seizures like your-" She paused, withdrawing the needle. "Girlfriend?"

"Sure. Whatever you guys want to call it." I looked over at Krystal, kissing her knuckles and chuckling softly.

"If you two exchanged something, that explains your eyes, too." Krystal said passively, looking between my eyes as she spoke. I raised an eyebrow, unaware of what she meant.

"You mentioned something earlier-"

"Right, hold on. Sorry. Alice, you have a-…ah, thanks." She took a small hand mirror from Alice and held it in front of me, revealing my appearance for the first time since the battle. I was surprisingly unblemished, no cuts or scrapes on my face, but my right eye had drastically changed in color. As if some of Violet's genetics had been carried over and affected me, I now had one silver eye with a hint of cobalt blue and another one the shade of amber. It was brown at its core, but had been lightened with the silver I carried to make a hybrid similar to the color of honey. Krystal pulled the mirror away and shrugged, leaning against the bed as Alice spiked a healthy dose of IV painkiller into my fresh bag of saline.

"She's a part of me now." I recognized, assuring to Krystal that her best friend wasn't gone. "I get to remember her…honor her the way she'd have wanted. With her happy memories."

"That's more than I could have ever asked for." Krystal smiled, leaning into me. "It just means she's not gone forever."

"I meant to thank you, by the way." I ran my thumb over her hand, brushing it lightly. "I was only able to survive that, seeing death again…because of you. I wouldn't have made it out alive if I didn't already know what I was dealing with. If I hadn't already been…somewhat familiar."

"I'm glad I helped in whatever small way I could." Krystal nodded, the color of her eyes shifting to a sky blue for a moment before returning to a deep cerulean color.

"So, Krystal…" I felt the first hint of chemical influence wash over my brain, muddying my thoughts and filling me with an artificial moment of peace. "Tell me another story. This time…I'll let you finish it."

***

The snow had finally fallen. While the past hours were ones of warning by a growing darkness in the sky, the grey clouds above us dusted every visible surface in a layer of white snow that fell in slow, meandering patterns to the ground. My wool coat kept me insulated while Krystal stood next to me in only a long-sleeved blouse for insulation, but the group as a whole did their best to avoid complaining about the frigid air. I let my right arm – my new one – reach out from the pocket of my coat and touch Krystal's hand lightly. She laced her fingers with mine, and while I couldn't feel the distinct texture of her skin against my own, I could feel where her fingers pressed. That was enough for me to feel warmed.

Val stood from his kneeling position, his right knee darkened with wetness after pressing into the snowy soil. The stone marker he worked on was completed, his strength playing a surprising role in carefully chipping a neat set of letters into the gravestone after hours of painstakingly careful work. He set his tools to the side, hoarsely clearing his throat and returning to Alice's side. She was in no better condition, holding Violet's ashes and the urn containing them with extraordinary care. The silence around us was peaceful, and let everyone come to terms with the situation in their own way.

Damn, y'all. Stop being so sad. Life goes on, I was just an artist. I mean, thanks, though.

I tried to avoid smirking at the thought of Violet being so carefree regarding her own passing, but it was noticed by both of my parents in the thousandth glance they had given me throughout the few minutes we had been standing outside.

"What'd she say?" My mother asked, holding onto my father's arm delicately. I shook my head, the tamed rows of silver waves around my head dusting the snow from my coat.

"Said to stop being so sad." I chuckled, inciting a brief and forced smirk from some of those in our circle.

"She did hate funerals, didn't she? Weird thing to have as a goth girl." Eric suggested quietly. We all chuckled, nodding.

I was remembered as a goth girl. Mission frickin' accomplished. High-five. Oh, right, I don't have arms. And you only have one real one. Ha!

I forcibly suppressed a growing smile, finding it wildly inappropriate that her thoughts strayed to such a level of humor in the deadly melancholy of the moment. Unfortunately, I also knew that it's exactly how she would have reacted to her own funeral, and did nothing to suppress the thoughts in my head.

"I think she got that from me." My mother added softly. "The goth look. I always wore black. Just…what I did. Black, reds, dark purples. She liked it. Made it her own. I think that…is what was so unique about her." She paused, sniffling. "She could make anything her own. Take something and make it new."

"Take something…" Alice chuckled, shaking her head. "Speaking of which, does no one remember her thieving?" A few of them nodded, the corners of their mouths finally turning upward.

"She stole every one of my left shoes one time. *Only* the left ones." Val reminisced. "All because I said her fangs were tiny and cute instead of menacing."

They WERE menacing! Just…a little more slender than some people's. Call me cute and tiny…hell yeah, I took your shoes. Cute and tiny. Who's ugly and big, huh?

I turned away for a moment, Krystal mistaking my suppressed laughter for tears with a comforting hand on my shoulder. She decided to speak up, which surprised me with how difficult it was to even get her outside prior to the event formally starting.

"She was my best friend. You were all my best friends, but she…understood what it was like to be different. She helped me understand that it was okay to be different. That it didn't make us any less. And that we were the best kind of misfits."

Oh, Krystal…I love you, too. You're the best.

I finally turned around, this time actually shedding a single tear and nodding in agreement, though I didn't know if the thought was Violet's or my own.

"When Kara died…the *first time*, and let's hope that doesn't happen again-" Jalix started. "Vi was such a help with Amy. They…bonded, immediately. I didn't really understand it. But a year after Amy was born…Kara explained that Violet was her daughter. And I guess it clicked. They knew they were sisters before any of us did. I think I admired that most about her. Her instincts. And…she got those from Kara. She got everything from Kara. And defied any other evil she faced…right to the end. Probably the most fearless of us all." He inhaled, tilting his head back and leaning into my mother in a moment of emotion.

That might be the shortest speech he's ever given. And…it was sweet. Thanks, Jalix. Still not calling you dad. Too weird.

"She was struggling when she found out about Kara being her mom." Tony spoke up, taking a step forward and inspecting the gravestone. Although it had been salvaged from our kitchen's expensive marble counter, it looked better than any I had ever seen in its pristine whiteness mottled with streaks of grey and black. "I told her that her anger wasn't worth it. To appreciate who she had. And that life was too short to feel undeserving of our love." He paused, placing a gentle hand on the grave. "I was right. Life was too short. But she knew that. And that's why she loved us anyway." Stepping away quickly after his last words, he lifted his dark sunglasses to wipe his tears and took a few steps away from the group to collect himself.

That was sweet, Tony.

My thoughts were more my own now, and I had wondered if something happened to usher Violet's reactions away from my own mind. It was a paranoia I had borne since I discovered her gift to me, and I consistently judged each period of her silence as a terrifying absence. She had come back each time over the past week, but it didn't make the wait any easier.

"I don't think I even have something to add." Sonya whispered, staring at the quote on Violet's marker. "We've all said what we've needed to, thought what we've needed to. We'll never be fully okay without her. Fully whole. But if there's one thing she taught us-" She swallowed hard, trying to speak clearly. "-it's that there's nothing to be gained by living in sorrow. She lived the things worth living for. Love. Faith. Hope. And life." All of us having said our piece, she nodded to Alice and indicated for us all to step away. Alice moved forward with the urn, unwilling to do what needed done. Although the ground wasn't broken to lower a casket or body into, it seemed to have a black hole in the area surrounding the marble slab that kept anyone from functioning within its sphere of influence. Alice looked at Violet's ashes again, silently saying another goodbye.

I get to become part of the earth, or ashes in the breeze that end up exploring all the corners of the world. Ashes that become atoms that will always exist.

Violet's words from our shared dream state entered my mind, forcing a scrunch in my brow as the words rattled in my head as something to be regarded as more than passing thought. I shook my head, staring at the words on her grave as I came to an epiphany.

Violet Annabelle Valencia Kane. 1988-2035. As unique a diamond as any one of us. May she rest in eternal peace.

"Alice, stop!" I exclaimed, rushing forward to touch the tip of the urn before she finished tilting it to scatter its contents.

"Wait. Hold on." I breathed, looking away for a moment in thought.

"You okay?" Krystal asked, taking a step toward me.

"Yeah, just…I have an idea. But I need you guys' help with it. Alice, I need, uh…"

Come on, think back to your chemistry lessons. Sodium, lithium, potassium…yes, potassium. Wait, potassium burns purple, it doesn't bond with that color in the visible spectrum within a solid state. Boron? I think it's boron. Alice might have some.

"What kind of laundry detergents do we have?" I asked excitedly, looking at Alice while the entire group looked at me in reserved trepidation.

"Amy, let's go inside. I think we-"

"No, just-…answer the question." I ignored Sonya's comment, knowing that I wasn't having a mental breakdown. "What do you use to wash your scrubs?"

"Uh…just…generic laundry pods and some stain removers." Alice answered hesitantly, returning the urn to an upright state as I moved it toward her chest.

"Chemicals, woman, chemicals!" I shouted, shaking her shoulders lightly.

"Uh, it's…sodium percarbonate to lift stains and some sodium tetraborate-"

"Yes!" I hissed excitedly. "Stay here."

I turned and jogged the few steps toward the large cabin, throwing open the door and making my way through the space until I found the laundry room. While I enjoyed the warmth inside the cabin, I whisked the box I needed off the shelf and ran back outside as quickly as I was able. The group, particularly my parents, had moved away from mourning and instead stood in stunned confusion at my outburst.

"I need your help, Krystal." I motioned for her to move toward me. "And mom and Sonya. You guys come here, too." The requested individuals silently complied as I did mental calculations beyond what I had done in recent years.

Come on, brain. It's basic ratios and stoichiometric conversions. You can do this.

Deciding on a number I was comfortable with, I reached into the white box and removed the small measuring cup, taking a scoop of the substance and shaking some loose until I had the amount I wanted. Nodding to Alice so as to confirm my sanity, I slowly poured the scoop of detergent into the urn and took a step back once the plastic spoon was empty.

"I need everyone to actually do what I say. Alright? It's the only way this is going to work. Alice, mix that together with the ashes, thoroughly. Just rotate the urn a bunch of times. Mom, Sonya, if Alice were to dump the contents, could you both sorta…hold it? In mid-air? We don't want her ashes touching the ground."

"Amy." Sonya said quietly, tilting her head in an almost scolding manner. "This is someone's funeral, not a science experiment."

Oh hell, no, this is absolutely a science experiment. You do what you gotta do, girl. I'm down to play the game.

"Violet wants this, too. I promise. Just-…can you make them float?"

"Yeah, we can do that." My mother nodded, gesturing to Sonya that it was okay for me to continue my insane ramblings. Alice had rotated the urn several times, mixing the contents as well as they could be without professional equipment.

"Okay. Alice, pour. Mom, Sonya…catch." While some of the finest particles of Violet's remains were lost to the gentle breeze, the vast majority of the grey ash mixture was suspended in the air as Alice shook the urn lightly. Empty, she put it on the ground. The two women with telekinesis molded the loose ashes into a cohesive shape, holding them together and suspending them four feet off the ground.

"Alice, as *hot* as you can get them. Everyone else might want to step back." I added, letting go of Krystal's hand so she could use her powers to keep us cool during the process. While the winter air provided an advantage, Alice's efforts wrapped the shape in flame until the searing heat melted an inch of snow into the ground nearly ten feet in every direction. I was lucky enough to stay close to the glowing orb, cooled with Krystal's help.

"Mom, Sonya, push your powers to their fullest. Compact it as tightly as you can, and don't hold back. Crush it with everything you've got, squeeze it as tightly as possible. "

"I see where you're going with this." Alice breathed, watching with extreme interest to see if my idea would truly work.

The ball of ash started to shrink, the dim red glow it was emitting from Alice's efforts now growing to a white light with a sun-like intensity. The ball grew smaller and more irregular in shape, until it was barely smaller than my fist and stopped moving despite Sonya and my mother grunting with effort.

"Krystal, cool it down as fast as you can. Now." I held my breath as the radiance dissipated, dimming the light until it was gone and letting the view of a jagged-looking grey rock replace that of a glowing ball.

Everyone ceased their efforts, the small object landing on the ground with an intense thud and everyone's suspenseful stares. I knelt down, looking up at the marble gravestone and smirking with the feeling of success. Picking up the object, I briskly walked to an area outside the radius of Alice's fiery energies and smeared wet snow across the surface of the rock. Sure enough, the grey coating of unused ash rubbed away easily and revealed the deepest color of transparent violet I had ever seen. While there were imperfections and unused elements within the rock, it was a gorgeous piece of magic that I proudly held in my palm in front of everyone witnessing.

"Is that…a diamond?" Krystal asked in awe.

"The detergent…" Tony realized. "It contained boron. When bonded with hydrogen from Alice's powers-"

"It makes a purple color." I confirmed quietly. "If her memories are still with us, all that was left was her body. Now even *that* can be with us forever." I looked down at the stone, heavy for its size, and closed my fingers around it.

"I know a guy in Vanaheim." Tony added again. "Jeweler. He could cut it for us. That way…we'd all have her with us." Tony's beautiful sentiment was disrupted by the sound of a car's engine growing closer and closer, forcing our heads to snap toward the road. The only one unmoving was Alice, who stared at the ground for a moment before speaking.

"Not a surprise guest. I…asked her here." She mumbled, a sense of concern draped over her eyes. "I'll explain in a few minutes." Our small circle moved to the side, a car making its way up the driveway and stopping a hundred feet from the edge of the cabin. Tamara exited the vehicle, apparently its only passenger, and walked to the trunk to retrieve something. Val made his way over to Krystal and I, his hands shoved deep into his pockets and his eyes watching Dr. Goodson carry a large silver case and a leather satchel up the driveway.

"You know…" He started, lightly running a hand over the mottled scar tissue on the right side of his face. "Violet and I talked, once. I remember, I told her that you and her would be the next generation of us. That you'd carry us forward when the older ones weren't around anymore. That you two would *both* bring the world back together." He looked between my eyes, smirking at the distinct colors. "I was more right than I knew."

"You do drop the odd pearl on occasion." I smirked, letting him bring my shoulders into his for a brief hug. Tamara silently approached Val, handing him the leather satchel and saying nothing until she took the large silver box and bestowed it to Alice.

"What you asked for." She said tersely. Alice took it from her hands, a delicate process of transfer, before Dr. Goodson started to walk away. She turned to Val after a few feet and decided to say something with respect to the object he held in his own hands. "I read it." She began. "I wasn't supposed to, and I did." She said nothing else, but as she walked away, we turned our attention to the two objects and Alice, who seemed to know what was going on.

"We should go inside." Alice decided. "Val, I'm not sure what *that* is, but if you want to-" A single gunshot echoed from behind us, setting everyone alight in an adrenalize-fueled haze before we spun around to see Dr. Goodson's body strike the side of her car before falling limp. An old, silver revolver fell from her hand as she collapsed, resting against the snow as its flurries began to bury the evidence of its existence. Each of us stood in stunned silence, a confusion wracking our minds in a period of indecision. Alice seemed to be the only exception in the group, bearing a look of regret more than of confusion.

What the hell…?

"Everyone, inside. Right now. I'll…explain all of that. I'll take care of the body later. Val…you stay here with Amy. Find out what *that* is, first. Then meet us inside." She beckoned to the leather pouch before cautiously hoisting the massive silver case onto her hip and making her way inside the cabin.

"What's she doing? The hell's going on?"

"I have no idea." Val returned, both of us whispering so as not to be overheard by the retreating party. He continued to stare at the object in his hands. "I have no idea what a lot of things are right now."

"Open it." I suggested. "Tammy…gave it to *you* for whatever reason."

We both looked over at the scene again, Dr. Goodson's body slumped against the front tire of her car. Val shook his head, too emotionally drained to have any further reaction, and started to untie the leather cord that held the pouch shut. We made our way to the front steps of the cabin and sat down, protected from the snowfall by the wooden overhang and sitting on a largely dry surface. As the last tangle of the knot was undone, Val reached inside and pulled out an aged journal.

Yellowed parchment was held together with a thick piece of leather, some of the binding glue having flaked off and fallen in crumbling pieces. He opened it, staring at the first page for far too long while his face changed shape repeatedly. His reaction started with surprise, then dived briefly into anger and sadness before finally settling on a confused sense of neutrality.

"It's…Schillinger's. From a long time ago." He mumbled, turning the page and letting his working eye roam over the contents contained within the journal's pages.

I watched in silence, unable to see the full context of the words, and waited patiently for him to explain what Schillinger's words involved. I waited for minute after minute, his hands hastily turning page after page until nearly an hour had passed of his frantic and disbelieving reading of some long text. His breathing grew heavier, forced from his nostrils in heated vapor that escaped into the winter air. He finally closed the book and set it next to him, clenching his jaw and exhaling heavily with a flow of tears.

"What's wrong? What is it?" I asked, picking up the journal before he placed his palm on it and shook his head.

"You don't want to read it." He said hoarsely, wiping his left eye with the sleeve of his coat.

"What *is* it?" I pressed, wanting nothing more than to read through the same words he had.

"Everything." He whispered, looking out at the landscape as snow started to once again cover the ground where Alice's fire had melted it. Violet's headstone was untouched by the process, a beautiful white testament to her life forever preserved in marble. "It was everything." I waited for him to explain, understanding that it would be a process. "He knew, Amy." He whispered again, his voice struggling to keep a steady tenor. "He knew…exactly what would happen. And when. He knew which projects would fail, which ones would succeed. He knew about Legacy, he knew about his own death. He had every detail of everything that would happen, mapped out and planned meticulously. To this very moment. He knew I'd survive. And he wrote the journal to me."

"To you? Not…mom?" I asked hesitantly. He shook his head.

"He knew she'd never read it. There's nothing Kara wants to hear of Schillinger anymore. But he knew I'd be too curious."

"That makes sense, but I mean…I'm asking what the point of it was. Just to…prove he *knew* he'd lose?" I asked in vain. He took in a deep breath and sighed, looking over at me solemnly. For the first time, his voice resumed its normal tone as he spoke again.

"He didn't lose." Val mumbled, his eye looking between mine. "He wanted this to happen. All of it."

"Wh-…why?" I was bewildered, now more curious than ever to read Schillinger's words.

"He said…he needed the world to understand how evil it was. That he had to create things so bad, so horrible, that the people who overcame them could lead the world into a better place. It's why he used Kilkovf and Legacy as his puppets. To show us the face of evil, of brutality. The face of what humanity looked like at its worst. He never wanted to accomplish the goals he told us. He wanted *us* to make the new world order. Free of…war. Of conflict. Free from the inevitable prosecution our virus would have brought. He wanted the world to be better than it was. And he did these horrible things to lead us here." He picked up the journal finally, opening one of its last pages and pointing to a sentence.

"…and here you gather at the place of Karalynn's death to mourn the loss of her first daughters; A loss that allows her remaining child, her Legacy, to claim the reigning crown of peace on a new world and purge my bloodline from existence so the evil I created would be eternally departed …it goes on from there." I mumbled, shaking my head in disbelief. "At least we knew he got a *few* things wrong." I tried reassuring Val. He looked at me, puzzled. "It says mourn the loss of her first *daughters*. Raven's not dead. Probably. Just gone."

"You're missing the point." He emphasized quietly. "He *used* Violet and Raven to win his war. He knew they'd die. He knew they'd go through hell and back. And he knew this a hundred years before they were born. He didn't know their names, their personalities, who they were. None of it. He knew them as *tools* to be used in the twisted shit he was working on. As Kara's daughters. Nothing else."

"We all die, Val." I said softly. "We all go through hell and back. It's the way of life. His ability to set up a course of events doesn't dictate our future." I lifted my right hand, holding Violet's diamond in my left, and set the robotic fingers across the back of his neck. "You still have a story to write with Alice. As I do with Krystal, as my mother does with my father. And there are thousands of untold stories that can go on because of us. *Nothing* else matters." I paused, letting my words sink in. "We dealt with the circumstances of the world we were given. That's…the most human thing we could have done. And we did it the best way anyone could have."

"Amy…if *we* followed his plan to the letter, if *we* went along with his grand scheme…" He waited for a moment, trying to find the right words. "Aerael, our family, Schillinger, Legacy. Who actually won?" I bowed my head for a moment, listening to the peaceful silence around us in Violet's place of rest.

"Everyone else, Val. Everyone else."

***

Krystal's left hand made its way slowly through my hair, stroking it gently as we shared a couch cushion in front of Alice's table. The room was filled with the crackling, whooshing sounds of the cheerful fireplace that covered each of us with a warm yellow glow of light. Alice stood in front of it, looking at the group around her before deciding to speak.

"I hid something. From…all of you. For that, I'm sorry. But for what I've done, I am not." Her eyes held a callousness that hadn't been seen since the darkest days of our virus's outbreak. "I, along with some help from Dr. Goodson, developed a mutagen we named New Dawn, a part of the Starlight project. She and I were the only two to hold knowledge of this effort, and after a long debate, we decided that I would be the *only* one…to keep this knowledge. That it was…too dangerous to remain in the hands of more than one person."

"You asked her to kill herself?" Kara asked in alarm.

"No." Alice responded coolly. "We both knew one of us would have to. So we flipped a coin and vowed to assent the results. She picked tails to live. Coin landed heads. So here we are." She paused, glancing at me instead of anyone else in the group. "You healed me, Amy. A few days ago. Determined that my paralysis was a damaged set of nerves in my cervical spine. You healed them, and now I can walk. If that's not a miracle, I don't know what is. And the world…the world *ahead* of us needs miracles." She beckoned to the table behind her, which held a collection of vials, syringes and bags of fluid I couldn't identify from across the room. "The New Dawn mutagen, without launching into a tirade about the details, will let us remain Vampyres. Exactly as we are, no significant changes. Now…this mutagen isn't contagious in any way, including bites and even direct blood transfusions. So everyone with the Starlight strain, the virus carrying the cure, is immune to it unless they're injected *directly* with this New Dawn RNA compound I created." She paused, the room keeping its silence. "I have ten vials here. One for each of us…and one was for Violet."

Hey, I get one for free now anyway. Perks of sharing a bloodstream. Long as you take one, Amy.

We all unintentionally looked at the large purple diamond on the mantle above the fireplace, twinkling with light as the flames below it flickered happily.

"This is a choice. A heavy one. But it's one we need to make. Become human with the rest of the world…or continue the way we are." Alice finished, no pageantry on her lips as the words left her mouth. No one spoke, a resounding lack of reaction from most members of the family. Krystal's fingers stopped their movement as I felt her thinking uneasily.

Curiosity. Uncertainty. Optimism. Bravery.

I looked over at her as she felt the familiar tingle of my powers, smiling gently and nodding once to me. I stared into her perfect eyes, framed by hair of a matching color in perfect waves that cascaded across her shoulders. There didn't seem to be any doubt, as she knew me too well to second-guess the feelings she was able to glean from me.

"Krystal and I would like to stay as we are." I said quietly, smiling at Alice. "We have a lot left to experience, a lot of good left in us to give to the world. And I want that long life spent with her."

"Krystal. You agree?" Alice asked plainly.

"I do." She smirked, nodding.

"That better not be the last time you say that." I whispered just loudly enough for her to hear.

Krystal grinned, pulling me closer into her body. As if the choice was meant to be done sequentially, the roaming eyes moved to my parents on the other end of the couch. They were whispering to each other so quietly that I couldn't hear their words, but my father said three words, kissed my mother gently, and looked over at Alice.

"We've lived beautiful lives. We'll live the rest with each other. But it's time for us to be human again." He affirmed.

Oh, no…

"Wait, you can't-"

"Amy." Krystal warned, keeping me from reacting too severely. I collected myself, looking over at them in confusion.

"You can't. I'd outlive you. I can't bury you two someday." I lamented.

"That's the way of the world, my darling daughter." My mother replied. "Children outlive their parents. But Jalix and I…we've had amazing lives. And we'll still have *many* more years with all of you. We'll make the most of them. I promise."

"It's everyone's personal decision." Sonya agreed, looking over at the two of us. "They have to have the freedom to make that choice. Or we're forcing something on them they don't want."

She's right. But…damn it. I'll never come to terms with having to bury them someday.

You already have. You knew the war would be hard. That they might not survive. At least, this way, it's their choice.

My thoughts coalesced with Violet's to form an understanding, and I nodded to show my acceptance. Sonya took the advantage while she was still in the spotlight.

"I'll take it. Superpowers *and* good looks? Think I'll hold onto that for a while longer." She smirked at me, trying to lighten the mood. It worked for the moment, but tension arose again when Tony and Eric looked at each other.

"No." Tony said simply. "I've lived long enough. Too long. Another forty, fifty years is plenty."

"Now's not the time to be a cynical asshole, man." Eric berated. "I'm taking it, and I know damn well you need to. You and I have done too much for Aerael and Vanaheim to stop now. We have a whole *country* to rebuild. It's…the ultimate challenge. How can you back down from that?"

"Because I'm not like you." Tony returned. "Life doesn't give me what it gives you and everyone else."

"Yep, the selfish prick at it again." Eric chuckled, shaking his head.

"Eric!" Kara scolded.

"Oh. I'm sorry, I can't tell him that he's being selfish, Kara? That he could do good with his life instead of throwing it away?" He returned, arguing with my mother.

"Are you going to tell me the same?" She replied.

"No, but-…" He looked over at Tony again in desperation. "Come on, man. I spent a long time without you. Trying to build a life that you could be a part of. We haven't always…seen eye to eye, but you're my brother. I need you, man." Tony sat in silence at Eric's request, his eyes fixed on the floor in front of him. He didn't say anything else, but it seemed as though he was thinking deeply.

"I can't make this call right now. Dropped on me like this. I need time. And I'll…consider it." He said, looking at Alice. She nodded, moving one of the vials to the side and laying it in another compartment of the massive case in front of her. Being the only two left, Val leaned forward from his chair and looked at Alice, speaking in short, simple words.

"I want what you want." He folded his hands, setting his chin atop his knuckles and acknowledging a surrender of his choice. "Your life is my life."

"Don't put that on me." Alice denied. "I can't-"

"Calm down." Val interjected quietly. "There's no pressure on you. My life, whether another thousand years or another ten, is spent at your side. I've already died. I've already gotten a second, third, tenth chance. So *your* choice…is the only one that matters here."

"The choice I want might not be the same one that you do." Alice sniffled, crossing her arms.

"You *are* my choice, Allison." He smiled, his eyepatch lifting slightly. "Until death do us part." She exhaled, wanting to keep her composure in front of the group, and took a step forward before kissing her husband gently. She knelt in front of him, speaking truthfully.

"I've been under so much pressure. Been through so much trauma and so many wrongs. And so have you. And I want to live a life where we can forget those bad moments and focus on the good. Not carrying them around until the end of time. But I can't ask you to-"

"Then so be it." He interrupted her, kissing her forehead and smirking. "As long as we can try some surgery on my face while I'm still a Vampyre. I'm thinking I could stand to be a little less ugly for the time we have left."

So many of them, choosing to be human. Choosing to have short, quick lives. Maybe it's something I don't understand because of my youth or my beliefs. Maybe they've been through more than I have, but I can't understand it. I just…love them.

"I've already given that some thought." I offered to Alice, trying to have a normal conversation so I didn't think about the mortality they would soon have. "I could assist if you'd like. Healing would go a lot faster." She nodded, exhaling heavily again and returning to the table. She picked up a small pile of empty syringes, carefully filling them with precision.

"We'll do it tomorrow. Here." She handed Krystal and I each an injection, followed by Sonya and Eric. "You guys take those. Tony…I can give you until after Val's surgery. After that, I'd like to destroy this as soon as possible." She closed the silver case and picked up a folder from the table it sat upon. Slowly, she extended it to me and failed to let go as I cautiously grabbed it.

"This is the formula for New Dawn."

She's…entrusting me with it?

"Do whatever you believe is right. It's the only copy." Alice nodded to me, letting go of the folder as I set it down on Krystal's leg and stared for a moment in numbed shock.

This is the future of the Vampyre race. To continue…or to die out. That decision, in my hands.

"We'll figure it out later." Krystal mumbled, holding up her syringe as if it was a toast. "For now…let's start the rest of our lives." I smiled, holding up my own briefly before I injected the solution and exhaled. Unlike the medicine we took to keep cravings at bay, there was no relief or satisfaction, and in fact, nothing whatsoever had changed as we disposed of the needles in the garbage can Alice held out to us.

Everything changed, Amy. You get to live the life of your dreams with the woman you love.

"Mmm." I mumbled aloud, as if agreeing with the thought.

Both of them.

"Only one thing left to do, then." Eric posited, standing up and taking the laptop that Alice handed him. "Amy, come over here to the table." I looked at Krystal quizzically as she shrugged, moving her legs so I could join Eric. Alice had moved away and sat next to Val in a loving embrace, the two of them talking quietly to one another.

I heard Tony's footsteps move across the floor before a cold breeze entered the room. Eric looked over his shoulder as Tony left, leaving the cabin and closing the door behind him.

"He needs time." I tried reassuring him.

"I know." Eric returned. "Him and his damn walks. Here, I just need to log in…" He opened several windows, most of them being programs that showed padlocks across their headings and prompted for multiple passwords.

"This isn't a normal laptop." I recognized, gesturing to the yellow security label below the keyboard.

Top Secret. For Official Use Only by Authorized Agents.

"No, it's not." He agreed, continuing to switch between typing and waiting for things to load. "I pulled this from the White House. Used it for a bit while you were asleep. Last piece of the puzzle." He stepped back after maximizing one of the windows across the screen, my own face showing on the bottom corner as a live feed.

"Eric, what is this going-" My jaw dropped, a picture of the most famous room of the United Nations dominating the screen while the dozens of people in its chairs all eagerly stared at me in wait.

The United Nations Assembly Hall. My god…I have to tell them everything that happened. How Legacy lied to them, how my family didn't betray them.

The screen split into two halves, the image of the hall and its representatives on the left while a man, suited in a clean blue attire and adorning only a simple red pin on his breast pocket, spoke directly to me.

"Madam President. My name is Arthur LaFleur, and I'm the Prime Minister of Canada. Are you able to hear me?"

Mada-…oh, shit. This just got real.

"I-…yes, I can hear you just fine." I paused to think of the proper way to decline the recognition of his title, but he took my brief silence as an opportunity to speak, instead.

"We're glad to see you alive and well. We're aware there's been a conflict recently in your nation's capital and, as I'm sure you can understand, we have *many* questions regarding the past few years' events." He cleared his throat, appearing to briefly glance at a teleprompter. "Over the past fifteen years, we have received information from those claiming to be the controlling parties of the United States' Government and its people. Before the battle began, we were contacted by someone only identifying himself as Legacy, who explained his standing as an impostor, and that the UN General Assembly should be held to discuss these ramifications. Do you hold the authority to speak from that perspective?" I drew in a breath, my mouth open for a few seconds and no words leaving it.

Let's do this, girl. This is the shit you were born for. We're ready for this.

"Yes. For these purposes, and until a proper election is held…I represent the spirit of the free nation of the United States of America and its people. *All* of its people, both Vampyre and human." The volume in the background increased, distracting the Prime Minister for a moment. Alice was kind enough to slide a kitchen chair behind my legs so I could sit rather than awkwardly hunch toward the screen. I noticed my family said nothing, and in a brief glance behind me, I realized that I had their full support.

"While we have our questions, the General Assembly has agreed to allow you to first explain the situation so that we may be alleviated of our concerns. Particularly those of a nuclear or militaristic nature."

"I can appreciate the gravity of those threats, Mr. Prime Minister, and would like to start by allaying those concerns in stating that no such threat exists. Our nation's nuclear weapons capability was negated during the attack with the destruction of both the person with its codes and the device from which they would be fired. As far as our military effort, the might of our nation is unlimited in its ability to defend its borders and protect its freedom, but that might is upon the will of the people, and not of an organized military force."

Holy actual shit, I was right. You really are nailing this. Good job growing up in politics and actually remembering how they work.

"Thank you for that information, Madam President. We appreciate that...level of transparency and recognize that it leaves you vulnerable at the moment." He paused, beckoning to me. "We'd be welcoming of any background information you'd be willing to share before we discuss anything else. A context, if you will." I nodded, clearing my throat and turning to look at my family once again. My mother's face was full of pride, matching my father and Krystal in their soft, kind smiles. I faced the laptop camera again, taking a deep breath.

"Four hundred years ago, a beast with no name infected my mother and her best friend with a virus the world had yet to see. Instead of succumbing to this affliction, they survived, and they thrived within the world with new abilities that allowed them to survive in conditions far beyond any human. This was at the cost of requiring blood for sustenance, a key nutrient of the virus they now shared. This monster pursued her. Across continents, it pursued her until she was forced to convert her own brother to keep him safe from the thing that they eluded. This...Creature. My mother began a life underground in hiding, gathering those in the most desperate of need to provide a second chance in this new city. Aerael, the city of light. The city was a birthplace for a resistance against the Creature and his own army as he began an attack on humanity behind the shadows of history's events. He betrayed the race that gave rise to him and sought to supplant them with one he believed to be superior. One that humans called the myth of Vampyres. My mother, my uncle, and their close friend now gave chase to the creature, who gave himself the name Robert Schillinger as he attempted to blend in with society as one of their own. During this pursuit, my mother added trusted members to her own family, each with their own unique abilities and talents until they finally achieved a shared city unparalleled with that of any human civilization. During this pursuit, my mother was captured by this Creature and his allies. In her imprisonment, she was raped and forced to conceive the first two of her three children. One of them was raised by this Creature, encouraged to assimilate with humanity as she drove a knife into its back with illicit, immoral, and supernatural sciences. Her other daughter, Violet Annabelle Valencia Kane, gave her life on the battlefield at Washington, D.C. to shutter the Creature's last hope at sabotaging the human race: a failed experiment known as Legacy. In doing so, she ended the war that started those four hundred years ago. And in doing so, she ended the threat of the very virus that created the apocalyptic country we became trapped within. While some of us will remain Vampyres to continue our rich heritage, the others will experience humanity once again, and the new virus within them will spread across the world as a biological immunity to Vampyrism's effects. They will change, and they will be human. But those Vampyres that remain…we will also be human. We are not another species, and we are not another race. We value passion and love and choice, and we treasure those who strive to uplift this Earth with their endeavors. We, as a people, will ensure that the gift of Vampyrism is guarded safely, given freely, and used with no respect to power or control. We Vampyres who remain will ensure that no other person ever be subjected to the evils of obedience under another tyrant. We are the guardians of freedom, of independence, and of personal liberty. We were Vampyres. But today…today, we become human."

There was a long pause filled with the applause of the chamber as the decades of threats, fears, and violence that pervaded their view of both Vampyres and the country we lived in dissipated in a matter of moments.

"Madam President-" The Prime Minister continued to speak over the applause, as it ceased to quiet down in the patient minute he gave the rest of them. "-we apparently have been gravely misinformed on your purpose, and I suppose I must ask that you clarify your intent here within the Assembly so we can appropriate any necessary assistance. Put simply, what is it that you plan for your country and your people?" I felt Krystal's cool hand on my shoulder as she took her everlasting place at my side.

"What we have always done. We will rebuild. Because we are Unbroken."

STARLIGHT

THE EPILOGUES

KARALYNN & JALIX

EPILOGUE

My knees held the same pain that had persisted over the past few days, but without anything in my pockets to take for it, I suffered with a smile on my face as the agent continued the tour. Without so much as a blink between the two of us, Kara reached into her purse and pulled out two prepackaged tablets of ibuprofen.

"Thanks." I chuckled, tearing open the packet. "Miss the days where my cartilage wasn't an issue."

"We've been human for six months. Relax." She laughed, elbowing my side. "*Miss the days.*" She mocked, apologizing to our real estate agent. "We're sorry, Clara. Just enjoying all of this a bit too much."

"Oh, it's not a problem!" She waved dismissively. "Couples are always happy purchasing a new home. Um, with that being said…" She looked around, grimacing. "Are you *sure* this is the one you guys want?"

"What do you mean?" I asked, flexing my right leg.

"Well…I mean, forgive me, but I know who you guys are. The…President is your daughter. You folks could have any house you want, literally." The real estate agent continued.

"This one's perfect." I confirmed with Clara, poking Kara's ribcage just to mess with her while she stretched. "Couple acres, enough for me in here to fix up so I'm never bored, lots of room for another kid."

"Oh! Are you two expecting?" She asked, looking at us both.

"Not yet." Kara replied. "But we're going to knock down the foundation trying. It'll be a boy this time, though. I can *feel* it." She waved her black manicured nails at me menacingly, as if she was conjuring some form of witchcraft over my ability to provide children.

"Mind if we have a few minutes alone here? *Unrelated* to the…making-a-kid stuff." I felt responsible for adding the statement, although it should have been unnecessary. Clara chuckled and nodded, walking through the front door to enjoy the summer air outside. "You sure about this one?" I confirmed, gesturing to the space around us. "There's a *lot* of work to be done here. The place was built in the nineteen-twenties. The basement is literally dirt. Like. *Soil.* There's no concrete down there. I would have to pour a new floor."

"Then pour away. We'll have a lot of time on our hands, and most of it is going to be boring unless we dive headfirst into another interspecies war." She joked. "Besides, I want to get into gardening. I always loved the arboretums in Vanaheim and Aerael. Maybe I'll start one big garden…" She meandered to the window, peering outside at the sloped ground that ran to a small stream at the bottom of the hill. "I could do fruits here…vegetables over there. Tomatoes in the middle because who the hell knows what they are."

"It's a fruit." I returned quickly, looking forward to the debate.

"Oh, really? Then why is it eaten like a vegetable? What other fruits do you put on a hamburger, hon?"

"I've had grilled pineapple on a burger once. It was actually delicious."

"On a burger? Pineapple doesn't even belong on *pizza*." She snorted, glaring at me.

"But a tomato does? Isn't that a fruit?"

"We're done. Go file the divorce papers, I've had it with you." She turned to walk away and cackled as I grabbed her waist and lifted her an inch off the ground, spinning her to face me and give me a close hug. "Mmm...you smell nice." She whispered.

"Still wanna divorce me?"

"Yeah, of course. But I'm keeping your shirts." I laughed, kissing the top of her head as we made our way outside. Clara let out a lungful of vapor, placing the device back into her pocket before confronting us.

"Well? What are we thinking?" She asked, moving her hands like either end of a weighted scale.

"Oh, we'll take it." I confirmed, looking up at the roof and wincing. "But let's have a few maintenance things put into the contract. New roof, poured concrete for the basement. And if they could set up a set of gardens on the south end of the house, I'll pay for pro landscaping and setup."

"*Krystal* will pay for pro landscaping and setup." Kara corrected quietly. "Our soon-to-be daughter-in-law."

"Meh. Either way, you get what you want." I smirked, pulling her in. "You happy?"

"Of course I'm happy." She smiled, caressing my face. "I love you."

"I love you, too, Kara."

KRYSTAL

EPILOGUE

Unknown to my beautiful bride, I could barely breathe at the sight of her, and the lacing on the corset of my elegant white dress didn't help my state of affairs. For the second time, I was lost for words, and each time I looked at her, I struggled to do anything other than cry at the magnificent, enchanting, and intelligent woman that looked into my eyes with pure love. I held her hands, gripping the bionic one slightly tighter so I didn't cause her any pain, and tried to recount what I had rehearsed an infinite number of times the night prior.

"Am-" I looked up and laughed, unable to get her name out before I choked up. Ever-loving and ever supportive, the electric tingle of her abilities crept from her fingertips to my own and soothed my soul in a thousand ways. "Amy…" I tried again. "I don't speak as eloquently as you do, and I struggled to find anything worthwhile to say. So I'm going to abandon what I wrote and just…offer you something." Her perfect pink smile grew, soft and alight with a happy glow. "We met by your abilities reaching into my heart. You calmed me, calmed my mind and body while I had seizures. Then you saw my soul. You saw me, bare and pure in a form only you could ever see, more than I'll ever know, myself. You saw who I was and you still loved that. And that's what I want to make my vow today. Everything you've touched is yours. Everything you've seen is yours. My soul, my body, everything…is yours. Forever. Everything I am and everything I have is dedicated to you completely. And I hope that's enough." She nodded, her silver and darkened goldenrod eyes gazing into my own before she replied.

"You said everything that I was going to say." She laughed, holding up her notecard. We both shared a moment, the audience and guests also finding it adorable that we had thought along the same lines. We recovered ourselves, the quiet snap of a photo being taken preceding her next words. "I said exactly the same. What I saw is all I want. Who you are is all I want. No expectations, no plans, and no demands of one another. Just you and I."

"Just you and I." I echoed, wanting nothing more than to kiss her already.

"You guys done with the mushy feel-good shit yet or can I marry you both already?" Val mumbled under his breath, his position behind us keeping his words hidden from the audience. We both nodded, and Val gestured toward the door. Sonya walked down the aisle briskly, her sunny yellow dress flowing a short distance behind her white heels. On a small pillow, I was able to finally see our rings for the first time.

"Yours is the one on the right." Sonya whispered to me, letting me pick up the one to my left and inspect it. A dazzling array of tiny purple sparkles mottled the woven titanium band in an unbelievable flash of lavender and deep plum, and was complimented with a traditional-looking centerpiece of magnificent violet diamond.

The perfect ring for Amy. It's so much more than I could have ever asked for.

Sonya stepped away, now that we were in possession of our rings, and allowed Val to speak up again.

"Do you, Amelia Lynn Kane, take this woman before you as your lawfully wedded wife?"

"I do." Amy whispered gleefully.

"You sure?" Val checked, asking the question at full volume. The room erupted in laughter as I slid Amy's ring onto her perfect, slender finger. It fit without question, as if it was meant for her, and her alone.

"And do-"

"I do." I gushed impatiently.

"Yeah, say the words whenever you want. Why am I here?" Amy and I both laughed as she gifted me my own ring, happy that Val complied when we allowed him to use his sense of humor during the ceremony. Our family seemed to enjoy it, and to us, that was all that mattered.

As the ring met the base of my finger, I was finally able to marvel at its beauty. It was simpler than Amy's in design, but meaningful in a thousand ways. No center stone was present, but two interconnected waves of blue and purple laced together to create a perfect symbol of my friendship with Violet. Amy's contribution was a third woven piece of titanium down the middle, adorned with three, simple, crisp stones of brilliantly clear-white diamond that touched both sides.

Oh, I'm going to break down crying long before we make it through.

I choked back tears looking at her, realizing the depth of planning she had in making these. For the hundredth time since we stood at the podium, we silently told each other how much we loved one another.

"As unconventional as it is, I'm going to say something, too." Val mumbled, speaking only to the two of us. We looked over at him, both of our eyes filled with glistening tears of happiness. "You two are forever. There will never be anything else that either of you can ever know. A marriage…is a process. It's a ceremony. It's a certificate. But love is something different. Love is forever. When things get tough, remember that, okay?" We both nodded to him, grateful beyond words that he would impart something so kind to us during the most important moment of our lives.

"Normally the line is *you may kiss the bride.* Since we have two brides, uh…just kiss." The audience leapt out of their seats, laughing and clapping as she and I collapsed into a singular person with our hands, our hearts, and our minds in the first kiss we would share as wives. Nothing had ever felt so right, and even the first kiss we ever shared seemed to pale in comparison with the emotional depth I felt for her in our moment of long-awaited bliss. She pulled away from me first to hiss a few happy words.

"We're married."

"We're married!" I returned, forsaking another kiss for an embrace. I pulled her into me and leaned into the crevice of her neck, letting myself cry tears of absolute joy.

"Come on." She whispered, looking at me with a sense of mischief. "I have another surprise." She took my hand, guiding us through the aisle as hands reached out to give us their congratulations and voices echoed in cheer around us. Even Kara and Jalix, despite Kara's growing pregnancy, tried to push their way through to us and was ignored by the rabid woman that tugged at my arm.

"I'm coming!" I laughed, trying my best to give brief hugs where I could. She finally pulled me from the crowd, running at my side through the chapel's doors and letting the waiting Secret Service members open the door to our limousine. She climbed in first, making her way as far back in the vehicle as she could while I struggled with the train of my dress.

"Amy-" I grunted, yanking on a strip of fabric. "What about the cake, and the rest of the ceremony?" She grabbed me under my shoulders and pulled me inside, the two of us barreling to the back and sitting in the spacious leather seats. I could see another of Amy's attaché in the passenger seat for protection as the doors were closed and the limo pulled away from the church.

"What's this surprise?" I asked, looking into her eager eyes.

"Honeymoon. Starts *right* now. Maui for a week, then the Bahamas for a cruise back to the States." She gushed, helping me remove the more cumbersome pieces of my dress. I took in a hefty gust of air as she unlaced the corset and finally allowed me to breathe.

"When did you have time to plan-…Mmm…" She kissed me again, reaching over to press a button and raise a privacy divider between the front and back halves of the vehicle.

"I said the honeymoon starts…*right*…now." She smirked, starting to undo her own dress.

"Oh." I realized, my eyes growing wide. "You literally mean-…Hmmph…" She attacked my lips again, covering us in the materials of our wedding dress and creating a blanket to shield us from anyone else's eyes.

VALTERIUS & ALLISON
EPILOGUE

I couldn't keep my husband still, his parental instinct becoming overbearing as he messed with the settings on his phone to find the best video results possible.

"Babe. We're right in front of the stage, it's fine." I whispered as the lights of the auditorium dimmed.

"See, the-...the damn lighting changed, now that'll mess with the exposure." He returned, aggravated.

"This is being *professionally filmed.*" I emphasized for the third time that morning. He looked over at me, one eyebrow arched.

"It is?"

Oh, I'm going to kill him. Wish I could still set things on fire.

"*Yes*. Dumbass. I said that repeatedly." I chuckled, joining the courteous applause as the school's principal walked onto the stage and approached the microphone.

"Good evening students, parents, guardians, and teachers, as well as our esteemed guests. I want to thank *all* of you for being here to watch South Boston Technical's graduating class of 2055!" Another round of applause echoed with the occasional loud cheer from an overzealous parent, which happened to be the man I shared a marriage certificate with. The principal looked around the room, acknowledging a thumbs-up from security at the upper end of the auditorium.

"First and foremost, I am honored to introduce our guest speaker for this graduation, the First Lady of the United States, Krystal Elizabeth Kane." It was my turn to be overzealous and stand out from the polite clapping that most others gave to my sister. As she walked out from behind the curtain, she gave the two of us a small, happy wave before doing the same to the rest of the crowd. Her silver blouse and long blue skirt were an unusual choice for her attire, but they complimented her well. Her hair was held up in a tight, modern bun with silver clips that gave her a professional appearance. Even from her walk, I could tell that she had gained experience being in the political atmosphere of Amy's standings.

"Good evening, everyone. I'm so happy to see every face in here, and I'm extremely excited to have our school systems producing high-caliber students like yourselves. I know the last thing you want is to hear a long speech, but thankfully that's the hallmark of my father-in-law, and I'll keep things much shorter so you can all get out there and celebrate tonight." She looked down at Jalix and winked, who quietly protested in his place next to Val.

"You know, I try my best to-" Jalix's quiet, protesting voice was drowned out by the microphone as Krystal spoke again.

"The first thing I'd like to do is recognize your class valedictorian, who I'm aware is giving a marvelous speech of her own in a few minutes. This phenomenal student took it onto herself to run as president of her chapter's honor society, and spent more than a hundred hours this year on volunteer work. She was accepted in April to the New Harvard School of Law, and starts in October as a pre-law student with a fast-track to law school under full academic scholarship."

"Man, she makes Annie sound like a queen." JD quipped from behind us.

"You'll get your chance, just like your sister. Two years, Krystal will be saying the same thing about you." Val returned, trying to get his son to do the impossible and remain silent for the ceremony.

"Not about *law school.* Ugh." JD articulated. I shook my head, trying to listen as my daughter's triumph was announced.

"If everyone could please give a resounding round of applause to Annemarie Vivian Valencia, class of 2055!" Krystal stepped back from the microphone while I stood up, clapping and looking for my daughter's seat. I finally found her, pointing and waving as she struggled with the honor cords and stoles that covered her graduation gown.

Ugh, I feel like she was a baby just days ago. Now even JD is sixteen. I'm getting old…

"We're getting old." Val quipped, turning to me as I smiled and laughed to myself.

"Yeah, you are." JD quipped.

"Jared, I will beat your *ass* when we get home-"

"I'm kidding, I'm kidding." I looked around for a moment during their exchange, curious as to where our other guests were. I sat down, leaning in to talk to Val while Krystal spoke.

"Where are Eric and Sonya?"

"Backstage." He replied quietly. "Wanted to talk to Krystal but didn't want to miss the show."

"Ah." I nodded, hoping to see them afterward. I watched Krystal speak, infinitely joyous in the way she addressed the crowd, and ran my hands through my hair as a slight headache started to become more noticeable. I looked at my hands, a few small hairs being combed from my scalp by my simple action. I looked at them closely, discarding them on the floor, but held onto one with a slight frown. In the light of the auditorium, I could spin the small fiber between my fingers and catch just enough light to see that it was gray.

AMELIA
EPILOGUE

"I'd like to conclude this State of the Union by addressing a concern that many of you have voiced, both in the polls and in your own ways." I paused, deliberating which pieces of the complex puzzle I wanted to address first. "Earlier this month, I used my powers to issue a Presidential Veto on the new bipartisan law that would eliminate term limits for presidents in the United States. Unfortunately, my veto was overcome by a congressional majority vote, and has come to pass. This legislation was not something that I agreed to, nor that I designed. And I understand that this, after the first formal elections held in 2038 for a United States President, is my fifth term." I paused to let the cameras capture what they needed to before I continued. "I understood and agreed with the need for a third-term exception to ensure the continuity of new legislative efforts and the rebuilding of our country, and the fourth tested the legal concept of one individual remaining in power. For eighteen years, I have faithfully and diligently served as your President, and I must make it abundantly clear that I am *against* any one person holding power over a people that do not want their leader in place. I am thankful and grateful to the American people for continuing to vote for my presidency in overwhelming majority, but in order to continue serving this country with its trust, I *must* implement a set of laws that tighten restrictions on term limits. I will be working with all parties to ensure it is done fairly and justly, and we will be discussing election within the scope of Vampyre lifespans as well as that of humans' to ensure equity and equality across all people." A courteous applause thundered from the crowd. "The State of the Union is unbroken as I stand in front of you. And I will make that my mission for as long as I serve you all. Thank you." I stepped back from the podium, waving for a few seconds and counting each moment in my head to ensure I was showing respect while managing to escape as quickly as possible.

"Very nice. Bit long, but very nice." Krystal muttered, wrapping her arm around my waist.

"Bit long? It took forever. Any idea how much stuff I have to talk about?"

"Yes, I do. You complain about it at dinner every night." She smirked at me, giving me a quick kiss on the cheek and beckoning for us to take our leave. As I stepped inside, I was delighted to see Alice waiting for us.

"Heyyy!" I squealed quietly, giving her a gentle hug around her shoulders. Krystal joined in without waiting for her own turn, letting the three of us share a happy moment after a droning, but largely positive speech. "I missed you at Christmas."

"Hey, you two. I was a little busy, special project. How are we holding up?" Alice asked. "I heard there's some political pressure on your back."

"It's-" I rolled my eyes and unclipped my hair to shake it loose. "It's basically fictional. There's a few news outlets that have done speculative pieces regarding my lengthy stay in office, but all the polls are coming back over *ninety* percent. Ninety. Percent."

"Sounds like you're complaining." Alice remarked as I led the way down the hall to one of my offices.

"I'm not, but…I feel like I still don't know what I'm doing. Most of what I'm suggesting is common sense, and I'm hiring staff that have common sense. Everything's somehow functioning. I'm doing *something* right, but I don't know what the something *is*." I speculated.

"Ha! That's the something you're doing right. The last time the government ran this country, there wasn't a drop of common sense around." Alice remarked, gesturing to her sister. "You remember."

"Yeah, I do. Not…everything worked at all, let alone worked well." My wife said with a chuckle.

Tell her she looks pretty! Did you not notice that dress?

"Krys, your dress is *gorgeous*. You look amazing." I complimented as we settled into one of the more private rooms of the White House.

"Aw, thanks. You always look better than I do. I have to compete somehow." She stuck her tongue out at me, pressing her lips together afterward in a blissful smile.

"Good to see that love is alive and well." Alice smirked, gesturing to my computer. "Check your email. Your personal one. I don't have all the fancy access to your government stuff." I furrowed my brow, marking her look of mischief and understanding that she had news for me. "Or I could just tell you, that would be faster." She laughed. "Sorry, I'm excited."

"Whatchya excited about?" Krystal enquired, pouring Alice a drink and handing her a glass of my favorite whiskey.

Oooh, she's lucky it's her sister. You gonna let just anyone dole out your booze to guests?

I shook my head at the internal comment, looking down at my ring as another reminder of Violet's more physical, more conscious presence. I felt a pang at missing her, despite how actively she still lived within me.

"Well…I got you guys your Christmas present from sixteen years ago." We both stared at her for a moment for several reasons. For one, she wasn't holding a gift, and for another, neither of us had any idea what we would have asked for as a gift more than a dozen years ago.

"That's…sweet. But you *might* have to remind us." Krystal tried to sound respectful, but we both knew that Alice didn't expect any special treatment from us. Alice rolled her eyes, glancing over as Krystal took up her place at my side. I wrapped my mechanical arm around her waist, placing my palm on her hip.

"I wouldn't expect you two idiots to remember. You mentioned it in passing, only had a discussion on it for about five minutes. Fortunately for you, I took it to heart."

What's she going on about? What present?

"The research lab I work in, we partnered with a think tank about five years ago. I registered as an employee for both sides. Frickin' human sleep meant I couldn't work more than twelve, fourteen hours in a day, but I came up with something. A solution." She stared at us as if her words had meant anything significant so far.

"A solution to…?" I started.

"The penis!" She gestured broadly, sweeping her hand past us both. "The testicles, actually. But you get my drift."

"We do *not* get your drift." Krystal asserted.

"Babies!" Alice emphasized, standing up from her chair. "You guys wanted a baby. You heard us all talking about it and mentioned you two wanted to adopt someday, but you wished you could have a kid of your own."

"And you…found us a penis?" I asked.

"Testicles, actually." Krystal corrected quietly.

"We're not interested in a donor-"

"That's why I'm here, you morons. Get that political junk out of your heads and listen to what I'm saying. I found the *solution* to that." She beamed, seeing the dialogue start to make sense to both of us.

"You're saying you found a way to make a viable fetus with two egg cells, without the need for a donor sperm cell?" I confirmed, wracking my brain for a logical method of how she managed to do it.

"Hell, yeah, I did." She said proudly. "The studies have been going on since the early two-thousands. But with today's tech and a bit of brains, we managed to get some working trials in a lab. The FDA – *your* FDA by the way – approved human trials for volunteers. It starts next month and my company is running it. If you want, I can get one of you on board."

Holy shit, are we having a baby?

I turned to Krystal, staring at her blankly. I knew that I had always been the one to provoke the discussion on having children someday, in the context of adoption, and knew she had a few reservations about the process since there were few unclaimed children in the U.S. anymore. Her eyes moved between mine, looking at me for an answer to questions I didn't know.

"Krystal, I…is this something you want to consider?" She stared at me, her face slowly paling.

"That is *not* the question I want to ask right now. Or even talk about."

Damn…I was hoping she'd at least have the discussion. I mean, we can wait. If it works, there's always another time-

"We *should* be asking which one of us is going to *carry* the baby." Her expression was still terrified, but it incited an ear-to-ear grin from me and a bouncing, joyful energy.

"Krys, are you serious right now? Like seriously, are you serious, Kryssi?" She laughed at my energy, nodding slowly as her eyes welled with tears.

"Yeah. Yeah, I am." Krystal swallowed, her sapphire eyes glowing with ecstasy. "I wanna have a baby with you." I tackled her, and in spite of the poor Secret Service agent that had to bear witness to all of this, I embraced her with all my might. "I wanna have a baby with you." She repeated into my shoulder.

"I want to carry." I pushed her back for a moment, explaining my train of thought. "I think with my healing-"

"If you think you need to convince me, don't. It's a deal." She laughed, wiping away happy tears. She settled for a moment after a thought crossed her mind. "Can you handle being the President while you're pregnant? Is that…legal or anything? Bit of uncharted territory." I took her hands in my own, our sparkling violet rings glinting in the winter sunlight that shone in beams through the windows.

"Krystal, I've been the first female president, the first openly gay president, the first Vampyre president, the first president to serve a fourth and *fifth* term, the first president to rebuild the U.S. from scratch, and the first president since George Washington to add four amendments to the Constitution. I can be pregnant, I'll *make* it happen!" I cackled.

"Amy, I-…Sorry, *Madam President*, I'll get you on the list tomorrow." Alice poked fun at me, which I returned with another overbearing hug.

"Easy. Human bones. Brittle." Alice groaned as I let go. "And mine aren't doing so hot." She grumbled, rotating her shoulder. "Getting old sucks."

"So we've been told." Krystal teased, not wanting to take her comment too seriously.

"There is *one* important piece of information I need for the records. During the process, fairly early on, you can decide on a sex for the fetus. It's not a hundred percent guaranteed, but when we start the developmental process, we use one method or another and each presents typically with a higher rate of one sex versus the other. So…boy or girl?" Alice asked, looking into my eyes.

"Girl!"

"Boy!" I erupted with a much different answer than Krystal, invoking a devious stare from my lovely wife while she cracked her knuckles and opened her mouth to make her case.

SONYA & ERIC

EPILOGUE

"Hi!" I started, looking eagerly at our newcomer. He closed the door behind him and made his way to the table in slow strides, plopping down at the table in front of Eric and I with little energy. "Welcome to the Kane-Hudson Center for New Dawn Vampyrism. I'm Sonya, this is Eric." I gestured as Eric waved hello and sighed behind my back. "We're going to do your interview today! Super exciting. How do you feel?" I sat down finally, staring at his half-open eyes.

"Good." He said, saying nothing further.

Don't be impatient, he's probably nervous.

"Good! Glad to hear it. So what brings you to our center?" I asked enthusiastically, always eager to hear people's reasons.

"Wanna be a Vampyre." He shrugged, again saying nothing more.

He probably feels shy. Doesn't want to talk about it in front of people he doesn't know. Humans can be a bit slow to trust.

"Ah, okay!" I started, unsure of where to take the conversation. "Why's that?"

"Wanna have cool powers and be able to like…do cool stuff. Jump off buildings and all that." He explained, finally using more than four words in a sentence.

His brain isn't as developed as yours, have some more patience. He might not have a great education or something.

"Okay, okay. That *is* certainly some cool stuff. Why…do you feel like these powers would benefit your community?" I glanced down at the list of questions I had, scanning the rest of the form with my eyes. He shrugged again.

"Could fight bad guys and all that. Be like. The guy that stops crimes and saves people."

He…I'm sure there's a reason he's like this. Maybe he's depressed, thinks Vampyrism would help his state of mind.

"Oh, okay. Um…do you plan on enlisting into the military?" I asked hopefully, uncapping my pen and hovering the tip over the checkbox.

"Nah, I don't think so. People yelling at me and shit? I'd yell right back, doesn't work with me."

"*Okay* so no, no military service." I sighed, putting a checkmark in the box next to it. Eric remained unusually quiet, standing behind me with no input. "Do you…have a job that would benefit from enhanced strength or-"

"Job?" He asked, scratching the shaggy brown hair under his beanie. "Do I need one of those, or…" He trailed the sentence off, leaving me without the words I needed to communicate effectively with him.

"No…no, not necessarily. Do you do community work?"

Does he look like he does community work?

I shook my head, trying to get out the negative thoughts and remain nonjudgmental, but it coincided with his answer, as well.

"I had to do community service for a couple months after I got caught spray-painting my girlfriend's house. Does that count?" I paused at his situation.

"Spray-painting a house isn't illegal."

"What I was spray-painting *onto* it was." He chuckled.

Okay, is…is it okay for someone to be hopeless?

"Mr…Cinder? Jake? Um…we have to meet a list of criteria for you to qualify. So is there anything you *can* offer us as proof that you or your community would benefit from receiving the NDM?"

"The what?"

"I'm sorry, the New Dawn Mutation. The…injection."

See, patience. You answer his questions, he learns something new, and you get to listen to more of his useless drivel.

"Oh. Uh…is it alright if I'm not a fan of needles?" He asked, scratching his arm and exposing a full sleeve of tattoos.

"You have tattoos." I pointed with my pen. "Those use needles."

"Yeah, but like…that's different." He countered intelligently.

"Alright, I'm done." Eric sighed, making his way around the table and pressing his palm into the corner. "Listen, Jake, buddy. You…are *useless.* In every way." Eric gestured with his hands for emphasis. "You have…no bearing doing anything more than eating cheese puffs and skateboarding in places you shouldn't be. On a generous day, I would give you a place at the dollar store cash register, and even then I doubt that you could count change correctly." Eric paused, not to think of more insults, but to take another breath to unleash what he already had in mind. "There is nothing on Earth that would make me inclined to increase a physical and mental potential that wouldn't be met in a quadrillion years. I hope that when you leave here today, you reconsider every aspect of the life you live and pray to whatever you believe in that both of your brain cells will someday meet and coalesce to form an independently thinking being. When *that* happens…give us a call." Eric extended a business card, looking over at my disapproving face.

"Yeah, for sure, man." Jake took the card, shook Eric's hand, and left the room while Eric watched to ensure Mr. Cinder properly found the elevator at the end of the hall.

"Did I just have a stroke?" I asked, hoping that Eric would answer truthfully.

"No, my friend. *You*...just encountered hopelessness." He chuckled. "Your illusion of everyone having potential has been officially shattered and hopefully, maybe, a sliver of your optimism has been replaced with realism."

"I just don't understand." I started. "Everyone has something they're passionate about, that they work toward. *Something.* Why...didn't he?"

"Lots of people are like that. They usually just don't even have the desire to walk in here. It's extra effort on their part." He patted me on the back as I finished filling out the form, denying his application for a mutagen injection and marking the reasoning in the empty box.

"Failed to...show...potential..." I paused, trying to think of the right words as I wrote them down. Eric whisked the form off my desk, holding it out for me to grab.

"Perfect. Not another word needs said." I laughed, taking the form from his hand and filing it in the cabinet behind me.

"We still on for dinner Friday?" He asked nonchalantly.

"Yep. My plans rarely change. Schedule is like clockwork."

"Awesome. Wanted to check. Girlfriend was asking about plans, but I figured I wouldn't have an open night 'til Saturday. I'm thinking we're gonna take a weekend trip." He explained.

"Oh, speaking of. How's she doing?" I pulled my phone from my pocket, buzzing with the indication of a text.

"Good. Started work at a new club that opened up. Gave her a signing bonus and everything for the routines she has." He sighed. "She's got a lot of regulars. I'm lucky I'm her favorite."

Results came back. Positive…two of them. Surgery tomorrow, but not sure how much it's going to help. Outlook is still a few years, hopefully. She'd love a visit.

"Oh, no…" I sighed, gritting my teeth and clenching my phone lightly.

"Aw, man…" Eric rolled his head back. "They got the results, didn't they?" I nodded, setting the phone on my desk and taking a moment for myself. "That bad?"

"She'll go into surgery tomorrow. Dual-diagnosis, according to Jalix." I wasn't sure what else to say, but I grabbed my keys and heeded the last part of Jalix's message. "I'm gonna go pay her a visit. See her before she goes in. Can you cover for me tomorrow? I'll probably wait 'til she's out of surgery."

"I can't cover you tomorrow, sorry." Eric paused. "I think I'll be visiting a friend in the hospital." I smiled, nodding to him and locking my office door before heading down the hall with a treasured friend.

RAVEN
EPILOGUE

I growled, my car taking too much of a beating for the unkempt road I drove upon and clunking for the fifteenth time as my tire navigated a pothole.

"Who the hell would live out here?" I grumbled, seeing the deteriorating house fall into view against the Pennsylvania countryside.

Overgrown gardens flooded the acres around the house, still blooming with plants and fruits, but in a disarray never intended by the person who built them. I slowed my car to a stop, getting out and checking the exterior for damage. Small stone chips marked up the paint and blemished my favorite car, but it was worth the drive to the destination. I swirled my keys around my finger for a moment, realizing that the house's occupant had no idea that anyone had arrived.

I made my way toward the door in long, slow strides, inspecting the gardens for any sign of what I was looking for. Invisible to the eyes of its occupant, I stalked to the front door of the house and knocked, waiting for several long moments before I heard any noise. A man inside groaned, several heavy thuds reverberating through the ground before he called out to me.

"Just...a second." His breathing sounded labored and difficult, and his voice was raspy from lung problems. After more than a minute of scuffling and thumping, a hunched man opened the door while clinging desperately to a walker in front of him. He stared at me for a long moment, meeting my eyes and waiting. In spite of his health, he still had a full head of grayed hair.

"Can...I help you?" He asked, taking a sniff from the oxygen cannula under his nose.

He has no idea who I am. Old man's senile. This is perfect, more than I could have asked for.

"Hi. I, uh...hope I'm not interrupting." I started pleasantly.

"Oh, no. Just...reading an old book. What can I...do for you?" His lips moved long after he was done speaking, struggling to get out the words he needed.

"I'm an old friend of Kara's." I explained. "I wanted to visit where she was buried. Would you mind showing me?" He hesitated, inspecting me.

"A...friend? Don't...recognize you. Too young...to know Kara." He rebutted.

"I'm...a Vampyre." I clarified confusedly. "We look young."

"Ah! Ah...yeah. Yeah, I know that." He nodded for far, far too long before looking up at me again. "What can...I help you with?"

"*Kara.*" I enunciated. "I would like to see her *grave*."

"Oh! Oh, Kara. Yes, we'll...uh...let me get my...foot out the door." He made his way out slowly, and in the desperation I had to escape the aged idiot, I held out an arm to help him down his front steps.

His walker finally touched the soil, and we trudged at a painstakingly slow pace, his heavy breathing being a focus of my rage. It was annoying beyond all comprehension, the hissing from his mobile oxygen tank only adding to the reminder that I was dealing with the geriatric shadow of an alleged hero long past. We walked for minutes, each ticking by while we passed garden after garden, row after row of plants that overgrew their intended boundaries.

I remained silent, choosing to focus on looking around to find the headstone before I also died of old age. Unexpectedly, he stopped, turning to the side and gesturing with his walker toward one of the gardens. This one was filled with a combination of lilies and roses, with a few carnations pushing their bright colors out of the ground where they could. With growing disdain, I put one of my expensive shoes in the soil and took several steps forward, picking up my pace as I finally saw a low-lying marker on the ground.

That's why I couldn't see it. It's damn near hidden.

I read the inscription, scoffing at the trivial remark they had decided to place upon my mother's grave. I looked over my shoulder, Jalix still ambling his way through the thick foliage while he battled with his walker. He wasn't even looking at me, trying to rip his mobility assistance from a knot of rosebushes.

"You…ugh…find her?" He called, almost having caught up.

"Yes. Yes, I found her." I grinned, lowering myself to the ground again and touching the soil. "I found *exactly* what I was looking for." I let myself have a moment of victory, having waited decades to finally seize my opportunity and do what needed done. "And now our work can continue. With no one the wiser. This…is why I played the long game. Saw further than anyone else. Predicted things. Just like my father did." I lauded. I chuckled, hearing more noise from Jalix as he made his way toward me. "Just go back to the house, old man. I don't need your help any-"

Quiet. Metal against plastic. Familiar sounds…

"You and your father both had the same problem, Raven." My blood ran cold, my crouched position giving me no quarter in seeing the man behind me. His voice was still aged and tinged with the damage of too many years on Earth, but incredibly strong in power. From where I was, it sounded like he had stood to his full height immediately behind me, having only used the walker for show. I snorted, nodding once.

"And what's that, Jalix? What problem did we both have?"

A nearly silent click. The safety of a pistol.

My heart jumped, realizing that I was in a fatally ill position for death threats, having told no one where I was and having no one that would come to my aid.

"You…suck…at your job." He growled. I hesitated, realizing that there was an opportunity for me to overpower him if I moved quickly enough. If I spun, if I lunged, there was a chance I could-

A single gunshot rang out across the Pennsylvania countryside.

"Be that word our sign of parting, bird or fiend!" I
shrieked, upstarting—
"Get thee back into the tempest and the Night's
Plutonian shore!
Leave no black plume as a token of that lie thy soul
hath spoken!
Leave my loneliness unbroken!—quit the bust above
my door!
Take thy beak from out my heart, and take thy form
from off my door!"
Quoth the Raven "Nevermore."

- Edgar Allen Poe

Acknowledgements:

I could fill another book with people I'd like to thank by name, but I have to stick with only a few because my editor said so.

First and foremost is my family, beyond a doubt. On a daily basis, I tell myself I couldn't possibly be any prouder of my younger brothers than I already am, but they have proven me wrong at every turn. I commend you both for always following what you love so deeply. I'll always be there for you.

The same goes for my supportive parents, watching me struggle to write during a military career, graduate school, and painful diagnoses; Your steadfast support is not forgotten. My grandmother, a best friend since infancy, is also worth a book in her own right, and for the guidance she's given me through hard times and challenges, I credit my success in large part to you.

To all those mentioned and to the incredible extended family who is equally supportive of my path (but I'm out of room for), I thank you deeply.

To my wife: On a serious note, which we both hate, your love and support has always been treasured. I'm lucky enough to consider you a centerpiece in my life, and I'm proud of the woman you've become.

To all of my friends and mentors, close and distant, near and far, from military, work, school, or fate, I don't forget the experiences I've had with all of you and the ways you've helped me grow.

And, perhaps most importantly, to my readers:
You are the core of the Sorrowverse. This series is full of pain, suffering, loss, addiction, trauma, and more, and it's not written blindly. For every reader who finds a personal connection with a character, a theme, an event, or one of its volumes, I hope you no longer feel alone in knowing that others have been where you are and have conquered their worst nightmares. My goal in writing is to create a connection between you and myself through the world I've created. Enjoy it, cherish it, and support it as it grows to help people escape reality or understand its consequences within these pages.
You are my legacy.

www.ingramcontent.com/pod-product-compliance
Lightning Source LLC
LaVergne TN
LVHW041058080826
845145LV00007B/1616

9781970018158